THE UNIVERSITY OF
WINCHESTER

Martial Rose Library
Tel: 01962 827306

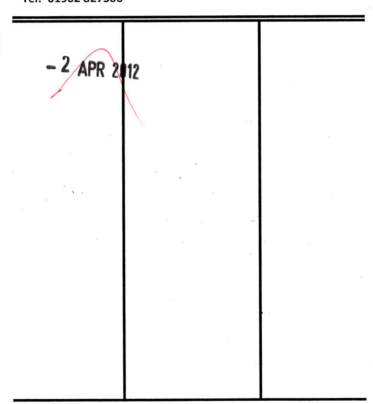

- 2 APR 2012

To be returned on or before the day marked above, subject to recall.

Composed Theatre

Composed Theatre
Aesthetics, Practices, Processes

Edited by Matthias Rebstock and David Roesner

intellect Bristol, UK / Chicago, USA

First published in the UK in 2012 by
Intellect, The Mill, Parnall Road, Fishponds, Bristol, BS16 3JG, UK

First published in the USA in 2012 by
Intellect, The University of Chicago Press, 1427 E. 60th Street,
Chicago, IL 60637, USA

A catalogue record for this book is available from the
British Library.

Cover: Scene from Trübe Quellenlage by Ruedi Häusermann.
Photograph by Sebastian Hoppe.
Cover designer: Holly Rose
Copy-editor: Macmillan
Typesetting: Mac Style, Beverley, E. Yorkshire

ISBN 978-1-84150-456-8

Printed and bound by Bell & Bain, Glasgow.

Contents

Acknowledgements

First and foremost the editors would like to thank the Arts and Humanities Research Council, UK (AHRC), and the Stiftung Universität Hildesheim for funding two four-day symposia in Exeter and Hildesheim, which formed the starting point and basis for this research and this publication. We would like to thank all those who attended and participated in these symposia, generously contributed to them and have left their mark on the research presented here. The Department of Drama, Exeter, the Institut für Musik und Musikwissenschaft, Hildesheim and the Universitätsgesellschaft Hildesheim further supported the research workshop events that were instrumental in establishing the notion and the network of Composed Theatre. The use of space and resources, the help from technical and administrative staff as well as the interest and support from colleagues at both institutions were all much appreciated. The tireless work of the research assistants Paul Edmondson and Karoline Kähler was another key factor in successfully preparing and conducting the project, which led to this book. We are also grateful to the Herder Kolleg of the Universität Hildesheim for its valuable support regarding the translations.

Many thanks go to Peter Hulton, who carefully and diligently documented the workshops, presentations and discussions preceding the book and ensured their accessibility through the Exeter Digital Archive, Exeter, and the Audio-Visual Archive at Hildesheim, and Sarah Crumb, who provided the exact transcripts from the lively discussions, which formed the basis for chapter 15.

Editing, writing and partly translating a publication in English as two non-native speakers, we needed patient, resourceful and sensitive editorial advice and received it in full from Sarah Evans (Exeter), Peter Thomson (Exeter) and Nita Shechet (Jerusalem), whom we thank very much. We are also very grateful for the translations provided by Lee Holt and Nick Wood. Any remaining flaws, however, are ours.

Introduction: Composed Theatre in Context

David Roesner

Since the beginning of the twentieth century, it has been an ongoing interest of composers like Arnold Schönberg, John Cage, Mauricio Kagel, George Aperghis, Dieter Schnebel, Hans-Joachim Hespos, Manos Tsangaris, Charlotte Seither and Heiner Goebbels – to name but a few – to approach the theatrical stage and its means of expression as *musical* material. They treat voice, gesture, movement, light, sound, image, design and other features of theatrical production according to musical principles and compositional techniques and apply musical thinking to performance as a whole. This idea is again flourishing among composers, directors and theatre collectives, as reflected in recent developments towards postdramatic forms that de-emphasise text, narrative and fictional characters, seeking alternative dramaturgies (visual, spatial, temporal, musical), and focussing on the sonic and visual materialities of the stage and the performativity of their material components.

At the same time, musical composition has increasingly expanded its range of 'instruments' to include live video, lighting design, live sound electronics, costumes and spatial arrangements, and has paid closer attention to the theatricality of the musical performer. Thus the interests in the musicality of theatrical performance and the theatricality of musical performance have given rise to a wide range of forms of what we propose to call Composed Theatre.

Following two symposia Matthias Rebstock and I organised in 2009 at Exeter and Hildesheim, to which we invited practitioners and scholars who work in this field, we seek to now establish the field of Composed Theatre in this book, providing terminological consideration and frameworks for analysis, all of which have not been widely used before and have not received in-depth academic attention. We have called on both scholars and practitioners, thereby providing a wide range of historical and theoretical perspectives as well as detailed case studies. It is one of the contentions of this book that Composed Theatre cannot be defined solely by its 'works' or outcomes. It can, however, be grouped and approached – despite the diversity of its outcomes – according to specific characteristics of its various stages of becoming: its conceptual, devising, rehearsing and designing processes.

In short, it is the process, not the performance that distinguishes Composed Theatre from other forms and thus defines the field.

Our book does not seek to define Composed Theatre ontologically or phenomenologically, but in the light of a genetic approach (see e.g. Feral 2008; Rebstock 2009; Roesner 2010), which aims to establish a set of shared criteria that are characteristic of most of its creation processes. These are particularly interesting not least because this kind of composing of theatrical media according to musical principles calls into question fundamental certainties about both musical composition and music-theatrical production.

Composed Theatre is situated within and expands on a context of previous research into earlier examples of this practice, particularly in the US and around the work of John Cage (e.g. Fetterman 1995; Kaye 1996; Sanio 1999; Deuffert 2001). However, work of this kind has proliferated in more recent European and particularly German developments due to a unique theatre system and a specific funding and festival culture, both of which facilitate this kind of experimental work. Our book explores this European strand. Here it is particularly Mauricio Kagel, another composer of the generation of the 'fathers' (Tsangaris) of Composed Theatre, who has received detailed academic attention, to which this book is also indebted (see e.g. Schnebel 1970; Klüppelholz 1981; Klüppelholz/Prox 1985; Tadday 2004; Heile 2006; Rebstock 2007). Kagel's often-cited notion that one can compose with "sounding and non-sounding materials, actors, cups, tables, omnibuses and oboes" (Kagel 1982: 121) is a point of departure and recurrent throughline in the research on Composed Theatre. Matthias Rebstock's chapter "Composed Theatre – Mapping the Field" (chapter 1) explores the historical developments and lineages of Composed Theatre in greater detail and David Roesner's concluding discourse analysis (chapter 16) extends this towards an in-depth interrogation of the main themes, features and characterisations of Composed Theatre today.

Composed Theatre is consciously in dialogue with a number of neighbouring or overlapping discourses. With its focus on process, for example, it aims to be a significant contribution to the current scholarship on artistic process (Bannermann 2006; Féral 2008; Porombka et al. 2006, 2008). While not all Composed Theatre is music-theatre, there is certainly a strong relationship with the development and discussion within experimental music-theatre (Heilgendorff 2002; Mauser 2002; Danuser 2003; Reinighaus/Schneider 2004; Salzman/Desi 2008; Schläder 2009). Beyond its immediate field of practices and by virtue of its continuous crossing of boundaries, *Composed Theatre* also explores questions of intermediality (Meyer 2001; Rajewsky 2002; Balme 2004; Chapple/Kattenbelt 2006; Müller 2008), new dramaturgies (Turner/Behrndt 2007), materialities and sensory perceptions of the stage (Lechtermann, Wagner, Wenzel 2007), the performativity of music (Godlovitch 1998; Small 1998; Cook 2001; Auslander 2006), the aesthetics of devising (Heddon/Milling 2006; Mermikides/Smart 2009) and, last but not at least, aspects of the postdramatic (Lehmann 2006).

With regard to the latter, it should be added that our notion of Composed Theatre is at the same time narrower and wider than Lehmann's more loosely grouped catalogue of performance phenomena. While on the one hand there is a strong connection between what Lehmann calls musicalisation of theatre (Lehmann 2006: 91–93) and what we offer here as Composed Theatre, this is only *one* of the strategies of postdramatic theatre Lehmann describes, and only very briefly.[1] Composing theatre suggests a shift in activity during the process of making theatre, a dramaturgical quality, a new perspective in creation, where Lehmann's term of musicalisation within the postdramatic is more an aesthetical and performative quality and is predominantly concerned with the musicalisation (and de-semantisation) of language.

One the other hand, Lehmann's category focusses strongly on examples of theatre and performance, whereas Composed Theatre also brings music-theatre, dance, staged concerts, sound installations etc. into view. Where Lehmann emphasises the musicalisation of theatre, Composed Theatre adds phenomena that would fall under the heading 'theatricalisation of music'.

Composed Theatre is not a genre – it is more a frame or a lens that brings quite disparate phenomena into view and collocates them. At the centre of this frame, the focus is on creation processes that bring the musical notion of composing to the theatrical aspects of performing and staging. Here we find mostly composers like those mentioned earlier, who work intentionally with a more rigorously musical concept of composition, which applies compositional techniques and concepts, often developed from models in the Western Classical Music to theatrical materials and actions.

On 'zooming out', however, we also can look at practices and process under the heading of Composed Theatre, where the application of musical ideas is perhaps less conceptual and strictly compositional, perhaps even not fully intentional. Directors such as Christoph Marthaler, Einar Schleef, Sebastian Nübling or Robert Wilson work more instinctively with musicalisation, for example, but are well worth investigating within the frame that is "Composed Theatre". In this respect this book is addressed equally strongly to theatre scholars and musicologists, to theatre practitioners and composers and will also be relevant for musicians, dancers, designers.

The book offers a range of approaches that provide multidirectional perspectives on the aesthetics, practices and processes of Composed Theatre. Rebstock's opening chapter of Part I provides a detailed historical account on the different developments in music, music-theatre and theatre that contribute to and mark the field at hand. Quitt and Meyer then offer two methodological approaches that investigate different borders of the field: Quitt's considerations on changing symbolic and meaning-making processes in the transition from what he calls 'descriptive art' to 'new art' cut to the core of the semiotic implications of Composed Theatre and uses an in-depth discussion of visual art to extrapolate key features of Composed Theatre as an experimental practice. Meyer on the other hand embeds the idea of Composed Theatre in the wider observations and consequences of an 'acoustic turn' that can be observed not only in the arts (see also Meyer's book of the same name, 2008) and investigates the phenomenological shift towards a more strongly auditory engagement with the theatre in three performances from the world of dance, music-theatre and theatre.

---

1. See also Demetris Zavros' chapter (chapter 10) in this book for a wider discussion of this connection.

We then turn to a series of case studies and reports from practitioners themselves (Part II) exploring the unique creation processes of Composed Theatre in more depth and conceptualising relationships between compositional thinking, creating performance, working with actors, dancers, musicians and materials, as well as negotiating new technologies. Complementing this are portraits and analyses of further key composer/directors whose works and processes define the current face and phase of Composed Theatre (Part III).

In its penultimate approach, the book documents excerpts from a series of lively discussions between some major exponents of Composed Theatre, focussing on its main characteristics, processes and principles.

This is further evaluated and contextualised by the final chapter, in which Roesner provides a extensive discourse analysis, which both ties together and opens up some of the main throughlines and questions of this book and the research that led to it. These are:

- What are the key characteristics of Composed Theatre?
- Why is it important to focus on its creation process in order to determine the field?
- What other terms are in circulation and how do they relate to the scope of this book?
- How do the different arts (music, theatre, literature, film) and media (actors, musicians, instruments, lighting, video etc.) interact and interrelate in the creation processes of Composed Theatre?
- How does a creation process which is guided by compositional thoughts and concepts affect the roles of the collaborators (composer, director, performer, designer, dramaturg, technician, programmer, etc.)?
- How does the transference or translation of compositional principles (such as polyphony, counterpoint, development of motifs, permutation etc.) to non-musical forms of theatrical expression (speech, movement, gesture, stage design, lighting etc.) impact on both (the principles and the stage vocabulary)?
- What role does improvisation play in the creation process and how is it influenced by forms of musical improvisation?
- What is the nature and the status of (musical) notation in the creation process in Composed Theatre?
- What are the institutional and educational frameworks for Composed Theatre and what is their impact on the creation process?

Composed Theatre offers answers to these questions in a cumulative way – emerging through the assembly of the many puzzle pieces that the range of contributions offers – but it also embraces the variations and even contradictions that the range of views, examples, definitions and convictions will provide. We offer *Composed Theatre* as a starting point, the beginning of an engagement with an exciting range of theatre forms and creation processes, rather than a definitive and closing statement.

References

Auslander, Philip (2006) "Musical Personae", *TDR: The Drama Review*, Volume 50, Number 1 (T 189), pp. 100–119.

Balme, Christopher (2004) "Intermediality: Rethinking the Relationship between Theatre and Media". *THEWIS* (http://www.theaterwissenschaft.uni-muenchen.de/personen_neu/professoren/balme/balme_publ1/balme_publ_aufsaetze/intermediality.pdf) [10 May 2006].

Bannerman, Christopher (ed.) (2006) *Navigating the Unknown: The Creative Process in Contemporary Performing Arts*, Enfield: Middlesex University Press.

Bayerdörfer, Hans-Peter (ed.) (1999) *Musiktheater als Herausforderung: interdisziplinäre Facetten von Theater- und Musikwissenschaft*, Tübingen: Niemeyer.

Chapple, Freda and Kattenbelt, Chiel (eds.) (2006) *Intermediality in Theatre and Performance*, Amsterdam: Rodopi.

Cook, Nicholas (2001) "Between Process and Product: Music and/as Performance", *Music Theory Online*, 7 (2001), at http://www.societymusictheory.org/mto/issues/ mto.01.7.2/mto.01.7.2.cook.html#FN8 [13 September 2006].

Danuser, Hermann and Kassel, Matthias (eds.) (2003) *Musiktheater heute: Internationales Symposion der Paul Sacher Stiftung Basel 2001*, Mainz: Schott.

Deufert, Kattrin (2001) *John Cages Theater der Präsenz*, Norderstedt, (FK) medien | material.txt.

Emons, Hans (2005) *Für Auge und Ohr: Musik als Film – oder die Verwandlung von Kompositionen in Licht-Spiel*, Berlin: Frank & Timme.

Féral, Josette (2008) "Introduction: Towards a Genetic Study of Performance – Take 2". *Theatre Research International*, 33, pp. 223–233.

Fetterman, William (1996) *John Cage's Theatre Pieces: Notations and Performances*, Amsterdam: Harwood Academic Publishers.

Godlovitch, Stan (1998) *Musical Performance: A Philosophical Study*, London / New York: Routledge.

Heilgendorff, Simone (2002) *Experimentelle Inszenierung von Sprache und Musik. Vergleichende Analysen zu Dieter Schnebel und John Cage*, Freiburg im Breisgau: Rombach Verlag.

Hiß, Guido (2005) *Synthetische Visionen: Theater als Gesamtkunstwerk von 1800 bis 2000*, München: Epodium.

Kagel, Mauricio (1982), "Im Gespräch mit Lothar Prox, Abläufe, Schnittpunkte – montierte Zeit", in Alte Oper Frankfurt (ed) *Grenzgänge – Grenzspiele: Ein Programmbuch zu den Frankfurt Festen '82*, Frankfurt: Alte Oper.

Kaye, Nick (1996) *Art into Theatre: Performance Interviews and Documents*, Amsterdam: Harwood Academic Publishers.

Kesting, Marianne (1969) "Musikalisierung des Theaters – Theatralisierung der Musik". *Melos – Zeitschrift für neue Musik*, Heft 3, pp. 101–09.

Klüppelholz, Werner (1981) *Mauricio Kagel 1970–1980*, Schauberg: DuMont.

Klüppelholz, Werner and Prox, Lothar (eds.) (1985) *Mauricio Kagel: Das filmische Werk I*, Amsterdam/ Köln: Meulenhoff.

Lechtermann, Christina, Wagner, Kirsten and Wenzel, Horst (eds.) (2007) *Möglichkeitsräume – Zur Performativität von sensorischer Wahrnehmung*, Berlin: Erich Schmidt Verlag.

Lehmann, Hans-Thies (2006) *Postdramatic Theatre*, London/New York: Routledge.

Mauser, Siegfried (ed) (2002) *Musiktheater im 20: Jahrhundert*, Laaber: Laaber.

Mermikides, Alex and Smart, Jacqueline (eds.) (2009) *Devising in Process*, Basingstoke/New York: Palgrave Macmillan.

Meyer, Petra Maria (2001) *Intermedialität des Theaters. Entwurf einer Semiotik der Überraschung*, Düsseldorf: Parerga Verlag.

Meyer, Petra Maria (ed) (2008) *Acoustic turn*, Tübingen: Fink.

Müller, Jürgen E. (1998) "Intermedialität als poetologisches und medientheoretisches Konzept", in Jörg Helbig (ed) *Intermedialität: Theorie und Praxis eines interdisziplinären Forschungsgebiets*, Berlin,:Erich Schmidt Verlag, pp. 31–40.

Müller, Jürgen E. (2008) "Intermedialität und Medienhistoriographie", in Joachim Peach and Jens Schröter (eds.) *Intermedialität: Analog/Digital. Theorien – Methoden – Analysen*, München: Wilhelm Fink, pp. 31–46.

Porombka, Stephan, Schneider, Wolfgang and Wortmann, Volker (eds.) (2006) *Kollektive Kreativität: Jahrbuch für Kulturwissenschaften und ästhetische Praxis 2006*, Tübingen: Francke.

—— (2008) *Theorie und Praxis der Künste: Jahrbuch für Kulturwissenschaften und ästhetische Praxis 2008*, Tübingen: Francke.

Rajewsky, Irina (2002) *Intermedialität*, Tübingen / Basel: UTB.

Rebstock, Matthias (2007) *Komposition zwischen Musik und Theater: das instrumentale Theater von Mauricio Kagel zwischen 1959 und 1965*, Hofheim: Wolke.

Rebstock, Matthias (2008) "Theorie der Praxis, Praxis als Theorie: Überlegungen zu einer 'praktischen Musik-Theater-Wissenschaft'", in Stephan Porombka, Wolfgang Schneider and Volker Wortmann (eds.) *Theorie und Praxis der Künste: Jahrbuch für Kulturwissenschaften und ästhetische Praxis 2008*, Tübingen: Francke, pp. 61–80.

Reininghaus, Frieder and Schneider, Katja (eds.) (2004) *Experimentelles Musik- und Tanztheater*, Laaber: Laaber.

Roesner, David (2003) *Theater als Musik: Verfahren der Musikalisierung in chorischen Theaterformen bei Christoph Marthaler, Einar Schleef und Robert Wilson*, Tübingen: Gunter Narr.

—— (2010) "Die Utopie "Heidi": Arbeitsprozesse im experimentellen Musiktheater am Beispiel von Leo Dicks *Kann Heidi brauchen, was es gelernt hat?*" in Kati Röttger (ed) *Welt – Bild – Theater. Vol. 1: Politik der Medien und Kulturen des Wissens*, Amsterdam: Rodopi, pp. 221–34.

Sacher, Reinhard Josef (1984) *Musik als Theater: Tendenzen zur Grenzüberschreitung in der Musik von 1958–1968*, Köln: Bosse.

Sachs, Klaus-Jürgen (1996) "Komposition. A. Einführung in Gebrauch, Bedeutung und musikbezogene Implikationen des Wortes", in Ludwig Finscher (ed) *Die Musik in Geschichte und Gegenwart, 2. Ausgabe, Sachteil, Bd. 5 Kas-Mein*, Kassel: Bärenreiter, pp. 506–08.

Salzman, Eric and Desi, Thomas (2008) *The New Music Theatre*, Oxford: Oxford University Press.

Sandner, Wolfgang (ed) (2002) *Heiner Goebbels: Komposition als Inszenierung*, Berlin: Henschel.

Sanio, Sabine (1999) *Alternativen zur Werkästhetik: John Cage und Helmut Heißenbüttel*, Saarbrücken: Pfau.

Schnebel, Dieter (1970) *Mauricio Kagel: Musik Theater Film*, Köln: DuMont.

Schläder, Jürgen (ed) (2009) *Das Experiment der Grenze: Ästhetische Entwürfe im Neuesten Musiktheater*, Berlin: Henschel.

Sichelstiel, Andreas (2004) *Musikalische Kompositionstechniken in der Literatur: Möglichkeiten der Intermedialität und ihrer Funktion bei österreichischen Gegenwartsautoren*, Essen: Die blaue Eule.

Small, Christopher (1998) *Musicking: The Meanings of Performing and Listening*, Hanover: University Press of New England.

Turner, Cathy and Behrndt, Synne K. (2007) *Dramaturgy and Performance*, Basingstoke/New York: Palgrave Macmillan.

Part I

History and Methodology

Chapter 1

Composed Theatre: Mapping the Field

Matthias Rebstock

Symptoms of Composed Theatre

In what follows, the question 'what is meant by the term "Composed Theatre"' will be addressed by taking a historical approach, looking for its traces and forerunners. The assumption is that, since the sixties, a field of artistic practice has arisen that is situated *between* the more classical conceptions – and institutions – of music, theatre and dance, and that is highly characterised and unified by making use of compositional strategies and techniques and, in a broader sense, by the application of compositional thinking. As a first step, this field can be exemplified by some of the main figures working in it and developing it: composers like Heiner Goebbels, Georges Aperghis, Manos Tsangaris, Carola Bauckholt, Daniel Ott, Robert Ashley or Meredith Monk; theatre directors like Robert Wilson, Christoph Marthaler or Ruedi Häusermann; in dance, part of the work of Xavier le Roy, William Forsythe and Sasha Waltz, ensembles and theatre-collectives such as Theater der Klänge in Düsseldorf, *Die Maulwerker* and the *LOSE COMBO* both in Berlin, *Cryptic* in Glasgow or the *Post-Operativ Productions* in Sussex; most of them having some roots in the work of composers such as John Cage, Mauricio Kagel, Dieter Schnebel or in the Fluxus movement.

By introducing the term 'Composed Theatre', the aim is to focus on this – necessarily non-homogeneous – field because within it, artistic processes are currently moving forward in a way that gain momentum from mutual influence and exchange of practices and positions, and that this, so far, has not been taken into account by academic research, which usually still focusses only on aspects, questions or positions relevant to the particular discipline of the researcher.[1] But as Composed Theatre is something that may be said to exist between art forms, so an interdisciplinary approach is required to describe and account for it. This *being in between* not only has consequences for academic purposes but also for the educational system. If it is true that contemporary theatre and performance in general – not just within Composed Theatre – challenges the separation of the art forms that had taken place in the second half of the eighteenth century, somehow recalling or bringing forward an integrated concept of theatre, then this should also lead to changes in an educational system in which interdisciplinary courses are still very rare. I will return to this problem towards the end of this chapter.

---

1. Fortunately, an increasing amount of interdisciplinary work has been published in this field over the last years so the situation begins to change.

But let us first go back to what is meant by the term 'Composed Theatre'. In the discussions during the two conferences on "Processes of Devising Composed Theatre" from which this book has emerged, it quickly became clear that the term 'Komposition' in German is very strongly linked to the field of music.[2] 'Komposition' in German usually means musical composition. In English, however, it means something being put together in a much broader sense, which is not *per se* linked to music at all. So obviously the concept of Composed Theatre needs some clarification here, because if 'composition' or being 'composed' was to be taken in the broad sense – as the Latin origin 'componere' (= 'place together') suggests – Composed Theatre would cease to mean anything precise at all, as theatre in this sense is always composed. So a first important specification is that the term has to be taken in its musical sense. That means, if the field of interest is characterised by the use of compositional strategies and techniques, these strategies, techniques and ways of thinking are typical of musical composition and, moreover, are applied no longer just to musical material but to such extra-musical materials as movement, speech, actions, lighting or whatever you have in the realm of theatre.

A second characteristic or symptom[3] of Composed Theatre consists in the aesthetic conviction of the independence and absence of hierarchy among the elements of theatre or, to put it another way, in the conviction that *in principle* no element should so dominate that the others would be reduced to illustrating, underpinning or reinforcing the first. Georges Aperghis makes this very clear when saying:

> The visual elements should not be allowed to reinforce or emphasise the music, and the music should not be allowed to underline the narrative. Things must complement themselves; they must have different natures. This is an important rule for me: never say the same thing twice [...]. Another thing has to emerge that is neither one nor the other; it is something new.
>
> (Aperghis 2001)

Similar statements could be found from most of the artists within the field.[4] Interestingly enough, there is a certain latent tension between this first conviction – which implies that each element is not only treated with equal rights but also accorded its own rules and strategies – and a second one, namely that the organisation and interaction of all such elements should follow musical or compositional principles. Thus, the relations between

---

2. See the discussion in chapter 15.
3. As we do not aim here for a sharp ontological definition of the concept of Composed Theatre, what I offer are not criteria in a logically strict sense but characteristics, some of which are true if we encounter Composed Theatre, but not necessarily all of them. In a similar setting, Nelson Goodman speaks of 'symptoms of the aesthetic' and I follow him in using this terminology; see Goodman (1976).
4. See in particular Heiner Goebbels in chapter 4.

these independent and equal elements and the overall structure of the pieces are governed by compositional means.

Thirdly, Composed Theatre is not only – or even not necessarily – characterised by compositional strategies at the point of performance but also – or even only – during the artistic processes of creation. A performance may not show any typical sign of compositional strategies; yet, without applying such strategies, the composer, the director or the ensemble would not have come to the same result. This means that dealing with the field of Composed Theatre requires a consideration, not only of the performances but also of the working processes if we are to determine in what sense compositional thinking drives these processes. Typically – though not in all cases – within the working process there are phases of experimenting, generating new material, structuring of material, structuring of progressions and combinations and finally creating the formal overall structure, and all these phases may be governed by compositional principles.

What can be seen as a fourth characteristic of Composed Theatre is that the working processes will generally differ from those within traditional theatre. What usually happens, to put it simply, is the separation of the different stages of production: text – musical composition – staging – performance. And for each step it is pretty clear who has the last say. Composed Theatre, however, very often is devised theatre, or at least works against hierarchical normsand with a more collective approach, leaving more space for each individual to bring in their own competences and personality than there is in traditional theatre work. The performers will very often get involved in the developing process of the piece itself, and the segregation of the different steps of production is less strict, thus giving way to a more integral approach of mutual influence and exchange. As a result it is very often unhelpful to attempt to distinguish between a piece or a composition on the one hand and a way of reading, interpreting and staging it on the other. Consequently Composed Theatre, fifthly, can be understood as a genre that basically exists only in its perfomances: it is only in the moment of performance that the different elements come together, and everything before that moment points to it. This directly affects the role of notation and scores within Composed Theatre. Constituting the necessary way to facilitate the performance, they cannot in themselves represent the work or the piece. The composition process is prolonged through the process of staging until the very moment of the performance. That is why so many composers in the field also take responsibility for staging and directing their pieces themselves (e.g. Dieter Schnebel, Mauricio Kagel, Heiner Goebbels, Georges Aperghis and so on).[5]

---

5. This insistence on the non-hierarchy of the elements excludes operas from the genre of Composed Theatre. In opera the music generally dominates the other elements. And operas are very rarely devised, opting to follow a traditional way of production with demarcated steps (libretto – composition – and finally a *mise en scène* which is 'just' an interpretation of the composition rather than a work of art on its own). Therefore, in this book, the field of opera is very rarely touched. This is not to say that operas could never be Composed Theatre, nor that compositional strategies are necessarily hostile to their production.

Thus, 'Composed Theatre' refers to the creative process and the performance of pieces that are determined by compositional strategies and, in a broader sense, by compositional thinking. But 'compositional thinking' is an elusive term. The quest is for a definition that is sufficiently broad to accommodate the needs of different art forms, but sufficiently specific to give full value to the musically derived concept of composition as the productive theatrical force. We are looking for something beyond the metaphorical. The musical titles Kandinsky gave to his paintings are just metaphorical. But what of Vsevolod Meyerhold's claim that theatre performances should be 'put together like orchestral compositions', or Dieter Schnebel's reference to 'visible music'? Is this more than a metaphorical way of speaking?

Things get more difficult as the concept of composition or compositional thinking, even if restricted to the field of music itself, is subject to historical changes. These changes take place in response to the other art forms and their techniques. For example, the musical techniques of *phrasing, interpunction* etc. are derived from an aesthetics that understands music as a kind of language, but this transfer from the realm of language to the realm of music is a matter, not only of terminology but also of thinking and understanding. And equally, when looking at the music of Ockeghem, Dufay or Josquin des Pres, one can easily see that the idea of building musical pieces on a system of complex proportions is heavily influenced by architecture – itself historically influenced by the idea of the 'harmony of the spheres' proposed by Pythagoras and his followers. So can there be anything specifically musical within 'composition', and what would that be when the realm of music in a strict sense is left and one enters the field of theatre? In the following these questions will be addressed from a historical perspective in order to cast some light on the developments through which the practices of today have been adopted. My assumption is that it is these common historical threads and aesthetic influences, more than a single clear-cut definition, that hold together the field of what we now call Composed Theatre with all its very different forms.

Richard Wagner and the *Gesamtkunstwerk*

It might be suprising to start with Richard Wagner, as opposition to Wagner's music-theatre and his pathos and heroism seems to be a position most representatives of Composed Theatre have in common. However, in his aesthetic writings Wagner was the first and certainly the most radical to claim that in theatre all elements should come together with equal rights. And Carl Dahlhaus points out that the most important achievement of Wagner's was yet something else: the 'aesthetic revolution' of Wagner was his claim daß das Theaterereignis nicht bloßes Mittel zur Darstellung eines Kunstwerks, dessen Substanz der dichterisch-musikalische Text bildet, sondern selbst das eigentliche Kunstwerk sei, als dessen Funktion man Dichtung und Musik auffassen müsse.[6]

Wagner with his *Gesamtkunstwerk* was certainly not the first to pursue 'synthetic visions'. Rather he is relying upon and developing the ideas of early Romantic writing, especially the idea of the unity of the arts and the overcoming of their separation.[7] But whereas, for early Romanticism, theatre was an inferior art form, Wagner put it on the same level as literature and music, an elevation that has been sustained until today. And at the same time his ideas of intermedial relations were of enormous influence on further theatre development:

Der Musikdramatiker setzt Worte, Töne und Bildentwürfe auf der Ebene der Partitur in Beziehung. Der Regisseur, wie ihn Edward Gordon Craig fünfzig Jahre später exemplarisch entwarf, betreibt diese intermediale Kompositorik mit dem Arsenal der Bühne. Der Schritt von dem, was Wagner ‚Gesammtkunstwerk' [*sic!*] nennt, zu Craigs Konstitutionsformel, die Theater als ‚Gesamtheit der Mittel' begreift, ist winzig.

(Hiß 2005: 56)[8]

Musicalisation of theatre

As early as in 1969 Marianne Kesting wrote a remarkable paper, "Musikalisierung des Theaters: Theatralisierung der Musik" (Kesting 1969).[9] She gives a historical outline of these two threads converging in the sixties in a fluid interplay of art forms such as Experimental Theatre, Happenings, Fluxus, Mixed Media, Instrumental Theatre, Experimental Music and so forth that can also be taken as a first peak of Composed Theatre. Reconstructing history along these two separate but converging threads is still a valid approach, one that is adopted

---

6. "[T]hat the theatre event is not just a means to present an art work of which the substance is the literal and musical text, but the piece of art itself of which text and music have to be regarded as its functions" (Dahlhaus 1971: 192). (In the following, if not stated otherwise, all translations of originally German quotes are by Lee Holt and Matthias Rebstock.)
7. For further discussion of the relation between Wagner and the early Romantic writers like Novalis and Schelling, see Hiß (2005: 27).
8. "The music-dramatic composer works out relations between words, sounds and drafts of images on the level of the score. The stage director, as outlined by Edward Gordon Craig fifty years later, undertakes this intermedial composition with the means of the arsenal of the stage. The step from what Wagner calls 'Gesammtkunstwerk' [*sic!*] to Craig's formula that theatre consists of the totality of its means is minimal."
9. "Musicalisation of Theatre: Theatricalisation of Music". Karl-Heinz Zarius takes a similar line; see Zarius (1976).

in what follows here. Of course, historical developments in theatre and music did not take place separately from each other. They touched whenever the separation of the arts was radically questioned: in Futurism, Dadaism, including the *MERZ-Bühne* of Kurt Schwitters, at the *Bauhaus* or in the writings of Antonin Artaud etc. But none of the great composers has ever formed part of one of these avant-garde movements[10] and mostly the different art forms were still so clearly distinguished that it makes sense to look first at theatre and then at music separately.

Theatre, which has always integrated other forms of art, became a model case for interdisciplinary art in the early twentieth century. This new kind of theatre no longer considered itself as 'represented literature'; it liberated itself from the primacy of language.[11] The theatrical reforms of the avant-garde are connected primarily by their fundamental critique of language. Language was toppled from its throne, where it had stood uncontested for centuries at the pinnacle of the hierarchy of theatrical elements. Edward Gordon Craig aimed for a reform, after which "the Art of the Theatre would have won back its rights, and its work would stand self-reliant as a creative art, and no longer as an interpretative craft" (Craig 1957: 178). Meyerhold sought to supplement spoken language by using biomechanics to transfer the laws of mechanics to the actor's body. In Dada soirées, meaning in language was banished by all means of textual collage, simultaneous poems and sound poems that emphasised language's qualities of sound and noise; the forms of abstract theatre practised in Futurism or by Oskar Schlemmer of the *Bauhaus* neglected to bestow any role upon language; and in Artaud's work, language was integrated into theatrical elements that were to be structured according to musical principles.

The crisis of language is intimately associated with the crisis of narrative. If the semantic dimension of language retreats into the background, then there is no longer a linear plot or story told on stage that has the power to determine the form of the theatre. This theatre requires other structural principles and new concepts of form. The ways to approach this problem are divergent, but what they do have in common is the search for forms of non-narrative theatre. Theatre is no longer the staged interpretation of a literary text, but rather an independent, creative art form: "The art of theatre is neither a spectacle nor a play, neither staging nor dance. It is the totality of elements of which these individual areas are comprised" (Craig 1959: 138). These forms of theatre all tend towards totality, towards the *Gesamtkunstwerk*, although not in Wagner's understanding of the term as, for Wagner, the text-based narrative was an essential feature of his musical drama. Here, totality refers to the entirety of the elements that comprise the theatre; it becomes a point of intersection, a site at which various elements come together in the presence of the audience: space, colour, light, movement, sound, language, etc. Meyerhold speaks of an "independent total theatre [...]

---

10. Kandinsky, however, asked Schönberg to join the Bauhaus. But Schönberg rejected as he was afraid of antisemitism in the city of Weimar; see Kienscherf (1996: 186).
11. For further discussion, see Fischer-Lichte (1995); Esslin (1996); Brauneck (2001) and Kesting (1970).

that should summon not just the spoken word, but also music, light, the 'magic' of the visual arts and the rhythmic movements on the stage" (Meyerhold 1930: 253). Meyerhold pushes the theatre in the direction of choreography and dance and deploys musical terminology in the description of what makes a production significant and revealing:

> We saw that we would have to piece together this performance according to all of the rules of orchestral composition. Every actor, taken individually, isn't singing yet; they need to be embedded in groups of instruments or roles; these groups again need to be interwoven in a highly complicated orchestration; the lines of the leitmotifs have to be raised up in this complicated structure, and actors, light, movement, even objects – similar to an orchestra – everything has to be conducted together.[12]

This idea of composing all elements according to a musical model also shapes the theatre experiments of Oskar Schlemmer at the *Bauhaus* and the visions of László Moholy-Nagy, whose 'theatre of totality' is "an organisation of precise form and movement, controllable down to the last detail, that should be the synthesis of dynamically contrasting phenomena (of space, form, movement, sound and light)" (Moholy-Nagy 1925: 155). For Moholy-Nagy, the human actor becomes completely superfluous, "because, however cultivated he may be, he can at most perform an organisation of movement that is at best related to the natural physical mechanism of his body" (Moholy-Nagy 1925: 154). Moholy-Nagy envisions a mechanisation of the theatre. The crucial idea here is that of a moving, sound-producing image. Narrative, text and actors do not play roles in this 'theatrical apparatus'; instead, there are moving surfaces of colour, light and film projections, mobile objects, etc. In contrast to Meyerhold and Schlemmer, Moholy-Nagy does not view the "synthesis of dynamically contrasting phenomena" as synaesthesia, understood as the metaphysical correspondence of specific colours with specific sounds or other stimuli; instead, Moholy-Nagy emphasises the contrasts of the elements: "I can imagine a total stage performance as a great, dynamic, rhythmic compositional process that combines the greatest colliding masses (accumulation) of resources – tensions of quality and quantity – in an elementally compressed form" (Moholy-Nagy 1925: 158).

In contrast to the *Bauhaus* and its abstract experiments in theatre, Dadaism sought to destroy this precise arrangement and organisation of different elements: anti-art, anti-work, anti-artist. At the end of a senseless and brutish war, Dadaists wanted protest rather than reform; instead of order, they sought a provocative declaration of chaos in art. The Dadaists were enthusiastic about noise and Bruitism, not in the sense of the Futurists and their apotheosis of war, but rather as a means to shout down the bourgeois order that had

---

12. Meyerhold/Tairow/Wachtangow: 'Theateroktober', in Hoffmann and Wardetzky (1972), here cited in Zarius (1976: 7). Alexander Tairow went one step further by creating production scores that precisely 'composed' the interaction between all of the elements.

led Europe into World War I and the battlefields of Verdun. Dadaist techniques therefore have less to do with composition than de-composition or the destruction of the status quo: "assemble, collage, transform, alienate, reduce, destroy, ridicule" (Goergen 1994: 6), techniques that John Heartfield described in 1919/20 as 'dadaing'. The de-compositional techniques of Dada are distinguished by their potential application to every kind of material; for example, one could cut up newspaper texts, or even musical compositions or images, and rearrange them in collages. In this sense, Dadaism pursues a 'negative total theatre'.

Dadaism developed two techniques that assumed major significance in the late 1950s, particularly through John Cage: simultaneity and the incorporation of the incidental. Hugo Ball reports, "Hülsenbeck, Tzara and Janco performed a 'poème simultan'. It was a contrapuntal recitation in which three or more voices speak, sing, whistle or otherwise produce sounds at the same time" (Ball 1916: 104). By presenting different texts at the same time, each of their respective meanings is on the one hand distorted because the audience cannot follow the individual poems; on the other hand, the overlapping creates a new text in which the fragments of the individual texts flow into one another and create unforeseeable relationships with one another. The effect on the audience cannot be predetermined; it is incidental and completely different for every member of the audience, depending on where his or her attention is directed and which associations these 'live collages' trigger for them.

In addition to Dadaist productions, Antonin Artaud's theatrical utopia exercised a major influence on various exponents of New Music and Composed Theatre.[13] Boulez was the first to make the connection between Artaud and developments in serial music, which at that time got into crisis. In 1958, Boulez wrote, "I don't feel compelled to puzzle out Artaud's language, but I have stumbled onto the fundamental problems of contemporary music in his writings" (Boulez 1972: 123). Artaud demanded a theatre that was liberated from the 'chains of literature', and that was to be created on and for the stage. And he also emphasised the totality of "all the means of expression utilizable on the stage, such as music dance, plastic art, pantomime, mimicry, gesticulation, intonation, architecture, lighting, and scenery" (Artaud 1958: 39). For Artaud, however, the term 'totality' is reserved for something else, for the totality of the human being and of life: "Renouncing psychological man, with his well-dissected character and feelings, and social man, submissive to laws and misshappen by religions and percepts, the Theatre of Cruelty will address itself only to total man" (Artaud 1958: 122). This totality aims for an ecstasy, for the 'cruelty' of human existence as a glance behind the mask of civilisation:

---

13. Cage became familiar with Artaud's writings in 1952 during his stay at Black Mountain College. Pierre Boulez had a more direct contact with Artaud. He was the musical director of the theatre company of Jean-Louis Barrault, who also met Artaud in the winter of 1934/35 and played the role of Bernardo in his production of *Cenci*.

Theatre will never find itself again [...] except by furnishing the spectator with the truthful precipitates of dreams, in which his taste for crime, his erotic obsessions, his savagery, his chimeras, his utopian sense of life and matter, even his cannibalism, pour out, on a level not counterfeit and illusory, but interior.

(Artaud 1958: 92)

Artaud wants to reconstruct the ancient connection between art and life in (religious) ritual through his theatre. To do this, however, the separation between the stage and the audience must be overcome: "We abolish the stage and the auditorium and replace them by a single site, without partition or barrier of any kind, which will become the theatre of action" (Artaud 1958: 96). It is precisely this connection between art and life that both the Happenings and Fluxus movements strove for with their respective theatres of action; indeed, their adherents viewed themselves as Artaud's successors. Yet their neo-Dadaist spirit stands in opposition to the requirements of exactitude and precision in Artaud's theatrical compositions, referenced above by Boulez:

Once aware of this language in space, language of sounds, cries, lights, onomatopoeia, the theatre must organize it into veritable hieroglyphs, with the help of characters and objects, and make use of their symbolism and interconnections in relation to all organs and on all levels. [...] Meanwhile new means of recording this language must be found, whether these means belong to musical transcription or to some kind of code.

(Artaud 1958: 90, 94)

For the generation of young composers and artists in Germany and Austria after World War II, the contact to these avant-garde movements from the pre-war years had been cut off by National Socialism and therefore had to be rediscovered.[14] At the same time a new type of theatre arose, primarily in France, that attached itself to several points of the theatre reforms of the early twentieth century, although it reacted in a unique way to the destruction and senselessness of war: the theatre of Beckett, Ionesco, Genet and many others, which Martin Esslin grouped together under the generic term 'Theatre of the Absurd' (Esslin 1996). Ionesco's *The Bald Soprano*, the subtitle of which describes it as an 'anti-play', premiered in Paris in 1950; *The Chairs* followed in 1951. In 1952, Beckett published *Waiting for Godot*,

---

14. The poet and composer Gerhard Rühm describes his situation in Vienna after the war as follows: "after seven years of enforced isolation, we young people, wanted to recoup everything that had happened during that time in the outside world, the modern art that had been denied to us. [...] We greedily devoured the fragmentary information we received about expressionism, dadaism, surrealism, and constructivism, passed it around, painstakingly stitched it all together; there was almost something sectarian, cultish, about the whole thing. First we had to find out the most important names and titles, just to know where we should take a closer look. That made every hint, the smallest citation, an exciting discovery" (Rühm 1985: 7).

which also premiered in Paris in 1953. And then there was *Endgame*, which, under curious circumstances for a French play, premiered in London in 1957.

Ionesco and Beckett both integrate the coarseness and grotesqueness of popular theatre and the gags and situational comedy of the vaudeville show. Vladimir and Estragon clearly refer to the tradition of the comic duo, even to the tragicomedy of silent films. Language plays a crucial role in the Theatre of the Absurd, but it is a language that revolves in emptiness, that can no longer move anything in reality, that does not set any narratives in motion and that is completely unsuitable as an instrument of perception. The language of this theatre engages in clichés and stereotypes; thus, for example, the text of *The Bald Soprano* is based on a collage of sentences from an English conversation book. It gets entangled in itself, disintegrates or falls completely into nonsense, as in Lucky's famous monologue in *Waiting for Godot*, which is a parody of an academic lecture. And in *The Chairs*, the longed-for speaker finally arrives, only to reveal that he is mute.

The Theatre of the Absurd eschews psychological motivations for its characters' stories, which follow patterns or archetypes, or remain – superficially – nonsensical. The individual stories do not come together into a coherent or evolving narrative; instead, these works focus on unfolding a basic metaphor over time, corresponding to the situational and pictorial character. This lends the works the form of a "complex poetic image, a complicated pattern of complementary images and themes that are interwoven in a manner similar to the themes in a musical composition" (Esslin 1996: 313). For example, the repetition of the exact same lines of text in *Waiting for Godot*, the structural meaning of pauses and the principle of variations upon motifs are all striking features. The structural principles of music permit the translation of basic, static, content-based situations into a regimented temporal framework.

The fundamental criticism of text and language as primary elements in the theatre has been levelled since the end of the nineteenth century. This critique led to a crisis of the psychological character and linear uninterrupted dramaturgy and has given rise to forms of theatre that were forced to secure the coherence of their works on the basis of other non-textual, non-dramatic approaches, integrating principles of structure and form that contributed to compositional approaches and ways of thinking.

Theatricalisation of music

Composing the non-musical: **Die glückliche Hand** *by Arnold Schönberg*

If we look at the complementary movement and look for music-theatre forms that start off by making the music itself theatrical or that which apply compositional means to theatrical elements, we inevitably find ourselves returning to the visions of Arnold Schönberg, and in particular the famous music of lights in his *Die glückliche Hand op. 18* from 1913. In a text that he wrote for the 1928 performance of this 'drama with music', he found a very precise and telling way to describe his vision of a new kind of music theatre:

Figure 1: Arnold Schönberg: extract of *Die glückliche Hand*, bars 127–131. Copyright by Universal Edition.

Mir war lange schon eine Form vorgeschwebt, von welcher ich glaubte, sie sei eigentlich die einzige, in der ein Musiker sich auf dem Theater ausdrücken könne. Ich nannte sie – in der Umgangssprache mit mir: *mit den Mitteln der Bühne musizieren*.[15]

Schönberg's libretto describes, in very symbolic language, a dream. A man, of whom it is said that he incorporates the 'supernatural', encounters a woman who gives him something to drink. He falls deeply in love with the woman as she had given life back to him. He touches her hand, but she goes away with another man. In the third picture the man comes to a kind of goldsmith's studio where he makes a golden diadem with only one stroke on the anvil. The workers around him get furious, but before they can attack him there is "a crescendo of the wind" accompanied by a "crescendo of the stage lights" as it says in the score. Finally in the fourth picture the man finds himself back in the situation he was in at the start, and everything in between turns out to have been a dream he is going through over and over again.

The "crescendo of the stage lights" is described very precisely in the score: "Es beginnt mit einem schwach rötlichen Licht, [...] das über Braun in ein schmutziges Grün übergeht. Daraus entwickelt sich ein dunkles Blaugrau, dem Violett folgt."[16] But it is also directly synchronised with the music, the crescendo of the wind and the acting of the man. For this Schönberg even develops a special kind of notation.

This passage is the most elaborate realisation of what Schönberg means with his idea of "composing using the means of the stage". However, this idea is decisive for the whole piece and for all theatrical elements. In a letter of 14 April 1930 Schönberg writes to Ernst Legal of the Berlin *Kroll-Oper* about the staging of *Die glückliche Hand*:

Der Aufbau der Bühne und das Bild wird aus tausend Gründen haarscharf nach meinen Anweisungen erfolgen müssen, weil sonst nichts stimmen wird. [...] Ich habe auch die Stellungen der Schauspieler und die Wege, die sie zurückzulegen haben, genau fixiert. Ich bin überzeugt, daß man das genau einhalten muß, wenn alles ausgehen soll.[17]

And in his text on the occasion of the Breslau-performance he points out:

---

15. "For a long time now I have been thinking of a form, of which I believed, it was in fact the only possible way a musician could express himself on the theatrical stage. I called it – in talking to myself: *composing with the means of the stage*" (Schönberg 1976: 236).
16. "It begins with a slight red light, [...] that changes through brown to a dirty green. Out of this a dark colour between blue and grey develops followed by violet". Cited in Kienscherf (1996: 183).
17. "The setting of the stage and the images will – for a thousand reasons – follow absolutely precisely my instructions. Otherwise nothing is going to work. [...] I have also fixed exactly the positions of the actors and the distances they have to cover" (Schönberg in Kienscherf 1996: 177).

Es würde gewiß zu weit führen, wenn ich alle Beispiele nennen wollte, die einen Begriff von diesem Musizieren mit den Mitteln der Bühne geben. Ich glaube aber sagen zu können, dass es jedes Wort, jede Geste, jeder Lichtstrahl, jedes Kostüm und jedes Bild tut: keines will etwas anderes symbolisieren als das, was Töne sonst zu symbolisieren pflegen. Alles will nicht weniger bedeuten, als klingende Töne bedeuten.[18]

Schönberg is clearly convinced that the effect the piece will have on the audience does not depend solely on the quality of the music but that all the elements in a performance of the piece contribute equally to the effect, and therefore he, as the composer, also organises these visual elements and fixes them in the score.

Schönberg who, as is well known, was also a remarkable painter, was strongly influenced by the synaesthetic ideas of the time.[19] And what we see in *Die glückliche Hand* is that he composes more or less equivalent processes in the music, the wind, the lights and the movement to reinforce the effect of the whole. So even though one can say that here, maybe for the first time, visual elements such as lights are (musically) composed in a rather strict sense, the theatrical elements do not yet hold their own, are not yet of equal status. In other words: what we see is not yet the *polyphony of the elements*. If we look for early examples of this idea, so crucial in Composed Theatre, we would have to turn to the scores of the *Mechanical Eccentric* by Moholy-Nagy from 1925[20] or to the writings of film-maker Sergei Eisenstein. In his essay "Vertical Montage", Eisenstein tries to develop a specific methodology for the montage of image and sound in film "by which correspondences between depiction and music are set up" (Eisenstein 1940: 271). But these correspondences no longer imply that sound and image should reinforce each other, but that they can carry different meanings and that, with this tension between the media or elements, a third meaning can be achieved.

Separation of elements: L'Histoire du Soldat *by Stravinsky*

In the field of music-theatre, Stravinsky's *L'Histoire du Soldat* (1918) was a milestone with respect to a new way of organising the different theatrical elements. In this piece – a kind of anti-Wagnerian-opera – we find text (narrator), music (small ensemble) and acting (including dance and pantomime) placed on a stage divided into three parts: music and text at the sides, the theatrical part in the centre. So while in opera all comes together

---

18. "But I think it is apt to say that it is every single word, every gesture, every beam of light, every costume and every image that does it: nothing should symbolize something other than what sounds usually symbolize. Everything should mean nothing less than the sounding notes mean" (Schönberg 1976: 238).
19. Other famous examples would be Scriabin's *Prometheus* op. 60 or his 'Key-Colour Scheme'.
20. Reprinted in Fiedler and Feierabend (1999: 305).

culminating in the singer, who performs text, music and a theatrical role all at the same time, here each element is visually but also structurally independent from the others. And it all comes together only in the perception of the audience, thus making the audience an active part of the performance. Stravinsky makes this anti-operatic approach even more clear as he rejects singing altogether. The text is an adaptation of a Russian fairytale. Charles Ferdinand Ramuz, who wrote the text, retained its epic form, so that there is neither dramatic dialogue nor psychologically delineated characters. Instead they are like archetypes. As Ramuz pointed out: "Wir würden die alte Tradition der Gauklerbühnen, der Wanderbühnen, der Jahrmarkttheater wieder aufnehmen."[21] Stravinsky's music follows this non-psychological approach in that he takes up forms of popular music (ragtime, tango, waltz) and works with them, alienates them etc. He consciously abandons Wagner's through-composed form, returning to single numbers that can stand on their own and that are interpolated into the narration. So the character of the whole piece is one of distance and alienation, adopting popular theatre and music forms and bringing art very close to the world of people's ordinary lives. *L'Histoire du Soldat* is, therefore, the first example of an epic music-theatre that became very successful in the twenties and thirties, especially in the collaboration between Bertolt Brecht and Kurt Weill, but that also had great impact on the New Music Theatre of the sixties and seventies: small forms, non-psychological characters, no (operatic) singing, no dialogue, separation of the elements, empathy with popular or trivial culture (cabaret, music hall, variety etc.)[22] and, last but not least, the emphasis on the visual and corporal aspect of making music. Stravinsky put the musicians on stage not only to demonstrate the separation of the elements of music-theatre, nor just for practical reasons, but in service to his conviction: "Wenn man die Musik in vollem Umfang begreifen will, ist es notwendig, auch die Gesten und Bewegungen des menschlichen Körpers zu sehen, durch die sie hervorgebracht wird."[23]

"Towards theatre": John Cage[24]

Although historic and aesthetic contexts are completely different, there is a striking echo of Stravinsky in John Cage's observation that "[r]elevant action is theatrical (music [the imaginary separation of hearing from the other senses] does not exist), inclusive and intentionally purposeless" (Cage 1955: 14). But Cage does not only mean that the visual

---

21. "We wanted to revive the old tradition of jugglers' theatre, of moving stages and fair-theatre", Ramuz in Hilty (1961: 67).
22. Especially in the work of Mauricio Kagel we find a lot of examples for this; see, for example, his *Varieté* or *Dressur* (both 1977).
23. "If music is to be fully grasped it is also necessary to see the gestures and movements of the human body by which it is produced", Stravinsky in Hilty (1961: 69).
24. Cage (1957: 12).

aspect of making music is an essential part of music. He is set on radically challenging the very concept of music and composition, and thus, by implication, he also challenges what has been said about Composed Theatre so far. In one way or another, 'composition' in music has always been understood as an intentional process of building meaningful musical structures and forms that guarantee the unity of a musical piece. And it is exactly this notion that John Cage and the composers of the New York School disposed of:

> Cowell remarked at the New School before a concert of works by Christian Wolff, Earle Brown, Morton Feldman, and myself, that here were four composers who were getting rid of the glue. That is: where people had felt the necessity to stick sounds together to make a continuity, we four felt the opposite necessity to get rid of the glues so that sounds would be themselves.
>
> (Cage 1959: 71)

This rejection of the old concept of composition is twofold: firstly, the aim is to avoid any kind of continuity between sounds or events, and, secondly, composing no longer has to do with the intentions of the composer but, quite to the contrary, the 'new' composer must develop a technique that will negate the interference of his intentions. Cage's concept of composition only becomes productive for the discussion of Composed Theatre if we view it together with the equally radical change in the concept of music. Already in 1937 Cage had denied that there was any difference between noise and music, thus embracing within the concept of music any kind of sound: "Wherever we are, what we hear is mostly noise. When we ignore it, it disturbs us. When we listen to it, we find it fascinating. The sound of a truck at fifty miles per hour. Static between the stations. Rain. We want to capture and control these sounds, to use them not as sound effects but as musical instruments" (Cage 1937: 3). With this *Credo* Cage puts himself in line with Edgard Varèse and also with futurism and its vision of a music of noises as described by Luigi Russolo in *The Art of Noises* (1916). But in the fifties John Cage went even further, opening music to any kind of action, with or without sound: "Where do we go from here? Towards theatre. That art more than music resembles nature. We have eyes as well as ears, and it is our business while we are alive to use them" (Cage 1957: 12).

For Cage, there are two approaches that lead to the theatre – one via the material and the other via the listener. By opening music to the sounds of everyday life – that is to the sounds of the environment (see *4' 33"*) and to the other arts – actions of any type can now be used as musical material. It is still music, though, because the only dimension that, elusively perhaps, remains fixed for Cage is that of time, the temporal shifts between (sound) event and silence. The second approach, via the listener, is based on Cage's fundamental conviction that human experience is total: it is not divided between the different channels of sensory perception, neither in everyday life nor in art. Music is not just what is heard but also what is seen; it is the comprehensive experience of an action. And therefore "relevant action is theatrical".

In 1952, Cage and David Tudor created a performance that pursued Cage's idea of indeterminacy to its logical extreme, an action that radically questioned the idea of a musical work. The *untitled event* took place during a summer course at Black Mountain College, an interdisciplinary art school founded by Joseph Albers along the lines of the *Bauhaus* in Dessau. The *untitled event* was also interdisciplinary: participants included the composers John Cage and Jay Watt, the dancer Merce Cunningham, the musician David Tudor, the visual artist Robert Rauschenberg, and the writers Charles Olsen and Mary Caroline Richards. Cage's composition consisted of nothing more than directions for periods of time ('time brackets') that prescribe to the actors when they act (or can act) and when they cannot. The actions themselves were determined by the actors without further discussions. During the action, Rauschenberg's *White Paintings* – which Cage also animated for his famous silent piece *4'33"* – hung from the ceiling; Cage stood on a ladder reading a text from Meister Eckhardt and later performed a piece for radio. Tudor played a piece for prepared piano, Olsen and Richards read poems, while Cunningham danced through the room chased by an angry dog. Rauschenberg projected abstract slides and a film. Coffee was served during the performance. The audience was apparently thrilled, and Cage was pleased because the performance met his desire for the absence of intentionality. It was "purposeless in that we didn't know what was going to happen" (Cage 1955: 15).

Here we see that, for Cage, the idea of non-intenionality is intrinsically linked with another idea that has become extremely important since: the idea of experiment or of the experimental. Cage at first, as he explains in his essay "Experimental Music" (Cage 1957), refused to call his music experimental. But later he accepted it. "What has happened is that I have become a listener and the music has become something to hear" (Cage 1957: 7). For Cage, music becomes something to hear only if the composer is in the same position as any other listeners insofar as, like them, he does not know in advance what exactly is going to happen, what there will be to be heard. And 'composing' means exactly that: the creation of such listening situations. This requires techniques to bypass the preferences and intentions of the composer and to avoid purposeful structures.

> Where, on the other hand, attention moves towards the observation and audition of many things at once, including those that are environmental – becomes, that is, inclusive rather than exclusive – no question of making, in the sense of forming understandable structures, can arise (one is a tourist), and here the word 'experimental' is apt, providing it is understood not as descriptive of an act to be later judged in terms of success and failure, but simply as of an act the outcome of which is unknown.
>
> (Cage 1955: 13)

Cage's idea of the experimental is still vivid in the field of Composed Theatre – as in one way or another it continues to inspire the majority of contemporary art. But the focus seems to have changed somewhat. Most artists and ensembles try to develop strategies that deliver results that are unforseen and non-intentional, and therefore "experimental" in the sense

Cage uses the term, be it by introducing chance operations or by researching the phenomenal qualities of certain artistic materials or questions etc.[25] But all this usually happens as one part of the process of devising. For the performance, however, most artists come back to the more traditional concept of composition, that is the 'forming of understandable structures' such that the composer/the performers do know the outcome – at least within a certain range of chance – in advance.

But even if the aspect of non-intentionality has lost some of its impact, other features of Cage's concept of composition and music are still extremely influential for the field of Composed Theatre. Most important is (1) the wide concept of music itself as outlined above. Music is not just any sound or noise but any event happening, any action being performed within a certain time span, be those actions artifical or environmental. Consequently, there is no difference between events to be heard or to be seen. Cage's broad concept of music shifts towards theatre, negating not only the separation of the senses but that of the arts, too. And if composition is not about making structures there is also no question of selecting some elements rather than others. Everything can happen simultaneously. In this way Cage's version of Composed Theatre is (2) the most radical realisation of the idea of non-hierarchy between, and independence of, the theatrical elements that is crucial to Composed Theatre.

As in the case of the *untitled event*, Cage's pieces since 1952 are no longer fixed objects but (3) processes. "To approach them as objects is to utterly miss the point. They are occasions for experience, and this experience is not only received by the ears but by the eyes, too" (Cage 1958: 31). The *untitled event* exists only in the very moment of performance. It is unique and unrepeatable. What the 'piece' is, or is about, what it 'means' is completely left open to the experience of every single spectator – and all of them will experience something quite different. So Cage's music – or theatre – (4) is directed to the perception and the individual experience of its spectators in the very moment of performance.

That Cage's pieces are, in fact, processes, also implies that they are not completed by Cage but left open for the performers. They are *indetermined*. For Cage *indeterminacy* is one way to ensure that his own intentions do not enter his pieces and performances. But for the performers it requires an involvement in the compositional process of a particular version of a piece, making them co-composers. For example, in his *Songbooks* (1970) Cage gives rules and instructions to work out singles pieces, but *how* this is done will very much depend on each performer, his or her experience, taste, capacities etc. That means that Cage asks for – and makes himself dependent on – a certain kind of performer who is willing to get involved in the development of the pieces themselves rather than 'just' giving good interpretations of those pieces. With this (5) Cage changed the notion of authorship, opening the way to a less hierarchical and more collective way of working.

Cage's aesthetics rapidly spread into different forms of art. The *untitled event* inspired a new interdisciplinary and performative form, the Happening. When Cage gave classes on

---

25. For such a research approach see the chapters of Jörg Lensing and Nick Till in this book.

experimental music at the New School for Social Research in New York in 1956, among his students were a few composers, including George Brecht and Toshi Ichiyanagi, but mostly fine artists, photographers and film-makers, among others Allan Kaprow, Dick Higgins, Scott Hyde and Al Hansen.[26] Cage's aesthetics triggered Fluxus and Performance Art and had a great impact on contemporary dance, especially through his collaboration with Merce Cunningham, Robert Rauschenberg and Jaspar Jones. Today, Cage's ideas are still especially efficacious in interdisciplinary contexts and therefore also in the field of Composed Theatre.

Total organisation of parameters: Composed Theatre and the spirit of serial music

If we examine early serial music, there seems to be very little that points in the direction of Composed Theatre. Serial music precluded any kind of extra-musical meaning, expression and subjectivity. Yet there are some features within the compositional basis of serial music that have become highly relevant for Composed Theatre. And it was the clash of this highly organised structural music with the aesthetics of John Cage and the early happenings that unleashed enormous productivity in the field of music-theatre in the sixties, making this period the true starting point of Composed Theatre. The central aesthetic qualities to which the serial composers devoted themselves were musical order and structure.

> Order means: the merging of the individual into the whole, of difference into unity. The criteria for order are evocativeness and disambiguity. The goal of ordering is to approach the conceivable perfection of order in general and in its particulars. [...] In total order, everything is equal in its individuality. The sense of order is founded in the disambiguity between the individual and the whole.
>
> (Stockhausen 1952: 18)

The doctrine that all parameters are equal, reified via serial organisation, is initially related here solely to musical material in the narrow sense, namely tones, sounds and, with the early pieces of electronic music, noises as well.[27] But it comes as a consequence of the emancipation of new materials that serial procedures and methods can be applied not only to tones, sounds and noises but also in principle to any material that can be arranged as scales and can be quantified in this way. One of the essential discoveries of serial music for composers was that the processes and strategies of composition are separate from the material used. Composition was understood as a set of specific methods of organisation that are no longer bound to specific material. And this step made composition with non-musical

---

26. See Kostelanetz (1973: 171–74).
27. See Karlheinz Stockhausen, *Studie II* (1954) and *Gesang der Jünglinge* (1956).

materials possible. Mauricio Kagel formulated this in his often-cited remark: "You can use sound materials. You can compose with actors, with cups, tables, busses, and oboes, and finally compose films" (Kagel in Prox 1982). So following the internal logic of serial music, European composers finally arrived at a point quite similar to one that Cage had already made in the early fifties, even if on the basis of completely different aesthetic beliefs, when he sustained that virtually everything could turn into musical material.

In his 1959 essay "Musik und Raum", Stockhausen depicts the development of electronic music as an immediate consequence of the principle of equality of all musical parameters.

Since 1951, we have been confronted in composition with the striving for an equality of all of the characteristics of sounds: all of them should be involved in the same degree in the formative process so that you can always represent new creations in the same light. It turned out, though, that this equality of tonal qualities is extremely difficult to achieve.
(Stockhausen 1959: 69)[28]

Such exact proportioning, especially within the parameters of timbre and dynamics, "demands automatic electro-acoustic processes" (Stockhausen 1959: 69).

And there is another decisive point in the theatricalisation of music that is associated with electronic music. Stockhausen's *Gesang der Jünglinge* was performed for the first time on 30 May 1956 in the large studio of the Cologne broadcasting centre. Stockhausen placed five groups of loudspeakers around the audience and allowed sounds and noises to be projected into the space and to move through the room. If spatial effects in music had previously tended to be a musical by-product or dramaturgical effect, now the sound space or sound movement became a component "essential for understanding the work" (Stockhausen 1959: 60).

In *Gruppen für drei Orchester* (1957), Stockhausen applied the principle of spatial loudspeaker distribution to three orchestras of identical instrumentation, and grouped them around the audience. It was only a small step to move from wandering sounds to wandering musicians, who then actually carried their sounds through the room.[29] This is where music came into motion, and movement "is the fundamental element of Instrumental Theatre and is taken therefore into account during musical composition. Movement on the stage becomes an essential feature for differentiating from the static character of a normal musical performance" (Kagel 1960: 123).

The rapid development of instrumental techniques, in the context of the emancipation of timbre as an effective parameter, also led – indirectly though – to a theatricalisation of music, and turned concert-going into a visual experience. Schnebel, for example, wrote the following

---

28. The problem is that the various parameters are scalable in very different ways; Stockhausen contrasts the 88 pitches of the keyboard with c.40 distinguishable note durations and c.20 timbres that could be played by a conventional orchestra.
29. See for example Dieter Schnebel: *! (madrasha II)* for three groups of a choir (1958).

about the performance of Boulez's *Polyphonie X* in Donaueschingen in 1951: "The conductor flailed out unusual tempo changes. The exorbitant difficulties of the instrumental parts created a game that somehow called to mind difficult gymnastic exercises" (Schnebel 1968: 8). There is also a theatrical element when a cellist, as in Kagel's *Match*, suddenly threads his bow between the strings and the body of the cello and draws it across the underside of the strings. Here the action that an instrumentalist must perform to create a specific sound receives more attention than the sound that is produced. The action is liberated from its mere functionality; it is emancipated and constitutes its own independent theatrical element.

The use of unusual instruments has a similar effect, whether it be the sirens set in motion with a hand crank in Varèse's *Ionisation* (1930/31), or the unusual percussion instruments, such as brake drums and anvils, that Cage uses in *First Construction (in Metal)* (1939). Such instruments entail a visual component; they belong to a specific context outside the art world, and they bear these associations with them as they are brought into the art world. In a similar way, the search for new sounds leads to the playing of traditional instruments in 'inadequate' ways; Cage for example often treats the piano like a percussion instrument.

One piece that combines all these elements is Cage's *Water Music* (1952). The pianist sits in front of an enormous score. There is a pail of water and a radio next to him and a duck-call whistle around his neck. He starts a stopwatch and turns the radio on. For 21 seconds nothing else happens. The pianist listens, as does the audience. Depending on where the piece is performed, the radio plays static, music or overlapping broadcasts. Later the pianist plays a few musical gestures, stands up to throw playing cards into the body of the grand piano, sits down again, waits. He blows the whistle and submerges the whistle, still whistling, in the pail of water, pours water from one vessel into another, stands up to prepare a few sounds, plucks a single note, waits. Various actions are repeated. The piece is over when the stopwatch shows 6'40".

Water Music can be considered an example of Composed Theatre. The objects used are heavily loaded with associations from the everyday world: the radio, pail, duck-call and playing cards. Without representing anything in particular, these objects incorporate their content into the piece. But these objects are used exclusively as musical instruments, on an equal basis with the piano. The actions required to operate these unusual instruments are just as unusual as the instruments themselves. The audible dimension of these actions appears to some degree as a by-product of visible actions – and not vice versa, as we are accustomed to, for example, from the movements that orchestral musicians make when they perform. When the pianist stands up and throws a few playing cards one after the other onto the grand piano's strings, the audible effect of this musical action is less striking than the visual element of its enactment. Heinz-Klaus Metzger notes

> Cage recognised at that time that one can scale the audiovisual compositions of actions, that a scale of purely visual actions can be constructed, beginning with a movement that is soundless, to gestures that make a little bit of noise, to the other extreme of a gesture that one can only hear and cannot see at all.
>
> (Metzger 1960: 260)

Cage, however, was never concerned about such scaling or even an exact composition of these relationships. Metzger is clearly arguing here from the context of serial music, for which the possibility of scaling is the prerequisite for being able to work with something as musical material. Even if Metzger's remark does not apply to Cage, the option of being able to compose actions serially, and especially the opportunity to contrast the audible and visible sides of these actions, played a crucial role in the development of New Music Theatre in Europe. Musical action, which was originally conceived as an organic whole in the making of music, turns out to be just as divisible into discrete parts as the individual musical sound.

Composition with stage sets: **Die Himmelsmechanik** *by Mauricio Kagel*

Mauricio Kagel's *Die Himmelsmechanik* (1965) provides a particularly clear exemplification of how composition shaped by the experiences of serial music goes beyond its influences and leads to its own form of Composed Theatre. The piece is identified by a subheading in the score as a *Composition with stage sets*. In an Italian-style theatre the parts of a stage set move about: "At first, grey-pink clouds drift by, then a blue vapour appears in which the sunrise totters upward. As if by accident, the moon appears for a brief moment. He comes back though, marries the sun, such that only the full moon remains" (Schnebel 1970: 173). And all the movements of these set pieces are precisely notated in the score, where they follow a compositional and not a narrative logic. If we study Kagel's sketches for *Himmelsmechanik*, it becomes clear that Kagel actually organised the procession of stage images in a very strict serial manner at the level of material organisation:

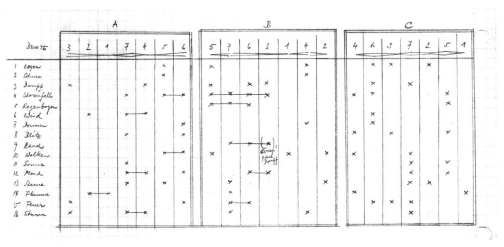

Figure 2: Sketch by Mauricio Kagel for the disposition of elements for *Himmelsmechanik*. Copyright by Paul-Sacher-Stiftung, Basel.

In the first step, Kagel de-composes the weather into 16 discrete elements, assigning a graphic symbol to each element. Twelve elements are represented with stage images only, that is, only in a visual way; rain and fire are represented acoustically *and* visually, and thunder and wind only acoustically. Kagel applies a quasi-symmetrical 'series' to the list of elements, read out from the middle: 3 2 1 7 4 5 6. Each one of these numbers determines how many elements appear simultaneously and at what intensity they will appear. Which elements would appear Kagel initially decided at random.[30] Ultimately, this sketch remained a preliminary study. That is to say that Kagel did not follow *this* material organisation during the composition process. What is crucial, however, is the compositional thinking shown here in the creation of theatrical processes, thinking that is deeply influenced by the experience of serial composition. If the structural procedure at the material level is completely separated from the results at the level of perception, it follows that serial procedures can be applied to other non-acoustic materials; whether to temporal distances or statistical occurrences that are serially organised, or to the procession of weather conditions, makes no difference, as this level of organisation exists below the borders of perception. The only prerequisite, as stated above, is that the affected processes can be scaled in discrete units that can be represented by means of number series. These elements of serial music go far beyond this music to exercise a critical influence on Composed Theatre, in which compositional processes are applied to non-musical materials and media without a second thought. Here, in a very literal sense, the various elements of theatre are composed.

Composition of body language and sign language: The Composed Theatre of Dieter Schnebel

At the end of this chapter, I want to give two further examples that illustrate the application of compositional procedures to theatrical material: *Körper-Sprache* (1979/80) and *Der Springer* from the *Zeichensprache* cycle (1989), both by Dieter Schnebel. *Körper-Sprache. Organkomposition für 3–9 Ausführende* is the first composition by Dieter Schnebel in which he completely renounces the acoustic dimension. *Körper-Sprache*, like Schnebel's more famous *Maulwerke*, is less a composition than it is a set of directions or handouts to the performers for the creation of a composition. As in *Maulwerke*, Schnebel composes a process rather than a result, one that can be written out into a work-like complex and performed, yet does not necessarily need to be so. Such a performance – and this is interesting in the context of Composed Theatre – does not necessarily lead us to believe that it has anything to do with music. An uninformed spectator, unfamiliar with Cage's broad definition of music, would probably say that it was a form of abstract dance or theatre. But the way in which Schnebel organises the process, how he structures the material panels that comprise the

---

30. For a more detailed analysis of the process of composition, see Rebstock (2004).

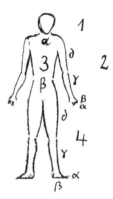

Figure 3: Section from the introduction to Dieter Schnebel: *Körper-Sprache* (1979/80). Copyright Schott Music.

composition, reveals that the piece is conceived through and through as a musical composition. And Schnebel's own debt to his experience of serial composition can also be clearly seen.

Schnebel starts off by subdividing the continuous field of possible human movements into discrete units in order to generate a matrix of combinatory possibilities to which any serial technique could in principle be applied.

In his introduction to the score, Schnebel writes:

> By means of such quasi-mathematical division of physical movements, we can create mathematical combinations: 1+2, 1+3, 1+4, 2+3, 3+4, 1+2+3, 1+3+4, 2+3+4, 1+3a, 1b+2a, 3b+4g etc. [...] This structure, with its seemingly pure formality and cool-headed analytical nature, facilitates on one hand acquisition and rehearsal as well as concentration; on the other hand, the structure corresponds to the limbs themselves and denotes empathy with the body's structure, its connections – and its life.
>
> (Schnebel 1980)

Almost exactly ten years after *Körper-Sprache*, Schnebel completed the *Zeichensprache* cycle, which premiered on 3 May 1989. *Zeichensprache* can be understood as a composed version of *Körper-Sprache*: the four regions of the body – head, arms, torso and legs – correspond to individual pieces. In contrast to *Körper-Sprache,* however, *Zeichensprache* no longer guides the performers to their own fully composed versions of the piece. One could say that *Zeichensprache* is a work instead of a process, meaning that Schnebel composes concrete actions and movements for a defined, straightforwardly performable piece. And, also in contrast to *Körper-Sprache, Zeichensprache* adds the acoustic dimension in the form of utterances, and Schnebel composes the relationship of these two levels with high precision. I will exemplify this with his piece *Der Springer.*

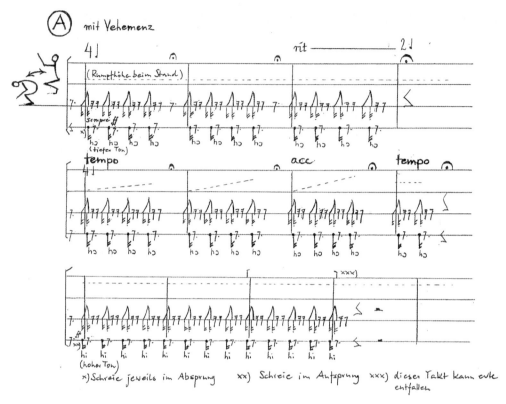

Figure 4: First page of Dieter Schnebel: *Der Springer* (1989). Copyright by Schott Music.

The piece begins with the exposition of the basic material: regular jumps from a half-upright position, with a sound uttered each time at the moment when the performer lands on the ground. From the audience's perspective, this material is viewed as a unit, as a gesture of strength and resoluteness, perhaps also as a sign of stubbornness.

Schnebel de-composes this homogeneous basic material into three levels that he then writes as three independent layers into the score: the height of the torso, the jumping movements, and the sounds. It is interesting to see how, from this original gestural-musical unit, these three levels are emancipated as independent elements so that one can perceive the alternation between homophonic and polyphonic structures, and finally how a highly expressive piece of Composed Theatre arises from this analytical, technically composed grasp of movement, one that proscribes every type of psychological or narrative motivation – which appears to be a basic prerequisite for the musical quality of non-musical material to appear at all in the foreground of perception.

In the first system, all three layers are synchronised, preserving the perception of a unified gesture. Schnebel plays here with just one element, namely the alternation between the metrical similitude of the jumps and the non-metricised pauses. In addition, there is a *ritardando* in the third repetition of the jumping blocks. In the second system, an additional element is added to this structure: torso height is introduced as an element in its own right. Everything else remains the same. Instead of the *ritardando*, there is an *accelerando* at the end of the third group. For the third system, there are three decidedly new elements that remain constant within the staves: the pauses fall away, creating a greater, less inhibited flow of energy; the vocal action is performed offbeat for the first time, at the beginning of the jump rather than at the end. And the vocal changes to 'hi' (to be pronounced as 'hee') instead of 'ho'. In accordance with the brighter vocalic 'i', a sound situated higher in the mouth, Schnebel now also prescribes a more upright torso position, enforcing a correspondence between physical movement and vocal colour.

The second part of the piece contrasts with the first one primarily in that, instead of the impulsive jumps, there is a flowing hop from leg to leg, accompanied by continuously flowing breathing that corresponds exactly to the individual hopping steps. The first line exposes the new basic material that then varies in the two following lines. Schnebel – and with him the performer – plays here in a virtuosic performance with rhythmical shifts between and within the individual layers, so that the levels finally fall apart completely and

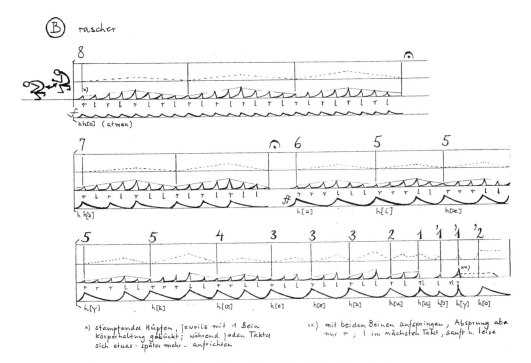

Figure 5: Second page of Dieter Schnebel: *Der Springer* (1989). Copyright by Schott Music.

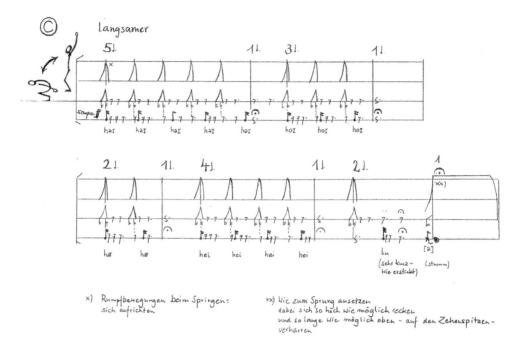

Figure 6: Third page of Dieter Schnebel: *Der Springer* (1989). Copyright Schott Music.

movement, having collapsed into its individual parts, stops. The length of the breaths is distributed differently over the number of hops; the hops become increasingly irregular in a series from right and left, and the torso movement varies in its own tempo through the rhythm changes. Finally, the tempo of vocal shifts gets faster and faster.

In the third and last part, a clear reference is made to the beginning of the piece. There is however a final separation of the originally whole gestural unit: the exclamation of sound, which has up to now always corresponded to the energy of the jumps or hops – either as an offbeat collection of energy or as a descending energetic landing – disengages from this causal structure and becomes its own independent voice: the vocal accent always shifts by a sixteenth note against the jump. And finally, at the very end, there is a single moment that is motivated by content: a brief choked sound and then a relaxed posture, 'as if to jump' – but perhaps also as a sign of victory?

Composed Theatre and Postdramatic Theatre

For the field of Composed Theatre the sixties and seventies have been a period of enormous innovation in which new ideas arose faster than they could actually be assimilated. And, as is well known, this dynamic was driven by an impetus to break down the borders between the arts on the one hand and between the arts and everyday life on the other. There is, for example, the Happening that found its place in the fine arts but that was heavily influenced by John Cage; the Happening works with all kinds of material and deploys diverse performance elements in its presentational mode, leading eventually into Performance Art. There is Fluxus that, at least at the beginning, was mainly pioneered by people from the arts scene, but was understood as musical performances by its representatives. There is the dance scene, for which the collaboration between Cage, Cunningham and Rauschenberg or Jones was highly influential. Or the *Judson Dance Group*, which worked with chance operations à la Cage, or the German choreographer Pina Bausch who, from the late seventies, integrated spoken text into her performances, bringing them closer to theatre. There is the whole field of new electronic media, manipulated to serve individual artistic visions and leading on to the creation of new fields of *mixed media, intermedia* or, later, *multimedia*.

Thus, even if we pick out just a few examples from this whole field of performative art forms, what we see is that the separation of the arts can no longer be determined by the old criteria that dictated that music should work with sound and time, fine arts with colours and space, dance with bodily movement etc. The concept of artistic material – which at least within music was of enormous importance to the evolution of New Music – loses its power: fine artists integrate temporal aspects, musicians integrate spatial elements, dance integrates language and film etc. As with the other art forms, Composed Theatre is then best understood through an exploration, not of the materials used, but rather of the strategies and techniques it employs, how these materials are treated. Looking at Composed Theatre from the perspective of the theatricalisation of music, basically two forms have emerged: one that composes the different and independent elements and means of the theatre according to musical strategies and techniques and another that works with the intrinsically theatrical aspect of performing music with one's body.

In the realm of theatre, Hans-Thies Lehmann has categorised developments since the early seventies as *Postdramatic Theatre* (Lehmann 2006). Some of the characteristics of this Postdramatic Theatre come very close to those of Composed Theatre. Indeed, where Lehmann speaks of the "musicalisation" of the theatrical elements, and points out that this not only means that music has become an ever more important part within current theatre but that the guiding concept was that of "theatre *as* music" (Lehmann 2006: 91), Postdramatic Theatre coincides with the idea of Composed Theatre. Unsurprisingly, then, some of the other symptoms of Postdramatic Theatre are identical with those so far identified with Composed Theatre; Simultaneity and non-hierarchy of the theatrical elements, for example. Consequentely some of the artists Lehmann includes in his Postdramatic Theatre are the very composers that we also name as representatives of Composed Theatre: Heiner Goebbels, Meredith Monk or John Cage.

As Lehmann tries to cover a very wide field of theatre practices over the last three decades, and as he is not trying to give a definition but rather a "panorama of Postdramatic Theatre" (Lehmann 2006: 68), it is not problematic for his project that some of the symptoms come close to contradicting each other. For example, he states that Postdramatic Theatre has the "structure of dreams" (Lehmann 2006: 84) but at the same time is characterised by the "irruption of the real" (Lehmann 2006: 99); and he says that Postdramatic Theatre is essentially a musicalised theatre but at the same time he suggests that it follows a "visual dramaturgy" (Lehmann 2006: 93). What is of interest for us, here, is only the question of how the concepts of Postdramatic Theatre and Composed Theatre relate to one another: Composed Theatre is part of Postdramatic Theatre because of the set of shared symptoms just mentioned, but Composed Theatre also transcends Postdramatic Theatre simply because it includes phenomena from music theatre, scenic concerts, musical performances etc.; that is, phenomena that Lehmann excludes because his focus is still on theatre and not on music, or more precisely the space in between music and theatre.

Where the two concepts overlap, Lehmann refers – besides the composers already mentioned – to the theatre of Robert Wilson, to Einar Schleef and his "choral theatre" ("Chortheater", Lehmann 1999: 233) and finally to the theatre of Christoph Marthaler. In the case of Wilson, it is arguable that he should be seen as a practitioner of Composed Theatre. Obviously the precision and the formal character of movements, lights and choreographies make his theatre very musical. But this seems to be true in a metaphorical way rather than in a literal sense. Wilson's artistic strategies and his thinking might more usefully be related to visual thinking than to compositional thinking. With Einar Schleef it is different. There is no doubt that the way he treats language, movement, gesture etc. is musically composed in a strict sense. In his *Ein Sportstück* (text by Elfriede Jelinek) we encounter scenes in which rhythm, intonation, articulation and dynamics are precisely and richly formed, led by musical rather than semantic demands. In that sense, it is a musical composition made with words, just as we find in the works of Kurt Schwitters, Hans G Helms, John Cage or Robert Ashley. Some of Schleef's scenes are even conducted by a hidden conductor, so that the onstage singers actually become a musical choir. And in the famous *7–8 Chor*[31] within *Ein Sportstück* we find a polyphonic structure between the rhythm of the physical movement of the choir (on different levels), the text, spoken by the choir in unison, and the rhythm that evolves from the bodies moving through sectors of light and no-light. These theatrical compositions by Schleef could be easily written out as scores, as David Roesner has demonstrated (Roesner 2003). Schleef himself, however, does not work in the way a composer would normally do. He does not compose 'in his mind' or 'on paper', creating a score in abstraction from the (sound) materials and in advance of his actors' interpretation of that score. On the contrary, he works out his compositions together with his actors in rehearsals and approaches the final result in constant feedback with what he hears and sees. And the precision of these results is achieved, not by a precise

---

31. David Roesner has named this part of *Sportstück* that way because the words 'sieben, acht' appear at the beginning of every repetition of the basic pattern. For a detailed analysis, see Roesner (2003: 193–201).

form of notation but by repetition, so that even the finest nuances finally sink down into the corporal memory of the actors.[32]

Where the concept of Composed Theatre is concerned, it is important to note that the question is not whether (in this case) Einar Schleef himself understands his way of working as composing in the musical sense, nor whether he *consciously* applies musical strategies. Obviously, there are differences between composers who explicitly compose and theatre directors who may work with compositional means in a more intuitive way. But these differences are not decisive in determining whether or not a piece can be categorised as Composed Theatre. This, finally, depends on the question if it is adequate and revealing to describe the piece or its working process in that way or not.

The case of Christoph Marthaler is, again, different, as Marthaler is a trained musician and had worked for many years as a musician and composer of stage music before he started his successful career as a stage director. That Marthaler's theatre pieces, especially the devised pieces, are driven and determined by the application of compositional strategies is quite obvious. His background in music is, perhaps, most evident in his use of repetitions or, more precisely, the constant and often provocative recurrence of the same material, sometimes in exact repetition, sometimes with subtle variations. These repetitions have a twofold function (as in musical pieces, too). On the one hand, they function structurally. Marthaler's devised pieces[33] do not follow a plot or story. They are situated in just one basic situation, similar in that respect to the theatre of Beckett or Ionesco. Typically it is some kind of waiting situation. The dramaturgy of the pieces – Marthaler himself often calls them 'Abende' ('evenings') – that evolves from these basic and static situations is mainly a musical dramaturgy, and working with repetitions is one of the basic strategies to organise the divergent material in such a way that it, nevertheless, holds together. On the other hand, of course, these repetitions are also part of the process of building meaning. The characters are waiting for something from the outside to come because they themselves lack any energy, any vision, anything meaningful and reliable enough to allow them to develop some sort of coherent action that could change their situation, help them 'escape'. Instead they are occupied with absurd, often slapstick-like activities and rituals that bring the theatre of Marthaler close to the Theatre of the Absurd in which both the reference to mundane activities and the repetition are characteristic. And, most notably, from time to time these isolated, lonely characters of Marthaler's theatre start to sing together with a beauty and perfection that is in stark contrast to their deficient individualities, and that momentarily gives a glimpse of a 'metaphysical horizon' of truth and sense that is extinguished as soon as they stop singing.

---

32. Georges Aperghis describes a similiar approach to musical composition and labels it "oral composition".

33. For example, *Murx den Europäer! Murx ihn! Murx ihn! Murx ihn! Murx ihn ab!*, Volksbühne Berlin, 1993 or *Stunde Null oder die Kunst des Servierens*, Deutsches Schauspielhaus Hamburg, 1995.

But it is not this direct use of music and singing that makes Marthaler's theatre an important example of Composed Theatre but the organisation of the different elements in general: choreographic elements, noises and the musical approach to language etc. One of the devices of Marthaler's theatre, for example, is the frequent transition between meaningful text or language and pure nonsense which, by the way, brings his theatre into a straight historical line from Dadaism. Very often this effect is simply achieved by several characters talking at the same time, a strategy that Marthaler himself calls 'Ballung' ('compression') and by which the focus slowly shifts from the meaning of *what* is said to the musical qualitiy of *how* it is said or rather *how* it sounds. The most impressive example of this is probably the speech that Graham F. Valentine performs in *Stunde Null oder Die Kunst des Servierens*. Here it starts with completely correct sentences – in fact, quotations of speeches that had been made by politicians, military officials etc. in 1945 after Germany had lost World War II, a moment of crisis that in Germany is often referred to as 'Stunde Null', that is 'hour zero'. At first Valentine starts to switch between different languages, mixing German, Russian, French and English; but the more he goes on the more nonsense phrases appear, and it is not surprising that these nonsense sections refer to a sound poem by the Dadaist Kurt Schwitters.[34] And, finally, characteristic of Marthaler's theatre are the elements of Instrumental Theatre. Here, he was influenced and inspired by Mauricio Kagel, John Cage and by the work of Fluxus, with whom he also shares his humour.

To return to the twofold function of the repetitions, Marthaler provides us with a good way to address a more general point about Composed Theatre: when we speak of compositional strategies, or when Lehmann speaks of musicalisation as a symptom of Postdramatic Theatre, this is not a revival of the old form–content debate we extensively find in music aesthetics of the nineteenth century. The application of musical or compositional thinking and acting within theatre is not much served by a determination to separate the formal or structural aspects of theatre from its content or meaning. On the contrary, what this theatre is about, what it makes us experience, is conveyed by means of musical devices. It is no longer the written text, the *drama*, that stands at the top of the hierarchy of theatrical elements but – in a non-hierarchical, postdramatic way – every element can be part of the meaning-making process, and can shift from the foreground to the backgound of perception of any single spectator or listener. And this constant shifting is facilitated by compositional devices and strategies.

Conclusion: Composed Theatre – mapping the 'scene'

As it was said at the beginning, Composed Theatre is barely recognised as a coherent field, largely because of the conditions in which it is produced and presented and the consequent

34. For a detailed analysis of *Stunde Null*, see Roesner (2003). For further writing on Marthaler, see also Hiß (2005).

problems it has in the competition for public attention and reputation. The situation, especially in German-speaking countries, which have nurtured some of the leading lights of Composed Theatre, is symptomatic. There, New Music Theatre (on the more musical wing of Composed Theatre) is not yet institutionally embedded within the theatres run by the state, the cities or the communities. It does not have the status, for example, of contemporary dance (the *Tanztheater*) that is featured in many of these theatres alongside the classical form of dance, ballet. Opera houses very rarely produce New Music Theatre, and if they produce New Operas they usually do so within the traditional aesthetic framework of nineteenth-century opera. Consequently, there is no institutional infrastructure for New Music Theatre, and therefore we mainly encounter it at festivals or in independent productions. There are – or have been – however, some institutions which promote this kind of theatre and have made it part of their specific profile: the *Hebbel Theater* in Berlin under the artistic director Nele Härtling (until 2003); *Europäisches Zentrum für die Künste Hellerau* in Dresden-Hellerau, founded by its artistic director Udo Zimmermann and continued by his successor Dieter Jaenicke, who, however, primarily focusses on dance; the performance series *Visible Music*, initially at the *Theater Bielefeld*, then at the *Nationaltheater Mannheim*, both run by the dramaturg Roland Quitt under the artistic directorship of Regula Gerber, who discontinued it in 2010; the *Forum Neues Musiktheater* as part of the *Staatsoper Stuttgart*, which was founded by its artistic director Klaus Zehelein in 2003 before being abandoned in 2005 by his successor Alfred Puhlmann, who, coming from *Staatstheater Hannover*, brought another format to Stuttgart, called *Zeitoper*, which is more focussed on New Opera, comparable with a series at *Theater Bonn* called *Bonne chance!*. Other interesting, not state-run, institutions are, or have been, the *staatsbankberlin*, founded and run by the dramaturg Berthold Schneider from 2001 to 2005; the *Gare du Nord* in Basel/Switzerland or the *TAM* (*Theater am Markt*) in Krefeld, which has specialised in the Instrumental Theatre of Kagel. Whilst, among opera houses or state-run institutions, the number of venues that give room to New Music Theatre is rather on the decline, there has been increasing activity in the free music theatre scene, and a growing interest at the big Festivals for New Music in these forms of music threatre. Almost all of them integrate at least some scenic works in their programme: *Donaueschinger Musiktage* in Donaueschingen, *Maerzmusik* in Berlin, *Eclat Festival* in Stuttgart, *Wittener Tage für neue Kammermusik* in Witten, the *Ruhrtriennale* in the county of Nordrhein-Westfalen, the series *Kunst aus der Zeit* within the *Bregenzer Festspiele* and the *Wiener Festwochen*. What might be seen in parallel with these showcases is the adventurous programming of the *Almeida Festival* in London.[35]

Within the realm of Postdramatic Theatre, which might partly be called the theatrical wing of Composed Theatre, the situation is somewhat different. Many of its representatives – Marthaler, Ruedi Häusermann, Frank Castorf – are featured at the big state-run theatres, most notably at the *Volksbühne am Rosa-Luxemburg-Platz* in Berlin. And there are networks

---

35. The Musiktheater-Biennale in München should be mentioned, but its focus is on New Opera.

that facilitate co-productions at prominent free theatres: *Sophiensaele* Berlin, *Kampnagel* Hamburg, *FFT* Düsseldorf, *TAT* Frankfurt, *Theaterhaus Gessnerallee* Zürich and *brut* in Vienna. This sector is also better covered by critical and academic writing , and earns much more public interest than New Music Theatre.

If, finally, one looks at the educational institutions that facilitate music, theatre and the performing arts it has to be said that – with some notable exceptions – most are slow to accommodate Composed Theatre. There is a similar tendency to quarantine music/opera from theatre, with most degree courses providing specialist training in one field or the other. Very few courses follow an interdisciplinary or transdisciplinary approach. But if the impression is right that for both theatre and music/opera, Composed Theatre could, over the coming years, make an important contribution to the dynamics of innovation, it is vital that our institutions, be they theatrical, musical or educational, be as open as our minds to the changes that this will bring.

References

Aperghis, Georges (2001) "Werkstattgespräch *Machinations*. Nathalie Singer im Gespräch mit Georges Aperghis", in Berno Odo Polzer and Thomas Schäfer (eds.), *Katalog Wien Modern 2001*, Saarbrücken: Pfau.

Artaud, Antonin (1958) *Das Theater und sein Double*, München: Grove Press.

Ball, Hugo (1916) "Cabaret Voltaire: Bildungs- und Kunstideale als Varietéprogramm" in Brauneck 2001.

Boulez, Pierre (1972) "Ton und Wort" in Boulez, Pierre (1972), *Werkstatt-Texte*, Berlin: Ullstein Verlag.

Brauneck, Manfred (2001) *Theater im 20. Jahrhundert*, Hamburg: Rowohlt [1982].

Cage, John (1937) "The Future of Music: Credo" in Cage 1973.

—— (1955) "Experimental Music Coctrine" in Cage 1973.

—— (1957) "Experimental Music" in Cage 1973.

—— (1958) "Composition as Process: I. Changes" in Cage 1973.

—— (1959) "History of Experimental Music in the United States" in Cage 1973.

—— (1973) *Silence*, Hanover: Wesleyan Paperback.

Craig, Gordon Edward (1957) *On the Art of the Theatre*, London: Heinemann [1911].

Dahlhaus, Carl (1971) *Wagners Konzeption des musikalischen Dramas*, Regensburg: Gustav Bosse Verlag.

Davidson, Donald (1980) "Actions, Reasons, Causes" in D. Davidson (ed.), *Actions and Events*, Oxford: Oxford University Press.

Eisenstein, Sergei (1940) "Vertical Montage", in Richard Tylor (ed.) (1994) *S. M. Eisenstein: Selected Works*, vol. 2, London: bfi publications.

Esslin, Martin (1996) *Das Theater des Absurden*, Hamburg: Rowohlt Verlag [1965].

Fiedler, Jeannine and Feierabend, Peter (1999) *Bauhaus*, Köln: Könnemann.

Fischer-Lichte, Erika (ed.) (1995) *TheaterAvantgarde*, Tübingen: A. Francke Verlag.

Goergen, Jeanpaul (1994) "DADA: Musik der Ironie und Provokation", in *Neue Zeitschrift für Musik*, vol. 155.

Goodman, Nelson (1976) *Languages of Art*, Indianapolis: Hackett Publishing Company.

Higgins, Dick (1984) "Intermedia" [1966] in Dick Higgins (ed.), *Horizons: The Poetics and Theory of Intermedia*, Illinois: Illinois University Press.

Hilty, Hans Rudolf (1961) *C. F. Ramuz, I. Stravinskij: L'Histoire du Soldat. Die Geschichte vom Soldaten. Mit Dokumenten des Werks und sechs Abbildungen*, St. Gallen: Tschudy-Verlag.

Hiß, Guido (2005) *Synthetische Visionen: Theater als Gesamtkunstwerk von 1800 bis 2000*, München: Epodium Verlag.

Kagel, Mauricio (1960) "Neuer Raum – Neue Musik, Gedanken zum Instrumentale Theater", in Alexander Gruber (ed.) (1970) *Mobiler Spielraum – Theater der Zukunft*, Frankfurt: S. Fischer Verlag.

—— (1982) "Im Gespräch mit Lothar Prox, Abläufe, Schnittpunkte – montierte Zeit" in Alte Oper Frankfurt (ed.), *Grenzgänge – Grenzspiele. Ein Programmbuch zu den Frankfurt Festen '82*, Frankfurt, Alte Oper.

Kesting, Marianne (1969) "Musikalisierung des Theaters: Theatralisierung der Musik" in *Melos* vol. 3, pp. 101–109.

—— (1970) Entdeckung und Destruktion, München: Wilhelm Fink Verlag.

Kienscherf, Barbara (1996) *Das Auge hört mit: Die Idee der Farblichtmusik und ihre Problematik*, Frankfurt am Main: Peter Lang Verlag.

Kostelanetz, Richard (1973) *John Cage*, Köln: DuMont Verlag.

Lehmann, Hans-Thies (1999) *Postdramatisches Theater*, Frankfurt: Verlag der Autoren. English translation: Lehmann, Hans-Thies (2006) *Postdramatic Theatre*, London/New York, Routledge.

Metzger, Heinz Klaus (1966) "Das Musiktheater John Cages" in Gianmario Borio and Hermann Danuser (eds.) (1997), *Im Zenit der Moderne*, Freiburg: Rombach Verlagshaus.

Meyerhold, Wsewolod E. (1930) "Rekonstruktion des Theaters" in Brauneck 2001.

Moholy-Nagy, László (1925) "Theater, Zirkus, Varieté" in Brauneck 2001.

Roesner, David (2003) *Theater als Musik: Verfahren der Musikalisierung in chorischen Theaterformen bei Christoph Marthaler, Einar Schleef und Robert Wilson*, Tübingen, Gunter Narr.

Rühm, Gerhard (1985) *Der Wiener Kreis*, Hamburg: Rowohlt Verlag [1967].

Schläder, Jürgen (ed.) (2009) *Das Experiment der Grenze*, Leipzig: Henschel Verlag.

Schnebel, Dieter (1979) *Mauricio Kagel. Musik-Theaer-Film*, Köln: DuMont Verlag.

Schoenberg, Arnold (1975) *Style and Idea*, London: Faber & Faber.

—— (1976) *Stil und Gedanke. Aufsätze zur Musik*, Frankfurt am Main: S. Fischer Verlag.

Stockhausen, Karlheinz (1952) "Kriterien der punktuellen Musik", in K. Stockhausen (ed.), *Texte zur elektronischen und instrumentalen Musik*, Köln: DuMont.

Zarius, Karl-Heinz (1976) "Beiträge zur Theorie des Instrumentalen Theaters" in Kultur Forum, Bonn.

Chapter 2

Composition and Theatre

Roland Quitt

Towards the beginning of the last century a fundamental shift occurred in the aesthetic use of symbols that has altered the functioning of the whole of art. As the most essential of today's premises about art still go back to that time, art, under ever-changing conditions, is still preoccupied with further evaluating problems and possibilities that were posed then and remain current. In this essay I am going to explore some features in the semiotics of contemporary theatre that can be derived from this historic transition. In the first section I will focus on some fundamental features of traditional art. In the second I will try to show how, during the course of a semiotic shift, some of these characteristics changed while others have remained the same. I will thus try to explain what exactly it is, from a semiotic point of view, that leads to art's transformation. Only then, in the third section, I will turn to the consequences that have arisen from this general transition for theatre in particular. If nothing else, I hope in this way to be able to provide some deeper understanding of the relations between features that since Hans-Thies Lehmann have become embedded in the term "postdramatic". In Lehmann's influential book these features are, for the most part, subjects of separate examination. Such an approach, however, fails to illuminate the nature of their semiotic interdependence, and it is for this reason that Lehmann himself fails to achieve his proposed objective, namely "developing an aesthetic logic" (or logical aesthetic[s]) "of the new theatre" (2006: 18). In the context of such an aesthetics, which I hope to be able to define more clearly, we will naturally also find all the particular questions surrounding the theme of this book – the notion of Composed Theatre. If Composed Theatre is not the primary subject of this text, I do hope that my reflections could serve as a preliminary that helps to clarify some of the terms for such discussion.

The logics of description

Description

Today, so much about the arts seems to be in transition, that it is unclear where old terms still fit their purpose. Aesthetic methods that had previously been tied to a specific kind of material – especially those relating to the material of sound – have become viable in other contexts. But traditionally, despite their acknowledged interdependence, it has been the material used by the artist rather than the method of shaping it that has been used to distinguish one art form from the other. Art using words has been called literature, art using sound has been called music and so forth. For the sake of retaining some basic conceptual tools, I will stick to such a terminology here.[1]

Whatever the material of an art form may be – it is the way in which it is organised that determines a work's aesthetic efficacy. Generally, we expect to find unity as well as diversity. More precisely, we expect there to be some sort of diversity which submits at some level to unity.[2] What we are looking for within the organisation of art, then, is a kind of complexity. That is to say, a work of art should present itself as a functional context which satisfies two principal requirements: in it there has to be some wealth of detail, but each detail should be positioned with a view to unifying the whole.

Within traditional art, this process of choosing and ordering details is usually responsive to some sort of external reference. An artwork provides us with a set of labels some of which allow the identification of what the artefact refers to, while others exceed such purpose. In the following, Rubens' painting *The Rape of the Daughters of Leucippus* will serve as my principle example for this functioning of art. In this painting it is the title, rather than any information given by the application of paint to canvas, which takes on the role of picking out and identifying the subject from the realm of the external.[3] Apart from that, by colour on canvas this event is provided with further labelling that outreaches by far the 'identificatory' features given by this event's historic sources. It is this further characterisation, that we would call Rubens' 'interpretation' of the event. While any painterly act of interpretation (the application of details that do not serve identification) would be unsuitable for, say, a sketch of a person being sought by the police (because the sole purpose of such an image is to assist in identification), it is its interpretative aspect (the application of further labels) which traditionally sets a picture that aims to be art apart from any other.

One of the aims of interpretation is to supply the recipient with a vivid impression of the object interpreted. Thus, by an abundance of labelling, it will strive for wealth of detail. It is such wealth of labelling that could be phrased as a work being 'descriptive'. In what follows, any art form that becomes involved with the principle of interpretation, I will call 'descriptive art', speaking of 'descriptiveness' to refer to the feature of being descriptive, and using 'descriptivity' when the semiotic principle of being descriptive is meant. And I will use

---

1. Within such a terminological agreement Dieter Schnebel's term 'visible music' were to be taken as metaphorical. This would not rebel against its basic concept of bringing attention to an art which is not *belonging* to sound but appropriating methods that formerly were reserved to sound.
2. Without diversity, unity would mean dullness; without unity, diversity would mean chaos.
3. Phoibe and Hilareia, the daughters of Leucippus, were abducted by the Dioscuri (Apollodoros III, 11, 2; Hyginius, Fable 80). In the case of this particular painting, the title had long been lost. It was rediscovered around the middle of the nineteenth century by the German poet Wilhelm Heinse. Before that, the painting had been assumed to refer to the "Rape of the Sabine Women". While during that time there was a feeling, that this painting in some ways presented a masterwork, there remained much bewilderment, because what the painting was seen to refer to could hardly be brought into accordance with its details.

Figure 1: Peter Paul Rubens: *The Rape of the Daughters of Leucippus* (around 1618).

'descriptive content' to refer to the totality of labels (identificatory plus non-identificatory) that a descriptive artwork employs.[4]

Composition

What a painter or poet wishes to propose regarding an object guides them in applying colours or choosing syllables. Description – labelling as an act of interpreting as well as identifying – in traditional art thus typically functions as an instrument for guiding the organisation of its material. Within art forms, however, there has remained one which resists this conventional guideline. The possibility of a process of aesthetic organisation which needs no outside reference to guide it first came to prominence on account of instrumental music from the era of Mozart

---

4. My use of the word description differs from Nelson Goodman's (*Languages of Art*, Indianapolis, Cambridge 1976). Goodman uses this term to differentiate signs that are provided by means of language from those that are given by visual means; pictorial labelling thus remains for him *per se* non-descriptive. Within Goodman's terminology, the term 'description' is therefore not associated, as it is here, with the specific procedure used to supply an artwork, be it linguistic or

and Haydn. While there remains an intuition that art in some ways can't be complete without bearing relation to the world, music since then has been constantly seen to challenge aesthetic reflection (Cf. Dahlhaus 1989). In today's colloquial language, the term 'to compose' – denoting an organisation of aesthetic material that gains its principles from somewhere beyond external reference – still refers primarily to the arrangement of the very particular material of *sounds*. Abstract as it is, it marks the dilemma of referring to a process that has no better explanation than that somehow, in some way, things are being 'put together' here.

I will not try until much later to touch on an explanation of the semiotic riddles that are posed by music. Problems, however, that are essentially 'compositional' in nature – because they are dealing with the organisation of aesthetic material beyond external reference – are not limited solely to music. Even in traditional pieces of visual art, for instance, the construction of an image can never wholly be reduced to aspects of external reference. A listing of all the labels contained in *The Rape of the Daughters of Leucippus* would thus fail to account for its strengths or weaknesses as a work of art: only by reaching beyond the descriptive can we discover further important elements of its aesthetic quality.

Any such experiment is likely to lead to a phenomenon that might tentatively be called a "feeling of balance". In painting, such a feeling is of a geometrical kind, revolving around the geometrical centre of the picture plane. The composition of a picture starts with the establishing of a point of focus away from the centre, leading to the creation of a

---

non-linguistic in kind, with a large network of interrelated labelling. The basic semiotic difference in the functioning of visual and linguistic signs, that Goodman emphasises, nevertheless remains relevant to what I call descriptive content: because an image does not follow a notational scheme (cf. Goodman 1976: 136, 137, and 159–164), a complete characterisation of descriptive content can, in such a case, therefore, only ever be approximated. Of course, descriptive content is only part of a much broader scope that amounts to an artwork's total content. Within the Rubens picture, the two horses can be understood as denoting the sexual energy of the Dioscuri – with a dichotomy between light and dark that encompasses both riders and horses as a way to associate them. While the lighter horse is rising up into the sky and, by its colour, is almost dissolving in it, it can be taken as signifying beatitude. Furthermore, as the Dioscuri remain divided not only by this dichotomy between light and dark, but also by one between the heroic and the profane, they can be seen as signifying two aspects within an inseparable dialectics of human erotic drive. Elements that function metaphorically like this can normally be distinguished from features within descriptive content which remain conspicuous by seeming peculiar and at the same time arbitrary in relation to the overall context of the descriptive. Yet, if the event that this painting identifies by its labelling can be taken to exemplify something else, this, of course, does not mean that the painting is *not* referring to this event. There remains a difference between these two levels of meaning. In order to understand the picture, one has to understand also which outside event it refers to. The propositions it includes concerning sexual libido, on the other hand, are of a kind that is more meant to be *felt* than understood, thus relegating the aspects of what could be called deeper meaning to the subconscious. If, in what follows, I do not pay respect to any such aspects of the metaphoric any more, this only expresses my hope that there remain some basic problems that could be solved without it.

counterbalancing focus on the opposite side. Regarding their function within composition, both elements can be said to refer to each other, so that, within a picture, there are elements of reference that do not reach to the outside but stay intrinsic to its own structure. Of course, any such situation of counterbalance is not restricted to pairs of elements as in the above example. One large element can just as well be opposed by a group of smaller ones, or, say, three elements can create mutual opposition by forming a triangle that is focussed around the centre. Moreover, by the different features that any element owns – size, shape, colour, tone, lightness or darkness – it will at the same time be part of oppositions on various levels, thus setting the stage for a rich network of multi-level relationships within a picture.[5]

What composition means, then, is a staging of discrete individual elements within an artefact, all of which refer semiotically to each other in such a way that together they form an ordered system of some complexity. Thus, even where art is descriptive, composition provides a further basic semiotic function, with the complexity that a picture needs in order to be art being already rooted within the compositional. What we are tempted to call "balance", then, is just another word for the kind of order that functions through its owning of some point of general reference, as is the case with the geometric centre within a painting. Moreover, the fact that, when concerned with such balance, we are tempted to speak in terms of 'feeling' is an important point: to own an aesthetic understanding of a work of art one does not have to analyse its level of composition but rather to grasp it intuitively, for composition, as we shall see in what follows, remains on the darker side of the multilevel appeal that aesthetic experience offers to our understanding.

Composition plus description I: Overlapping

Even if we were to inspect Rubens' *Rape of the Daughters of Leucippus* only in terms of its outside reference, it would be impossible to avoid noticing elements that actually are rooted within the compositional. As concerning the proportions of a horse's chest and of its head, or of the extension of a rider's upper body to his foot, the picture contains elements that conflict with our knowledge of external reality. Furthermore, there are elements which barely seem to be justified in terms of outside reference at all: the black blur behind the back of the standing

---

5. In the Rubens painting, the dark element on the upper right (the horse of the riding Dioscuro plus his chest-armour) is opposed by the slightly lighter element on the left (the brownish body of the other Dioscuro extending into the brownish cloak on the ground). Yet the lighter element on the left does not suffice to counterbalance the dark on the right, so to the right of the standing Dioscuro, there is another small dark element. As to forms, there is a tipped triangle (which – in the form of a heart – also relates to symbolic content, just as the red between the legs of the central girl does), being counterbalanced by the strong lining produced by the contrast between light and dark at the left side of the dark horse. While the body of the lower girl helps form the triangle, by her outstretched right arm she also takes part in creating a line that outreaches it. One could go on with such detailed descriptions for a very long time.

Dioscuro, which draws the eye by its very darkness, is only whimsically integrated by the painter into the descriptive by the placing of a tiny black line around this Dioscuro's waist, thus indicating that the shape can be understood as a cloak. However, while this particular painting contains plenty that cannot satisfactorily be explained on the descriptive level, thus enforcing a recognition of considerations that might well belong to the compositional, it has to be seen as exceptional. In most descriptive art, compositional elements are hidden. In order to achieve this concealment, descriptive art uses a strategy – one which Rubens evidently felt licenced to play fast and loose with – which involves an 'overlapping' of the compositional and the descriptive. This strategy requires that the structural elements should simultaneously satisfy the demands of both internal and external references. No compositional element can be introduced that does not also serve the painting's descriptive needs. The functional complexity that is characteristic of this kind of art combines, through the technique of 'overlapping', the descriptive and the compositional, with the semiotic richness of detail contributing to both. In this kind of art, though, it is description that conceals composition and not vice versa: what is consciously perceived at first glance is only the first. Why then, if composition works autonomously, but only in the background, does descriptive art need composition at all, and how does composition interrelate with description?

Composition plus description II: Art as metaphor

If the object of a painting were a historic event, interpretation would set in where labelling outreaches features that are proven to meet with historic reality. To know, such a picture engages in interpretation, is to know it engages in assertions outreaching the proven. Accordingly, its labelling would not be understood by the onlooker as asserting truth (else he would hold any such art to be a mere fraud), but only possibility.

Rather similar, if the object of a picture were to be only a myth, its assertions will take on the form "It is possible that." If Apolloginius and Theodorus – the sources of the event Rubens focusses on – did not bother to tell, surely it remains in accord with their story to assert that Leucippus' daughters were blonde and had braided parts of their hair on the day they were abducted. Surely also, if this story should be 'fiction' and, hence, should itself be centring on mere possibility, Rubens' painting remains all the more occupied with only the possible.

Yet, descriptive art is not just about possibility but is also meant to appear *credible*. Consider, in such respect, a picture of the sinking of the Titanic that would show a second ship of some size being present at this event, a ship that could have saved many lives, while we know that in fact those weren't saved. It is not impossible but would seem highly improbable, as we know from what is presented as fact, that such a ship should have been present. But if this picture would be disturbing by rebelling against what is purported as fact, we would take it as to assert that until now we just have been fooled by what has been presented as fact and that within the possible there remain relevant details which, for some reason, never have been revealed.[6] Descriptive art, then, does not have to submit in its labelling to our previous conception of some object identified, and the credibility it strives for is not just a matter of its labelling.

Instead, our feeling, that a picture appears credible is set forth on a rhetorical level to which composition plays the decisive role. It is the most basic law for art that it must achieve complexity. But this follows from the fact that art is responsive to the world and that our world itself is endless in complexity. In ontological terms composition thus functions semiotically as a metaphor for our understanding of life. As an artwork's compositional structure, by being functionally ordered, corresponds to our notion that the world is ordered, any descriptive work of art carries some claim to portray the world as it is. It is owing to the effect on our subconscious of its hidden compositional imperatives that a descriptive painting persuades us that it is reaching beyond mere possibility. And it is in this way that compositional complexity eventually emerges within descriptive art as a value in its own right.

New art

Description banned

As we have seen, description, as an artistic principle, is heavily dependent on the equally important principle of composition, because what is possible must also appear credible. As we have also seen, composition's pursuit of credibility is linked ontologically to assumptions we make about the nature of things, our belief that both art and the world are in some sort of complex order. But while in art any such order is self-contained and can, within varying degrees of consciousness, be experienced as a system of integral harmony in which nothing remains without meaning, when we leave the field of art and enter into everyday life it is a mere assumption that things are ordered in any comparable way. As long as we live we are caught up in life's problems, never achieving full harmony, and, however hard we strive, we never achieve a full understanding of the world's physical and metaphysical functioning. Furthermore, it is only on the theoretical level that we are concerned with an order which, supposedly, exists independent of us. If order is to exist on the *practical* level, it is we who have to create it.

Descriptive art, then, works on a level that has been called 'the ideal', a metaphysical term which can be boiled down to the notion that art gives us a picture of a possible world in which all problems are solved. The contemplation of art, then, gives us a glimpse of the world as it should be, perhaps emboldening us to resume the task of ordering things and to take control of our life.

---

6. In more complicated ways a similar argument could be made for the case of a picture that is relating to myth.

Figure 2: Julian Schnabel:
Circumnavigating the Sea of Shit (1979).

Such an emboldening is generally short-lived, though, and withdrawing from the world to turn to the perfect order of art also bears aspects of escapism. It is granting us with what Herbert Marcuse has called "den Trost des schönen Augenblicks" ["the comfort of the beautiful moment"] (1965: 63) – some moment of relief that spares us to become active and change our own rather chaotic world for the better. In relation to our task of mastering the world, descriptive art is thus trapped in a double bind. Its unresolved role is to confront reality or to escape it, to help or to obstruct the achievement of freedom.

With the growth of mercantile society in the nineteenth century, art, like everything else, became insistently subject to market forces. Some reappraisal of its function was inevitable. One of the earliest substantial critiques of the priorities of art under pressure from market forces appeared in 1849, shortly after the failed German revolution. In *Art and Revolution* Richard Wagner emphasises that art has "sold itself completely to industry" (Wagner 1976: III 44) and has come to serve merely on a level of escapism. In this writing Wagner also lays the philosophical foundation for a radical change in relations between art and reality.[7] At the beginning of the twentieth century, then, a fundamental change in the principles governing

---

7. Within the new programme that Wagner proclaims for the arts, their function is to act on society in order to bring about a revolution that puts an end to capitalism (*Art and Revolution* 1976: III 9–41.)

Figure 3: Wassily Kandinsky: *Black and Violet* (1923).

artistic production is pushed through – in pursuit of an entirely new relationship between art and the world, the avant-garde banishes the principle of descriptiveness from artistic canon. In the course of technological innovation at that time new kinds of art join the old. The rejection of descriptiveness, however, forces art in all its forms to ask new questions about their methods and modes of symbolic signification.

Until that point in time, and with the problematic exception of music, the arts had relied on descriptiveness to provide the link between composition and external reference, which it had done so effectively that both were generally assumed to be the two sides of the same coin. Deprived of descriptiveness, this unity vanishes and the thought rises that they might not only be distinct as features, but also as functions, and thus can be handled independently. Future strategies in art would split up into relying on two opposing logical methods, one centring on the traditional idea of composition, the other on external reference. In their opposition, they form what could be called the heart of the avant-garde and will later be put to the service also of postmodernism:

- Much in the spirit of *l'art pour l'art*, which can be seen as a forerunner of and preparation for the semiotic shift, the approach that retains the traditional concept of 'composition' seeks to rid itself not only of any adherence to description, but of the whole semiotic function of external reference. Kandinsky's painting *Black and Violet* will serve as my main example (see below under *Avant-garde Type P*).
- Conversely, the approach that seeks to maintain 'reference' to the world (see below under *Avant-garde Type W*) rids itself, together with descriptiveness, of any former concept of composition. Yet, we will see, that composition is not given up by this method, but only in some ways transformed. Malevich's painting *Black Circle* will be my main example of this second type of semiotic method.

Type-P-semiotics: Code provided

The understanding of signs relies on grasping the codes they refer to. In most art the relation between sign and code is fixed by convention. With the passing of time codes may change or even get lost and artworks become subject to misunderstanding. Some codes, however, seem to rest on laws of perception and cognition. The centre of a picture plane, for example, corresponds to the centre of our visual field; it seems like a natural point of reference to which we relate everything else that is brought to our sight. For the type of avant-garde semiotics which I call type *P* – with *P* standing for 'code provided' – it is characteristic that basic traditional codes remain untouched. In fact it is these codes that works of this semiotic type held all the more on to as everything else was subject to change.

The idea that art could be self-contained or 'absolute', which means that it would only be constituted by internal references, is a semiotic phantom that has haunted the theory of art since the heydays of 'absolute' music: when descriptivity is disposed of – so runs the basic thought – art will be stripped of external reference and become autonomous, because all that is left will be the rich network of internal references that is created on the level of composition. During the times of the avant-garde this kind of concept is followed either explicitly or implicitly by the kind of art that turns to the new semiotics of type *P*. Traditional forms of 'absolute' music serve as an orientation for finding new ways for the other arts here. However, if art seeks to free itself of external reference, it cannot avoid semiotic trouble. Kandinsky's *Black and Violet*, painted in the early days of the avant-garde, might help to illustrate this point.

Black and Violet borrows from music a technique of variation that is based on entities that, in music, are called 'motifs'[8] – sonic constructs that can be identified as belonging together because they share structural features (e.g. in terms of pitch or rhythm) and,

---

8. There is a significant difference between the meanings of 'motif' in music and the visual arts, since a motif in visual arts necessarily belongs to the realm of the descriptive or symbolic.

therefore, stand in relation to each other. In *Black and Violet,* one could say, triangular, circular and arched forms also appear as motifs inasmuch as they are variously recurrent and stand in relation to each other. Semiotically, though, there is a decisive difference between motifs belonging to the acoustic and those belonging to the visual. While a musical motif as a scheme inflected by pitch and rhythm is an abstraction of relations that are interior to the work, a visual motif carries greater referential baggage. As an abstraction, a triangle is also always an abstraction of triangular things in the external world, just as a circle *refers* to the group of things that are circular. By the very nature of their specific material it is not possible for visual arts to take possession of semiotics belonging to the acoustic without, even if involuntarily, changing them. Abstraction, then, as the term is used within the painterly and figurative, is not a means to allow an artwork to confine its reference solely to itself, but only a particular way of relating it to more general aspects of the external.

This problem, however, is not the only one that art faces when it attempts to do away with external reference in an effort to create a world of its own. Within the descriptive, as we have seen, composition is always related metaphorically to a suspected ontological order. But for any non-descriptive work (for example, a work of 'absolute' music) this will still be the case – as long as there is no change in the concept of composition itself. Doing away with description, then, does not suffice to solve the problems confronting the advance of the arts over the second half of the nineteenth century, and if the lure of descriptiveness was one of those problems, then, whatever the artist's intention, composition is another. Any system of order presented by an artwork cannot help being taken as relating to ontology. The main dilemma to the idea that art could be 'absolute' is composition as a concept of order itself.

As it developed, avant-garde art of the semiotic type *P* remained preoccupied with this problem. In the 1950s, this led to the paradoxical end represented by John Cage's idea that having no order at all is not only also a system of order, but the most desirable and closest to perfection of all.[9] Introducing a compositional system that – either by mathematical calculation or simply by chance operations[10] – is organised to avoid any recognisable hierarchy within principles of inner interrelation, this led up to a type of artistic work in which each element has the same – indifferent – relation to any other. Logically such a system must be seen as one that is not creating but avoiding order, because where everything refers to everything the concept of referring as a singling out loses its meaning. However, there remains a rhetorical dimension to this kind of art. With respect to the interrelation of its elements it does not organise complexity but chaos, yet, its appeal is still based on the fact that we will be searching in it for order. This appeal comes into play once the work has been

---

9. Cage's phrasing of Thoreau "The best form of government is no government at all", as it appears in *Song-Books* (1970), is not meant as a statement of merely political but also aesthetic anarchism.
10. Within music, in this respect their is common ground to the aleatoric and the serialist.

declared to be art and presented as such. The recipient, then, is confronted with the task to 'create' internal relations where by the method of composition there are none. Paradoxically, in such an artwork, where everything points at nothing, the appeal for the recipients is that everything will point at everything, and they will therefore be able to find a truly endless cosmos of inner references. The mystic density one can experience in such a work, then, is just the other side of its provoked arbitrariness. It is here, at the moment when art seems to get closest to the condition of autonomy, that the semiotics of *P* dissolves into a new kind.

Type-W-semiotics: Code withheld

Unless we shy away from the metaphorical, any geometrical opposition within a picture can be seen as "creating a conflict" within it. Metaphorically, then, Kandinsky's *Black and Violet* reaches further into the external world than I have admitted. The basic "conflict" between the two large elements left and right of centre is enhanced by a symbolism of war, and many of the painter's abstract motifs combine to emphasise this reference. One sees faces, ships, menacing knives, even tips of weapons striking heads. Kandinsky's introducing of the notion of war into such a painting does not, however, licence us to call it a picture about war. It is, rather, a picture centred on the problem of composition, with the notion of war figuring metaphorically to illustrate that it is the idea of conflict that is the basis of the composition's semiotics. *Black and Violet*, then, is a painting about painting. It contains a proposition about painting, and what it proposes is that, once the curtain of descriptive content has been raised, what remains of a painting is only its composition, and what composition boils down to is a structuring of the canvas that amounts to creating a site of opposition.[11]

Malevich's *Black Circle* dates from the same year as Kandinsky's *Black and Violet*. It is also a painting about painting.[12] Yet, it is a painting of a different kind. *Black Circle* holds back from offering propositions, relying rather on raising questions. And if Kandinsky proposes that all there should be left to art is just the traditional concept of composition, then that's precisely what Malevich raises to question.

However novel it may have seemed at the time, there is nothing difficult about using a picture to raise questions. Take any graphic object, for example, an x-ray, declare it to be art by putting it into an artistic context such as an exhibition or gallery, and, given that it is not

---

11. If painting really achieves its goal of being occupied with nothing but painting here, it manages to do so only by referring to the *concept* of painting. Thus, it is ultimately relying on such things within the external that are called painting, and its basic self-referentiality, therefore, remains an illusion.

12. There is some common ground between this painting and Rubens' *Rape of the Daughters of Leucippus*: both are dominated by a circular form positioned outside the geometric centre. But Malevich provides no counterbalancing formation, whereas Rubens uses the outstretched arms of the lower and upper girl to create an arched line at the lower right that both touches and counters the circle.

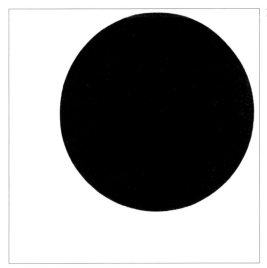

Figure 4: Kazimir Malevich: *Black Circle* (1923).

taken to be art for any commonly accepted aesthetic qualities, anyone who looks at it will automatically question whether it properly belongs there. Not everything that is called art *is* art, of course. To declare something to be a work of art involves two propositions: firstly, that it is meant to function symbolically, and secondly, that in its symbolisation it achieves a certain degree of complexity. Looking only at the simplicity of its structure, *Black Circle*, it might be argued, is too simple to rate as art, but the questions it raises are not simple. They relate to the concepts of complexity, balance and handicraft, but most of all they challenge the concept of art's relation to the world. Is art there to please or to disturb? And if the title *The Rape of the Daughters of Leucippus* signifies that the picture is a representation of the rape of the daughters of Leucippus, what does the title *Black Circle* signify? Surely not that the picture is a representation of a black circle, for what is to be seen here is not a painting of a circle but a painted circle. So if we have a picture that is not picturing anything, can we still rightly call it a picture? If it can be said that, in a 1926 exhibition, *Black Circle* must have provoked complex questions about painting and even about 'art', its functional complexity is comparable, however different, with that of Kandinsky's *Black and Violet*.

If there is a form of art, that can be said to raise questions, this is because such art is meant to provoke a rather conscious process of scrutinising its material, that differs from former ways of doing so. It requires an act of *speculative thinking* in order to grasp the code which gives its elements an aesthetic function. While in former art this code had been agreed upon by convention, such agreement is now given up by the artist, as *Black Circle* obviously hurts any 'feeling of balance' evolving from the habitual effort to gain unification from focus on a geometric centre. Missing functionality, the viewer thus gets entangled in fundamental questions about art, and eventually he is to find out that it is these questions rather than the answers what it is all about. It is the complicated network of such questions itself that provides the picture with its functionality.

Painted, like *Black and Violet*, in the wake of the rejection of descriptivity, *Black Circle*, too, reveals art's traumatic obsession with itself owing to questions of its survival now that its function can no longer be taken for granted. By the late 1950s, though, art had regained confidence and greater scope for reflection, focussing on ecology in land art, problems of media and epistemology in pop art, and it develops various strategies to react to other specified situations of social concern. Because since Malevich the notion of 'picture' has become problematic examples other than paintings might make the point more clearly. In Joseph Beuys' *Schlitten* (Sledge), impressions of coldness and darkness in the assembled objects may lead us to think of existential human distress as one factor that unifies the whole assemblage as a work of art. With *Jason II*, as the title shows, Beuys is bold enough even to refer back to classic subject matter.[13] By virtue of the fact that the semiotics of *W* embraces works that declare itself to be art, some self-reference is necessarily involved, but such work is not exclusively self-referential. The unavoidable questions posed by Malevich and Beuys – 'why is this art?', 'how is this art' – have resonances beyond art itself.

Withholding the code that provides for an artwork's functionality, works belonging to the semiotic model *W* have the form of riddles. They do not present an aesthetic order but it is only through the viewer's attempt to solve the riddle that such an order may be found. This is possible only due to the self-reference that consists in presenting an object as a work of art which otherwise would not be received as such. If a forgotten painting by Rubens or Kandinsky were to be found in a trash-filled attic, it could readily be identified as art, but the same cannot be confidently said of *Black Circle* and certainly not of Beuys' *Sledge*. Stored amid the rest of the attic's detritus, none of them, in fact, would *be* a work of art because there is nothing to declare them one. With type *W*, then, artworks are no longer properly addressed as *objects* but as *situations*.[14] If composition, even under such conditions, remains what it always has been, namely a means of achieving complex functionality through internal relations within a work, now it is a situation (consisting of an object, a place and a time) that is composed. And since the object is now only an element of an enlarged context, it may or may not contain in itself elements of composition – as Beuys' *Sledge* does and Beuys' *Jason II* does not.

If the new semiotics of *W* do not so much abandon principles of composition as apply them in new ways, the same is true in the matter of aesthetic experience. The recipient's aesthetic experience remains one of progressive insight during an act of contemplation, with more and

---

13. Of course, the first question here is, "How can the tub be brought in line with the title?", and the second, "What features of the tub are relevant in this context?"
14. Because of this 'situationist' approach, contemporary art ages much more rapidly than traditional art. It is only by an effort of the historical imagination that we can recover some faint inkling of the rhetorical impact made in the early twentieth century when *Black Circle*, or Duchamp's *Fountain*, were declared to be works of art.

Figure 5: Joseph Beuys: *Schlitten* (Sledge) (1969).

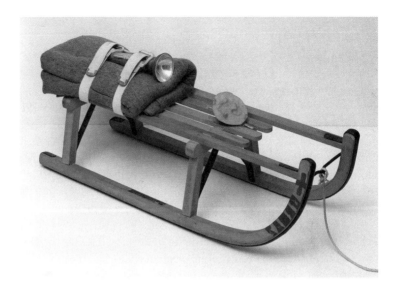

more of a work's details revealing their possible function. As with traditional art, this process is not subject to the closure of scientific analysis. Instead, its specific appeal arises from an emotional response to endlessness, a kind of *feeling* that there is always more to know, more interrelationships to be perceived. But type *W* departs from traditional art in its challenge to aesthetic experience. In two distinctive ways, it blocks off the route to escapism and disallows a response of passivity. In the first place, a gallery filled with everyday objects – an old sledge, a torch, a bathtub – does not offer refuge from the world. The objects that confront the visitor do not belong to an alternative cosmos, but to the everyday banality of this one.[15] Secondly, the semiotics of type *W* call for speculative thinking as an *active* response. Within *W*, art revises its former relation to the world, becomes active in it itself by calling for such response and by turning to the forgotten rhetorical means to challenge, to surprise and even to raise anger.

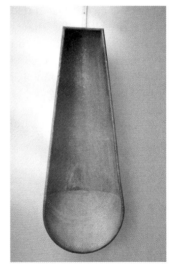

Figure 6: Joseph Beuys: *Jason II* (1965).

---

15. Art of type *W* is always metaphorically posing the question of how we might achieve order within the real. The answer proposed by Wagner, and picked up by Beuys, Cage and many others since, was that we can do so only by transforming utility values into aesthetic values, so that eventually there would be no difference between art and the world. The revolution that Wagner envisages

The postmodern type

In the early years of the avant-garde, the semiotic principle of *W* was characterised by the simplicity of an object or assemblage of objects being presented as art. After all, if the 'artwork' were as lavish in material details as it is in Rubens or even Kandinsky, how is the recipient to know that he is to abandon former ways of unifying the parts with the whole? In retrospect, the 1970s can be seen as a time of crisis for the avant-garde, which led to its giving way to postmodernism. This crisis was essentially semiotic in nature. As has been seen, the built-in problem with *P* was its inability to free itself of metaphoric reference, so that the "beautiful moment" which it was set on defeating would always defeat it. In taking steps to overcome this problem, towards the end of the 1950s *P* effectively defeated itself and dissolved into the semiotics of *W*, which was thus confirmed as the mainstream of avant-gardism. But *W* had problems of its own because of its substantial dependence on rhetorical means. It is not easy to surprise people who are expecting to be surprised. Once the art world became habituated to its strategies, *W* lost much of its original rhetorical power. It had been an objective of *W* to destroy the view of art as mere entertainment or pastime, but as the riddles and teasing of *W* turned into a commonly accepted strategy it had become just that.

It was during this time that *W* departed from its former simplicity in regard to the number of elements it employs. The result was an increasing uncertainty whether it follows the logics of *W* or *P*.[16] These were the circumstances that gave rise to the emergence of a new semiotic type of art, which is essentially tied to postmodernism. This is a hermaphrodite because it combines the semiotics of *P* and of *W* with two concepts of composition working simultanously. So not long after it had been dismissed by the avant-garde, *P* was revived as part of the new type *P+W*. With this new type of semiotics, first appearing in the 1980's, the aesthetic programme of the avant-garde came to an end (comp. Julian Schnabel's assemblage *Circumnavigating the Sea of Shit*, p. 62).

---

in *Art and Revolution* would replace capitalism with socialism and purposive rationality with aestheticism. While in the industrial age man is enslaved by the machine, so Wagner's reasoning goes, man should, instead, enslave the machine, so that there will be no need for him to waste his life in 'making a living'. The world would then be inhabited only by artists employed in transposing it into some kind of brotherly *Gesammtkunstwerk* (*Art and Revolution* 1976: III 144–177)

16. Beuys, for example, also created very complicated installations, that, if only on first view, might seem semiotically comparable with traditional art.

The theatre

Multi-mediality

In *The Empty Space* (1968), Peter Brook attempts to describe the minimum requirements of theatre: "I can take any empty space and call it a bare stage. A man walks across this empty space, whilst someone else is watching him, and this is all that is needed for an act of theatre to be engaged" (1968: 9).[17] However unexceptionable this statement may be, it is not so much theatre's *minimum* as its *maximum* potential that raises questions. Typically, theatre is more than this minimum of just 'movement in space'.[18] It may very well include various other elements – like language, music or even film. In most instances theatre will be 'multi-medial', and a work of multimedia will be theatre, if it includes theatre's minimum requirement, namely movement in space. But whenever theatre operates multimedially, it does so without obvious hierarchy. Language, music, film etc. become equal parts of it. They are neither minor nor extrinsic to its essential functioning.

Whether confined to a single medium or active across media, a work of art has the same basic responsibility: to create but one coherent whole. In multimedial art, then, no one medium can be allowed to gain autonomy and to function independently of the rest. The bourgeois age, however, gave rise to an aesthetic that no longer took language to be equal to the other elements of theatre but instead granted it supremacy. This development was propped up by a reliance on Aristotelian theory. While Aristotle's reflections on drama had been carried out within the narrow confines of poetics, it is mostly in respect as to classifications of literature, that they are paying interest to theatre. This perspective lead to the demise of the literal meaning of 'drama' (δράμα), which had been referring to just any visible *action* or *thing done* that could be perceived on the stage. In this sense, a drama performed is nothing more than a thing done in the presence of onlookers. But if several 'things done' can be strung together to form a 'plot', it is the theatre's 'plot', prefixed by the means of literature, to which 'drama' then became synonymous.

It was with this literary mainstream in mind that Richard Wagner in 1849 pointed out an aesthetic problem: in a theatre that is governed by literature, stage action and its theatrical adjuncts are reduced to a merely decorative function – appendages to the text. Theatre, Wagner complained, had become "a branch of literature", more precisely, "a form of poetic art like the novel or the didactic poem, with only one difference: instead of simply being read, this text is supposed by a number of persons to be memorised, declaimed, accompanied by

---

17. Consider the difference of this description to the one given by Eric Bentley only a few years earlier: "The theatrical situation, reduced to a minimum, is that A incorporates B while C looks on" (Eric Bentley, *The Life of Drama* 1964). Brook does not speak of 'incorporating', but only of performing a movement.
18. I take 'movement in space' to comprise every discernable change that might be observed on stage, including the movement of muscles that change the expression to an actor's face.

gestures and illuminated by theatre lamps" (Wagner 1976: III 157). Wagner raises the claim, this unsatisfactory situation could only be overcome by a new form of theatre. In it, all differing elements – such as stage action, language, architecture – are not to create closed functional systems in themselves anymore, but to "consume" and "obliterate" each other "as devices in favour of the achievement of a unified purpose of all". (Wagner 1976: III 60). This is, perhaps, the first reflection in history on the functioning of multimedia performance.

Semiotics of body

It is perhaps nowhere more obvious than in theatre, that the semiotics of description is linked with the function of escapism. With the lights dimmed in the auditorium and the revelation of a three-dimensional set in which real people are moving about as they do in real life, the spectator's world is obliterated and replaced with another. An actor will be the more acclaimed, the more he succeeds in making an audience forget who he is. Stage design enhances his suggestive power to create an appearance of reality to what really is only 'play'.

All such scenic elements – brought together and unified by the concept of 'plot' – contribute to what has been called 'narrativity', and since narrativity comes down to the semiotics of description theatre can no longer rely on it.

Because this remains an area of critical confusion, it seems important to stress that the challenge to narrativity is not just one of many characteristics of contemporary theatre. Insofar as the rejection of descriptiveness was the hallmark of the new semiotics of art, the attack on narrativity is the most fundamental feature of today's theatre – all the other features are just consequences of it.[19]

As in other arts, it is the semiotics of P and W which have provided models for the future of theatre. Since stage design is naturally related to the visual arts, much of its functioning within new theatre is exemplified by my references to Kandinsky, Malevich and Beuys. Instead of going into further detail here, I will first turn to the semiotics of visible action on stage, later to the semiotics of language and musical sound.

It is not 'playing', but the concept of what commonly would be dubbed 'role-playing' that creates the basis to descriptivity in theatre. To play at seeing a ghost does not bear descriptive content. But to play at seeing a ghost, plus playing at hearing that this ghost speaks with the voice of one's father, plus playing at hearing also, that this father is calling for revenge because he was murdered, is – by the very complexity of all this labelling – creating descriptive content. However, if this combination of actions would make up some of the 'role' of Hamlet, what I mean by the term of 'role-playing' is not reserved to roles that are prefigured by a dramatic text. Any consecutive situation of playing will be subsumed by the

---

19. Twentieth-century theatre did not become self-referential, as Hans-Thies Lehmann supposes, because it wilted "under the impression of new media" (2006: 23), but rather because, together with all new media, it is part of the totality of art, and any art that is intolerant of description can take reference to the outside only by a detour that also employs self-reference.

onlooker into *one* context of playing. It is impossible then, to combine situations of playing without inducing the concept of playing a role.

If 'role-playing', then, emerges only from a combination of actions, how could we define the kind of actions that form its basis? In other words: what do we mean if we speak of the simple action of 'playing at something'? Anyone would agree that there is a difference between a person who is sad and a person who is playing at being sad. Yet, if played well it is impossible for the onlooker to distinguish both – the significant difference is only that of a mental state, and mental states, by their very nature, can be perceived from the outside only by conclusion from actions that indicate them. Hence, playing at being sad amounts to engaging in a kind of action which in everyday life can be taken as *indicator of* this particular *mental state*. Accordingly, if an actor, through control of his facial muscles, takes the action to achieve a look to his face which in ordinary life indicates sadness, he cannot be said to play this look, for the look is real, yet, he can be said to play at being sad by voluntarily presenting such look. Thus, while actions on stage always are real and it is impossible to *play* them, if they are of a kind which in everyday life will indicate a mental state, they can be used as a means for playing, with what is played being the state, not the action.[20]

Admittedly, on the theatrical stage as in everyday life there also are situations of 'playing at something' that are not tied to mental states. A person can 'play at driving a car' by performing the alleged movements (like turning an invisible steering wheel etc.). But because in such a situation an onlooker can tell the playful pretence from the real, any playing of such kind is typically excluded from 'serious' theatre, even in children's theatre it will be received as a moment of burlesque. The notion of 'playing' then, in the way it is typically employed on the theatrical stage, amounts to a concept that is twofold: it means to engage in an action which in an everyday context indicates some kind of mental state, and means to do so voluntarily while in effect one does not possess this state.[21] In everyday life, to 'play at something' is the same as to pretend it, thus, to make another person believe something that is false. In theatre, to play at something is embedded in the agreement that engaging in such an action embodies a voluntary act of reference, which semiotically converts the indicative quality of

---

20. Mental states may be divided into emotional states, attitudes and inner activities. To produce tears will indicate the *emotional state* of being sad. To make the sign of the cross will indicate two interrelated *attitudes*, a momentary one of sensing some direct communication with God, a more steady one of believing that Jesus of Nazareth came to the world to be a messiah. To look for some time at the page of a book indicates the *inner activity* that we call 'reading'. An attitude, normally, is indicated also by uttering a sentence: we will take a person as *meaning* what he says, unless surrounding actions provide contraindication that he is a rather ironic sort of person, and we will take such a person to *believe* what he says, unless surrounding actions indicate he were a notorious liar.

21. In order to include opposing theories of acting, this assertion could be weakened to the point, that an actor may indeed *possess* this mental state at the moment, but still produces it *voluntarily* for an outer purpose.

actions. Playing the mental states that add up, say, to the role of Hamlet is not pretending to be Hamlet, but *presenting* him by the use of conversion of indicative quality. For the onlooker, however, the person presenting Hamlet nevertheless tends to vanish behind the character presented. By descriptivity's force of delusion Hamlet's world will block out and replace the real one.

Plainly, a theatre that wishes to escape descriptivity, must avoid role-playing.[22] As any art, it may then turn to the semiotic models provided by the avant-garde. Imagine a theatrical performance that showed nothing more than a person running round and round in a circle, and compare this to a second performance where the running person were to eat an apple at the same time. Neither running nor eating an apple are actions indicating any mental state. Consequently, there would be no 'playing' at all to both of these performances.[23] In its provoking simplicity the first performance would not find explanation within any reasoning of P. Being led to pose questions of the type "Why is this art?" the spectator would be in a situation much similar to that created by Beuys' *Jason II*, in that such a performance would pose a riddle, giving the spectator only very limited clues towards understanding their meaning.[24] The semiotics would at first view not be so clear with the second performance. Is it following model P in that the dynamics of syncopation between running steps and bites provide for its complexity? Is it following W in that the combination of running and eating an apple might carry echoes of the expulsion from the Garden of Eden? Or is it following model $P+W$, with both, syncopation and symbolism, providing for its aesthetic functioning? Whatever theory will prove successful in producing the most convincing results will be the one that interpretation finally turns to.

In practice, however, the deciphering of a theatrical performance's intentions will rarely be problematic because even where a performance will engage in riddles, it will make it clear in how it is structured that it is doing just this. Thus, if a piece adheres to type P its combinations of actions will remain complex as it does in Kandinsky's painting, and, as

---

22. Actually, as I will show later, such a radically non-descriptive theatre very rarely has happened. See the section titled *Irony* on page 76 of this book.
23. The action of eating an apple might have any number of mental causes: the eater feels hungry, the eater is bored, the eater is taking part in an experiment on the effect of eating apples. And if we should say that a person running or eating an apple must surely have the *intention* to do so, that is trivial: any intention could hardly be only played while someone is actually following it. Actions which by themselves do not indicate mental states, however, may do so if they are combined with actions that do: Running on stage while eating an apple is unlikely to convey a mental state to the spectator – since it is a complicated and rather stupid thing to do and the spectator has no usable reference point in everyday life. But running on stage while glancing behind now and then may well be taken, on stage as in everyday life, as an indicator of the attitude of "believing one is being chased".
24. Theatrical events of such simplistic kind were first staged by Italian futurism and subsequently appeared under the banner of Fluxus. Generally, the semiotics of W relates to the theatrical branch that is commonly called performance art.

with Kandinsky there will remain much handicraft, professionalism and perhaps virtuosity to it. It is no coincidence that performances of this kind are mostly to be found within the theatrical branch of dance. On the other hand, if the guiding principle is that of type *W* the piece is likely to consist of actions, which, were it not for their presentation on stage before an audience, would not be perceived as art. There is no obvious need for professional actors in theatre of this kind. Typically, the actions of the performers are of considerable duration, simple in themselves and appear unrelated to each other. This is a theatre that combines the ritualistic with the playfully trivial or platitudinous.[25]

Semantics

In a theatre that follows the avant-garde rejection of descriptiveness, language is particularly problematic, not only where it creates literary plot and militates against multimediality, but also because two sentences may already suffice to form a nucleus of descriptive content. It is for this reason that the semiotic shift away from descriptiveness affected literature more directly than it affected any other art form. If written language is typically received by the eyes and spoken language by the ears, Dadaist sound poetry was designed to reconfigure literature as music and Dadaist lettrism to reconfigure it as graphic art. Both are *reflecting* semantics, nevertheless they are not employing semantics any more, because they abstain from full propositions. Yet, many a poem by Paul Celan, René Char or others might be cited as evidence that the semiotic shift did not require an abandonment of literature, because these poems largely consist of simple, stand-alone subject/predicate sentences, monadic isolates that avoid descriptiveness by their failure to relate to the sentences either side of them.

The problems posed by language are met with much awareness within Brecht's theatre. Yet, within Brecht, there remains an open avowal to maintain literature as an ultimate authority for theatre's functioning. In Brecht's dramatic writing moments of self-reflexivity and ellipsis contribute to what he termed the *Verfremdungseffekt*, which was designed to weaken the descriptiveness of language. Brecht's actor, on the other hand, is held to change his attitude to the text as well as to the audience. He is asked to no longer only act out and give sensual expression to what on such basis nonetheless of descriptivity remains contained, but to step back from his role and reveal himself to the audience, thus problematising descriptive content and submitting it for critical scrutiny. The mistrust that literature evinces here against itself is profound, and the new function that the actor assumes within Brecht's theatre is the unpleasant one of the notorious killjoy. It is as if, by some emergency measure, from the audience were to be snatched away Marcuse's "beautiful moment", which such art cannot help but create, however sceptical of it became.

---

25. Once again Wagner was a pioneer here. No history of modern performance art should ignore *Parsifal* – his *Bühnenweihfestspiel*.

Irony

Of course, descriptive qualities, not only of language, are still prominent in contemporary theatre. In theatre schools actors are still primarily trained to interpret literary texts and to "become" someone else. Those abilities are, of course, also serviceable in the commercial media of cinema and television. Theatre's problem, then, is that it remains in the hands of professionals whose ideas were formed in institutions not so much interested in theatre as a contemporary form of art (only a whimsical section of the population is interested in that) as in providing an illustrated education in the historical texts of Shakespeare, Schiller, Chekhov etc. The progressive theatre has always had to work within such confines, and has to be satisfied with stretching rather than abolishing them.

Characteristically, much of what has been taken to be 'progressive' in theatre is in fact a compromise with the aesthetic needs which the semiotic shift has produced for the art of theatre. Brecht's new idea of acting introduced a way for such a compromise: the use of irony. Speaking, the Brechtian actor disrupts the appearance of *meaning* what he says. Performing other actions that indicate mental states, he formalises them in such ways as to counter the illusion that it is him as a person who owns them. He thus tries to fight delusion and continuously reminds his audience that he only *presents* his character.

Irony was not a preferred form for the avant-garde. However, with Brecht theatre turned to irony as a way of coping with material circumstance. Then, postmodernism provided an opening for the authentic irony of the 1980s. In what felt like refreshing air to breathe, there was an epidemic of theatrical creativity and experiment that even spread widely to the institutions. If Richard Wagner had already predicted "a gradual dying out of the actor's profession" (Wagner 1976: V, 46), with the idea of role-playing being invested with the irony that is essential to postmodernism, there was once again a real place for the professional actor.

Whilst irony cannot, in itself, destroy the old notion of role-playing nor the concurrent one of, as Wagner put it, speaking memorised literature while being "illuminated by theatre lamps", it can go some way towards absorbing them in aesthetics of a higher order. In its mode of composition today's theatre is responsive to the postmodern semiotics $P+W$. The discrete elements that it employs function in two ways at the same time: on one hand they try to achieve a "scenic rhythm", on the other a scenic "assemblage". It is a theatre that asks us to sense its rhythm and enjoy its self-reference, as well as to understand its riddling address to its subject matter.

Within this combined semiotics it is type W that allows for irony. By that, a performance can include descriptive elements without becoming descriptive in its basic functioning. Imagine, for example, that Beuys had accommodated Rubens' *Rape of the Daughters of Leucippus* on his *Sledge*. Let us also suppose that the viewer is meant to see the Rubens canvas, not as merely *any* descriptive painting, but as *this* painting, with all its descriptive associations. The reassembled *Sledge* would be comparable with the ironic forms of today's theatre. It would not be possible to understand *Sledge* without getting partly involved in descriptivity. Yet, within the elements of the assemblage, Rubens' canvas would be just as discrete as the other elements are. For the assemblage – wooden sledge, torch, blanket – the canvas would be yet another entity and there would be no code for the function of the features within the overall composition. Accordingly theatre creates *subsystems* when it adapts the semiotics of *P+W*: it can allow role-playing but never in permanence, otherwise the subsystem would become the system itself.

Typically, in postmodern theatre, role-playing is a burlesque activity, implicitly undermined as soon as it is employed. Theatre that makes a concession to role-playing is, at the same time, making fun of itself and reflects on its delusive tradition rather than submitting to it.

Semiotics of sound

Although the semiotic shift registered with the force of an explosion on the art world of the early twentieth century, a subterranean fire had been smouldering for some time before, largely unnoticed. It had been ignited by Wagner's essay *Art and Revolution* and fuelled by his *Tristan und Isolde* (composed 1854–9, first staged 1865). Notably, the long middle Act seems more prepared to dispense with both language and plot development than had been attempted in any previous theatrical work. In the subheading Wagner describes *Tristan*, not as an opera, but as a *Handlung*, referring to the ambivalence of the Greek word δράμα. As a theatrical term *Handlung*, would normally indicate a 'plot', but just like δράμα, it may also mean 'action'. Since *Tristan und Isolde* is a work in which plotting is of revolutionary insignificance, but 'action' and the 'act' of loving are crucial, Wagner draws attention away from an expected to an unexpected meaning of the word.[26]

Wagner's dramatic theory, which is also an aesthetic theory of general kind, aimed to revive an older meaning of δράμα as that which "really is moving before our eyes" (Wagner 1976: IX 94). His aesthetic work has been of seminal contribution to the outlined semiotic shift. It has undermined art's foundations and laid the grounds for a semiotic revolution. All this is ignored by Lehmann's concept of 'postdramatic theatre' which is unhistorical and based on a limited scope of the meaning of 'drama' and especially 'Musikdrama'. To speak of 'postdramatic theatre', when, in fact, it is about non-descriptive theatre, means to obscure historic and semiotic relations instead of clarifying them.

On Wagner's stage, language looses most of its grip over stage action – by being altogether silenced or being turned into pre-Dadaist sound poetry. His proleptically multimedial vision was of different semiotic elements which "consume and obliterate each other as devices in favour of the achievement of a unified purpose of all" (Wagner 1976: IX 17), but it was achieved in large part by what might be called a stage trick. It may be true that where in the Bayreuth theatre 'the eye roams' there is a new sort of equality between the semiotic

---

26. Since Act Two of *Tristan* is largely concerned with the act of sexual intercourse, the German word *Handlung* has particular resonance.

levels involved, but this is brought about architecturally, by the sinking of the orchestra pit.[27] A new manipulative force that is taking the place of a former is thus technically removed from the spectator's view. In Wagner's late work, orchestral language, secluded from "what is really moving before our eyes", takes possession of the dictates which – as he himself was the first to criticise – were forced upon theatre formerly by literature. The paradoxical state that stage action, as theatre's basis, remains contingent to theatre, hence does not only apply to Wagner's theatre as well, but also to every post-Wagnerian product whose success rests on the closure of a musical score.

Today, a non-descriptive theatre wishing to exploit the semiotics of sound is therefore more likely to be found within theatre's institutional branch that employs professional actors than the opposing one that employs orchestra and professional singers. In order to dispense with implications of descriptivity, this tradition has in various ways turned to acoustic means that are extending beyond the function of language. In visual art, a rose both *is* a rose and *signifies* a rose. It needs no description. Similarly, in aural semiotics, a scream will be and will also signify a scream. There is no need to describe it, and it is impossible to 'play' or 'pretend' it. Music is comparably situated within an actors' theatre. However, if in such theatre no musical score usurps the whole, semiotics of sound mostly remain within the scope of later theatre's irony. They form quotational subsystems, identifiable, say, as a Schubert song or a 'lick' in the style of Jimi Hendrix.

The semiotics of music have only a small part to play in the postmodern theatre, if only because most composers for the theatre still consider music to be a self-contained art. They fail to reckon with the fact that sound is only one aspect of the total composition of a theatre piece. Any music that has a potential outside life – in a concert performance, say – does not truly belong to Composed Theatre, and certainly not if it strives after a musical complexity independent of the complexity of the theatrical totality to which it belongs. Even Richard Strauss's *Elektra* and Berg's *Wozzeck* – among the very best scores written for the theatrical, rather than the operatic, stage since the semiotic shift – ask only that their music be heard and their text understood. In that respect, they belong more to the concert hall than to a theatre that wishes to avoid the trap of descriptiveness.

Our contemporary theatre has made a discernible move towards the condition of music. Yet, this is not because it uses music as an element or material but because the semiotics of *P*, that originally was attributed only to music has become prominent within theatre, just as it has within other art forms. Since Kandinsky and Schönberg, there has no longer been a fundamental aesthetic difference in terms of the artistic approach between music and other arts. Today, what we came to call 'sound art' accounts for the semiotics of *W* within the realm of the acoustic. However, it would be difficult to make a convincing claim that there is now a new tradition, one that applies to theatre the semiotics of sound in a way that is not

---

27. The term *Mystischer Graben* (mystical abyss) is applied by Wagnerian apologists to the orchestra pit at Bayreuth, but the abyss, with all its implications, may have mystified, but was never mystical.

safely ironic but of the essence of theatre itself. This is all the more strange in the light of such avant-garde innovators as John Cage, Dieter Schnebel, Vinko Globokar, Frederic Rzewski and others, creators of what promised to be a genuine music theatre. The avant-garde blazed a trail, but academic tradition has proved stubborn, and the institutional preference for the arcane semiotics of opera remains potent. Educational prejudice may not be the only problem, but it is probably the biggest one. Now that descriptiveness is no longer an aesthetic priority and 'art' is widely recognised as simply a matter of composition, any artist has become a 'composer'. So long as there remains a costly and specialised 'music theatre', there is only limited scope for an educational system that does not link the composition of sound with the composition of space, light and body action. Perhaps one should remind the traditionalists of Richard Wagner who was the first to move to the combination of both.

References

If not stated otherwise all translations are by the author.

Brook, Peter (1968) *The Empty Space*, New York: Touchstone.
Dahlhaus, Carl (1978) *Die Idee der absoluten Musik*, Kassel: Bärenreiter/English: (1989) *The Idea of Absolute Music*, Chicago/London: University of Chicago Press.
Marcuse, Herbert (1965) "Über den affirmativen Charakter der Kultur", in *Kultur und Gesellschaft I*, Frankfurt/Main: Suhrkamp.
Lehmann, Hans-Thies (1999/2006) *Postdramatisches Theater*, 4th edition, Frankfurt/Main/English: (2008) *Postdramatic Theatre*, London/New York: Routledge.
Wagner, Richard (1887–1911/1976) *Gesammelte Schriften und Dichtungen [GSD]*, 10 vols. Leipzig.

Chapter 3

'Happy New Ears': Creating Hearing and the Hearable

Petra Maria Meyer

One makes a cross-check: if during the performance of a piece of music in a concert hall a sound rings out (a chair that falls over, a voice that doesn't sing or the coughing of an audience member) then we feel that something in us is torn, there is a break in some substance or a rent in some law of association; a world falls apart, a spell is broken.

(Valéry 1991: 71)

Historically, music has always been an indicator of changes in listening habits and perception. These changes have also influenced other art forms that work with musical structures and compositional processes. In as much, music is a significant element of theatre, dance, performance art, of radio and film art. Also in sound installations in the field of fine arts, if nothing other than everyday sounds are heard in a concert hall and 'a chair which falls over, a voice which does not sing, or a spectator who coughs' are declared pieces of music. They are acoustic events with which 'the world disintegrates' and which French philosopher Paul Valéry cites as a cross-check. The legendary *4'33"* by composer and Nestor of New Music, John Cage, performed in 1952 in the Maverick Hall in Woodstock (USA), became an acid test through which the world opened itself anew.[1]

Pianist David Tudor entered the stage, sat at the piano, opened the lid and closed it again. This procedure was carried out three times. Not once did he place his fingers on the keys, not one sound was heard. Nevertheless, a composition by John Cage was performed, in an interpretation by the pianist David Tudor, who allowed the piano to be silent – *Tacet*[2] – it is silent. The composition has a real time of 4'33" and is divided into three movements, which the pianist structures in gestures. Thus, a new audible space was opened up and a new auditory experience was cultivated towards 'everyday sounds', which have always surrounded us, by nothing more nor less than a temporal frame with which the frame of concert music was broken. Since 'Tacet' concerts no longer have to consist of musical notes, and silence and sounds are no longer treated as opposites. Moreover, it has become clear that reality and 'life' consist of many musical events that 'art and life' can intertwine and music can become theatre – not least due to the use of gestures. John Cage has always been

---

1. Cf. in detail: Meyer 1998.
2. The Latin word *tacet*, meaning silence, in music indicates that in an instrumental piece or folk music the voices in the movement or for the rest of the piece pause or are silent.

particularly close to the theatre arts, not only due to his long co-operation with dancer and choreographer Merce Cunningham.[3]

> You see, at the beginning, the music experts didn't want to accept my work as music. In the thirties, they said frankly that what I was doing was wrong. But dancers accepted it. And so I became almost immediately accepted in the theatre world, and the theatre encompasses the fine arts, poetry, singing. Theatre is where we are at home [...] I think the thing that differentiates me from others, [...] what made it different, was that it was theatrical. My experiences are theatrical.
>
> (Cage in Furlong 1992: 91)

From the musicalisation of theatre by Adolphe Appia through the theatricality of music by John Cage, the 'instrumental theatre' of Mauricio Kagel up to the 'optical music' of Robert Wilson, on to the 'conceptional compositions' of theatre by Heiner Goebbels or the multitude of forms in which Christoph Marthaler stages theatre as music, theatre has shown itself a model medium of new compositional processes in interaction with music and the acoustic arts.

For the world of tonal music, litmus tests existed even before Cage. Here, one can refer to futuristic concerts using self-constructed sound-makers[4] and the 'musique concrète' of Pierre Schaeffer and Pierre Henry, which in the 1940s used randomly found sound material, machine noises or animal sounds as compositional material, and manipulated these electro-acoustically. This also revolutionised music. Today, it is possible to say that atonality and twelve-tone music did not drastically change music. Rather, the multimedial 'emancipation of sounds' and music's discovery of silence were innovations which paved the way to acoustic material dissolving its boundaries in many, widely differing arts and media. In the course of these changes, which included tones made by the body, the sounds of breathing, sighing or screaming, which dealt with a sound poesy of the Dadaists, with Lettrists or representatives of 'poésie sonore' and with a 'théâtre du cri' of Antonin Artaud in theatre, poetry and acoustic arts, the listening experience and the ways things are heard and listened to have all altered to some extent.

The further line of thought is three-part. First, the efficiency of the sense of hearing will be established, while conducting a differentiation of the various ways of hearing or listening. Secondly, a fundamental 'acoustic turn' will be noted, which owes something in particular to a medial-technical change. Both parts indicate compositional processes within new frame conditions of hearing and audibility in theatre, which thirdly will be reflected using concrete examples. Composed Theatre is always an exercise in listening.

---

3. Cf. in detail regarding the cooperation between Cage and Cunningham: Meyer 2001: 183–252.
4. Cf. Luigi Russolo's *The Art of Noise/L'arte dei Rumori* (1913) and his noise-generating devices called *Intonarumori*.

Hearing, listening and 'close listening'

In Ancient Greek thought, where the foundations of occidental thought, speech and even history are to be found, the sense of hearing was highly esteemed. This seems physiologically plausible since the sense of hearing shows a particular perceptiveness for temporal processes and is capable of paying attention to the smallest dynamic differences. Erwin Straus in his seminal book *Vom Sinn der Sinne* [Of the Meaning of the Senses] formulated this precisely by saying: "In seeing we detect the skeleton of things, in hearing them their pulse" (Straus 1956: 398). While the eye is particularly adept at measuring, at estimating spatial dimensions with regard to recognising structures and at recording all that is permanent or constant, the sense of hearing's capabilities lie equally clearly in its increased ability to perceive temporal changes. Since the ear can perceive the smallest of sounds and amplitudes, it can recognise minimal changes. Always trapped in time, in a state of tension between remembered past and expected future, the ear records events at the moment they are executed, in their very creation. If the eye is particularly responsible for grasping static situations, the ear is for dynamic processes. While the eye adheres particularly to present conditions and even tends to dominate the present, the ear opens itself up to temporal processes, to continuous events, which transcend analytical division. In contrast to the sense of sight, which observes what is seen from a distance and often has to keep its distance to see at all, the sense of hearing is an external sense, which is characterised by an absence of distance. A listener is always in the thick of things. The external sound space presses into the interior, the listener is surrounded by the sounds, is penetrated by them.

Since hearing is operative not only to the front but all around the listener, it can follow sounds in all directions in a given space. With the help of a reverberation or an echo the ear can also determine the size of a space. It can differentiate simultaneous acoustic sounds in a space. One talks of the 'cocktail party effect' in order to make clear that hearing can pick out and understand a single voice from the miscellaneous sounds of heterogeneous, acoustic mixes. In this respect anthropologists regard the sense of hearing as the sense of time and space par excellence. And from a psychological point of view, the sense of hearing records spatial-temporal situations like no other sense.

In this context then it makes sense to differentiate between hearing as a physical process and listening as a psychological act. Furthermore, different types of listening (and perception) can also be distinguished. Listening to signals is practised by humans and animals.[5] The ear is the 'preferred sense of attention', which Paul Valéry claims keeps watch where the eye can

---

5. Roland Barthes differentiates between three forms of listening: (1) listening to signs or evidence (2) a decoding listening and (3) a listening which would not be thinkable without a psychoanalytical discovery of the unconscious and which is geared towards 'signifiance'. Cf. Roland Barthes, 'Zuhören/Listening', in Barthes 1990: 249–63. In my thesis I follow partly Roland Barthes and expand his theories however with recourse to other philosophers.

no longer see (Valéry 1993: 33). A second type of listening in the sense of deciphering a code and its signs or essential contexts can be understood as specifically human. According to Roland Barthes, this second type of listening is also particularly religious (1990: 254). The Ancient Greeks opened their ears to the sounds of the leaves on the Dodona oak trees and deduced prophecies from these natural sounds.

One must add an attitude to one of Barthes' marked practices of listening, which attempts to postulate and detect a 'beyond' of the meaning (Barthes 1990: 253), that is, it tries to shake off dark, unclear, dumb meaning. It is this attitude through which the worldly events of life are listened to. A common sense of listening and examination from Heraclitus via Leibniz, Herder to Nietzsche becomes more sensible for a "total sound of the world" (Nietzsche 1967–77: 817).

If theatre is staged not only from the *opsis*, that which is seen, but also from the *akoe*, movement which is heard, then this sensibility is evident from Greek tragedy, which according to Nietzsche was born of 'the spirit of music', to productions by Einar Schleef, who by using a particular sense of rhythm staged multiple voices in each dialogue in exact vocal instrumentation and choral intensity. Being aurally open to the richness of changing melodies in different languages as well as the acoustic accents of diverse cultures is a quality to be found from Peter Brook to Ariane Mnouchkine to Heiner Goebbels. In theatre, however, not only are the many-voiced and broad range of vocal tones in varying situations made audible, but the auditorium can be staged as part of the listeners' space, thus opening up as an acoustic circle. Theatre-makers know how to design their surround-environments diversely in terms of acoustics. They constantly draw upon their audiences' particular hearing abilities in different ways when they introduce sound objects from different directions and, like Robert Wilson, use them as striking key sounds. Wilson, who in stagings such as *Black Rider* or *Alice*, structures heterogeneous, associatively linked time-spaces in dream logic, thereby follows a particular perception of hearing, which has also been deliberated in philosophy.

Where a 'common sense of hearing' ensues from the organ which does not shut down at night, one can find from Leibniz to Nietzsche an inclusion of diurnal and nocturnal *petite perceptions* (Leibniz) of dream perceptions and of the unconscious. The sense of hearing permits no fixed demarcation between waking and sleeping, between waking consciousness and dream consciousness.

Friedrich Nietzsche in particular developed a physical-philosophical, seminal 'philosophy of hearing' as well as an 'acoustic-gestural paradigm'.[6] Since the sense of hearing is a perception which of its essence is non-distant, it remains involved with body, life and soul. With regard to the new definition of 'common sense' as a 'physical common sense' it therefore plays a central role. It does not however become the new primacy of the senses. Seen both physiologically and philosophically as the physical aperture to the world, the sense of hearing is inextricably

6. Cf. also in detail regarding Nietzsche's "Philosophy of Hearing": Meyer 1993: 53–117.

linked to the other human sense organs in such a way that removing the ear would result in a limitation of one's ability.

Even Henri Bergson in his time and image philosophy of the physical, which has considerably influenced film theory (cf. Deleuze 1989 and 1991), remains strongly oriented towards the acoustic phenomenon field, without taking a one-sided slant towards just one sense organ. He constantly draws examples from the acoustic field in order to clarify limited cognitive ability due to physically measurable, chronometric time, setting this in opposition to an uncountable and immeasurable 'experienced time', perceived through the great diversity of discoveries and perceptive experiences. In this context Bergson reminds us of the striking of a clock, which may be perceived in two ways. Taking in the sound in the sense of measured time, the hearer would count four homogeneous strokes in space and come to the perceptive impression of a total of the sounds heard: the clock has struck four, it is four o'clock. However when attending "to every single awakened perception" the hearer reaches a completely different impression of the sounds: "instead of lining up next to each other, they merged into each other" and sound like a "musical phrase" (Bergson 1994: 96). If the 'spatial time' suggests that different points in time appear homogeneous, 'experienced time' creates the experience that there is no homogeneity in the real-time experience, since there can never be two identical points in time. With each repeated chime of the clock, nothing is repeated since the second sound differs from the first in that it *is* the second and as such is perceived by one's consciousness at an altered configurative level. Due to this fact, the second sound has a different quality for the perceiver from the first. The "durée", designated by Bergson as a "qualitative diversity" (1994: 81) of time, which is experienced as a qualitative process of change and creation, is thus particularly accessible to the sense of hearing, requiring however a different type of listening than the deciphering type.

When theatre no longer serves to represent a plotted dramaturgical course or narrated time, but rather seeks to make time an experience, then it creates 'time within time', experienced in ever changing ways, as Vladimir expresses in Samuel Beckett's *Waiting for Godot*. From Beckett to Wilson, decelerated courses of movement and events as well as multifarious games with repetition and variation in reduced, even minimalist stage compositions reveal that theatre artists increasingly compose theatre with a changing attitude as regards listening. In this context, Bergson's bias towards the creativeness of time appears to be seminal, for it corresponds to the central value which has been adapted by a no longer identity-constituting, difference-generating repetition used today in compositions of widely different media (Cf. here: Meyer 2004: 227–37). "Would it be repetition? Only if we thought we possessed it, but since we don't, it is free and we are too" (Cage 1987: 141).

A qualitative and difference-oriented listening attitude also corresponds to a third form of listening, exemplified in various contexts by Roland Barthes. This form of listening is aimed at significance (Barthes 1990: 249). It does not owe itself to the appearance of a *significat* as the effect of recognition but is rather the effect of the "mirroring of the signifiers which are continually competing to be heard, which continually produces new ones without ever causing the sense to shut down: this phenomenon of mirroring is called *significance* (it differs from 'meaning') [...]" (Barthes 1990: 262/263). With regard to this "field of art" (1990: 262) Barthes refers to the difference between listening to a piece of classical music and a composition by Cage. If based on his education and sensibility the listener of the classical piece is required to decipher from the piece what he can – since the composition is usually encoded, just as the architecture of the same era – then he or she is required to do so differently when listening to Cage: "[...] with Cage's music however I hear each individual sound one after the other, not in its syntagmatic expansion but in its raw and quasi-vertical significance" (Barthes 1990: 263).

In other studies, Barthes clarifies this significance by naming it *signifiance*.[7] In contrast to the sign-theoretical meanings of Ferdinand de Saussure's *signifiant* and *signifié*, semiotically, *signifiance* is something which 'happens to a signifier', which sensually generates meaning, that is, it is that which appears due to the mostly neglected materiality and mediality of the sign-carrier and can trigger another associative chain of reference.[8] The graininess of a voice (*Le grain de la voix*), the dynamic of a movement, the idiosyncrasy of a gesture or the outline of a piece of handwriting are significant here since a signifier refers to a movement of the body (Barthes 1990: 258), which originates from the voice or the gesture of a musician when playing – something which Mauricio Kagel did systematically in his 'instrumental theatre'. The shift in attention of a signified to a *signifiance* corresponds to the shift in attention undertaken by the composer Kagel: to produce from the tones to be composed the musical practices, the notes and sounds via gestures.

According to Barthes, a central significance of listening as a sensually generated sense, which is not the same as meaning, has only become possible since the discovery of the unconscious and of a different kind of psycho-analytical listening with evenly suspended attention. Listening is no longer performed only in complete consciousness and as an intentional act. An altered hearing ability rather has the function of "gauging unknown spaces" (Barthes 1990: 261). Barthes argues that in this sense not only the unconscious is to be heard but also the implied, the indirect, the omitted, the additional, the extended and polysemy, overdetermined and the overlapping. Significance, which in this sense unfolds within this inter-subjective space, requires "attention" to the "in-between of body and discourse" (Barthes 1990: 259). It is geared less towards that which is said than that which is not said or even prohibited. Nothing that is said or makes a sound is to be heard. Rather, this type of listening is directed at whoever is talking and at how something is heard. The way and manner in which and through which something is heard is at the same time formed by a media-technical modification.

---

7. "Qu'est-ce que la signifiance? C'est le sens en ce qu'il est produit sensuellement" (Barthes 1966–73: 1526).
8. Cf. here in detail: Meyer 2001.

'acoustic turn'

In the nineteenth and twentieth century, not only optical media such as photography and film altered their perceptions and commemoration culture. The advancement in sound recording and playback technology, powerful loudspeakers and Dolby Surround systems were part of a sensual generation of meaning, which today enables a multifaceted art and culture of listening. The range of artistic approaches composed of notes, tones and sounds, which work with the whole diversity of the acoustic world, is correspondingly multidisciplined and multimedial. These arise from acoustically altered, social frame conditions. Radio communication, telephones, radios, audio books, Walkmans, podcasts, 'audio on demand' and other auditive potentials and offers of web-based communications have made this central position of the acoustic dimension within the cultural change to a sensual certainty.

The resultant central importance of the audible, the increasing acoustic designs in various social fields and a constantly growing range of acoustic arts allows us to speak of an 'acoustic turn'.[9] Although artistically and media-pedagogically this 'turn' has long been completed, academically it is still slowly being processed. While due to the primacy of the optical, hearing and the auditive elements in audio-visual culture were too long ignored, artists have been contributing to the dawning of a perception-consciousness for some time and have opened up an experimental field of new ways of listening in completely different media.

On the radio, poets, composers, artists and theatre-makers have brought forward in audio plays, acoustic art, sound art – the names vary – individual artistic forms generated from media-specific technology, which have advanced to seminal art forms and have aesthetically completely altered not only radio but also theatre, film or sound installations.

Cinema and theatre are particular listening spaces for acoustic stagings in which sound design and soundtracks are becoming increasingly important. The common elements of a temporally limited theatrical or musically composed structural sequence, which radio plays, film and theatre plays all have in common, have led to diverse bi-medial concepts. Soundtracks become audio films in radio, radio plays are performed on stage and often presented as performance art. Theatre or audio play dramaturgy has changed to intermedial dramaturgy. Composition has become a multimedial structural principle. Composers such as John Cage or Mauricio Kagel composed theatre, film and/or radio plays in equal measure. Kagel's 'Componere' became the artistic practice of organising time, which he applied to a wide variety of material and media. He composed using "sounding and non-sounding materials, actors, cups, tables, omnibuses and oboes" (Kagel 1982: 121).

In the following I would like to treat various, more concrete examples in greater depth. They originate from three different areas of theatre, from dance, music and straight theatre,

---

9. Cf. Meyer 2008. The symposon of the same name, at the Muthesius Academy of Design and Fine Arts in Kiel, held in 2006, was the basis for this publication.

and should make clear the overall relevance of acoustic and compositional concepts for theatre as well as their diversity.

In the theatre of the twentieth and twenty-first century there was and has been acoustic staging at all levels. The structuring of both time and space, a creation of atmosphere, an atmospheric design or the creation of tension, as well as characterisation have been attempted acoustically. In dance also, the acoustic level has taken on a central significance. A heightened awareness that dance allows the use of what happens in the visible stage-space in interaction with acoustic events within various listening spaces, can also be found in the dance theatre of the 1970s. The example of a neglected choreography by Pina Bausch should also support the relevance of a third form of listening, which Roland Barthes "ultimately (regards) as a small theatre, in which those two modern deities wrestle with each other, evil and good, power and desire" (Barthes 1990: 260).

Bluebeard – Listening to a Tape Recording of Béla Bartók's Opera 'Duke Bluebeard's Castle', a choreography by Pina Bausch

The dance theatre of Pina Bausch pursues psychological and physical interests, consciously eliminating the division between dance and theatre. Choreographer and dancer Pina Bausch, who died in 2009, played with signs of signs of a cultural behavioural code, referring theatrically to the social system and social – particularly gender-specific – roles, in an excessive presentation, recognisably alienated. By means of the language of movement, she also transcended cultural encoding by stripping off all masks in an attempt to refer back to traces of a body memory. At the end of the Expressionist dance movement she set an internal scene of soulful-thoughtful processes in opposition to a decorative theatre scene and the illusion of a plotted ballet. In her choreography, this led not only to unusual series of movements, through which the intensity could be released, but also to other acoustic and musical concepts.

Even the title of the choreography 'Bluebeard – Listening to a Tape Recording of Béla Bartók's Opera "Duke Bluebeard's Castle"', which Pina Bausch staged in 1977,[10] emphasised the audio-visual structure. Since Pina Bausch's choreography lasts approximately 120 minutes, whereas Bartók's opera only lasts 60, one surmises someone has approached the opera to which Béla Balázs composed a libretto as a 'stage ballad', on which the opera is based[11] in a way that orients itself towards the genre of tape composition. Originally introduced into the world of sagas as a fairy tale by Charles Perrault, the Bluebeard material

---

10. Cf. in detail with regard to this choreography paying special attention to the concept of space: Meyer 2010: 31–54.
11. Cf. Béla Balázs, Herzog Blaubarts Burg. Anmerkungen zum Text/Captain Bluebeard's Castle. Comments on the Text, in Balázs 1968: 34–7.

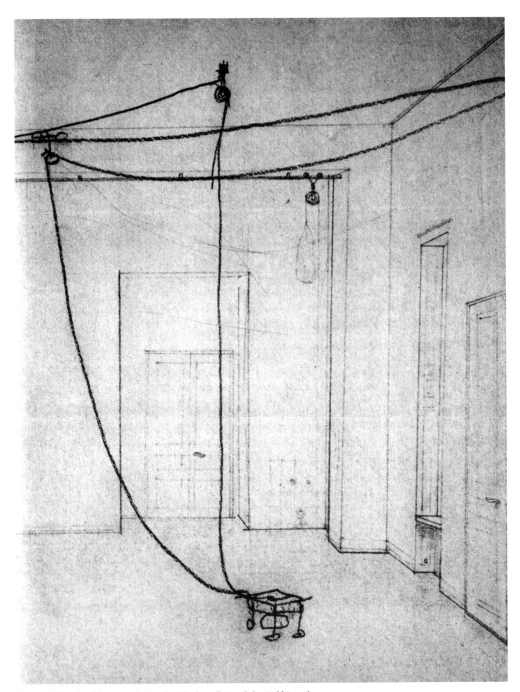

Figure 1: Sketch of the stage design for *Bluebeard's Castle* by Rolf Borzik.

was taken up by Ludwig Tieck and in 1797 became a folk tale with widespread effect. In 1910, Hungarian author Béla Balázs, who today is better known as a film critic and was at the time particularly interested in fairy tales came back to the material, and his friend Béla Bartók composed the music. The opera was first performed in Budapest in 1918.

In the opening sequence of Pina Bausch's choreography one sees dancer Jan Minarik start the tape recorder and approach a woman lying on the floor. The floor is covered with leaves and the female dancer, who also characterises Judith, is lying on her back.[12] She holds both arms stretched upwards while Jan Minarik lies on top of her. Together they slide noisily across the stage, then he gets up and stops the tape recorder, rewinds and starts the musical sequence again. He once again approaches the woman lying on the floor, lies on top of her again and they slide across the floor, again and again.

A 'sound machine' becomes the stimulator of desire and in equal measure memory's energy source. Since both the musical course and the continual plot course stops and re-starts, a different intensive temporal ordering of physical movements is created, which can also be understood as memory movement. In variations of the Freudian process, to remember, repeat, work through, one could talk in this case of repeating, working through, remembering. This process allows an intensive penetration into the memory movement of the body, which Pina Bausch tried to release in the rehearsal process with her dancers.

Via this dual process, which draws on human body memory as well as on a distorted, thereby altered reproduction technique of a tape recording as memory medium, not only memories and expectations due to a foreknowledge of Bartók's opera are damaged. Rather, an enormous increase in the intensity of the movements is effected. Observed from a media-studies point of view, the disturbance in the technical reproducibility brings about an increased development of awareness of the media technology on the stage, causing a reflecting upon the media-specifically different intensity of repetition and difference in theatre. Since for each reproduction – which varies from slightly to considerably in its beginning and its end, never exactly repeating the same musical sequence – the same, but never identical, scenic action is performed several times on stage. Thus the choreography simultaneously transfers the reproduction technique to the repetition structure of theatre, where only difference is always repeated. Another qualitative time experience, which enables an intermedial interplay, becomes equally manifest: with the aid of the tape recording montage an emphasis of time is just as possible as a manipulation thereof via fast-forward or slow-motion, forward and backward leaps in time, simultaneity of the past and the present. In the interaction with the choreographed movements, these time phenomena can be experienced as *durée* in the sense of Henri Bergson.

---

12. The relationship not only changes between the stagings but parts are performed by different dancers also within the staging: for example, by Beatrice Libonati and Malies Alt or Meryl Tankard.

This conception of a particular memory space uses an intermedial procedure to help us recall Bartók's opera in our cultural memory in a new manner, while opening up new time-spaces for dance via altered compositional procedures. If in Pina Bausch's choreographies one usually finds collages of various musical interjections from different genres (easy listening, jazz or classical music), here an opera is played from a tape recorder and composed anew using the 'cut-up method'.[13] The opera becomes the raw material, from which altered forms of a tape recorder composition can be generated in a self-referential process. Not only compositional but also psychological possibilities can thus be exploited. A tape may contribute to repeating the associative sequences as well as interrupting and diverting fixed associative series. In this sense, media technology becomes thematic and scenic. It begs the third form of listening in the sense of Roland Barthes, which focusses on what happens to the listener as well as on power and desire in theatre.

Although Bartók's composition here experiences a transformation, is dismantled and composed anew, each fragment retains the remembrance in the material. Basic thematic focal points in the story of Bluebeard, who kills his wives and is the prototype of desire and power, are strikingly sensualised. The painfulness of the scene depicting a failing sexual relationship increases rather than decreases with each repetition. This heightened painfulness also becomes perceptible at the acoustic level. Emotional connotations of the rustling leaves give rise to associations of rape and complement the sounds of the basses and cellos from the tape, which surge at the listener's ear with a melody similar to a folk song. A multitude of body sounds, of a body sliding and running over leaves, of seething and heavy breathing, of various bodily contacts etc. are presented along with the rich palettes of colour, sound and sensation of Bartók's non-illustrative yet suspenseful, intensive music. Here, dance puts the effect of the body itself on stage audio-visually. These acoustic accompaniments and vocal sounds and cries which accompany the tumult in the body, the noise potential made audible by the physicality of a human body and the materiality of things, directly oppose the transcending power of opera music in their concrete worldliness. Using an intermedial intervention Pina Bausch brings the music back down to the ground of the physical aspects of being human and the world of things and equipment.

Along with the moveable tape machine, which the Bluebeard figure[14] Minarik uses violently against the Judith figure, "direction vectors, speed and time" (de Certeau 1988: 218) are quasi-integrated into the spatial concept of the stage designer. In a multitude of ways, the audience experiences compositionally, scenographically and choreographically

---

13. In the 1950s the 'Cut-Up' method was propagated by the painter Brion Gysin and the writer William S. Burroughs. In doing so, the film montage technique was transferred to the process of writing for the first time. Tape recording compositions in relation to this process as well as filmic games – such as the non-camera film – followed in the 1960s. See also: Burroughs 1986.
14. Character concepts have also changed under the new medial conditions of theatre arts. In this context one increasingly assumes dynamic concepts, which set themselves apart from a long-dominant tradition via a change in terminology of figuration and transfiguration.

Figure 2: Scene from *Bluebeard – Listening to a Tape Recording of Béla Bartók's Opera 'Duke Bluebeard's Castle'*, a choreography by Pina Bausch. Photograph by Ulli Weiss.

that something is being done to this place and that space is being constructed in such a way in performance.

Scenographically the tape becomes the musical sounding body and handy object on the stage conceived by Rolf Borzig, since above and beyond its function as a prop it becomes a co-actor, enabling a transformation of Bartók's opera. Along with this transforming and rendering conscious of the media-technical composition of music, thanks to an intermedial strategy, a choreographic work is created in the performance space generated by the movements of the dancers. Here, the audio-visual emphases of the physical aspects of the human body and of the space itself are essential. Borzik's space concepts for choreographies by Pina Bausch always offered lots of space to walk, skip, strut, shuffle, hurry along, run, for walking steps and sliding bodies. In this case it always concerns the specific movements themselves and their acoustic expression, their audio-visual course in performance. The spatial concept of the scene as performed is accordingly expanded via a leaf-covered floor space, used and danced upon with sounds, which is quasi-penetrated by natural and cultural space, inside and outside.

In thematisation of the choreography *Bluebeard – Listening to a Tape Recording of Béla Bartók's Opera 'Duke Bluebeard's Castle'* as a prototypical example of acoustic and compositional practices in the field of dance theatre is self-evident simply because the space-time feeling of Bartók's opera is decidedly altered and the transcendental power of the music forms a paradox to the process of the tape composition. At this level of the perception, Pina Bausch's choreography proves itself also to be in opposition to a deciphering listening. The dismantled opera corpus allows no recognitive hearing. Instead, it enables a new encounter with a listening space 'tuned' by Bartók, which is enriched with sounds and voices of the physical space of action.

If Pina Bausch enabled a remembering of the new, which John Cage had already strived for using non-determination, via strategies of difference-generating repetition in intermedial interplays of tape compositions and dance, Heiner Goebbels exploits repetition differently again in order to release the richness of the acoustic.

Die Wiederholung/La Reprise/The Repetition, a theatre composition by Heiner Goebbels

The Repetition, a multilingual musical theatre production, which the composer, musician and radio playwright Heiner Goebbels produced in 1995 in the 'Bockenheimer Depot', the auditorium of the Frankfurter Schauspielhaus and the TAT (Theater am Turm), is based not on a libretto nor on a dramatic text, but on a text- and music-collage. The title refers to the philosophical reflections from *Die Wiederholung* (*La Reprise/The Repetition*) and other texts by the Danish philosopher Søren Kierkegaard, who wrote as a poet under several pseudonyms. Excerpts from different texts by Alain Robbe-Grillet also appear as does a transformation of the film script *L'année dernière à Marienbad* by Alain Resnais and a musical key text amongst the intertextual references: the song *Joy in Repetition* by Prince. Accordingly, Heiner Goebbels subtitled the performance text of *The Repetition*: 'nach Motiven von / *based on* / *d'après* Kierkegaard, Robbe-Grillet & Prince'. Additional musical set pieces by Johann Sebastian Bach, Ludwig van Beethoven, Franz Schubert, Johannes Brahms, Frédéric Chopin und Heiner Goebbels himself were also included. Together they constitute a quasi-heterogeneous text material spanning existential philosophy and *nouveau roman* and musical material, which in this theatre composition ranges from the classical music of the eighteenth and nineteenth century up to the rock/pop and jazz of the twentieth.

The cast can be seen as the consistent equivalent of a programmatic musicalisation of the theatre. It is moreover multilingual, due to a multiple duplication of the language sounds: Marie Goyette is a French-speaking, classical pianist, John King an English-speaking musician and Johan Leysen a German-speaking, Dutch actor.

Here, too, the author follows the concept of figuration and transfiguration, for the roles of the actor and musician on stage are not the representative embodiment of characters. Far more, they are actors who appear using their own names. In the course of the piece, the repeated, and thus constantly varyingly de- and re-semantised text material is divided

Figures 3, 4 and 5: Marie Goyette, John King and
Johan Leysen in Heiner Goebbels' *Die Wiederholung
/ La Reprise / The Repetition*. Photographs by Wonge
Bergmann (3–4) and Harmut Becker (5).

between them. Their corporeality is the medium for scenic figuration and transfiguration, the voice is a changing instrumentalisation of repeated text material.

Like Pina Bausch, Heiner Goebbels also uses repetition not only as a focal point of content but as a basal structuring principle, relinquishing coherence in a linear context, in order to generate sensual meaning in a different manner. Kierkegaard's central question of a philosophical experiment, "whether something loses or gains due to its being repeated" (Kierkegaard 1955: 3), here becomes a test of theatre as a medium of non-repetition par excellence.

The listener is thus manoeuvred back and forth between attitudes of listening via repetition and differentiation of a text in various languages. The attention of the listener is shifted from the sense of the word to the sense of the sound and at other times from the sense of the sound to the sense of the word according to the comprehensibility of each word. Repetition thus proves itself to be an iterative dislodging in an acoustically musical linguistic movement of transformation. This shifts from one actor to another, from a female voice to a male, from one language to another, from a foreign language to one's own, from a linguistic 'abroad' to 'home', from the rather silent and sounding language to a spoken language. Although the text is repeated, the difference triumphs, which can only be experienced thanks to the repetition. The effect of that which has been sounded and said twice is multiplied, without its novelty value wearing off. In fact, the repeated text is represented in varying ways by the difference in the vocal structures of the two languages German and French. Thus Søren Kierkegaard's perception of the relation between repetition and remembrance can be physically experienced through hearing: "Remembrance and repetition are the same movement just in opposite directions. For what we remember, has been, is repeated backwards, whereas the actual repetition is remembers ahead" (Kierkegaard 1955: 3). What is seen is quasi the gestural and proxemic sensualisation of the process by an actor.[15] A remembrance stimulated by repetition from the very beginning characterises the events at the same time as time markers, whose sense of relation changes in the course of performance time.

An aesthetic of interruption can also be found in Goebbels' staging, in which an auditively and visually multiple 'play' of fade-ins and fade-outs takes place. It operates sometimes tentatively and sometimes with abrupt clarity. A change between accelerated, dynamic and stopped courses of events, 'instants immobilisés' according to Robbe-Grillet, at the same time combine thematic motifs with compositional processes.

In this context, one is reminded of Cage's 'Tacet'. A silent stage minute is quasi set free in a silent scenography consisting of one minute of stillness, a minute of an absence of movement within a halted event, which Johan describes in the performance as 'one minute's non-motion'.[16] When this sequence is introduced with the words, "from the auditorium you

---

15. A detailed analysis of Heiner Goebbels' composition *The Repetition* has been published elsewhere: cf. Meyer 2001: 267–324.

16. This and all other citations from the performance text *The Repetition* are taken from the manuscript kindly provided by Heiner Goebbels.

hear not the faintest sound", then the audible occurs as a de-staging in the auditorium and around it – or not. Not only does Heiner Goebbels' theatre composition generate sensual sense but is also a meta-theatre of self-reflection. In this self-reflection, the relation between theatre and music as well as between classical or rather 'serious' music and popular music is included at diverse levels.

'Prince and the Revolution' was not just the name of the band at the beginning of mega-star Prince's career; it is also the title of a lecture by Heiner Goebbels, which, significantly, has been published, five times in different forms. This seems justifiable inasmuch as the composer accuses the classical new music of a wilful ignorance with regard to the rock and pop sector, thus causing a considerable delay in musical form principles, which had already been inventively tried and exceeded in other musical areas. According to Goebbels, it is disco culture in particular and an experimental subculture to which innovation drives can be attributed. From this he draws the appropriate compositional consequences: an openness and sensibility of perception for a permanently changing musical reality become conceptional.

In working with available material, de- and re-contextualisation, according to Goebbels, is only acceptable as a new artistic practice as long as it is not randomly re-worked. The foundation for this should be a reflected process equipped with a consciousness of history and regard for the material (see Goebbels 1989). In the age of collections, of *nouveau roman* and of the king of crossover, Prince, nothing less than such a compositional concept of a composer is performed self-reflectively by the theatre composition *The Repetition*, which so to speak puts itself to the Kierkegaardian test of "whether something loses or gains due to its being repeated". Here, Goebbels opts for the revolution of repetition in Robbe-Grillet's work and the revolution of the mix in Prince's, this particular musical personality who combines "soul, motown, rhythm & blues, country, folk rock, jazz" (see Goebbels 1989) in his own particular way, a unique way which shows itself in the mix, the sound, the microphonisation of the voice or the use of echo, in the macrostructure of the arrangement and the microstructure of each detail. This is what the 'revolutions' of Robbe-Grillet and Prince have in common: they are transgressions, excess in the manner of how something sounds, is combined, mixed, interwoven, how it becomes dynamic, energetic, effective, exciting and surprising, beyond revolutionary content and ideals.

Repetition, in Goebbels' music theatre production of the same name, proves itself to be a different ordering of the interlacing of various events using a reduced range of permutable elements. As in Pina Bausch's choreography a spatial concept by Erich Wonder supports the stage action. A curved wall on the revolve ensures that the room itself begins to move, it is altered, it withdraws from view and reopens partly or in full to the audience's gaze. Varying views of the space, perspectives and panoramas are created due to time becoming spatial and space becoming temporal as the revolve is used as space journey with no particular direction, clockwise or counter-clockwise. The theatre machinery runs in no one particular direction but rather in various directions simultaneously. Mutually connected sequences occur discontinuously, cues emphasise the heterogeneity of the audible and visible. Thanks

Figures 6 and 7: "I knocked, didn't you hear?" / "Yes: I said come in" (Repeated lines from different scenes from Heiner Goebbels' *Die Wiederholung / La Reprise / The Repetition*). Photographs by Wonge Bergmann (top) and Hartmut Becker (bottom).

to repetition there even occurs a sense-stimulating shift in attention and a reflection-provoking paradoxical time specification.

The musical treatment of language in Goebbels' staging is seminal for spoken theatre. Differences between the sounds of the various languages serve to emphasise a constantly varying time dimension from one language to another. This is further elaborated in the switches between emphatically slow, even hesitant speech to rapid, witty exchanges.

In Goebbels' work the word material in this manner is mainly determined by its temporality and thus dealt with as music, as opposed to the usual manner of dealing with word texts, in which the temporal dimension has virtually no effect on the content of the words. This structuring principle of repetition simultaneously connects the unfolding of text time to the remembrance time of the observer who is quasi challenged to recall so that, what has previously occurred through remembering penetrates that which occurs later. Thus the perception of the repetition varies due to this time-based penetration. This variation provokes the observer to listen in a different manner and challenges him/her to be more open to what sensually occurs on the level of linguistic signs.

Here, composer and radio playwright Heiner Goebbels clearly draws on his radio experience. Acoustic art in radio works with language, sound and music as acoustic materials with equal rights. This art has experimented with many forms so that the similarity of language and music may be experienced: that they are sounding events in time. More recent theatre productions also draw thereon.

Letter to the Actors, 'Theatre of the Ears' by Valère Novarina

Following in the footsteps of Antonin Artaud and Samuel Beckett, French-Swiss writer, director and painter Valère Novarina programmatically named his theatre a 'Theatre of the ears'/'Le théâtre des oreilles' (Novarina 1996) declaring the actor to be an oral and sonorous excretion organ. Novarina wants a "pneumatic actor" (1993: 95) and harks back to pneuma, which in Ancient Greece comprised body and spirit, undivided. Thus in this sense the actor's breath is his spirit. He takes language as material which of itself knows where it should go, knows as language whereof it speaks and therefore requires no cognitive author subject that gives it access to reason. Rather, he aspires to an understanding arising beyond the intellect: a physical, existentially anchored hearing and listening that takes over from the abstractly comprehending understanding. A staging of Novarina's *Letter to the Actors*, a play, which director Philip Tiedemann staged at the Düsseldorf Theatre in 2005/2006,[17] should in conclusion serve to clearly exemplify the characteristics of the 'Theatre of the Ears'.

---

17. Original performance under the direction of Philip Tiedemann, 4 March 2006 at the Düsseldorfer Schauspielhaus.

Figure 8: Scene from *Brief an die Schauspieler* by Valère Novarina, directed by Philip Tiedemann.

The first thing the audience perceives in this play, however, is writing. At the opening a curtain covered in writing can be seen (see figure 8). The letters are blue on a whitish-transparent background, which like a shower curtain resists the penetration of the glance while ever hinting at what is behind it. In this way from the very beginning the semi-transparent curtain allows an act of seeing that is linked to the imagination and inner vision. The audience simultaneously hears a simple percussive tone sequence to which the actors move. Each actor wears a blue-white leotard that covers their whole body, leaving only their face to be seen. Yet it is not only the faces, which serve to tell apart the shapes in, the same colours and clothes. Varying colour distributions of white-blue to blue-white, varying letters on their backs mark the difference rather than the individuality of these actors who otherwise remain nameless. Already on the level of outward appearance such anonymous heterogeneity is enacted. This serves to abstract from a psychologically realistic character conception to the benefit of an intensity of physical processes. Accordingly the audience's

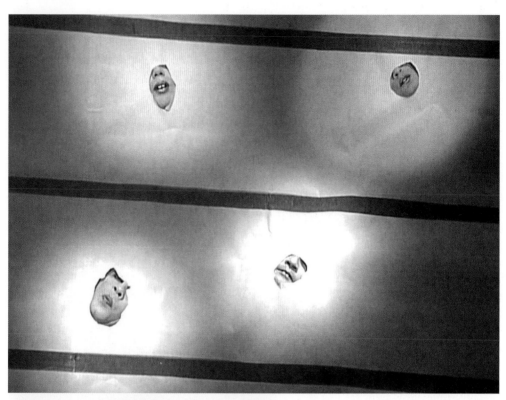

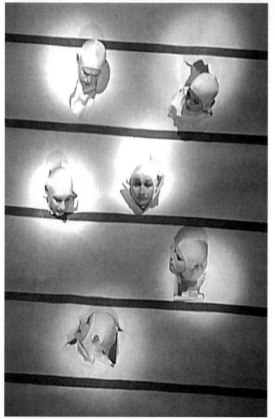

Figures 9 and 10: Scenes from *Brief an die Schauspieler* by Valère Novarina, directed by Philip Tiedemann.

attention is directed to other events. A strongly built man wears mainly white and appears particularly physical as a result. The colour white emphasises physical shapes and plays upon shape, in particular revealing breathing to the onlooker's gaze; blue on the other hand distinctly covers up any unevenness. Franz Lehr made his mark on the scenography with characteristic costumes and an idiosyncratic set.

After the curtain opens the letters on the actors' back come together for a moment to form the word 'play'. In the scenographic space of the theatre it is literally a question of an audio-visual 'Hör-Spiel',[18] which in the interplay of media makes the audience read and listen in turn. An angled piece of writing paper, designed as a white sheet with blue lines to correspond to the costumes, is accordingly the central stage element of the scene. Programmatic words, beginning with 'The Text', are projected onto this particular white surface. There follows a laser beam onto the paper surface, piercing through this point from behind.

The point becomes a hole, the ending of a sentence, a beginning that pushes out over every sentence. Then the opening is enlarged to a mouth aperture (see figures 9 and 10). One after another several round holes are made in the paper through which can be seen mouths which the actors push through from behind to finally pronounce the word 'text'. They do this polyphonically, voices as instruments, thus supporting the undertaking to re-encode the writing sheet into a score or the notation of a sound poem composition. With the continuing enlargement of the holes, through which heads finally emerge, the writing sheet expands more and more to the scenography. The paper of course is ripped, the actors crawl through and take their seats on a transformed performance text scaffold. There they hang like musical notes on a score, forming together at times a 'body' and group into ever changing audio-visual images (see figures 9 and 10).

What Novarina means by "pneumatic actor" (1993: 95) may thus be sensually experienced. Here the body is clearly used as a resonance body, as an instrument. Audible breathing sounds form initial sounds of varying intensity. The physical action of expressing is varied, at times immensely increased, when words are eruptively expelled from the body, making it shake. In evident correspondence to variations on acoustic arts the spoken material, in Tiedemann's staging, is deformed and deconstructed, transferred into sound associated forms composed as a rhythmical flow of language in vocal polyphony.

One singled-out scene serves as an example of the kind of listening attitude that is expected of the audience. In this indicative scene the scaffold becomes a climbing frame for a children's game and an experiential area, prior to language acquisition. It becomes a "trotte bébé" (Lacan 1975: 63) in the sense of Jacques Lacan. A burly, particularly physical actor in a mainly white leotard hangs by a belt from the scaffold (see figures 11 and 12).

He tilts back and forward and makes sounds, cries, chuckles, while next to him an actress translates the pre-language utterances apparently into understandable speech. It is not

---

18. The German word for radio play means, translated literally, 'hear-play' or 'hearing-play'.

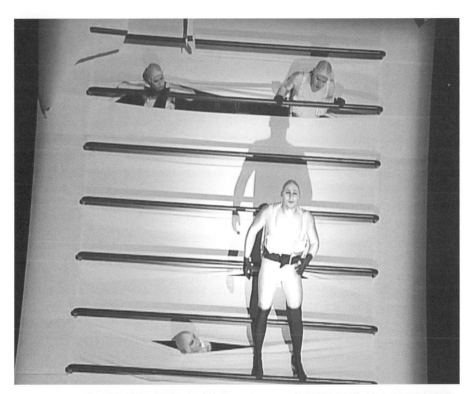

Figures 11 and 12: Scenes from *Brief an die Schauspieler* by Valère Novarina, directed by Philip Tiedemann.

difficult to perceive the scene as an acoustic re-staging of the visually oriented act which Jacques Lacan introduced as the primal scene of self-recognition and self-delusion: "the mirror as formative of the function of the I" (Lacan 1975: 61–70).

In contrast to the merely illusionary given wholeness in the mirror, described by Lacan, in Tiedemann's elaborated scene it is an acoustic reflection of the sound material in the form of coded speech that can be penetratingly felt in all its delusion. In the scene the smooth slickness with which the mirror stadium is able to charge up the imaginary with an illusion is missing.

Here the actor is visibly and audibly tormented, emphasising this effort in sound, physiognomy and gesture by punishing himself not only with his hands but also with his tongue, smacking himself therewith. "Of all the animals we are the only ones who have this hole", the translator says finally, enabling the theatre-goer to listen in a deciphering manner. Paradoxically it becomes evident in this scene – wherein single utterances are translated into a generalised, codified spoken language – that Novarina is attempting to restore words to tones and body sounds. Here it is insistently sensualised that words do not fall from the heavens, they are expressed physically. These tones sensually generate sense: *signifiance*. They may be perceived in the form of signs, symptoms or sound poetry, but in no case do they translate into a meaningful language of words. The translation is shaped by the discourse in between. Let us at this juncture repeat and recall further reflections of Roland Barthes regarding the third manner of listening, following the psychoanalytical turn: significance, which in this sense unfolds in the inter-subjective space, requires an "attention to the in-between of body and discourse" (1990: 259). Accordingly, Novarina's play also displays an interwoven meta-theoretical text level.

Philosopher Valère Novarina provides a meta-theoretical, self-reflecting level that is connected with the communication medium of writing, the medium of inscribing regulations, of theory par excellence in addition to the sound poetry level of the performance, in which the body shows what it does. If the theatre-goer at the beginning of the episodic sequence is confronted with writing, which in Tiedemann's staging of Novarina's *Letter to the Actors* is the first thing to appear on stage, it would seem that the theory, *theoria*,[19] has been there before the piece. The etymological relationship between theory and theatre seems to be implied here. In Novarina's work the *theoria*, subject since Plato to the primacy of the optical, experiences an *acoustic turn*: here, the theatre stage is reconverted to a listening stage.

Conclusion

An acoustic turn, implemented in various ways, is to be noted in all forms of theatre. Based on altered acoustic and musical practices a compositional practice for dance, music and theatre forms becomes seminal in equal measure. This practice no longer offers staging

19. Cf. Heidegger 1954. Heidegger makes clear that Theatre is "the view, the look in which something is shown" and that "to have seen this look is knowledge" (Heidegger 1954: 48).

which are faithful to the original text or a traditional dramaturgical structuring of the plot. Rather, through repetition strategies, intensities are experienced which are accessible due to a physical knowledge of the world and a new way of listening.

Differences and similarities may now be summed up. In Pina Bausch's choreography the medium of technical reproduction is used not only to remind of the new – as with Goebbels – but also to make painfully aware of the compulsion to repeat. In Goebbels on the other hand technological reproduction has the particular function of breaking through an established level of fiction. Differentiation, shifts of attention and new experiences of qualitative time, which may be released through repetition, can yet be found in all the examples of dance, music and spoken theatre cited here. Repetition is also structural in all these examples; it is used contextually and is recognisable in its double function.

If repetition within the framework of conventional structures serves to constitute identity through citations, repetition which may be iterated in the sense of Jacques Derrida is also associated with otherness (see Derrida 1988: 291–314) in Heiner Goebbels' staging concept the ongoing new creation of contexts becomes particularly manifest. When in Philip Tiedemann's staging of Novarina's *Letter to the Actors* the sounds are translated into conventional speaking language, another aspect becomes audible. The translation can be understood because it cites coded spoken language and draws upon discourse; at the same time the production of sounds refers to the body, the physical. Two different aspects of performing are experienced. In order to perform on stage representative language which relates to the world, the performance consists of pneumatic sound sequences in the form of acoustic and physical events in the world, appearing no longer symbolic but rather symptomatic. All the theatre pieces cited here were developed out of an altered listening attitude to the world; they all stimulate a new kind of listening as a way to experience and understand anew the physical, the psyche and life, existence and the world.

(Translation: Colin Moore)

References

Balázs, Béla (1968) *Ausgewählte Artikel und Studien*, Budapest: Kossuth Könyvkiadó.
Barthes, Roland (1966–73) *Œuvres complètes*, Tome 2, Paris: Seuil.
—— (1990) *Der entgegenkommende und der stumpfe Sinn*, Frankfurt/Main: Suhrkamp.
Bergson, Henri (1994) *Zeit und Freiheit*, Hamburg: Europäische Verlagsanstalt.
Burroughs, William (1986) *Electronic Revolution/Elektronische Revolution*, Bonn: Expanded Media.
Cage, John (1987) *Silence*, Frankfurt/Main: Suhrkamp.
De Certeau, Michel (1988) *Kunst des Handelns*, Berlin: Merve.
Deleuze, Gilles (1989) Das Bewegungs-Bild, Kino 1, Frankfurt/Main: Suhrkamp.
—— (1991) *Das Zeit-Bild*, Frankfurt/Main: Suhrkamp.
Derrida, J. (1998) *Randgänge der Philosophie*, Wien: Passagen.
Furlong, William (1992) *Audio Arts*, Leipzig: Reclam.

Goebbels, Heiner (1989) "Prince and the Revolution", in Albrecht Riethmüller (ed.), *Revolution in der Musik: Avantgarde* von 1200 bis 2000. Kassel: Bärenreiter, pp. 103–29.

Heidegger, Martin (1954) *Vorträge und Aufsätze*, Pfullingen: Klett-Cotta.

Kagel, Mauricio (1982) "Im Gespräch mit Lothar Prox, Abläufe, Schnittpunkte – montierte Zeit", in Alte Oper, Frankfurt (ed.) Grenzgänge – Grenzspiele: Ein Programmbuch zu den Frankfurt Festen '82, p. 121.

Kierkegaard, Søren (1955) Die Wiederholung, Düsseldorf und Köln: Meiner.

Lacan, Jacques (1975) *Schriften I*, Frankfurt/Main: Olten.

Meyer, Petra Maria (1993) *Die Stimme und ihre Schrift. Die Graphophonie der Akustischen Kunst*, Wien: Passagen.

—— (1998) "Als das Theater aus dem Rahmen fiel. Zu John Cage, Marcel Duchamp und Merce Cunningham", in: Erika Fischer-Lichte, Friedemann Kreuder and Isabel Pflug (eds.) *Theater seit den 60er Jahren. Grenzgänge der Neoavantgarde*, Tübingen: Francke, pp. 135–95.

—— (2001) *Intermedialität des Theaters. Entwurf einer Semiotik der Überraschung*, Düsseldorf: Parerga.

—— (2004) "Intensität der Zeit in John Cages Textkompositionen", in: Günther Heeg and Anno Mungen (eds.), *Stillstand und Bewegung. Intermediale Studien zur Theatralität von Text, Bild und Musik,* München: epodium , pp. 227–37.

—— (ed.) (2008) *Acoustic Turn*, München: Fink.

—— (2010) "Der audio-visuelle Raum: Pina Bauschs Choreographie, Blaubart – Beim Anhören einer Tonband-aufnahme von Béla Bartóks Oper *Herzog Blaubarts Burg*" in Sabiene Autsch and Sara Hornäk (eds.), *Die Kunst und der Raum – Räume für die Kunst*, Bielefeld: Transcript, pp. 31–54.

Nietzsche, Friedrich (1967–77) *Sämtliche Werke. Kritische Studienausgabe*, ed. by Giorgio Colli and Mazzino Montinari, München: de Gruyter.

Novarina, Valère (1989) *Le théâtre des paroles,* Paris: POL.

—— (1993) "Letter for the Actors", *The Drama Review*, 37/2 Summer 1993, pp. 95–104.

—— (1996) *The Theater of the Ears (Le Théâtre des Oreilles)*. Translated by Allen S. Weiss, Los Angeles: Sun and Moon Press.

Straus, Erwin (1956) *Vom Sinn der Sinne*, Göttingen: Springer.

Valéry, Paul (1991) "Poésie Pure (Notizen für einen Vortrag)" in Paul Valéry, *Werke, Bd. 5. Zur Theorie der Dichtkunst und vermischte Gedanken,* Frankfurt/Main: Insel Verlag, pp. 65–74.

—— (1993) *Cahiers 6, translated by* Bernhardt Böschenstein, Hartmut Köhler and Jürgen Schmidt-Radefeldt, Frankfurt/Main: Fischer.

Part II

Processes and Practices: Work Reports and Reflections

Chapter 4

'It's all part of one concern': A 'Keynote' to Composition as Staging

Heiner Goebbels

Keynotes suggest that you have the key to something. And all the questions which have been raised in the editors' proposal for this publication are indeed questions at the centre of what I am doing as a director and a composer. But the unconscious truly rules at the centre of an artistic work, so one does not really know exactly what one is doing and that's fine – sometimes. And especially when it is fine, you no longer need to ask for an explanation. Hence my problems when defining the mostly unconscious relationship between composing and directing.

Composing as a director

In the past I used to answer the question about the relationship between composing and directing by taking advantage of both professions in order to get a creative distance towards the other medium: composing as a director, directing as a composer.

In the first case I compare my process of composition with what I have experienced to be a director's work (in collaborations with such directors as Ruth Berghaus or Matthias Langhoff or Hans Neuenfels or Claus Peymann). A good director discovers the personalities, talents and creativity of the performers and organises the process in a way which relates to the drama. For my process as a composer it means: not having the score ready, but working with musicians from a very early stage, to invite them for improvisations, being attentive to the options they propose as musicians; ready to discover what else they can offer, which are the unique qualities of the individual musicians or of an orchestra or an ensemble.

I collect those experiences, biographies, characters, options and bring them together in a compositional process, which will be a very precise score in the end – my works are never improvised finally – but as a method of research on material an experimental improvisation is the best possible tool.

Songs of Wars I Have Seen, for example, a composition which was performed in April 2009 in London by the London Sinfonietta and the Orchestra in the Age of Enlightenment, was very much dedicated to the personalities of the musicians; not only, because in this composition the (female) musicians were asked to speak texts by Gertrude Stein during the performance of the music, but also because of the way they were able to treat their instruments.

In an ideal process I try to compose like a director, who is able to discover and develop (and not to oppress) the qualities and the options, which come up with the individual performers he works with. I never start with a complete musical vision or score.

Directing as a composer

On the other side, I direct like a composer: I work very formally and consider theatre as a very musical process. I firmly believe in the musical space of an aesthetic experience and rather think about the rhythm of scenes, the harmonic or contrapuntal relationship of the theatrical elements and the different levels between a 'visual' and an 'acoustic' stage. Once I have chosen the text I reflect the sound of a language– the sound in different languages, the rhythm, the melody of a spoken text.

Just recently I saw an early film by Rainer Werner Fassbinder on television: *Die Bitteren Tränen der Petra von Kant* (*The Bitter Tears of Petra von Kant*). I was stunned by the musicality of the speech of Hanna Schygulla, just spoken speech without any music or any other sound. If it had not been midnight and I had not already been in bed, I would have tried to notate the pitch of the language. It was so purely and beautifully musical. She pitched her speech like singing.

That is how I listen to language, especially to languages I do not understand, while working with French actors, with Greek, African, Japanese or English musicians. It enables me to discover the musical quality of a spoken text.

I also work on the polyphony of the media, their contrapuntal function and look for the rhythm of a performance, the chords of the colours – since colours also have a very strong acoustic resonance when they come to life.

The best way to define a musical approach on theatre is to be conscious about form, to undertake research on forms. It doesn't mean it is formal – forms always mean something, forms always have a very strong impact on our perception, more perhaps than the perspective reduced to semantics and topics. The idea of a 'form' can be very rich and open and does not have to not be reduced to 'symmetry', 'repetition' or 'rhythm'. In particular, the German theatre in the second half of the twentieth century has ignored the 'formal' approach and the institutions for the education of actors, as far as I know them, do not provide much training in form for the young students either. They speak about topics, characters, psychology, figures, and 'Einfühlung' [empathy] instead. Through this ignorance of form, I think we are very much in danger of being constantly and unconsciously influenced by the quasi 'natural' form, which consists of the professional conventions. There are so many conventional habits in body language, in expressive gestures, in speech training, in 'that's, how we do it'. But in order to avoid being a victim of the conventional, 'natural' idea of theatre any form is helpful: we know this from the work of directors like Einar Schleef, Bob Wilson, Michael Thalheimer and others. And most of these 'forms' come either from the visual arts or from music. In the last thirty years, theatre has been influenced most by composers or by painters or by choreographers – not as much by theatre directors in the centre of this discipline.

Bob Wilson: 'It's all part of one concern'

Bob Wilson is a set designer, a lighting designer, a painter and visual artist, a sound designer, a playwright, a performer, a director of operas and theatre; he is even a furniture designer, an architect, a collector of arts, a video artist and also a designer of exhibitions. He was once asked what these different disciplines mean to him. And – as the reader may know he is a man of few words – he said: "It's all part of one concern."

He did not explain what that means, but you may find clarity in his aesthetic approach of reduction, of clarity, of minimalism, of creating a space for the imagination in all those disciplines. At the same time it is evident that he never mixes these different elements. He insists on a total separation of elements and separates each element from all the others. He separates the movements from the language – because his performers do not do what they speak about, or if they do they do not do it in a naturalistic but in a very formal or aesthetic way. He separates the language from the bodies – because the performer's voices are never heard in a direct way, they're picked up with little microphones and amplified by speakers, and consequently the sound never reaches the spectators in a direct communication. He separates the bodies from each other – by creating different light zones on stage, with which he can create a distance even between people who are standing next to each other. He even fragments the different parts of the performer's body – by focussing the light so precisely that an isolated hand or head or shoe of a performer can start to tell the story.

It is indeed surprising for somebody who says 'it's all part of one concern' to separate all those individual disciplines and create such a space in between – which is so fundamental and so essential for our imagination.

Romeo Castellucci: 'I don't make a difference'

Romeo Castellucci is an Italian director, for example he directed the Dante trilogy at the Avignon Festival 2008 – a trilogy which is so rich in sound, in images, so powerful in its performance, in the experience for the audience especially because there is hardly a word of Dante to be heard. All topics and motifs have been translated into other media: into sound, video, light, images, and the use of space, dogs and children. In an interview with *Theater der Zeit* he said:

> I don't notice these different art forms so much as different or distinctive languages. Of course they are different disciplines in which I work [...], but I don't make a difference for example with regard to the visual arts; for me there is no contradiction between theatre and visual arts.
>
> (Castellucci 2008: 17)

And with respect to music he added:

> Sounds are truly carrying a form already; they don't accompany a form; they are a form themselves and in this way and this mode they are directly dramatic.
>
> When you do not exclude the visual imagination of sounds, they create spaces, they create colours, but you have to be careful not to put everything on top of each other. In conventional ways of directing opera very often the directors do not create any space for the form which lays within the music itself; instead, they superimpose ideas and ideas and images up to a degree where the imagination of the listener and the viewer is collapsing, because there is no space left.

My early experiments with stage concerts were dedicated to the idea of developing a format of performing art, in which the music comes to its best presentation inspiring the imagination – to develop exactly, what Romeo Castellucci describes with music already having a form by itself and not only illustrating something.

Anything, which comes late, can only ever be illustrative

"What came first, what were the important steps, at what point did musical ideas come in and how did they impact on the theatrical realisation?"[1]
With regards to conventional production methods, in an institutional production of theatre or music theatre anything which comes late in the process is only going to be illustrative; it does not have the power to change anything else which has already been established during the rehearsal period. When the original light is set up in the last three days of a production you can only light what is already there, you cannot change the staging by means of the light anymore.

That is why I work with all elements from the very first moment. I work with light, sound, and amplification. Even when there is no audience I amplify as if there was, because the amplification is a force in itself, sound design is an art form in itself, and I never would accept a rehearsal, where this has been just ignored and somebody says 'we do not need it yet'. It changes the way you speak on stage when a microphone is amplifying this for a potential audience of 500 or 1000 people. So I rehearse with the microphone from the very first moment just like I rehearse with the light and with everything else. I respect those elements as artistic partners and forces, not just as tools.

"At what point did musical ideas come into the play?"
You could expect from a composer to bring in the music quite early in the process. But because once I have established such a working method, and established a flexible way in

---

1. The following sub-headings are cited from an early position paper by Matthias Rebstock and David Roesner, which formed part of the invitation to this publication and the series of workshops and presentations, which preceded it.

which the whole team (the technical, the visual, the acoustic team and the performers) proceed, I tend to be very open for a long time, things can even come late, because we start early: the first very early rehearsal period happens one year before the premiere, for three to five days.

I do not have a complete vision of a piece when I start it. I have a question. But looking back at this working method, which I developed and employed over the last fifteen years, most of the things which you see in my pieces (in *Ou bien le débarquement désastreux, Schwarz auf Weiss, The repetition,* in *Eraritjaritjaka, Hashirigaki* or in *Landscape With Distant Relatives* and also in my recent pieces *Stifters Dinge* and *I Went to the House But Did Not Enter*) most of the things you see – not hear, but see – are created in the first three or four days of these experimental workshops, where everybody can 'sort of' do what he or she wants. If I would have the music already written before these early workshops I would set the music as a priority. I definitely do not want to do this.

In these first periods of production I even work with 'blind music' or 'blind texts'. It has been said about Fellini that he shot some of his films like this. Because he had not written the text yet he asked the actors just to count numbers – "Quarant'uno, quaranta due, quaranta tre!!!" – and it was only later that he wrote the text and synchronised it with the images. When I improvise with an ensemble I ask them to play something they have in their repertoire. Then I notice which register of music is interesting, who is moving in which way while playing the music, or maybe I already have an idea about the character of music I ask for – starting with the question what impression does a certain energy create in this costume and in this light together with this stage at this very moment.

I never would stage a piece, if I knew already how it would work. I really want to be surprised by the process, surprised by my team, surprised by the result.

At what point did musical ideas come into play? On a conscious level, probably very late, unconsciously it might be there already. It might already be part of the question with which I start. It might be there as a temperature. It might be there as a reaction to the first sketches of the set designer or the first ideas of the material and colour in the space we rehearse. Consciously it does not come too early.

"What is the relationship between music and the elements of performance?"
Let me explain that with *Stifter's Dinge*, a performative installation piece with five pianos and without any performer on stage. There are the three water tanks, three water basins, and in the background five pianos, metal sheets, pipes and tree trunks and everything is being handled or played by machines. There is even a stone which is dragged by an engine to create stone grinding sounds. All sounds except some bodiless voices are created in the performance at the very moment. In one specific scene you hear the sound of a shutter of light. The light has (with the sound of its shutter) a musical function. At the same time you hear a recording with the voices of Indians in Papua Guinea; an incantation for the southwest winds. The light actually reacts musically and visually to the voices and works as a punctuation of the scene.

Let me describe how we created this: I had a keyboard, which was designed by my friend and colleague Hubert Machnik as an interface to all the engines (via MAX MSP) On this keyboard I could control nearly everything in a musical way: one key to set the stone in motion, another key to move the stone backwards. F sharp was used to make it go faster and G sharp stopped it. Another key was used to start the rain, one for the light shutter to go on and off, etc. and all that in addition to providing the musical access to the mechanical pianos.

This made it possible to work in a musical way, composing the visual, the space and the sound elements from this keyboard. A keyboard was used to direct like a composer. Probably this musical approach represents a way of working, probably all these decisions (when to emphasise a light or when to move something) go through my body as a director as much as they went through my body as a keyboard player in the rehearsals of this piece.

I did music theatre before the keyboard. But it allows you to do things rather uncontrolledly or to let your body (as a composer/director) react to a material or an image. I savour this option of working unconsciously after a long period of conceptional work. And the biggest advantage of working with a team since ten, fifteen, twenty years ago is: you don't have to speak. You speak a lot in advance and hopefully come up with clever and intelligent concepts, but it's very important that you have the space and the option and the confidence in the team to react and create directly without explaining. And everybody has that in my team, including the sound engineer or the costume designer: she can just go on stage during the rehearsal and put a hat on the actor; or the set designer can go on stage and move things or lights around while I work with the actors or with the musicians. We have a completely different, concentrated but also relaxed way of trying things out. And after maybe a certain period of irritation in the beginning, everybody notices, that this is a much more pleasant and open way, more open to inspirations for everybody, than the hysterical silence in the authoritarian way of directing.

With regard to the relationship between music and the other elements of the performance let me refer to a specific scene of the music theatre piece called *Eraritjaritjaka* – with a string quartet and one actor, with texts of Elias Canetti from his notebooks and *Crowds and Power* (1960). It is a moment when the actor leaves the stage and is being followed by a video camera and the image is projected on the backdrop of the stage. The actor is leaving the theatre, goes through the foyer to a car and is being driven through the city towards his apartment. As soon as he enters the apartment, the string quartet is starting to play a string quartet by Maurice Ravel – the only string quartet by Maurice Ravel – live on stage.

It is a very important decision for the success of this work and the special attraction of this video/movie sequence that it is made only with one hand camera following the actor for about forty minutes. But for this movie we also reversed the relationship between music and action. When you think of the conventional relationship between film and music you never have the music as the starting point. We are used to the fact that the music is there to underline images, enforce emotions and illustrate moods, prepare tension etc. (The same is true for most of the music on stage by the way). This habit, this one-way-relationship between music and film / sound and film (or music and theatre) has been industrialised by the film industry. And what Adorno and Hanns Eisler wrote in an early piece of research on this phenomenon is still substantial now, seventy years later.

> The prerequisite of melody is that the composer be independent, in the sense that his selection and invention relate to situations that supply specific lyric-poetic inspiration. This is out of the question where the motion picture is concerned. All music in the motion picture is under the sign of utility, rather than lyric expressiveness. Aside from the fact that lyric-poetic inspiration cannot be expected from the composer for the cinema, this kind of inspiration would contradict the embellishing and subordinate function that industrial practice still enforces on the composer. Moreover, the problem of melody as 'poetic' is made insoluble by the conventionality of the popular notion of melody. Visual action in the motion picture has of course a prosaic irregularity and asymmetry. It claims to be photographed life; and as such every motion picture is a documentary. As a result, there is a gap between what is happening on the screen and the symmetrically articulated conventional melody. A photographed kiss cannot actually be synchronized with an eight-bar phrase.
>
> (Adorno/Eisler 2007 [1947]: 4)

We tried to put the relationship Adorno and Eisler describe here on its head in a way, in that the music was actually in first place to develop the film. So once the actor enters his apartment, you hear the string quartet of Maurice Ravel and whatever he does for the next thirty or forty minutes is staged, bar by bar, following Ravel's score. When the actor enters his apartment and starts opening and reading letters and the newspaper and peeling onions and cooking scrambled eggs and sorting through his laundry, watching TV and doing lots of everyday things, we did not try to find an appropriate music afterwards to accompany that; we try to provide him and his structure of movements and activities a sort of musical energy and tried to follow the musical form, one which is driven by aesthetic compositional aspects. This also means 'directing as a composer' (here like Maurice Ravel). The camera movements, the framing of moments, images and situations – all have been developed by following the score and its dynamics.

"Are you working on your own or with a group? How do you negotiate results, ways to go on, selection of materials etc.? Who is taking the decisions?"
I have been collaborating strongly with a set designer for more than ten years, with a costume designer as well, with a sound designer for nearly twenty years now, and actually even with the same technical team at the same theatre, Théâtre Vidy in Switzerland, since 1998. I do not have a complete vision of the piece, but I always have a starting point and great confidence that I can share this starting point or initial question with my team so that they can start working independently. The sound designer, the set and lighting designer, develop their own autonomous languages during the process towards the creation.

'It's up to you!'

Brecht once wrote a letter to Hanns Eisler sending him a poem, which he wanted him to set to music. It was completely striking for me that Brecht left certain questions, even questions regarding the text form, to Hanns Eisler, saying: 'it's up to you!' And this 'it's up to you!' is a very important attitude, with which I respect my team. I raise certain questions and try to trust in what the others think about them in the context of their artistic disciplines as they translate them into their medium.

References

Adorno, Theodor and Eisler, Hanns (2007 [1947]) *Composing for the Films*, New York/London: Continuum.

Castellucci, Romeo (2008) "Das Haus muss brennen. Romeo Castellucci im Gespräch mit Lena Schneider und Frank Raddatz", *Theater der Zeit*, 09/2008, pp. 16–20.

Chapter 5

'Theatre in small quantities': On Composition for Speech, Sounds and
Objects

Michael Hirsch

W hen I was asked to reflect on the aspects of Composed Theatre within my own compositional work, I have to acknowledge, that I have not developed any coherent theory in this context. I do not even represent a particular genre or a clearly definable style of music theatre. Elements of Composed Theatre, or of theatrically conceived composing can be found in my work in the most diverse genres, forms and quantities. This ranges from the form of opera, which is quite rooted in its genre tradition, via different forms of experimental music theatre to instrumental chamber music, which nonetheless contains trace elements, as it were, of theatre. These may be integrated into the music by means of small actionist irritations or through a special, quasi-scenic constellation.

As I am going to demonstrate in the following, even musical genres which on the surface seem to lack any optical or scenic element as for example my speech compositions and even some of my tape music, contain strongly theatrical elements.

I wonder in this context why that might be. Why do theatrical elements keep sneaking into my pieces, even if I planned them as 'absolute music'? One reason may well be that the dissolution of boundaries between the arts has become a natural achievement of the history of the arts of the twentieth and twenty-first century. Elements of music, visual arts, literature, film and theatre can be found in the installations of visual artists, in the performances of theatre practitioners as well as in contemporary music. Consequently, the reservoir of all art forms is open to a composer even when he writes a purely musically conceived piece of chamber music. A sound, a word, a gesture, a noise and an action then constitute a texture, that may be conceived purely musically, but is of a music-theatrical nature due to the diverse origins of its elements.

Speech composition

Speech composition is a particular form of dissolution of boundaries between the arts. At first sight, music that consists not of the sung but of the spoken word is hardly different to what has become known in the area of literature as 'concrete poetry'. Fundamentally, it is primarily the composer's self-image, which defines such a work of speech art as music and not as literature. But on close inspection, for example of the sound poems of Josef Anton Riedl, one can discover that they follow exclusively musical criteria. Their auditory gestus is entirely characterised by the sound world of both Riedl's electronic music and percussion music however much they may appear to resemble the sound poems of literary authors. In my own *Lieder nach Texten aus dem täglichen Leben* [*Songs after texts from real life*] (1992–95) those purely musical criteria are joined by an underlying semantic level, which keeps shimmering through or erupts. This composition for one speaker toys with the continuous oscillation between the semantic and the purely phonetic level of language. If one subtracts any semantic information from language, its musical potential comes to the forefront. Now, the *Lieder nach Texten aus dem täglichen Leben* are based on originally documentary materials, i.e. on entirely non-musical sources. Taped interviews, accidentally overheard or secretly recorded speech acts were transcribed in such a way, that the individual deviations from written language were advanced further and further and finally composed from a solely compositional angle into formal developments.

Elements of semantically intelligible language grow rampant from the thus developed abstract speech music, so that the act of listening sways back and forth between musical hearing to linguistic hearing, playing with comprehension and non-comprehension as well as with the boundaries between language and music.

Extra-musical reality manifests itself here in a twofold way: on the one hand through the fragments of the original material that remain intelligible, on the other – and this is the more significant aspect of this piece – through the moulds of individual intonations, that are musically portrayed here, which coagulate into musical form and become exaggerated through different levels of transformation.

I would like to use the original material of the first song, the transcript of a TV interview, to demonstrate my approach. The sister of a man, who gained notoriety in Germany by robbing a bank, followed by taking hostages and murder, spoke in a TV documentary about his childhood. She described psychological problems, which manifested themselves as speech impediments: "When he was embarrassed somehow he would begin to, like, stutter. [...] he couldn't say certain sentences: for 'roll' he would say 'woll'"[1] and so forth.

The first musical-compositional step started already when transcribing the interviews: I did not transcribe the sounds she made into correct speech – as one would normally do with an interview – by transcribing them into written language as accurately as possible and by omitting all mistakes, stutters or other deviations. On the contrary, I paid particular attention to any deviations from written language, and emphasised them by means of exaggeration. These could be deviations through dialect – in the case of this woman this was a dialect from the Rhineland. But there are also deviations, which are more difficult to define, that emerge from other irregularities of the speech act, such as distorted or drawled vowels due to a particularly emotional component. Or, words are being de-familiarised by sloppy speaking (e.g. 'sumtames' ['meinchmer'] instead of 'sometimes' ['manchmal']). I have emphasised many of the minimal discolourations, which occur in speech involuntarily, by means of exaggeration. As an additional act of de-familiarisation I then, sometimes violently,

---

1. "Wenn er verlegen war irgendwie, fing er auch an zu stottern, oder so. [...] Er konnte manche Sätze nicht sagen: Für 'Brötchen' hat er dann 'Brönnchen' gesagt".

removed the orthography from the written word. By combining such manipulations, a phonetic complexity such as 'Whaenhesem BAArrassd sumhow' ['Wännerfa LEEJgnwaa Eeagnqui ...'] emerged from the sentence "When he was embarrassed somehow ..." ['Wenn er verlegen war irgendwie ...']. In writing, the original sentence is barely recognisable at first sight. However, if one hears it presented acoustically, anyone who has a good command of German will certainly understand it. And he will probably even be able to identify the Rhineland dialect. For the notation of such transcripts I do not use the phonetic alphabet or any other objectifying characters, but limit myself to the material of the German written language. The text should be read according to German rules of pronunciation. Consequently, the piece can only be realised by a German-speaking performer. Beyond this, I have introduced a small number of additional indications: stressed syllables and sounds are emphasised by CAPITALisation, strongly stressed ones by putting them in **BOLD**. There are also staccato signs for sounds, which are meant to be articulated particularly short, and horizontal bars for more drawled sounds. Such techniques of transcription obviously do not render the documentary material of the interviews into a composition. The described liberties in the process of transcription certainly lead to some musical decisions. But the actual composition process only starts after that. With regard to this particular piece I decided to go for a very simple abstract manipulation: I read the whole transcribed text backwards and notated it. That does not mean that I simply put the letters back to front, but tried to make it phonetically exact, just as if one would play a tape in reverse. Just one example for this: the sound 't' in German is aspirated, that is, the plosive 't' is followed by a kind of 'h'. So in the backward version the 't' becomes a 'h-t'.

The German word 'stottern' [to stutter] became 'schtotan' in the liberal transcription and ultimately, in its mirrored version, 'naHHToHHTSCH'. (Here again, the duplication of the 'H's and the emphasis through capitalisation represent a conscious exaggeration, which results in a kind of laughing speech.)

I had two reservoirs of material now: on the one hand the liberal transcription, which for the (German-speaking) listener still contains reasonably comprehensible language. On the other hand the mirrored form, in which the material appears as an entirely abstract sound music. Hence the compositional work consisted in crossing the two levels of material and rendering them into a musical form.

Is such a speech composition 'Composed Theatre'? I think it at least touches on aspects of it. Firstly, it is a composition by means of the theatre. A music for actors. In addition, those aspects, which transcend a purely musical perception, are certainly to be apportioned to the theatre rather than to literature. The semantics and characteristics of the language fragments are not recognisable in silent reading. It requires the interpretation by a speaker. Besides, the kind of transcription of the interviews focusses more on the individual diction of the person than the 'literary' content of the text. Consequently, *Lieder nach Texten aus dem täglichen Leben* are small character portraits, which continue to shine through the abstractly musical sound world of the linguistic phonemes.

As an aside I should mention that my temporary preoccupation with speech compositions like these also has biographical reasons: other than being a composer, I have continually worked as an actor and speaker. It therefore suggested itself that I should also write pieces which unite these activities with my compositional work. So I wrote those pieces for myself as the interpreter. Nonetheless I tried to notate them in such a way that they could be realised by other interpreters without my assistance (which has since happened).

The *Lieder nach Texten aus dem täglichen Leben* are admittedly an exception within my work insofar as they are the only piece for an entirely unaccompanied speaker. Normally, I have combined speech with other musical means, be it instrumental music or musique concrète.

My piece *Hirngespinste, eine nächtliche Szene* [*Woolgathering, a nocturnal scene*] is an example for the combination of instrumental music and speech composition. *Hirngespinste* is a composition for two players with accordion. One of the players is an accordionist, his part was written for Teodoro Anzellotti, the other is an actor, his part was created for Robert Podlesny. Both parts are not synchronised with each other with the exception of a few points of coordination. In the separate scores the notation corresponds with the respective profession of the player in question: the musician's part is fixed in traditional musical notation whereas the actor's part consists of a small collection of stage directions and a speech composition.

By casting the two players' parts with a musician and an actor the elements of theatre and music are separately juxtaposed. Accordingly, the function of the accordion is different for both players. The musician uses it exclusively as a musical instrument while the actor uses it as an extension and amplification of his body by translating his own breathing into movement of the accordion bellows. Through the interaction of the two performers a musical scene is created, which is not explicitly music theatre since it lacks a decidedly scenic component, but which transcends the expressive ambit of pure instrumental music. In addition to the concretely physical and psychological expression of one part and the absolute musical character of the other, there is a semi-scenic constellation: the players sit in profile to the audience, back to back. For the audience this constellation creates the image of a singular figure with its mirror image in its back. Thereby both parts are able to rub off their respective characters on to each other, in a manner of speaking. As different, even contrary as they are in structure and material, they coalesce to a single dramatic figure, which they represent in different aspects.

The poetic starting point is a kind of dream or sleep situation (hence the subtitle 'a *nocturnal scene*'). This is admittedly only a vague point of reference, from which a cocoon of musical chains of associations develops. Adhering to the principle of the associative chain the composition relinquishes any stringent, logical, cohesive material. The composition process occasionally resembles the kind of 'automatic writing' undertaken in literature by the Surrealists. In addition, the composition was conceived through a number of approaches in that the fragments which were written first were photocopied, pasted together anew as modular components and finally overwritten with further material. The speech composition of the actor's part developed in a similar process of aggregation in several approaches. An initial unconscious murmur develops into a kind of dream language accompanied by the actor at first with the air noise of the bellows, eventually also with sounds from the accordion.

Later I developed the text material from *Hirngespinste* in a piece called *Dialog* [*Dialogue*]. This is a duo for two speakers, who are accompanied by an installation of small CD-players, which play a musique concrète rich in associations.

Musique concrète

Musique concrète continues to play a significant part in my work, most often in combination with other genres. Even though it is merely played through a set of loudspeakers, it still has a strong theatrical aspect for me. Corresponding with Dieter Schnebel's notion of 'visible music' one might introduce the notion of 'audible theatre' here. This applies in particular when it is possible to recognise at least partially where the sounds stem from originally. Here a similar phenomenon to the one I demonstrated using the example of my speech composition ensues: this iridescence between recognition and non-recognition, between the quasi-semantic contents of a sound and its abstract-acoustic appearance. The affinity to the theatrical in my musique concrète works results in particular from the fact that most often they deal with noise material that is clearly the outcome of a physical action. Usually it consists neither of electronically generated sounds nor static soundscapes, but predominantly of material sounds which depict things in motion: rolling balls, dropping objects, burrowing, shaking and crumpling sound actions, which often have been recorded in a kind of studio performance and were edited only to such a degree that the actionist background was still clearly identifiable.

Such acoustic action can even have an immediate emotional expressiveness in which a unique theatricality is inherent: the sound of bursting glass for example has a quite unmistakable effect, immediately evoking the concrete action of throwing, smashing, destroying, and thus takes an urgent gestural shape by purely acoustic means. Nonetheless, musique concrète is – when it is not in combination with other genres – purely tape music. (I use the expression 'tape music' even if tapes are no longer used today, but other storage media such as CDs or hard drives instead). As tape music it is in turn more remote from the performative character of the theatre than most other genres. Hence there is the inevitable problem of how to present musique concrète: any performance of music when realised by musicians on stage always has a certain 'performative' character, which enhances the immediate experience of the music for the listener through his empathy with the performing musician. Any concertgoer will always look for a seat from which he can see the musicians. Staring at loudspeakers in performances of tape music is always unsatisfactory. This is why I usually add a scenic live-performance to my finished tape music pieces. This is how my piece *Duo* came into being: by juxtaposing the small study in musique concrète with a small musical scene for two performers on stage as an optical counterpart. Here, the rather marginal acoustic actions of these performers serve as connecting links to the actual composition, which comes from a CD through a set of speakers.

In my *1. Studie* [*1. Study*] from *Das Konvolut, Vol. 2* the musique concrète is confronted with a group of five performers which seem to do little more than the audience, namely listening. Their mere presence on stage however makes them stage characters. In addition, certain tensions and relationships are evoked by means of the given constellation of the group and by some minimal physical actions. Hence this scenic aspect of the performance hangs in the balance between being a mere projection surface for the listening audience or the nucleus for a potential theatrical action.

My open music-theatre piece *Beschreibung eines Kampfes* [*Description of a Fight*] (based on Kafka) began with a piece of tape music to which I added a small acoustic-scenic performance. This then developed further and further until it grew to a full music-theatre project. Usually I use musique concrète as a playback tape in other pieces. Particularly in opera and music-theatre projects I used the associative richness of this genre to afford the theatre with an additional atmospheric space. One might call this an 'acoustic set design'. In my opera *Das Stille Zimmer* [*The Silent Room*] the musique concrète is integrated into the composition for singers, actors and orchestra as an eight-channel-playback. This opera on the whole was an attempt to form a unity out of different forms of music and theatre. The cast of singers and actors confronted opera with 'straight' theatre. The actors' parts contain both 'normal' theatre and experimental speech compositions. Again the orchestral part is enriched by elements from the musique concrète level, which at times also stands alone autonomously. This approach takes opera, as the most encompassing of all art forms, as a starting point. Basically any aesthetic means of expression can be integrated into this form. Even though the pathos of Wagner's notion of the 'Gesamtkunstwerk' ['total work of art'] seems dated, its essential core, the great potential of opera as an art form, remains current when it is scrutinised and renewed with the achievements of more recent art forms.

Konvolut[2]

Combinations of different, even diverging aesthetic elements play an important part in my work, not just in grand opera, but also in the smaller projects. Quickly then, the question of the most suitable form of notation for such heterogeneous elements of different provenance suggests itself. If one is to notate all levels in a score that synchronises everything, one has to also notate non-musical material by and large in traditional musical notation. Mauricio Kagel, for example, often notates the steps and movements of the performers in rhythms

---

2. The German word 'Konvolut', from lat. *Convolutum* = 'rolled up' has no direct equivalent in English. It refers to a bundle of different heterogeneous documents, which may consist of different media (note from the translator).

similar to a drum part. Similarly, spoken language is often notated rhythmically. Personally, I prefer notating non-musical elements at first with other means, which are more compatible with their own potential. In particular, spoken language has an inner wealth that is impossible to translate into traditional musical notation. If one wants to realise the complex and largely unconsciously uttered *rubato* of spoken languages even just approximately into written notation, the resulting score would be so rhythmically complicated that it would overwhelm musicians too, not just the usually musically untrained actor. Hence I notate language solely with alphabetic letters and a few additional signs. Some complementary performance notes enable the actor to savour the natural wealth of speech rhythms even in musically abstract speech compositions.

Likewise, I feel that the elements of theatrical action and scenic play can hardly be integrated into a musically notated score without significant losses. Here I prefer verbal instructions or descriptions of working processes, which are meant to lead to a scenic result. The electro-acoustic level of the musique concrete, finally, has its own, distinct form of documentation in the pre-recorded CD, which is entirely detached from the score.

As a consequence, this diversity of notational forms means that the conventional form of the score, in which all parts are synchronised in a way that can instantly be grasped, is no longer sufficient for my music-theatrical projects. This is why I use a form that I call 'Konvolut'. The Konvolut is a collection of documents and notes. The Konvolut as an alternative to the score enables the co-existence of conventionally notated compositions with concept pieces, verbal scores and stage directions. Verbally defined models for improvisation, electro-acoustic compositions on CD, scenic actions and self-contained compositions notated in traditional scores as well as pieces with mixed forms of notation are being composed into a macrostructure in a kind of meta-polyphony. The synchronisation happens through an individually devised system of cues. According to each project a unique balance between dependency and independency of the levels arises.

From time to time I work on a project in which the initially pragmatic choice of the Konvolut form becomes the topic of the project itself. Presumably there will not be any fixed notion of genre for the future final product, since the weighting of the genres will shift constantly within it. As a whole it will probably be ascribed as music-theatre. I am talking about a work complex, which is meant to encompass a yet indefinite number of 'Volumina' [volumes] under the heading 'Das Konvolut'. These will be self-contained singular pieces as well as amount to an extensive, full-length music-theatre piece when performed together. The title 'Das Konvolut' describes both the form of the project as a whole, as well as the form of the individual volumes. Hence, *Volumina 1-3* do not consist of self-contained scores but are also designed in a Konvolut form themselves.

Volumen 1, written for the Kammerensemble Neue Musik Berlin commissioned by the Berliner Festspiele (MaerzMusik 2002), consists of several autonomous pieces, which run simultaneously in a total time of twelve minutes. There is the monodrama *Opera für eine Sängerin und CD-Zuspielung* [*Opera for female singer and CD playback*]. This is a small opera in its utmost reduction, as it were. The function of the orchestra is held by a small CD player with small active stereo speakers positioned next to the singer. The singer's stage is the table at which she is seated. The monodrama consists of a twelve-minute sequence of very short numbers, entitled with 'scene', 'recitativ' or 'aria' respectively. The phonetic material for the singer's part is taken from opera seria libretti by Metastasio.

Simultaneously to this a piece is performed called *Improvisation für große Trommel und CD-Zuspielung* [*Improvisation for bass drum and CD playback*] in which the percussionist develops a dialogue with his CD track. The *21 Stücke für Piccolo-Flöte und Es-Klarinette* [*21 Pieces for Piccolo and E Clarinet*] and the five parts of the *Streichtrio* [*String Trio*] establish a traditional chamber musical level within *Volumen 1*, while the *Improvisation für Tuba* [*Improvisation for Tuba*] finally represents more of a scenic-atmospheric reflex towards the total event. The CD playback that belongs to the singer and the other CD, which is in dialogue with the percussionist, are composed in such a way, that they not only serve as an accompaniment for the monodrama and dialogue partner for the drum part, but also result in an autonomous electro-acoustic composition in combination with a third, self-contained CD: a six-channel-composition, then, spread over three stereo CDs and characterised with a certain blurriness due to the approximate concurrence of their entries. The coordination of the performers and CD players, which are dispersed in space, is controlled by a loose system of a few acoustic signals.

The acoustic layer provided by the three spatially dispersed CDs emanating from three sets of active stereo speakers sets up a compositional web, which the other instrumental, vocal and theatrical elements are woven into and relate to each other in various ways. This is because even the parts which are performed live – however different the may have been designed in material and form of notation – have (in contrast to Cage's simultaneous pieces) been conceptualised from the beginning in relation to each other and attuned to each other in various ways with regard to their dramaturgy and tonality. Hence the simultaneity achieved is situated in a field of tension between an autonomy of synchronously running structures on the one hand and a compositional plan on the other, which has always envisioned the sum of these structures as a whole, despite their autonomy.

Volumen 1 will have to be performed as a kind of overture in the foyer of the theatre in a full production of *Das Konvolut*. The spatial arrangement of the different levels in a foyer adds a further aspect to the simultaneity: the total result takes shape in different ways depending on where one is situated as an audience member. If one decides to stand next to the singer for the whole duration of the piece, one will predominantly experience a scenic monodrama with instrumental accompaniment. If one finds oneself nearer to the percussionist, one would perceive the event more as a solo concert for percussion and chamber ensemble, in which the singer is merely integrated as an added timbre, etc.

The different aesthetic elements, out of which this first 'Volumen' of the Konvolut is constructed, are not at least sketches, which can be developed further in various ways in forthcoming volumes.

Volumen 2 of the Konvolut is a sequence of small music-theatrical sketches or studies, while *Volumen 3* contains amongst other things a veritable opera – my thirteen-minute long

La Didone abbandonata. Volumen 1–3 could – according to my current plans – be the first part of the final project. Then there would be an interval, during which *Volumen 4* could be played: this part is a pure noise composition for percussionists and CDs entitled *Holzstück I–IV* [*Wood Piece I–IV*]. Like the opening *Volumen 1* this volume could be performed in the foyer. The ensuing second part of the evening (presumably *Volumen 5–7*) is not even at a conceptual stage. So we are talking about a work in progress, which is completely open ended. Its dramaturgy thus corresponds to the chosen form of documentation and notation of the 'Konvolut'. Where and to what extent this is going to grow unchecked is entirely open at this stage.

(Translation: David Roesner)

Chapter 6

... To Gather Together What Exists in a Dispersed State ...[1]

Jörg Laue

---

1. This text is almost identical with the one of the lecture-performance I gave in the course of the workshop series on *Processes of Devising Composed Theatre*. While I presented this text and several videos, images and sounds simultaneously in the course of the lecture-performance, for this publication I only pasted a few images into those passages that explicitly refer to the shown visual material.

"Als Mr. Cage etwa ein Jahr alt war, ließ sich sein Vater – ein, wie wir wissen, veritabler Erfinder – die Entwicklung eines der ersten U-Boote patentieren. Gerade dessen genial einfaches und in mehreren Tiefseeversuchen erprobtes Ortungssystem aus aufsteigenden Luftbläschen aber verhinderte eine Serienfertigung wegen erwiesener militärischer Untauglichkeit. Das Patent des behördlich so bezeichneten *Cage'schen Faraday'schen Unterwasserkäfigs* geriet bald in Vergessenheit. Und erst als der Zufall es wollte, daß Mr. Cage sich Jahrzehnte später an eben jenem Tag, als er die New Yorker Premiere des Zeichentrickfilms *Yellow Submarine* gesehen hatte, den Nachlaß seines Vaters hervor nahm, tauchte es wieder auf. Sogleich entschloß er sich, den Beatles die pazifistische Verwirklichung des väterlichen Patents zu gegebener Zeit mit einer kleinen Komposition zu danken."[2]

Preliminary remark

Before I start I would like to make a little preliminary remark reflecting on my Exeter experiences four weeks ago:

I had already progressed a good deal in my preparation for this Hildesheim session when, in the course of the Exeter workshop sessions, I learnt that *devising theatre* is a (more or less) precisely sketched term, which describes a certain theatre-practice or conception of theatre, whereas in German we speak of *postdramatisches Theater* (and not only since Hans-Thies Lehmann, as he himself admits, see Lehmann 2008). To me it is interesting that something is expressed by a verb in English, while in German it is expressed by an adjective, which indicates a kind of temporal shift between the genres, a progression so to say. Already this displacement, with all its implications, seems, to me, to be worth a *keynote* itself.

I couldn't find that specific meaning of *devising* in any dictionary, which not only resulted in a bit of a naïve definition, but maybe even in a failing of the use of the term.

In our final discussion in Exeter we'd been talking for a while about how Composed Theatre could be defined in regard to its conditions and processes. And Matthias, if I remember and understood it right, made an important and efficient distinction between

---

2. This brief text was part of the performance *Faraday's Cage*, which I did together with LOSE COMBO feat. Kammerensemble Neue Musik at St. Elisabeth-Kirche Berlin in 2006.

an ontological definition-approach on the one hand, and a practical and process-orientated definition on the other hand, which seem to be incompatible.[3] (Maybe this distinction is even one between verb and adjective).

And me – meanwhile I had learnt about the meaning of the term *devising* in a theatre-context and at the same time had a phrase – or rather a definition of Adorno's *Ästhetische Theorie* in mind: *Definitionen sind rationale Tabus* (Adorno 1973: 24). *Definitions are rational taboos*, I thought, shouldn't we instead go on *devising* this term in a process-related sense rather than finding a definition, which *per definitionem* has got a final, a definitive, that is, an excluding and limited meaning. But this, might be, was again just a failing, a displacement of the term from its theatre-context into the context of philosophical thought in terms of art.

But anyway, in case I used the term *devising* in a naïve manner, but surely in an unknowing way, afterwards this seemed to me an efficient failure, thus I decided not to change anything in the already prepared parts of my workshop-session concerning that term – not least because I'm very much interested in failures, incidences and coincidences in my work, which I mostly consider to be much more productive than a precisely defined knowledge. "Know how to forget knowledge, set fire to the library of poetics", as Derrida says in *Qu'est-ce la poesie?*, "gewußt wie man das Wissen vergißt, die Bibliothek der Poetiken angezünde" (Derrida 1990).

Lecture performance

In one of his conversations with Daniel Charles John Cage said: "We must construct, that is, gather together what exists in a dispersed state. As soon as we give it a try, we realize that everything already goes together. Things were gathered together before us; all we have done is to separate them. Our task, henceforth, is to reunite them" (Cage 1981: 215).

> Ich hoffe in diesem Performance-Vortrag zeigen zu können, daß mit diesem kurzen Zitat bereits eine Menge gesagt ist.

Within this lecture performance I hope to demonstrate that a great deal is already expressed by this brief quotation.

As Andrzej Wirth, who was my professor at university, was preparing a speech that he had to give on the occasion of getting an award for his life's work earlier in 2008, he asked me for a brief text that should explain the influence of the American avant-garde theatre on my work.

I sent the following *Drei kurze Absätze für Andrzej* to him:

---

3. See chapter 15: "Composed Theatre – Discussion and Debate" in this book.

Als wesentlich einem musikalisch aufzufassenden Zeitvergehen verpflichtete Performances profitieren meine Projekte unter anderem maßgeblich von der Bezugnahme auf zwei kompositorische Konzepte, die auf den ersten Blick weit auseinanderliegen mögen: einerseits das polyphone Denken Johann Sebastian Bachs, wie es sich in der Verwendung von *obligaten Stimmen* ausdrückt; andererseits das radikal-demokratische Materialdenken John Cages, besonders wie es sich in seinen späten Kompositionen in der Verwendung von *flexiblen Zeitklammern* zeigt.

Dabei widerspricht die organisatorische Strenge Bachscher Polyphonie nicht etwa dem hohen Maß an Entscheidungsfreiheit und -verantwortung, welches der Umgang mit Cages flexiblen Zeitklammern erfordert. Sondern in Gegenteil findet in den Performances, die ich mit der LOSE COMBO realisiere, beides als *Präzision des Zufälligen und Unvorhersehbaren* autonomer und gleichberechtigter *Performance-Stimmen* zueinander. Bei dem in meinen Arbeiten realisierten Konzept *performativer Polyphonie* ergänzen und bedingen Unvermeidlichkeit und Flexibilität einander.

Die Impulse, die von Cage – und eben nicht nur von seinem kunstphilosophischen Denken, sondern ebensosehr von seinen Kompositionen – ausgingen, kommen meines Erachtens in ihrer Tragweite bis heute – zumindest jenseits der (engen) Musikwelt – noch nicht annähernd zur Geltung (was selbst bei Bach kaum anders ist). Implizit und explizit versuche ich diese Impulse in meiner Arbeit aufzugreifen und fortzusetzen.

In preparation for this workshop I asked Andrzej Wirth for a recording of a roughly translated version of that brief text, as follows:

The performance-pieces, I realise with LOSE COMBO, are obliged to a passing of time, which is essentially musical. They benefit from the reference to two compositional concepts, which – at first glance – may seem to be far apart: on the one hand the polyphonic thinking of Johann Sebastian Bach, as you will find it in the usage of *obligate parts*; on the other hand John Cage's concept of a radically democratic use of material, especially in the way it is realised in his latest pieces applying *flexible time-brackets*.

Yet there is no contradiction between the strictness of organization in Bach's polyphony and the great extent of discretion and responsibility, as it is required by the use of flexible time-brackets. Quite the opposite: both concepts come together within the performances-pieces I do: they are merged as a *precision of the accidental and unforeseeable* of autonomous and equal *performance-parts*. In accomplishing the concept of what I call *performative polyphony*, unavoidability and flexibility complete and require one another.

From my point of view the enormous impulses, which were initiated by Cage – not only his philosophical thought in terms of the arts, but also his compositions – aren't yet recognised for its outstanding impact, especially beyond the (narrow) scope of contemporary music. (By the way, this is more or less the same with Bach.) What I'm trying to do in my work, implicitly as well as explicitly, is to pick up and carry on with those impulses.

Bevor ich fortfahre, möchte ich mich dafür entschuldigen, daß ich auch
weiterhin die ganze Zeit ablesen werde. Das hat vor allem mit der gewählten
Workshop-Form zu tun.
Before I go on I would like to apologise for reading all the time, even further on.
This mainly has got to do with the chosen workshop-form.
Ich habe eine ganze Zeit überlegt, wie ich diese Workshop-Session entwerfen
könnte, welche Form sie mit Rücksicht auf meine künstlerische Arbeit
haben könnte, ob ich einfach von der Arbeit berichten, oder sie
besser demonstrieren sollte?
It took me some time to think about in what way I could devise this workshop-
session, what form it may have, in regard to my artistic work, whether I should
just talk about the work, or superiorly demonstrate it?
Aber ich habe dann entschieden, beides zu tun – das eine und das andere, das
eine, indem ich das andere tue, das andere, indem ich das eine tue, und zwar in
Form eines Performance-Vortrags.
But I decided then to do both – the one and the other, the one while I'm doing the
other, the other while I'm doing the one, that is, in form of a lecture-performance,
eines Performance-Vortrags weitgehend über Prozesse des Entwerfens eines
Performance-Vortrags, mit Rücksicht auf das, was Processes of Devising
Composed Theatre heißen könnte,
a lecture-performance mainly on processes of devising a lecture-performance,
taking into consideration what *Processes of Devising Composed Theatre* may mean,
and that is, in two languages, at least at first.
und zwar in zwei Sprachen, zunächst zumindest.

In two languages – although I was informed right from the beginning that the working
language at both workshop places – Exeter as well as Hildesheim – would be English. It
certainly – more or less – would be possible for me to explain something in English, but
not to demonstrate the process of devising a lecture-performance on *Processes of Devising
Composed Theatre*, because devising a performance to me always has got to do with –
transformation. In this case: *translation*.

Lecture performance, Composed Theatre, performance – with regards to its devising I
can't see a difference, in principal. One of the main things I'm doing in my work is different
kinds of transformations of material. Later on I will give an example of a transformation
process concerning one of my performance-pieces, which at the same time will give you an
example of what I call performative polyphony.

But now I have to go back right to the beginning.
Aber jetzt muß ich noch einmal zum Anfang zurückkehren.

Mostly for devising a project there is a more or less coincidentally chosen (that may sound like a contradiction, I know) starting point, which generally refers to a certain topic or a wider topical context. Or sometimes there is a formal or thematic request, a given task, as for this event. I am thankful for such situations – because this prevents me from having to make an initial decision, thus the beginning is always a haunting thing. And, by the way, everything in a way remains a beginning all the time. But besides, and at the same time, there are also leaps, *leaps* that are leaping the permanently beginning.

> In genau diesem Moment des Schreibens über *Anfang und Sprung* hat solch ein *leap* stattgehabt.

At that particular moment of writing about *beginning and leap* such a *leap* has taken place.

An essential part of the work is giving its persistent beginnings a quality of a continuous leaping, which becomes a kind of flow, a decelerating movement, which makes one forget beginnings as well as leaps.

The fact that the topic "Processes of Devising Composed Theatre" is already set at the beginning – or to be more precise, even before the beginning, as a starting point that sets a task – is a good thing, because it is not more than four words to think and talk about. It is not more than four words that are sufficient to establish even more ways to devise a lecture-performance. Generally this is my approach: taking the beginning as a given occasion, taking it seriously, and then, let's see where it is drifting and what it is touching upon in the working process.

From its very beginning the whole process is guided by coincidental beginnings/leaps that will lead from one detour to another.

And as you can clearly see, I got on such a detour right from the start. Taking the beginning seriously may also mean simply missing it. Quoting John Cage, I neglected to talk about those four words, explicitly.

Somehow, even *to be asked* is a way of setting a task. In the case of the quoted *Drei kurze Absätze für Andrzej* the starting point, on the one hand, was just to be asked; and on the other hand, there was a theme: *influences of the American avant-garde theatre*. As you have heard, I didn't know to say that much about it. Being asked to relate my performance-work to theatre, I preferred to write about composers. At least for that reason it seemed to me to be a good beginning for this ongoing lecture-performance, which has become a demonstration on *gathering together what exists in a dispersed state*.

> Wie Sie sehen können, bin ich noch einmal am Anfang, mit einer kleinen Verschiebung allerdings, einer Transformation sozusagen, das explizite Thema dieses Performance-Vortrags betreffend.

As you can see, I'm back at the beginning again, though, with a little displacement, a transformation, so to speak, concerning the explicit subject of this lecture-performance.

Displacement, in its various meanings, is another important subject concerning the working processes of performative polyphony. But, while demonstrating, I have to postpone talking about it, because I owe you at least one more reason for having chosen those *Drei kurze Absätze für Andrzej* as a – displaced – beginning. It's not just because of its thematic impact, but also because those paragraphs are an obvious example of something that *exists in a dispersed state*. That brief text was definitely never meant to be a part of a performance or a lecture-performance or a speech that *I* would do. Using disseminated material, practising displacements and replacements has got a lot to do with *gathering together what exists in a dispersed state. As soon as we give it a try, we realise that already everything goes together.* That is, right from the beginning, from one displacement to the next.

A long time before I began to write down this lecture-performance it seemed very obvious to me to begin by quoting another lecture-performance – at least to give a short introduction into my work. For several reasons – and I already mentioned a few – I had to postpone that former beginning, instead I'm starting to introduce it right now.

Last year I went to South Africa for a six-month residency. In Cape Town I was invited to present my work in an already imposed, formal structure called **20:20** at the Western Cape section of the *Visual Arts Network of South Africa*. **20:20** stands for a strictly defined limitation: twenty seconds for twenty images. I did exactly, as follows, except for one word:

> For this presentation I wrote down a brief text, built out of 20 sentences, out of exactly 20 words each.
>
> Maybe it's impossible to count and to listen to them simultaneously, but you need not, I promise, I did count.
>
> First of all I have to apologise for reading, and for my deficient English too (this was sentence number three).
>
> There is an order of the sentences and of the images as well, but there is no calculated relation in between.
>
> I decided to present 20 images, each ten seconds, twice, while I was reading and presenting 20 sound-pieces, just once.
>
> And I decided not to give any further information on the images and sounds, because there weren't enough words left.

> In 1994 I founded the collective LOSE COMBO that does live-art-projects that combine the genres of performance, concert and installation.
>
> Working simultaneously with video, sound, texts and site-specific installations, the projects are often based on selected historical or literary material.
>
> Informed by John Cage's concept of chance music dealing with flexible time-brackets, the material is developed into complex polyphonic compositions.
>
> Organised in a kind of performance-score, each image, live and recorded sound or light-movement becomes a 'voice' of the composition.
>
> With regards to a specific experience of a decelerated passing of time each material gets its own space of time.

In 2004 I began a project-series called *Ghost Stories of Media* that conjures abstruse aspects of selected media or medial phenomena.

Part one, *LOSE COMBO's BLOOMSDAY,* is related to James Joyce's novel *Ulysses*, and focuses on questions of telegraphy and biometrics.

Part two, *HERTZ' FREQUENZEN,* is dedicated to the accidental discovery of electromagnetic radio waves in the late 19th century.

Part three, *FARADAY'S CAGE,* deals with the phenomenon of magnetism, which is the starting point of history of media itself.

Part four, *BRAUN light,* focuses on the hardly mentioned disappearance of the picture tube and the loss of its light.

Last year I started a new project-series called *time-labyrinths* that investigates the complex non-linear structure of the perception of time.

The first part, *HYDRA'S TRACES,* is a concert and performance-installation in two parts that lasts three hours during dusk.
   Its first half includes a brief comment on the performance-structure and a concert of Morton Feldman's extended trio-piece *Crippled Symmetry*.
   Its second half deals with different aspects of *Hydra* – not just the mythological monster, but also astronomical and biological aspects.

That was 6 minutes and 40 seconds – a precisely framed space of time. To speak in musical terms: a fixed time-bracket within lots of (more or less) fixed time-brackets, sentences as well as images, which can even be described as *sequential measures* or *visual bars*. The images as well as the layered sounds, as technically organised material, are to be fixed at a given time, but the placement of the sentences remains flexible, in this case until its performance.
   I'm not sure whether this example is suitable to give any impression of what *a decelerated passing of time* may be. Maybe it is too short to mark the difference between that kind of experience and a simple boredom, which emerges from the everyday passing of time.
   In other words, evoking a shift/change resulting in a decelerated experience of time sometimes needs some more time.
   But furthermore, and first of all, that specific experience is the result of a compositional practice, which has got to do a lot with a certain usage of time-brackets – flexible as well as fixed time-brackets, which are to be handled in as flexible a manner as the working process will ever allow.
   In the course of this final practice the different performance-materials, which were developed in broadly separate work steps (texts and video-sequences as well as multi-channel sound-installations or instrumental compositions), have to be layered by taking care of particular time-brackets, durations and extensions, but not with regards to any external references, except a – usually ascertained – space of time, which becomes the decelerated one.

So as not to demonstrate the first after the second work step, I will postpone explaining more about this compositional practice concerning the organisation of different performance-materials, but – as already announced – go on giving an example for a transformation process of a single performance-material.

The result of this transformation process is a piece for piano, flute and percussion I did for the performance *BRAUN light*. It is called *rgb*. As I mentioned before, the thematic starting point of this performance was the rarely mentioned disappearance of the picture tube and the loss of its specific light – its light beyond the function of generating images – that is images that normally make one forget the quality of the picture tube light, instantly. In a sense the performance is about what Heiner Müller calls: "Das Verlöschen der Welt in den Bildern – The dissolution of the world into images" (Müller 1971: 14).

At the end of the nineteenth century, the German physician Ferdinand Braun succeeds in the groundbreaking development of the so-called cathode ray tube, which enables the magnetic control of light-points, out of which images are to be generated.

Figure 1: *New York Times* article on the first electronic television.

In the early thirties of the twentieth century, Baron Manfred von Ardenne, a German natural scientist and engineer, presents the first electronic television ever at the *Berlin Radio Exposition* – a sensation, worldwide.

Figure 2: Ardenne's cathode radio television.

Its screen is a square, about 5 by 5cm, which is equal to 10.000 pixels. During that early moment the Ardenneian, so-called cathode radio television allowed for the transmission of movie-pictures only.

Figure 3: First video-still shot by Ardenne.

This is supposed to be the first video-still in the history of electronic television – a photo shot taken by Ardenne himself during his first transmission experiments. To be more precise it is the adapted scan of a reproduction of that photograph. This is apparent not only because the shape of the reproduction isn't a square anymore, but because the process of transformations must have begun even before I found it in a book. (By the way, I didn't find out anything about the name of the movie, nor about the actresses' names.)

This first video-still ever is the graphical basis for the *rgb*-piece for the *BRAUN light* performance. Skipping a few work steps, I took the scanned video-still – a coloured scan of a brown-coloured reproduction of a black and white photograph of Ardenne's black and white TV transmission – then I took the image, with its millions of colours, and reduced its huge amount of pixels to just 10.000 by using the rgb-colour-mode for digital image editing, which – as you all know – is, at the same time, (the name of) a common colour-TV-mode.

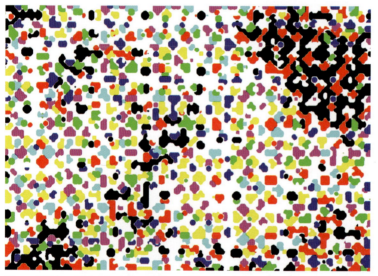

Figure 4: Video-still in adapted resolution and in *rgb*-colour-mode.

In other words, I adapted the resolution of the first electronic TV transmission to the supposedly first video-still, which is a document of this transmission. What you can see here is the result of that transformation step: about 10.000 computer-rgb-pixels – red, green, blue, its mixed colours yellow, magenta, cyan as well as black and white. For some reasons (I'd like to skip) it is indeed less than 10.000 pixels, but anyway it is a similar resolution to the one Ardenne's screen worked with. Maybe you can still identify the image?

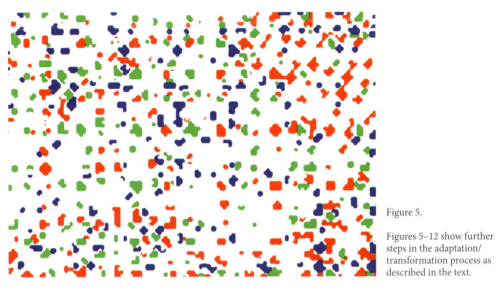

Figure 5.

Figures 5–12 show further steps in the adaptation/ transformation process as described in the text.

In a next work step I simply isolated the three basic colours of the pixel-image: red, green and blue – three colours for three musicians, which at the same time are the three image-generating colours of a colour TV picture tube.

Figure 6.

In the following work steps I isolated each colour and assigned it to one of the instruments: red for the piano

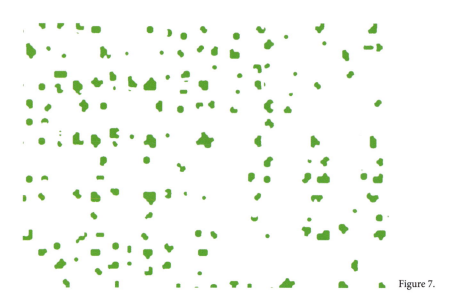

Figure 7.

green for the percussion

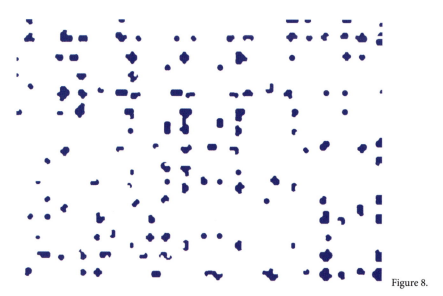

Figure 8.

and blue for the flutes. These are the blue pixels of the transformed video-still. For a moment I will just go on with the part of the flute. But it's the same transformation procedure according to the piano and the percussion part.

Figure 9.

These are the flute-pixels again. I simply changed their blue colour into grey, while the shapes of the pixels stay the same. In its approximate centres I placed the scaled-down identical pixels in their original colour. Or the other way around: I scaled-up the empty spaces in between the blue pixels.

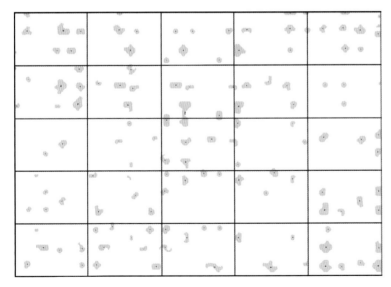

Figure 10.

In a next work step I divided the coloured-within-grey-pixels-images into 5 by 5, which is equal to 25 segments of the same size each. Each segment retains the proportions of the basic pixel image as well as the video-still. Every single segment becomes the graphical basis for one sheet of an instrumental part – in this case, of the flute. The 25 sheets are numbered sequentially, as follows: first row: one to five, second row: six to ten, third row: eleven to fifteen, and so on.

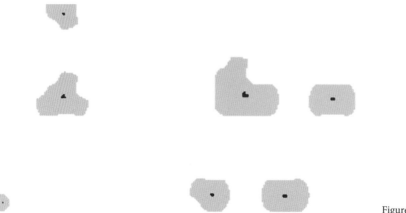

Figure 11.

This is the left segment of the top row. The distances between the grey pixels keep the proportions of the former basic colour pixels, as well as the proportion between the scaled-down blue pixels and the grey pixels – where they are centred remains the same all the time.

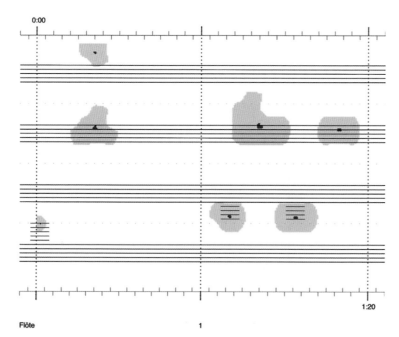

Figure 12.

This is the first sheet of the flute part, using the left segment of the top row.

Every single sheet has got 4 staves. In the case of the flute-part four staves at once contain the whole range of all flutes – piccolo to bass flute. (In the case of the piano-part four staves at once contain the whole range of the piano; in the case of the percussion-part two staves at once contain the whole range of the glockenspiel. It is a glockenspiel for the simple reason that the percussion part is orientated by the range of the percussion-instrument, which is used in Morton Feldman's composition *Why Patterns?* – the piece that we played in the second part of the *BRAUN light* performance. However, the percussion player is free to use different percussion instruments, and not only the glockenspiel. The piano player is also free to play inside-piano, and not only to use the keyboard; similarly the flute player is free to create sounds by using any articulation-techniques that the several flutes may provide.)

There is an exact graphical relation between the sizes of the staves and the ranges of the instruments, that is to say the spaces between the lines in a stave as well as between the ledger lines vary from one instrument to another. In other words, the vertical dimensions of the graphical segments are exactly covered by the ranges of the instruments.

Every single segment lasts 80 seconds. From this, follows the whole sequence of 25 segments, which are to be played conjoined one after another, lasting exactly 33 minutes and 20 seconds. That is a precisely framed space of time, a fixed time-bracket within 25 fixed time-brackets, which can even be described as visual bars or a kind of *raw time-pixels*. Within those 25 fixed time-brackets there is a big amount of flexibility because of the temporal arrangement of each instrumental part.

Each coloured pixel marks the pitch of a single sound event. Within a time-bracket of 80 seconds every grey pixel marks a time-bracket wherein such a single sound event may take place. That means at first that the duration, as well as the exact moment of every single sound event, remains basically flexible within a marked space of time.

At the same time there are several possibilities as to how to interpret the four staves, which result in an 80-second time-bracket:

Each musician is free to decide whether he would like to play:

- one stave after another, which means every stave lasts 20 seconds; or
- two staves at the same time twice, which means 40 seconds two times; or
- four staves at the same time, which means 80 seconds at once; or its mixed versions
- two single staves after another and two staves at once (20 + 20 + 40 seconds); or the other way around
- two staves at once and two single staves one after another (40 + 20 + 20 seconds); or
- one single stave at first, two staves at once and another single stave at the end (20 + 40 + 20 seconds).

These six different possibilities imply 216 possible combinations of the three instrumental parts for just one 80-second time-bracket. That gives 5,400 possible combinations for the 25 segments of the whole *rgb*-piece.

Depending on the musician's basic decision as to how a single segment is to be played, the durations of the grey-pixel-time-brackets vary. In other words, they become flexible, but they nevertheless keep a precise marking of the maximum duration of a single sound event.

Reading the top stave of the first sheet of the flute-part as a single one that is to be played within 20 seconds means that the sound event marked above the top stave would take place approximately in between second 2.5 and second 4.5. That implies a maximum duration of about 2 seconds. In this way of reading, this sound event would definitely be the first sound of the flute.

Reading both upper staves simultaneously, which is to be played within 40 seconds, the same sound event would take place approximately in between second 5 and second 9; it could be the first sound of the flute to be heard, but it doesn't need to be because the first sound event marked in the second stave could even take place before.

Reading the four staves simultaneously within 80 seconds, the sound event marked above the top stave, which would now need to be realised in between second 10 and second 18, definitely wouldn't be the first sound of the flute anymore, because the first pixel assigned to the lowest stave in this case would take place in between second 0 and second 4, approximately.

There is a chronology of the segments, and there are kinds of junctions, which require decisions every 80 seconds (by the way, there are even a few possibilities to re-decide within an 80-second time-bracket), while the chronology of the sound events marked by the pixels may change, or become indeterminate, as well as the moments of its realisations and its durations.

Because the pitches are only fixed relating to four staves simultaneously (in the case of the flute and the piano), respectively relating to two staves simultaneously (in the case of the glockenspiel), a lot of decisions concerning the temporal arrangement necessarily also entail decisions concerning the pitches. Apart from the fact that the coloured pixels may also mark non-tempered pitches this is the main reason to abandon any clefs.

But because I want to continue talking a little about the layering of separately developed performance-materials, and its particular time-brackets, I won't go on talking about pitches, clusters, noises, timbres etc. anymore. I will also omit further tricky – and occasionally paradoxical – details that have to be considered concerning the arrangements of the time-brackets.

The *rgb*-piece is one separately developed sonic performance-material, which becomes one layer of the *BRAUN light* performance. With regards to its 33:20 time-bracket it is a completely autonomous performance-'voice' in the sense of performative polyphony. As well as the trio, which is one layer of the performance, its parts are layers of the piece as well as of the whole performance. That is, the three parts of the *rgb*-piece are to be realised independently from one another. This means that each part should just be played in relation to its particular time-brackets, but not with regards to the pixels of the other parts or its common (transformed) starting point. Besides an arrangement concerning the basic characteristic style of the trio as well as of the whole performance, which is almost given by its time-passing calmness, there are no further directions. That is to say that for the musicians being aware of the piece, as well as of the performance, means not listening to, or caring about what the others are doing. To them it is just important that there are pixel-precise time-bracket-structures, which, at the same time, leave room for a huge range of flexibility. These structures require a high degree of precision because of their principally unlimited possibilities of realisation. While the decision as to when the *rgb*-piece is to be played in the course of the performance is fixed at a given time; in the case of the musicians, their decisions remain open until their actual realisation.

Besides Heiner Müller's text *Bildbeschreibung* (published as *Explosion of a Memory* in English), which we divided into two parts that are to be read by two performers, there is also a third sonic material: a six-channel-audiotape, which lasts 57 minutes. The duration of the tape (which I consider to be some kind of *devised silence* – but that would be another issue …) marks the fixed time-bracket of the first part of the *BRAUN light* performance. As well as the three sonic performance-materials – trio, text, audiotape – there are also layers of the performance: the tape itself is layered by hundreds of sounds, which mainly result from lots of electro-acoustic transformation processes of just two samples, both lasting a few minutes.

It was only by chance that I learnt about receiving funding for the *BRAUN light* project while I was in the middle of nowhere in Argentina, where I held a workshop on *Strategien des Nebeneinanders, Strategies of Juxtaposing* – what to me means a mode of layering and placement in terms of organisation of material. For that incidental reason, and with regards to the thematic starting point of the project, I brought two Argentinean everyday-life sound-samples with me, on which, coincidentally, TV sounds are to be heard in the background. *We must construct, that is, gather together what exists in a dispersed state*. Out of these recordings I generated hundreds of sounds for the *BRAUN light* audiotape. That is, I transformed a few sounds out of those two samples, and afterwards transformed lots of sounds out of the transformed sounds … and out of those … and so on … That transformation process resulted in a huge amount of sounds of derivates of derivates of sounds, which singularly last about 3–7 minutes. Thereby a single sound – or often a series of almost similar sounds –is usually not developed with any other sounds, which already came up, in mind, even less the resulting audiotape. I just care about the particular sound I'm actually working on, what it means, just listening, changing a little bit, listening again. Producing sounds for an audiotape and organising the tape out of the sounds – that is mainly placing, layering, editing and mixing – are totally separate work steps.

By the way, this is the same with the visual performance-material, especially the videotapes. But I won't talk about it anymore in the course of this prepared lecture-performance because too much time has passed in the meantime.

(I'm sorry that the tendency of this lecture-performance on *devising a lecture-performance on gathering together what exists in a dispersed state* has increasingly changed to a lecture on a specific performance. This is not because I'm reading all the time – musicians normally read too, and performers (at least in LOSE COMBO performances) read aloud as well. So I guess this change (or displacement) is mainly to do with the usually intended purpose of

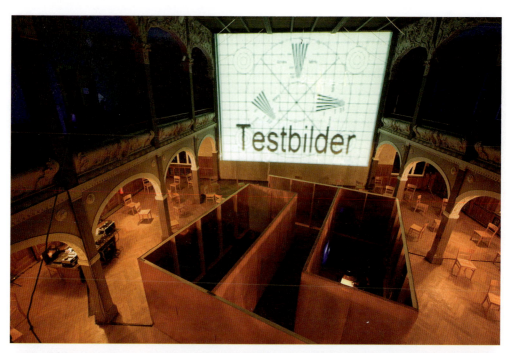

Figures 13, 14 and 15: LOSE COMBO feat. Trio Nexus: BRAUN *light*, *performance | concert | installation*; Villa Elisabeth, Berlin 2008 Copyright david baltzer/bildbuehne.de.

a lecture, which is to inform. Lectures are meant to aim at a comprehensible result, that is to say they never start without an aim, a target so to speak. In a way the starting point of a lecture even inverts to its opposite. Thus a lecture, layered or not, goes straight along a *time-line* describing a horizontal movement, with information and comprehension almost always in lockstep. While a performance, which is layered because of the time-brackets of its separately developed materials that were gathered together, becomes a *time-space*. Within that kind of time-space there is no need for any external aim. It is just taking place. In a sense its vertical dimension prevents one from aiming at anything else, and therefore enables a decelerated passing of time).

More or less at the beginning I mentioned that I don't see a difference between devising a lecture-performance and a performance, in principal. However, concerning its perceptions and experiences there might be outstanding differences.)

But I have to come back: while the development of each single performance-material normally needs a lot of time, usually a couple of weeks, the layering of the several materials, that is placing and moving and trimming, the whole assembling-process, takes place within a few days. And the result of this process is always just *one* out of a virtually infinite range of possibilities. The main thing is working out one supposable good possibility. It almost always feels like there isn't enough time. But at the same time *everything already goes together*. For that reason I usually prefer to come to an end abruptly, at an unforeseeable moment, that is surprising in the course of the working process, even to me. Although there are just a few days, and, one might think, too little (mostly technical) rehearsals, at the end of it all a performance is devised a lot faster than I could have ever imagined.

And that is the same with a lecture-performance.

References

Adorno, Theodor W. (1973) *Ästhetische Theorie*, Frankfurt/Main: Suhrkamp.

Cage, John and Charles, Daniel (1981) *For The Birds*, Boston and London: Marion Boyars.

Derrida, Jacques (1990) *Was ist Dichtung?*, Berlin: Brinkmann & Bose.

Hans-Thies Lehmann, Karen Jürs-Munby and Elinor Fuchs (2008) 'Lost in Translation?' in *The Drama Review*, 52:4, pp. 13–20.

Müller, Heiner (1971) "Traktor" in H. Müller, *Geschichten aus der Produktion 2*, Berlin: Rotbuch.

Chapter 7

From Interdisciplinary Improvisation to Integrative Composition: Working Processes at the Theater der Klänge

Jörg U. Lensing

Material, improvisation, composition

Something that has bothered me since I was a student of musical composition about the cliché of the contemporary composer was the romantic notion of the lonely genius writing his score at his desk, taking this unalterable masterpiece into rehearsal with a standardised orchestra and mercilessly monitoring the performance according to the specific notational signs, that determine the rendering to the last detail. This pursuit of perfectionist art was and still is lifeless for me. It becomes evident when dealing with 'sight readers' but even more so, when working with performers, who are not musicians. The music business has developed an almost industrial culture of creation and reproduction, which largely separates the interpreter from the creator. If many rehearsals with many musicians are necessary, they are undertaken by a conductor who is usually not the composer. In opera, creation and reproduction become even further detached due to the existence of the musical director and the theatre director. The only thing left for the composer in these standard formats is writing the music. Naturally this leads to a desire to prescribe in precise detail, what one wants. This unfortunately prevents almost entirely any form of feedback. Where in the ongoing process, which is geared towards the imminent première, are the possibilities to change the piece, rewrite it, react to suggestions, query oneself?

For these reasons, I have created my own work environment at the beginning of my career in music-theatre; an environment in which one interacts with the interpreter and arrives at a form in this collaboration, at a *particell*, at a score. And even the score is by all means still subjected to change and becomes more precise during the process of performing. Unfortunately, musicians are rarely prepared to participate fully in such a collective and time-consuming process. The 'market' is so lucrative for them that they are rarely able or willing to focus exclusively on one project only over a period of three to four months. The main argument is here: "If I turn down too many jobs for this period of time, I am going to be off the radar in the future."

Actors and particularly dancers are familiar with forms of collective creation. In theatre and dance – and here in particular in independent ensembles – it is quite customary to sign up for a project for three to four months full-time, during which part of the time is dedicated to the development of the piece.

During my 22 years of working with my ensemble Theater der Klänge [Theatre of Sounds] in Düsseldorf, Germany, I have developed and perfected a model of creation in three phases. Once the topic, the questions of content, the possible formal solution and potential formal stimuli are present, we gather together an ensemble, which almost invariably consists of a mixture of musicians (composers), actors and dancers. The first day of rehearsal is a day of blue sky thinking, talking and envisioning. Envisioning also includes watching videos of our own work as well as that of others, where the present formal solutions seem useful or applicable to the chosen topic. Other than that, the space, the stage and my notebook are empty. Or, to put it differently: the canvas is blank, ready to be painted on!

On the second day, the performers already become co-creators by reacting to the given stimulus by offering specific theatrical and musical ideas. For this, they have anything they need at their disposal in our rehearsal space, which has been optimised for these processes. The standard is a quadraphonic sound system, a video projector, a programmable lighting system with 24 lamps, a music instrument storage, a storage for cloth, a costume department, a shelf of masks. We ask them to develop miniature scenes, to sketch them out with their colleagues and to improvise towards as finished a stage-aesthetics as possible. The mornings are for training, agreements, selection of décor, sound and costume and a short rehearsal. After a communal lunch break, the scenes are performed as if it was an actual performance! For this we separate the studio into a stage and an auditorium by means of lighting. All the performers who are not involved in this scene, the composer, choreographer and director are the audience. The agreed interpreters are the actual performers. Sometimes we call the scene off after one minute, if it does not transmit any theatrical idea – and in this case we immediately discuss the intention and possibly a spontaneous change of idea for the presentation. Some scenes run for 45 minutes, fuelled by supportive shouts from the 'audience', when the improvisation between the performers and the audience as participator works.

In this way over four to five days of rehearsal per week and up to eight theatrical sketches per day we quickly generate comprehensive rehearsal transcripts. I rarely ask someone else to do the actual documenting, so that I can notate an abbreviated and concise form for the respective scene, while transcribing the seen and heard.

From the process itself, during which there is a lot of discussion between the scenes about what we have seen and heard, an aesthetic approach to the given topic and the desired form emerges bit by bit, which the collective begins to accept, is engaged in and inspired by. Even quite original ideas, however, which did not really resonate, may disappear in the archive of the rehearsal transcripts. Inspiring approaches, which trigger a chain of new scenic ideas, are the source of the actual form-finding and aesthetics, which subsequently defines the specific work. The recognisable 'signature' consists in the repeatedly wanted, the selection, the demand for particular aesthetic 'forms' as well as the dismissal of the unwanted, that which is ugly in my ears and eyes, which hangs over the individual topics and forms, as it were.

A lot of it has to do with a shared performance and reception space, with a sense of humour, with comprehensibility and plausibility and with figurative embodiment with an aim to make believe. With regard to the more abstract pieces it is to do with the plausibility and logical consequence of what the formal language evokes.

In any case, this first phase, which may well cover half of the rehearsal period, concludes with arriving at a 'book of material', which has often contained up to 200 scenic-musical ideas on the topic. One-tenth of these reach the selection for the composition of the piece, often extended and enriched by five to ten scenes, which have been developed as hybrids from various scenic ideas. This shortlist of twenty to thirty formal parts, already organised into a sequence, becomes the 'rehearsal *particell*' for the second phase of rehearsals, which usually lasts only two to three weeks. This is used to scrutinise the material again. Some of it we may not have gone through for weeks.

Three questions are important in this second phase:

1. Does the component or scene work when it is repeated, possibly with a different cast?
2. How can this component/scene be compacted, so that it becomes essential and omits anything superfluous (the 'parasites')?
3. Who of the available performers is the most credible embodiment for each part?

Here too, a narrative form-finding differs significantly from a more abstract process. In a more abstract work, people can be brought into play at any point in time so that each performance is optimally cast. In a linear narrative work, bit by bit the ideal cast must be found, which can carry a canon of characters throughout the whole piece consistently, even if particular scenes had been improvised more convincingly by other performers. This process itself is quite unusual even in theatre and dance companies, so that with regard to the more substantial textual or vocal parts there can be some resentment amongst the performers, that they have not been clearly cast even at this advanced stage, and that consequently they have been unable to memorise their texts or scores. For this reason, we continue to improvise with text and with the musical running order at this stage. It is more limited, since it is already clear what and how something should be said, but still open enough that person A may improvise the lead on a Tuesday while person B rehearses the same part and scene on Wednesday. In general, it becomes particularly transparent in this alternating process, who plays what in the most credible and vibrant way, and how parts work in their polished versions.

The third and last phase of rehearsals is the 'repetition'. The parts have been allocated, the text is fixed, the notation is made and the cues and medial transitions are agreed. Now it is about perfecting and internalising. Only at this stage can the costumes be tailored and the masks designed, but also the creation of costumes as well as the finding of the masks are now developed – based on the range of ideas from the first phase – into a coherent concept for the characters and their embodiment or the planned abstract formal trajectory. Now, it is not as if suddenly everything from the second phase is instantly available in the third phase. Rather, the third phase is used to render everything clearer, more contoured, more precise what had just been approximate, sketched or suggested. I like to compare this process with the development of photos in the fixer. Gradually, the picture is getting clearer and clearer.

Unfortunately, it is also only in this third phase that the music is added professionally. While in the early stages, it was mainly the composer, or ideally the musician-composer, who

Theater der Klänge: HOEReographien

5 Sonate (Trio)

Jenny, Hana, Caitlin

Exposition	Aufgang mit Engführung Thema A	Asynchron Thema B	Motivisch synchron	asynchron
Hana		-- -- -- C (Jenny)	A	B
Jenny	A Feld hr, b Feld hl A´Feld vl, c Feld vr	A -- A´ C (Hana)	A B	A B
Caithlin		-- B A´ C (Hana)	B	A
Musik	1 Feld rhythmisierter Klang			

Durchführung	
Hana	Thematische Variationsarbeit zunächst auf Motivvertauschungsebene, dann zunehmend auf Gestaltenebene mit Reverses, Gestaltverbindungen Fremd, Gestaltverbindungen bekannt (fragmentarisch) und Impulsfolge. Kontaktmöglichkeiten auf Gestaltebene nutzen.
Jenny	
Caithlin	Reduktion auf eine Grundgestalt bei allen
Musik	1 Feld freie Klangsteuerung

Reprise	Synchron a b a' c	Motivisch synchron	Engführung	Synchron Thema B choreografiert von h.r. in einer 3er Linie auseinandergehend
Hana	PdD PdD Aa' 1 2 >	PdD PdD B	Thema A	Thema B
Jenny	Aa PdD PdD 2 3	PdD PdD B	Thema A	Thema B
Caithlin	PdD Ab PdD 1 3	A PdD	Thema A	Thema B
Musik	1 Feld rhythmisierter Klang			

Thema A = Jennys Thema (bestehend aus 12 vektorisierten Bewegungen)
Thema B = Hanas Thema (bestehend aus 12 vektorisierten Bewegungen)

PdD = Pas de deux
hr = hinten rechts
hl = hinten links
vl = vorne links
vr = vorne rechts

11 Sonate (Trio)

Figure 1: Extract from the prompt book of *HOEReographien* (2005).

was involved in the creation, it is not until the third phase that the interpreting musicians join in. This usually happens, as mentioned above, in the conventional form. Sheet music – sight-reading – perfection through rehearsal. Only in the last week of rehearsals we have complete runs, complemented by a lighting design. In the last three days before the première these runs are normally in the evenings to get into the rhythm of the performances.

The première is usually also the day on which the prompt book is finished, which looks more like a score for scenic composition, than a traditional director's script (see figure 1[1]). At this stage it is quite sensible to work with an assistant for the script, whose job it is to bring the score/the prompt book into a definitive and comprehensible form. This is quite similar to the process of creating the fair copy.

'Integrative' theatre: How we integrate the various elements and put them in (compositional?) relation to each other

The more abstract pieces described above have by and large been what I call 'integrative' compositions within the wider range of productions of the Theater der Klänge. The basic idea behind this concept is the conditional nature of the artistic means and their mutual interaction. None of the used means 'serves' another, but instead they are autonomous, equal and work together. It follows: the result is more than just adding up the individual media.

An example from the current work on the *Suite Intermediale* (see figures 2 and 3) may illustrate this. In the scenographic setup for this work, the implementation of sensors and transformation of data generated by the sensors into control data for lighting and sound plays an important role. The space – and during the process of creation this means our rehearsal studio – functions as an electronic instrument, which only waits to be played and played on!

This also means that the sound which will be heard is no longer fixed beforehand and that the figural lighting design, seen in the form of video projections is dependent on what the sensors (in this case, cameras and microphones) capture, and how what they capture has an impact on the design of the sound and the video projections. In other words, the performer walks into a quiet, 'empty' space, which is barely lit, just enough for audience and cameras to identify him and the colours he wears. It is only the sounds he creates (the sounds of the floor through his steps, breathing noises) and his visual presence that provide sound and images for the computer, which now develops this input through algorithmic forms into structures evolving in time. These temporally evolving musical and visual structures in space are significantly modulated by the specific action/movement dynamics of the performer(s). Here, of course, they are selected, approved and channelled/interpreted by the audio composer and video composer, who are inevitably on stage in this live process and thus become part of the performance.

---

1. All images and plans provided by and printed with permission of the Theater der Klänge.

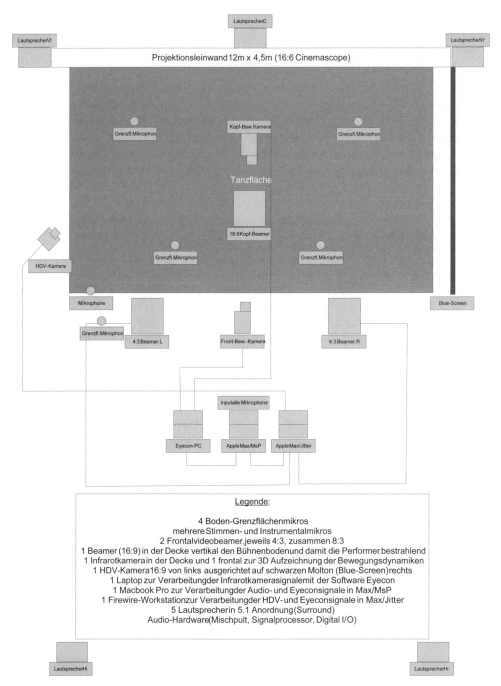

Figure 2: Technical setup for *Suite Intermediale* (2010).

Figure 3: Still from *Suite Intermediale* (2010).

Conversely, this approach also means a much greater responsibility and development of competency for the performers. It is not enough to repeat a predetermined pattern of movement or a fixed (musical) text. Rather, a level of competency with formal structures, possible improvisation techniques, scope for action and reaction and a sense of dramatic timing need to be developed through training. The live performance is rendered into a tightrope walk between agreed form and spontaneous improvisation. Certain effects are calculable. In particular, the possibilities for variation in each performance continue to surprise especially those involved in the performance, since an audience usually comes only once and therefore always perceives the performance as a fixed end result.

What remains and how can it be handed down?

It is precisely the form of integrative compositions I have described above which shifts the script/text/score into the computers. Algorithms replace the traditional score. For the performers, there are formal processes that are the condensed result of many improvisations and the assembly of individual results into dramaturgical sequences. The video recording of individual performances fixes momentous variations of these formal sequences together

Figure 4: Trio from *Figur und Klang im Raum* (1993).

with the algorithms linked to respective points in time in the computers involved. Since these also partly influence the immediate lighting, that is, the control of the installed lights and moving lights, only the stage setup as an instrument can be fixed (see, for example, the plans for *Hoereographien* and *Suite Intermediale,* figures 2 and 5) as well as the programming in the computers and the software used, but: the computers, software and hardware are evolving. This means that for example the first of these integrative compositions for the Theater der Klänge from the 1993 *Figur und Klang im Raum* (*Figure and Sound in Space*, see figures 4 and 6) is no longer performable in its original form today! A reconstruction by means of modern technology on the basis of the existing scores and video recordings is conceivable. But is that what we want? Is such a reconstruction not 'historicizingly' anachronistic? Just like the notion of the work in electronic music and 'musique concrète' ultimately implied, which medium would capture and reproduce this form of music, namely the tape, so will this form of intermedial, algorithmic composition, also ultimately only survive in derivatives, here the video recording. The method, the approach and the found solutions can be developed as models and be varied and progressed in new collectives.

Outlook

Similar to the evolution of jazz as a partly notated, but mostly improvised music, of which the 'best results' were recorded and published on records, the above-described form of composition will not remain in the consciousness of the audience by means of a 'live'-tradition, but through recordings. In how far these can really give an idea of what the spatial event in the performance by live performers was, is questionable, but may serve the next generation of artists, who want to take up such approaches to intermedial composition as a model for their own creations based on the then existing technical possibilities.

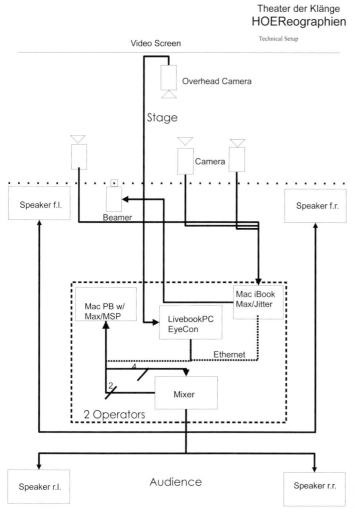

Figure 5: Technical setup for *HOEReographien* (2005).

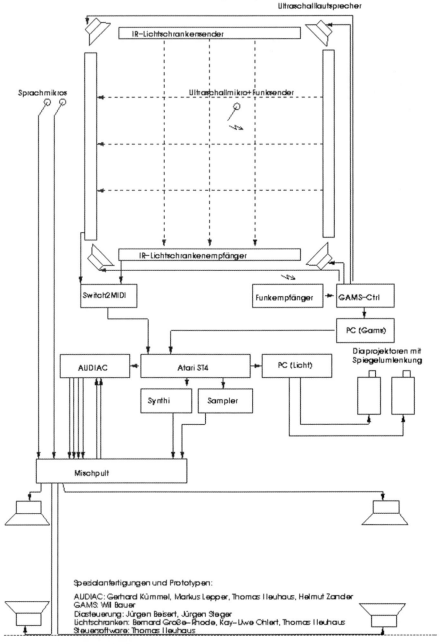

Figure 6: Technical Setup for *Figur und Klang im Raum* (1993).

If there was a meta-notation, which would manage to fix the various aspects of lighting, sound, action and musical notation regardless of specific programming languages for certain technical systems, handing down in the sense of how this was possible for musical scores in the past in relation to a defined orchestra would be conceivable.

It is however my observation, that the ambition of most composers who work towards these systems, shifts to the effect that they no longer just make fair copies of scores, but become a performative element themselves of the activity with a working ensemble at a given time. The possibilities of the theoretical construction of music, which were provided by notation, which was developed particularly by the generation of composers in Germany after the Second World War into advanced graphical notation for concepts of musical theatre, has been extended since the mid-nineties by electronic, interactively acting and reacting systems. This implies possibilities of composition, which were previously unthinkable, and combines approaches to improvisation for performers and musicians, like those also developed and tested by the post-war generation, then still in interaction with manually operated machines.

Moreover, I believe that such medially 'composed' actions will not be advanced only by composers. In this field choreographers, directors, visual artists, programmers, video artists and music composers meet in varying combinations, which is why there are fluid boundaries between dance, the theatre of images, intermedia performances and new music theatre.

After hundreds of years of the separation between artistic disciplines and fields in the conventional theatre this is to be welcomed, and gives us reason to anticipate exciting developments and results!

(Translation: David Roesner)

Chapter 8

'Let's stop talking about it and just do it!': Improvisation as the Beginning of the Compositional Process

George Rodosthenous

A piece of melancholic string music – perhaps a solo cello
Salome's monologue
One back-light
A silver tray
Go!

'If you had looked at me, you would have loved me...'

The beginning as loss of innocence – 'dive in'!

I mprovisation is synonymous, I find, with the loss of innocence. When starting a new piece of work, when a piece of text is spoken, a movement is created, a body changes position – there is no return: only forward-facing flow to the next event. The canvas has been splashed and now the only way forward is to continue creating shapes, mixing the colours and adding more layers. In this report, I would like to share some questions, issues and strategies that I have encountered during my piano improvisations, directorial journeys and the research project *From Improvisation to Composition* (2009). The project was funded by the School of Performance and Cultural Industries (University of Leeds), Echo Arts, Dance-Gate Dancehouse Lefkosia and the Ministry of Education and Culture (Cyprus). It took place between the 26–31 March 2009 in Nicosia (Cyprus) and a public sharing of the work was presented in Howard Assembly Room (Leeds) on 10 June 2009.

A blank canvas, an empty manuscript, a bare stage can all be rather frightening points of departure. How can we approach a new piece of theatrical composition when there is nothing in existence? When working with an ensemble of performers, how do we ensure that there is a common understanding of the desired artistic vision? How much (and what kind of) training do we need to achieve this?

Kent de Spain states that "improvisation is a form of research, a way of peering into the complex natural system that is a human being. It is, in a sense, another way of 'thinking', but one that produces ideas impossible to conceive in stillness" (De Spain 2003: 27). Very often, while devising work, we get carried away discussing in depth, and in real detail, the mechanics of a scene. However, there are other ways to get started. By using a prop,

Figure 1: *From Improvisation to Composition*, Howard Assembly Room, 10 June 2009. Leo Town (left) Tom Colley (right). Photograph by Georges Bacoust.

a gesture, a musical idea, improvisation can really function as a non-threatening starting point. Diving-in the initial material, using and developing an initial stimulus can help create a sense of liberating freedom for the performer/ensemble which can unlock new 'readings' of a particular idea. This freedom – this creative dialogue – is crucial in allowing for an inter-disciplinary awareness to be developed between the bodies in the rehearsal room – in real-time. Thus, we can examine whether an idea works, whether the timing of a (sub-) section is the right length or whether the overall structure makes sense for an audience. In newly formed ensembles, this exchange can actually negotiate the boundaries and the range of the ensemble's expressive means. 'Evaluating while doing' should be part of the arrangement here: to be able to feel in- and out-of-control of self-developing material. To absorb, analyse and make use of a series of accidents, 'non-relevant' contributions, surprises, pre-mature codas or even ego-management processes. All these can develop a single gesture (or a sequence) which can be the initial turning point leading to the larger structure of the piece.

Chris Johnston also believes that the act of improvisation is actually research. He asserts that "[w]hile more cerebral exercises such as writing or composing allow for greater control over decisions, improvisation can deliver the shock material. With its spontaneous, unpredictable processes, improvisation can deliver the right-brain gifts that sneak in under the radar. It's arguable that improvisation is in fact inseparable from the creative process" (Johnston 2006: 5). Working with performers who have a more developed sense of 'improvising' can be very beneficial in providing a faster pace of rehearsing. Especially, when rehearsal time is very constrained, improvisation skills can help create an environment where the actual focus of 'listening and responding' and 'being present in the moment' can produce new 'shocks', 'accidents' which can shape the work in unexpected ways. In a way, that endless source of energy can help overcome creative block(s) at the difficult initial stages of the rehearsal process. It can also ensure that everybody is working together and sharing the same understanding of what it means to be actively present in the space. In my experience, it is useful to refer to Viola Spolin's 'Seven aspects of spontaneity' (Spolin 1999: 4) and Anne Bogart's 'Viewpoints' – Tempo, Duration, Kinesthetic Response, Repetition, Spatial Relationship, Topography, Shape, Gesture and Architecture (Bogart and Landau: 36–54) – for exercises that aim to create a common working language for the ensemble.

Experience, energy, control

The extensive use of improvisation as part of 'the beginning' and its 'emotional mapping' can become a defining strategy, which feeds into the creative process of theatrical composition. This usually involves asking the performers to create a map of their journey. 'Emotional mapping' borrows techniques from the hot-seating exercise, but it also involves responding to the questions using more parameters. These might be pieces of costume, props, colours, texts, sounds and music that assist the performer shape their character. In addition, this technique can be related to the creation of movement material following Michael Chekhov's 'psychological gesture' techniques (Chekhov 1991: 58).

When the performers are comfortable with this first step of creating the character, then we can ask them to construct a map of their journey in the piece, in colour. At this point, the director can align their vision with the performers and also ensure that there is enough range to create an exciting juxtaposition of simultaneous events. In this respect, 'emotional mapping' can help us understand better the actual process of improvisation as composition: building a larger structure using smaller cells (stimuli) and motifs. In a collaborative environment such as the theatre, this knowledge can be transferred from one discipline to another. Some of the ideas from the rehearsal room can be shared with the composer, designer, lighting designer, choreographer at rehearsal and can be used to shape the overall *mise en scène*. And when I improvise, I feel it is very valuable to be aware of the larger overall structure: to know exactly where the work starts and, if possible, where it will end. Still, new working methods, links and approaches to the non-homogenous and/or multi-disciplinary backgrounds of each or newly formed ensemble must be established anew with every new composition.

Working with performers who are more experienced in using improvisation as part of the creative process has a different quality of energy. The desire to show-off, to impress or to 'steal' the scene is no longer a predominant threat in rehearsal. Rather, their contribution becomes all-encompassing and serves the basic principles of improvisation – to develop an open platform where the work will be created live. In such environments, there is sometimes

Figure 2: *From Improvisation to Composition*, Howard Assembly Room, 10 June 2009. Ashley Scott-Layton, Tom Colley, Leo Town, Riccardo Meneghini (from left to right). Photo by Alkistis Olympiou.

the issue of who is having the control of the process. The immersion in the activity of creating material could become a trance-like moment, where there is the danger of the performers losing their perspective. And it is at this point of diving-in that the following questions can assist us to structure the improvisation:

- What is the context for this activity?
- What dictates the next flow of events?
- Do we re-act, initiate, respond or become a non-contributor?
- Does 'being aware of the others' mean being 'less aware' of ourselves?

A director improvises live – conducting the body

Eugenio Barba calls himself an improvising director. He has worked extensively with improvisation in his Odin Teatret and his concept of 'directorial improvisation' is a fascinating way of working with performers. If we take music improvisation, for example, the actual improvisation is either a solo activity or a dialogue shared by the ensemble. But, we might encounter some difficulties while applying this concept to theatre. A director cannot improvise himself. So, we need to envisage that a director can only improvise live by using his actors as his 'instruments'. This offers new possibilities, structures and discoveries. In his extremely articulate book, *On Directing Dramaturgy: Burning Down the House* (2010), Barba writes about improvisation and describes his processes explicitly:

> I proposed variations, accelerations and decelerations, modified the directions in space, moulded the volume of the actions (reducing or widening them), reversed the order within a sequence and eliminated fragments of it: the beginning could become the end and a central passage the beginning. I did not worry about meaning. I wanted to arrange a dance of sensory stimuli which had an impact on my nervous system, I called this process *the score's elaboration* or *distillation*.
>
> (Barba 2010: 54)

A crucial development in the journey from improvisation to composition can be the manipulation, refining and honing of the actions of the actor resulting in the fine-tuning of their physicality. During this stage of the compositional/devising process, these methods can be associated with the term I have coined as 'conducting the body'. It is borrowed from traditional music practice and adapted to describe the process of shaping the improvisation in theatre. When our material involves dealing with live human bodies in space, then a 'conductor' is required to direct and guide those bodies. The conductor/director could, if required, 'conduct the bodies' and improvise 'live' ensuring that the structure of the improvisation is being refined, in real-time, by an outside-eye. As a result, the conductor can become an integral part of the improvisational process and this can be another way to establish tempi, structures and dynamics within the performance and its final outcome.

In my practice, after setting some boundaries and limitations, I allow the performer to propose material freely. If the performer has misunderstood some of the parameters of the improvisation, I stop him/her, explain the exercise again and let him/her start afresh. If the material is going completely against what I had in mind, or is not 'within' my vision, I still let it run. Within the diversity that the performer (knowingly or unknowingly) brings to the rehearsal room, there can be seeds of material that can be juxtaposed to my 'vision'. So, those moments can clarify certain issues for the director: what the material 'could have been' or 'should never be'.

> [T]he extreme freedom of improvisation,
> where everything is acceptable,
> the rules are there to be broken and to be re-invented on the way.
> A mistake can be changed to an intentional feature of the work,
> repeated, developed, discarded or abandoned.
>
> (Rodosthenous in Warner S. (ed) *Howl for Now*, Route 2005: 59)

Graph(s), colour(s) and structure(s)

In an improvisation, we have the opportunity of allowing the structure to be determined in unpredictable and unorthodox ways. One of the ways to incorporate improvisation in the compositional process is by setting some 'flexible structures', where the performer/improviser can see the overarching intended shape of the performance and work around these structures. These 'flexible structures' will then form specific points of reference (or synchronisation) and the ensemble would have to fill in the gaps from A to B and so forth (as in *aleatoric* music).

A graph, or a kind of notational device can assist them find the overall shape and use their creativity to inhabit the gaps with the improvised material. One of the exercises I use with my performers involves giving them a structure created by 'transitive verbs' (Caldarone and Lloyd-Williams 2004: xvi) and then they have to negotiate/fill-in the activity in-between the suggested actions. Caldarone believes that "[a]ctioning heightens the actor's spontaneity" (Caldarone and Lloyd-Williams 2004: xiii) and that it "facilitates efficient communication" through the following cycle of events: Stimulation, Spontaneity, Specificity, Self-confidence, Synchronisation (Caldarone and Lloyd-Williams 2004: xiv). Even if less experienced performers might not be able to 'action' exactly the verb that is requested from them, there can still be a difference in their performance by simply being aware that their intentions need to be clear at all times. In order to demonstrate how a 'composed score' can be used as a basis for a sequence, I would like to use the following solo score designed for a short exercise:

Attack
Confront
Provoke
Pause (for 5 seconds)
Ridicule
Entice
Sing a lullaby (for 20 seconds)
Seduce

This exercise might (or might not) involve verbal material, but it can serve as the beginning of a more complex movement sequence. With the addition of music and music's power to carry extra-musical meaning(s), a simple improvisation might become a significant moment in a character's emotional journey, or even a structural device to develop the narrative or flow of events. In my production of *Hippolytus* (2008), this exercise has been used extensively to create 'The Rejection Scene' (see Figure 3), where Hippolytus blocks the sexual advances of his stepmother Phaedra.

Using the score can open up different interpretations of the same 'actions' and it is rare that two performances of the same score are ever the same. To ensure that the whole group is aware of the proposed/desired overall structure, then a different form of graphic notation can be used to provide a map for the improvisation. This graph follows from the 'emotional mapping' I proposed earlier and can include colour(s) to provide an overall sense of changes in intensity, quality and dynamic which are crucial in establishing variation within that set structure.

Barba often insists that his actors perfect the technique of repeating an improvisation. He concludes that

[p]erseverance, concentration, and knowledge of procedures for remembering were necessary to fix an improvisation. I demanded that the actor render perceptible concrete or imagined situations, real or psychic events, the landscapes and epochs that he had crossed in the inner reality of the improvisation [...]. An aspect of their craft consisted in making an inner process perceptible through precise vocal and physical actions.

(Barba 2010: 29)

We need to consider whether it is actually possible for our performers to keep a mental record of the journey and/or whether it is actually important to be aware of the 'notation' of a previous improvisation. Of course, with the advancement of technology it is practical and easy to record improvisations for future reference and development and this has its own benefits, especially over a longer rehearsal period. After all, it is not always useful to

Figure 3: The Rejection Scene from
Hippolytus (dir. George Rodosthenous),
School of Performance and Cultural
Industries, December 2008. Lauren
Garnham (left) Tom Colley (right).
Photo by Georges Bacoust.

have an 'exact' repetition of a previous improvisation. But, this device also helps us to get an overview of the whole journey within a sequence and make adjustments to ensure that clarity, contrast, conflict and consistency are achieved.

'Where is the music, maestro'?

When referring to musical composition, Peter Stacey has developed six 'techniques of relating music and text'. These are very useful to adapt for theatre composition as well. In his article 'Towards the Analysis of the Relationship of Music and Text in Contemporary Composition' (1989), he classifies each technique and analyses its relationship. These are "direct mimesis, displaced mimesis, non-mimetic relationship, arbitrary association, synthetic relationship, anti-contextual relationship" (Stacey, 1989: 22). During the initial improvisation sessions, it would be beneficial to consider the ways that music can re-invent and re-interpret a piece of text and the relationships it develops across the overall structure. The co-existence of body, voice and text can then inform the creation of visual imagery for the final *mise en scène*.

There are many examples of borrowing musical structures to create a piece of theatre. This demonstrates that a musical form can influence our way of thinking (or improvising) giving us specific structures. In this respect, music works as a way of thinking about improvisation. Working with and against the music can provide inventive ways to help the performers change their patterns of speaking, develop their characterisation and create atmosphere. One can use a very naturalistic style of delivering a rather poetic text and working with/ against the music can help them achieve moments of emotional truth and variation in the delivery patterns. Using music in improvisational exercises can often help the performers relax, bond and also feel more comfortable with each other. In some cases, especially at the beginning of the rehearsal process, it is very useful to use music as underscoring for a scene and this pushes the performer to a higher level of 'emotional state', thus raising the impact of the performance itself. It is also beneficial for the more musically orientated performer to perceive patterns, shapes or little motifs in the music soundtrack which can help them develop something new in their physicality or even vocal delivery. So music can also function as a way of working within improvisation.

By breaking up the natural rhythm of a text, changing its tempo, stressing specific words at unusual places, we can move beyond a 'literary' reading of the text and not allow the very first impressions to guide our decisions. By treating the text as musical material and experimenting with the musicality of its sound, we allow the performer to improvise with the text, until it makes 'musical sense' and then try to find ways of keeping that approach 'fresh' so that it feels like a new discovery every time. The use of music as another stimulus can punctuate a sub-text and its importance within the overall dramaturgy of the piece and create a richer level of emotional impact. This simultaneity of additional stimuli, sometimes, causes problems in rehearsals because some performers feel that the music overpowers them and that the result could be overwhelming for the audience. It is something that needs to be handled carefully, because a disagreement in taste, quantity and volume levels of music can create unnecessary tensions since performers might feel that they are forced to 'compete' with the music.

'Get the understudy in. Now!'

'Working with the understudy' (or stand-in performer) to repeat and develop material that has been freshly improvised can usually provide new insights into adding detail and refinement. This can be another way of approaching the material by having different members of the ensemble taking the lead in specific sections, or sequences in order to add their own nuances to the interpretation of the material. At that point, we can make rehearsal notes and try to apply the best interpretative solutions/suggestions. This technique does provide for a good alternative when there is a blockage in the performer or when his/her actions are getting a bit stale and repetitive. By asking another member of the ensemble to repeat a scene, the chemistry of that scene is completely re-created and new discoveries happen instinctively because the familiarity (with the material or each other) that existed and was taken for granted a moment ago is no longer there.

This way of 'working with the understudy' can be used in two ways. The understudy can be asked to try and replicate exactly what the other performer did. This will show how alert and observing they have been during the rehearsal process. Since they will be re-creating pre-existing material, there will be a form of prioritising performance events (either because of being unfamiliar or not fully aware of the detailed nuances). This can re-enforce the details that need to be re-worked or improved. A second way is to allow the understudy performers to completely improvise the scene. This can lead to new breakthrough material that can be extracted and re-worked. In any case, asking understudy performers to improvise an already existing scene can provide new insights to the material and an escape from stale repetition.

There is no such thing as an accident:
just a cheeky deviation,
an afterthought,
a planned re-visitation of the falling chord,
the 'wrong' note,
the out-of-sync movement,
the mumbling of the words.

Take it and make it into something substantial,
something that counts.
Don't talk about it, just do it –
in this game,
not everything must be explained or
articulated (with words).
Allow the mind to shape the structure
in real-time:
listen,
look
and choose
what's coming next.

Ethics and credits: Is our material included in the actual performance?

It is undeniable that the improvisation process as part of the compositional process can raise some ethical questions/implications regarding the ownership of material. Even though the above suggestion might seem naïve at first glance, copyright issues that might arise out of the creative freedom of improvisation and the (either implicit or explicit) collaborative agreement can complicate the process. There have been recent court cases where in a specific process the actors' improvisations contributed to the director's and the writer's input and involvement in such a way that it was impossible to distinguish who did what, why and when.

It is always an awkward moment when, as a director, you remove some of the performer's contributed material from the piece (especially towards approaching the first performance, or even after). It creates a sense of exclusion and some performers take this at heart. They have the need to be co-authors of the performance with their material, which might be personal (at times, too personal), as part of the performance. A way to avoid this situation is to encourage the performers not to perform their own material themselves. This might even become a necessity when dealing with deeply personal material. Even if there are benefits of having performers presenting auto-biographical material, there is always the danger of not thinking about the overall structure and dramaturgy of the piece and worrying about giving equal performance time to all. But, this should not become a limitation or a factor that causes tensions during the process of refining the material and getting it ready for performance.

In conclusion, improvising material for devised work is a unique and very rewarding process because it extracts material from the performers (who are actually performing the piece) and gives them joint ownership of the final creation. My improvisational process leads to a kind of collective *in situ* compositional process. Its musicality (the sense of musical structure and – to a degree – notation, of musical underscoring, of conduction, of musically approaching language) is what sets it apart from other techniques of improvisation in devised theatre (which may have little or nothing to do with musical composition). As with any piece of devised performance though, a crucial question remains unanswered: 'who is ultimately the copyright owner of the work': the director, the dramaturge or the ensemble of performers itself?

References

Barba, Eugenio (2010) *On Directing and Dramaturgy: Burning the House*, Oxon: Routledge.

Bogart, Anne and Landau, Tina (2005) *The Viewpoints Book: A Practical Guide to Viewpoints and Composition*, New York: Theatre Communications Group.

Caldarone, Marina and Lloyd-Williams, Maggie (2004) *Actions – The Actors' Thesaurus*, London: Nick Hern Books Limited.

Chekhov, Michael (1991) *On The Technique of Acting*, New York: HarperCollins Publishers.

De Spain, Kent (2003) "The Cutting Edge of Awareness: Reports from the Inside of Improvisation", in A. C. Allbright and D. Gere (eds.) *Taken by Surprise: A Dance Improvisation Reader*, Middletown: Wesleyan University Press.

Johnston, Chris (2006) *The Improvisation Game: Discovering the Secrets of Spontaneous Performance*, London: Nick Hern Books Limited.

Spolin, Viola (1999) *Improvisation for the Theater: A Handbook of Teaching and Directing Techniques*, Evanston: Northwestern University Press

Stacey, Peter F. (1989) "Towards the Analysis of the Relationship of Music and Text in Contemporary Composition", *Contemporary Music Review*, Vol. 5, London: Taylor & Francis.

Warner, Simon (2005) *Howl for Now*, Pontefract: Route.

Chapter 9

Hearing Voices – Transcriptions of the Phonogram of a Schizophrenic: Music-theatre for Performer and Audio-visual Media

Nicholas Till

Forum Neues Musiktheater, Stuttgart Opera; ISCM World New Music Days, July 2006

This project entailed an investigation of the use of new interactive audio-visual technologies for music-theatre, exploring the dramaturgical implications of combining the real and virtual within music-based theatre. The project employed live performance and electronic sound and images to examine the phenomenon of the technological uncanny, investigating cultural anxieties about mechanisation in modernity, and in particular cultural representations of the mechanically disembodied voice from the nineteenth century to the present.

The project was part of a collaboration between the Forum Neues Musiktheater of Stuttgart Opera, the Centre for Research in Opera and Music Theatre at the University of Sussex, The Steim Centre in Amsterdam, and the Tempo Reale Studio in Florence (the late Luciano Berio's electronic music studio). Each centre contributed a piece of work made to the same brief and drawing on a collection of new Max/MSP and Jitter programmes developed by the Forum Neues Musiktheater.

The Sussex project team consisted of Nicholas Till (project director); Kandis Cook (visual director); Lee Gooding, Paul Vincent, Andrew Duff (video material); Sam Hayden, Ed Hughes, Tom Hall, Alice Eldridge, Joe Watson (sound materials); Frances Lynch (performer). Development of the project was funded by the UK Arts and Humanities Research Council.

Preparation

Project brief

The Forum Neues Musiktheater brief for the project was as follows:

All four commissioned compositions and their stagings are subject to the same conditions for the instruments and performers employed and the working materials. The challenge of a deliberately small cast with at most three singers, instrumentalists, dancers or actors is joined with a conscious limitation of technological means (two laptops, eight-channel sound system, one camera, two video projectors) which is intended to encourage and focus reflection on the essential conditions of narrative forms in musical theater and how they are communicated by means of technology. The possibilities of performance in non-conventional or not established theatrical settings should also be considered.

Each institute develops its project independently. The developmental process is, however, accompanied by an exchange of technological know-how and of the tools developed by the institutes, in particular a library of interactive audio-visual Max/ MSP and Jitter programmes developed by the FNMT, as well as through joint meetings of the producers to discuss aesthetic and dramaturgical questions.

A critical practice

I have described my practice as a maker of music theatre works as a 'critical practice'. I attempted to define the concept of a critical practice in a manifesto for a post-operatic music theatre in 2004:

> By 'critical' we acknowledge firstly the Kantian sense of 'critique': the method by which a discipline examines the grounds of its own possibility, as modernist art critic Clement Greenberg put it, "not in order to subvert it, but to entrench it more firmly in its area of competence".
>
> (Till 2006: 16)

Writing in the aftermath of the Second World War, Theodor Adorno framed this for music as a distinction between a critical and an avant-garde practice:

> Music ought to be composed with a hammer, just as Nietzsche wanted to philosophise with a hammer; but that means testing the soundness of the structure, listening with a critical ear for hollow points, not smashing it in two and confusing the jagged remains with avant-garde art because of their similarity with bombed-out cities.
>
> (Adorno 1999: 27–8)

My practice consistently interrogates the unspoken but ideologically powerful assumptions that underpin the modes of representation of conventional operatic forms. There is, for instance, a pervasive metaphysics of subjectivity at work in operatic singing, which derives its potency from the interplay of interiority and transcendence. It is a historically bounded subjectivity that was already in question by the early twentieth century, when such conceptions of subjectivity came under attack from the fragmenting and anti-humanising effects of industrial capitalism. It continues to be challenged by current theories of the posthuman subject in an increasingly technologised age. Any practice that simply assumes the continued validity of a nineteenth century metaphysics of humanist subjectivity is indulging in unreflective nostalgia. A consistent element in all of the works I have undertaken has been to engage critically with this metaphysics of subjectivity. In this project we explored the potential for the combination of live performance and audio-visual technologies to disrupt notions of centred and coherent subjectivity, which is also brought into question by the project's engagement with representations of schizophrenia as an illness that fragments the sufferer's sense of identity.

The 'critical' element of the project also engaged the relationship between the real and virtual in theatrical performance. Audio-visual technologies have been used in the theatre for almost one hundred years, and are now a commonplace of both theatrical and musical performance. But in general, artists employing sound and video technologies in the theatre have employed technology as an expansion of the sonic and scenic canvas, rather than as an independent dramaturgical element. One of the aims of our project was to consider how complexities of time-space and presence-absence relations brought about by the introduction of virtual technologies into the theatre space impact upon the fictions of liveness and musico-dramatic continuity that underpin the dramaturgy of most forms of music theatre. The real and virtual occupy different ontological spaces, and the juxtaposition of these different spaces of representation demands careful attention. In particular, when audio-visual media are employed in ways that draw attention to the gap between live presence and repetition/reproduction they may deconstruct the underlying metaphysical fiction that the sound accompaniment to the live presence in conventional operatic forms is 'noumenal' (i.e., unheard to the characters) rather than 'phenomenal' (to use the terminology of Carolyn Abbate in her book *Unsung Voices*). In this project we sought to destabilise the audience's sense of what is originary in time or space, creating deliberately uncertain relations between live and screen sound, between pre-recorded and live sound, between what the audience hears, what the live character on stage hears and what the filmic character hears.

Finally, we determined to engage some broader cultural representations of technology critically, considering in particular the experience of what I call the 'technological uncanny'. The technological uncanny is a symptom of our anxiety about the effects of technology upon conceptions of the human, a literary trope which first emerges in romanticism (e.g., E.T.A Hoffmann's *The Sandman*, Mary Shelley's *Frankenstein*). In particular, we were interested to investigate the vocalic uncanny as the effect of voice technologies (telephone, phonograph, radio, voice synthesiser) that permit the recording, transmission and imitation of disembodied voices (Ronell 1988). The technological uncanny is an effect that arises through the blurring of nature/culture distinctions, both at the phenomenal level (the electronic that *sounds* human, or vice versa; the anthropomorphism of machines) and the conceptual level (do we hear technologically produced sounds/images as phenomena of nature or culture; as 'mediated' or 'immediate'?). Cultural representations of the technological uncanny include the figure of the 'double' and the idea of 'the ghost in the machine' - the notion that a machine might have a conscious life of its own (Miller 1985; Heumann 1998; Royle 2003). This latter phenomenon is increased in theatrical performances that employ live interactive technologies, when it becomes difficult for the audience to be sure of who is in control of the performance: the performer; the person sitting at the lap-top or sound console; the machine itself?

Sources

Arising from these conceptual concerns, we agreed on a broad thematic approach to the work that was informed by a reading of literary and theoretical texts relating to the technological uncanny. These included Adolfo Bioy Casares' novella *The Invention of Morel* of 1940, in which an inventor constructs a machine that can record and project lifelike audio-visual holograms of people. But in doing so the machine drains the people it thus captures of their actual life. The novella is a classic of twentieth century technophobia, and from it we determined a basic dramatic idea in which the audio-visual technologies employed were to be figured as, in some sense, invasive and malign.

A second crucial source for the work was Friedrich Kittler's *Gramophone, Film, Typewriter*, a book about the way in which new technologies mediate, and thereby alter, our relationship to the world. The book includes a page of musical notation described as 'Transcription of the phonogram of a schizophrenic, 1899', in which the speech of a person suffering from schizophrenia had been documented for analysis by being recorded and then notated musically from the recording (see illustration).

The text of the score is as follows:

> The world, the world, the world, the world, fire, fire.
> Steilers Fritz, Steilers Fritz, Steilers Fritz Fritz, Fritz, Fritz, Fritz, Fritz, is
> Antichrist, for he has said so.
> My son, Wilhelm II, aia.
> Why not then, why not then, hey?
> Steilers Fritz, Steilers Fritz, Steilers Fritz.
> Steilers Fritz, Steilers Fritz, Steilers Fritz
> Ah, above, ah above, ah above
> Near, near – near, near, near, near
> Ah, what do I see there, fire burns there, yes, as fast as a train
> Rather, rather, rather, rather, rather, rather, rather
> Why do I feel so bad, why do I feel so bad, why do I feel so bad?
> Because I will be buried alive, because I have said, I would …

I introduced the score fragment to the project team at an early meeting in January 2006 and suggested that it might provide a starting point for the project. The page of music seemed valuable for a number of reasons:

- It provided a found 'score' that obviated the need for construction of a narrative and character-based libretto, which is usually required to enable the expressive word-and-drama setting of conventional operatic forms (see further discussion below).
- The 'I' of the text is decentred and displaced through the mediations of technology and notation in a way that challenges the expressive 'I' of operatic subjectivity.

Notenumschrift eines Phonogramms mit einem Schizophrenen, 1899

Figure 1: Illustration from Friedrich Kittler, *Grammophon, Film, Typewriter*, Berlin: Brinkmann und Bose, 1987. Reproduced by permission of the publishers.

- It related directly to the project's main themes of technology and mediation, in particular technologies of the voice.
- It related the uncanny effect of technologically reproduced voices to the typical condition of 'hearing voices' of schizophrenia.

The content of the text itself is familiar from the literature and iconography of schizophrenia: extreme paranoid anxiety (the fear of being buried alive – which is also a familiar trope of gothic literature); hallucinatory voices; apocalyptic religious mania (the reference to the Antichrist); belief in relationship to public figures or royalty (the reference to Kaiser Wilhelm II); fear of modernity, in particular modern technologies. On this last point Emil Kraepelin, who was the first psychologist to identify and categorise the symptoms of schizophrenia in the 1890s, noted that schizophrenic patients often described the hallucinatory voices they heard as "the call of a telephone", or "a phonograph in the head" (Kraepelin 1919: 7–8). In our production we suggest visually and sonically that the patient's fear of the speed and power of a train might have been conflated metonymically with fear of the mechanical apparatus of the recording machine itself, with its whirring cogs and wheels, and with the confusions caused by its ability reproduce disembodied voices.

Although an initial, and rather obvious, response to the text was to construct a fictional biography from the fragments of a life that are hinted at in the text, the enigmatic nature of the fragment itself seemed to be of greater interest. Further research determined that not only was there no identifiable source for the page (Kittler cannot recall where he found it!), but that I could also find no wider reference to the practice of using phonogram recordings to record the speech of patients suffering from mental illness. The project therefore developed as a series of historical and practical investigations of the found page of music itself, exploring the different possibilities that it offered both thematically, musically and dramatically. And the finished form of the work itself was similarly constructed around a series of performative, filmic and sonic investigations of the found 'score', in which the live performer confronted her historical alter ego on the screen, engaging in a dialogue with her until she herself was absorbed into the screen world.

Historical research

In the hope of gaining better understanding of the historical context of the score fragment I undertook extensive research into the history of the diagnosis of schizophenia. The first identification of what we now recognise as schizophrenia was made in the 1890s by the German psychiatrist Emil Kraepelin, who labelled the condition *dementia praecox*. His results were published in a series of books between 1896–1914. Kraepelin's main concern was to establish secure grounds for diagnosis of the disease. To this end he listed the symptoms exhaustively, from mental confusion to behavioural and gestural traits, and symptoms such as speech disturbance. In his book entitled *Dementia Praecox &*

Paraphrenia Kraepelin devotes six pages to the analysis of abnormal speech traits under headings such as: "erailments in Linguistic Expression", "Derailments in Finding Words" (Kraepelin 1919: 67–73). His books are full of tables, graphs and diagrams that 'measure' the physical symptoms of schizophrenic patients, and illustrations of the crude mechanical devices that were employed to secure these measurements. It is likely that the transcribed phonogram recording is an instance of such methods, used to document the "derailments in linguistic expression" of a particular patient, although there is no record of Kraepelin himself employing a phonogram in his enquiries.

Kraepelin's extensive catalogues of symptoms are characteristic of the general tendency in medicine towards scientific analysis of human of abnormality at the end of the nineteenth century. Technology played an important role in such analysis. Photography enabled visual analysis of movement, and was used, for instance, by speech therapists to analyse the positions of the mouth in speech. The French psychiatrist Charcot used photography to document different kinds of psychic disorder (Didi-Huberman 2004), and the English scientist Francis Galton based his attempts to establish the physiognomy and genetic characteristics of criminal behaviour on analysis of photographs of criminals (Kemp and Wallace 2000). The use of a phonogram to record the speech of a schizophrenic patient is therefore very much in accord with such practices. The use of musical notation as a means of transcription for analysis is ingenious, and was probably related to the contemporary movement to set words musically in a way that was closer to the pace, rhythm, pitch and intonation of natural speech. The composer Leoš Janáček, for instance, believed that speech melodies were indicators of emotional states, and notated the everyday speech that he overheard in his notebooks musically, often offering an analysis of the presumed emotional state of the speaker from what was thus recorded (Wingfield 1992). Other experimental methods of notating the voice included the notation of *Sprechtgesang*, first developed in the 1890s by the composer Engelbert Humperdinck, and employed by Schoenberg in *Pierrot Lunaire* (1912). This latter relates the phonogram text to the soundworld of expressionism, which itself evolved as an artistic attempt to convey extreme psychic states.

In our fragment both science and art are being employed to effect an objective analysis of the condition of a mental patient. In effect, the patient's illness is being technologised. Our project is not about schizophrenia or madness; even less is it about the madness of a particular individual (a much too well-worn operatic trope, in particular when associated with female characters). Rather, the piece is about the reification of the subject through technologies of transcription.

The working process

New artistic forms demand new working processes. Bringing an opera into being usually involves some familiar hierarchical stages: the identification of a subject or 'story' (usually derived from a literary source); the writing of a libretto; setting the libretto to music; the musical and theatrical realisation of the composer's intentions. Each stage of the process involves an act of interpretation – an attempt to convey the originary meaning of the narrative. But each stage also introduces another layer of replication, and hence redundancy. Without resort to a Cagean aesthetics of chance it is difficult to avoid intentionality. But one can to some extent subvert the process.

Although we started with a number of clear conceptual and aesthetic concerns that we hoped to carry through with rigour, the choice of found musical material was the first move in sidestepping some conventional approaches to music-dramatic composition. The metaphysics of operatic form are also closely wedded to the hierarchies of operatic production since the fiction of coherent dramatic subjectivity is underpinned by the subjectivity of the composer him or herself. Herder, whose ideas initiated many key ideas of German romanticism, believed that one ought to be able to regard each artistic work "as the impression of a living human soul" (Abrams 1953: 236) , and the American musicologist Edward Cone once suggested that in opera after Wagner, "the continuity of the orchestral sound and of the musical design constantly refers to an all-inclusive persona surveying the entire action from a single point of view", like the "omniscient author" in a novel (Cone 1974: 29, 35). For this project we needed to find a means of circumventing such an authorial (authoritarian?) voice so that the musical material would appear to be generated by the found score, the performer, and from within the apparatus itself.

Six people were therefore responsible for producing the sonic material: composer Ed Hughes, from the Music Department at Sussex University, was responsible for much of the vocal material, and for the overall sonic structure of the piece; composer Sam Hayden, also on the Sussex faculty, developed the Max/MSP patches that were supplied by Andreas Breitscheid of Stuttgart; computer programmer (and musician) Alice Eldridge from the Informatics department at Sussex developed the programmes associated with the interacive audio-visual elements; Sussex graduate Tom Hall worked on some of the pre-made electronic material; sound engineer Joe Watson worked on the spatial placement of live sonic materials. A significant amount of the vocal material was developed from improvisations by singer Frances Lynch.

The structure of the working process

The research and concept-making for the work progressed alongside the development of musical, dramatic and visual material in a process of constant dialogue. The practical development of the material consisted of:

1. A series of practical investigations of the 'score' – a process which involved our performer Frances Lynch attempting different modes of performing the score, and the musical team producing different workings of the material (e.g., in response to the question 'what would the text sound like as a song by Schumann?'; 'what would it sound like if it were

a lost number from *Pierrot Lunaire*?'; what would 'fire burning as fast as a train' sound like?). These different readings were all captured to provide source materials for the sonic components of the performance. This stage of the development also involved discussion and analysis of visual illustrations from Kraepelin's books on schizophrenia. One graph, for instance, evoked the response that it looked like a John Cage score. We made a series of recordings of Frances attempting different readings of this 'score', which became the basis for an episode which we designated 'The John Cage Interlude'.

2. A series of practical experiments with the Max/MSP patches provided by Andreas Breitscheid of the FNMT. These involved in particular different live treatments of some of the vocal material we had previously generated. We also downloaded some commercially available voice-synthesising programmes, and employed these to process synthesised vocal versions of the text (which played a part in the final section of the performance, which was intended to convey the idea that the performer's voice had itself become synthesised).

3. Practical experiments with audio-visual programmes that permit live interaction between digital images and sounds, or between the live performer and digital images or sounds (see below).

4. A series of practical investigations into different modes of presentation of the video material. In particular we were interested to identify what methods were most effective in achieving the uncanniness of the virtual 'double'. Discussion here revolved around the question of whether 'ghostly' visual appearances are less or more uncanny than a more conceptual approach. (For the latter a point of reference is the work of the performance arts company Station House Opera, who have developed a series of works employing live performance and projected images of the same performers carrying out simultaneous actions which converge and diverge to the point where they confound the viewer's sense of what is 'present' in both time and space).

For several days we explored the relationship of live presence and projected images, using CCTV images of a live performer projected onto suspended projection fabrics of different thickness and opacity, creating multiple images that dissolved the clear time-space presence of the performer. We also investigated the effect of creating an alternative space that was permanently present on a single screen, and that might be viewed as simultaneous or displaced in time, and might or might not imply spatial contiguity (e.g., when the performer left the stage space and immediately entered the screen space). As we were working we received instructions from Stuttgart that for practical reasons they required us to use only one screen, which determined for us which method we could employ. Although imposing limitations, this directive did mean that we were forced to concentrate on the nature of the real-virtual/live-screen relationship more intently. In particular, we became interested in the possibility of spatial *mise en abyme*, with further screen images appearing within the main screen image.

Development of musical material

All of the sound and musical material in the piece derives from the fragment of the score, from the voice of the performer, and from a few key elements that are invoked from the supposed memory bank of the machine (e.g. the sound of a piano, which accompanies the patient's recollection of a Schumann song that becomes confused with the music of the phonogram score; the wheels of a speeding train, that accompany, and eventually merge with, the whirring machinery of the phonogram, filmed in close up as the patient suffering from schizophrenia speaks into it).

Much of the sonic material was developed following general discussion of the overall effects we sought to convey. For example, I quote from an email from me to Ed Hughes after the work-in-progress showings in May of 2006:

> There's a whole other dimension that we've got to find – of space, atmosphere, deconstructed echoes of things half remembered, unlocatable emotions, structures carrying the piece along inexorably, the machine lurching out of control, shudders of nameless anxiety, gobbets of material spun around inside the machine and spat out, disembodied presences, hints of parallel universes, terror (hers or ours?).

Specific sonic materials were produced according to an evolving written 'scenario', produced after the initial exploratory stages of the project by myself and the visual artist collaborating on the project, Kandis Cook. This included descriptions of the dramatic action, a 'shooting script' for the video elements, and, in some places, quite specific verbal descriptions of the sonic effects sought, as well as more conceptual instructions, for example:

> Sound quality: the sound should always be on the cusp between the natural and the electronic – blurring the boundaries so that we are uncertain whether we are listening to humanly or naturally originated or machine-produced sound. The sound shifts its location between the theatre space, the space of what is represented on screen, the inside of Woman 2's head, the inside of the audience's head.
>
> Mechanical slide 'click-whirr' sound to accompany slide-change – sound is like a cross between some old mechanical contraption and a fierce, dangerous electrical spark.
>
> Tense electronic rasp-churn … as if something is gnawing away inside the machine. Combined with niggly bleep – pitched, but pitch indistinct – perhaps captured from piano harmonics – continues through next sequence in some sort of insistent loop.
>
> A distant electronic thud-crunch – quasi door-slamming sound – sound echoing down the corridors of the hospital and the corridors of the mind.

A crucial component of the sonic material was a recording of singer Frances Lynch reciting the notated text, made on an Edison Class 'M' electric cylinder phonograph of approximately 1897. At the centre of the performance is a film sequence in which the historical patient records the text on this phonograph, for which the sonic accompaniment attempts to convey the effect of the voices in the head of a person suffering from schizophrenia. Kraepelin notes different descriptions of hallucinatory voices: one patient is supposed to have heard "729,000 girls"; another described how "sometimes they shout as in a chorus or all confusedly"; "the patient is everywhere made a fool of and teased, mocked, grossly abused; everyone is occupied with him; the workshop screams" (Kraepelin 1919: 7–9). In this section we see the original patient on screen speaking into the phonograph, whilst the performer ventriloquises the complete text. The sonic treatment combines a pre-recorded montage of voices (all derived from the voice of the performer), in which voices interject and throw mocking questions and challenges, to which the live performance of the text serves as a response. The sonic accompaniment here also incorporated sections of the cylinder recording that we had made, and live treatment of the performer's voice, which was distributed throughout the performance space on five-channel speakers, creating the effect of some of the hallucinatory symptoms described by Kraepelin.

Work-in-process showing

Built into the project from the start was a work-in-progress showing at the Battersea Arts Centre in London in May 2006, approximately half way through the development of the work. The presentation was put together pragmatically to show some of the different interactive programmes we had developed. These included animated Victorian graphs, taken from Kraepelin's published clinical studies, that responded to sonic input, a movement-capture programme that allowed the performer to manipulate the vocal sounds that she was making, and a programme that permitted a sequence of still images to change according to sounds being produced. At least one of the programmes (the physical sound manipulation) lacked a clear dramaturgical purpose within the narrative, but we included it nonetheless so as to be able to illustrate the process.

The narrative of the BAC performances was as follows:

A female performer enters a stage as if for a conventional concert recital. A virtual audience applauds. Behind her is a screen displaying an empty room with a phonograph machine on a table. Behind the phonograph is a screen on which are projected graphs and tables. The song the singer sings has an accompaniment derived from a song by Schumann, but the sung notes and text are from the found score. She seems to be unaware of this disparity, but we hear virtual laughter as if of an audience at a different performance (the original audience who might have witnessed the schizophrenic patient's rendition? Public demonstrations of people suffering from mental illness were common in the nineteenth century). The graphs and tables on the screen in the screen are animated to respond to the music in real time. Half way through the song a disembodied voice takes over the song, cutting the performer off in mid-flow. The voice continues and the performer walks off the stage. On the screen her double, wearing Victorian costume, enters the space. She proceeds to record a spoken rendition of the text (sonically located from within the screen space), which is then played back as the sound of the phonogram recording. The on-screen woman leaves the space and the singer re-enters. She holds a copy of the 'score', from which she proceeds to read. As she picks out certain phrases the on-screen woman re-appears. The singer repeats certain phrases from the text, conveying a sense of distress as she realises their meaning. The phrases she sings are treated to render her voice electronic (sounding at first like the voice synthesis programmes that are used to generate train announcements, but becoming increasingly artificial), and the playback capture of her voice is also manipulated by her gestures. A CCTV image of the singer appears on the screen within the screen. She repeats the phrase 'buried alive' with horror, as if in recognition of its significance to the situation she finds herself in, and walks off stage. Her virtual image remains on screen (requiring a bit of trickery in the invisible substitution of an identical pre-recorded image for the live image). A collage of sounds and images referred to in the text (a burning house, Kaiser Wilhelm, etc.) in which the images change in response to the sonic input. The singer re-enters wearing the Victorian dress worn by her on-screen double. She sings a final (wordless) song of release and walks out of the theatre, leaving the image of her modern alter-ego trapped on the screen.

To show work-in-progress is essential to our method, since in addition to one's own evaluation, informed audience response to whether one's ideas are working is invaluable. A number of useful observations were made about the overly schematic nature of the structure, and about the lack of a developed sonic element (as noted in my email to Ed Hughes, quoted above). Visually it was agreed that the somewhat literal video imagery lacked interest and variety, which led us to consider a range of more varied and atmospheric visual material, ranging from the notion of 'found' nineteenth century film footage to ghostly emanations made from video blurr and fuzz and digital deterioration of CCTV footage. Something of the 'uncanny' effect of the *mise en abyme* spaces, of temporal and spatial ambiguity and the presence/absence of the 'double', was lost in this process – a familiar instance, perhaps, of the desire for aesthetic and dramaturgical interest to override the rigour of a conceptual research process. A basic dramaturgical discovery was also made. In the BAC version the 'singer' was apparently unaware of the screen or of her double. This raised some logical issues: if the stage space was meant to be a concert platform, why was there a screen on the stage, and from where did the invisible piano emanate? Dramaturgically we realised that the singer needed to acknowledge and engage directly with the screen and its contents, and that this would also allow for dramatic interplay to take place between the live performer and her screen double (although in other respects it somewhat reduced the uncanny effect of the singer being unaware of her screen double).

But perhaps the most important outcome of the BAC showing was the realisation that the audience was unable to discern either the liveness or the interactivity of the live interactive elements, meaning that our assumption about the 'uncanny' effect of these interactions was not working.

Working with interactive technologies on stage

The realisation that the audience could not discern the element of liveness in the interactive programmes (something that is also evident in most musical performances that employ such programmes) made us revise our approach to these. In part this is because the programmes themselves are not sufficiently sophisticated to register visual movement or sonic details precisely enough. One can, of course, make the relationship clearer by the use of, say, more exaggerated gestures; but then the very obviousness of the relationship means that it loses its ambiguity – the play of uncertainty that is crucial to the uncanny effect. In the event, we found that certain processes were achieved more effectively by being cheated: the gesture and sound processing was thus achieved by the programmer wiggling her mouse in accord with the gestures of the performer to achieve an effect that was both more reliable, and yet also less literal.

In general we found that the time it took to programme the Max/MSP and related software that we employed slowed down the process of immediate response and improvisation that is essential in a rehearsal situation. Alice would come along to a rehearsal with a new programme that she had written, and we would experiment with it. Inevitably we would find that one aspect was more interesting than another, but Alice would be unable to make the necessary alterations on the spot to enable us to develop the more interesting aspect; she would have to go away for a few days and come back with a new patch, by which time we had often moved on in our ideas.

Process and product

The finished piece makes the process of its own development evident, even showing material that was, in a sense, 'discarded' – for example, the attempt to convey a Schoenbergian setting of the score. The exposure of process is not uncommon in modern art practices. One thinks of the reworked canvases of Cy Twombly; the laying bare of process in conceptual art; the recursive erasures of Samuel Beckett. This mode of representation is also perhaps closer to the procedures of performance art, in which the element of fictional representation is less clear (although such work often plays on precisely the ambiguity about what is fictional and what is 'real'). In *Hearing Voices* the dramatic framework represents the process of exploration of the score itself: Frances Lynch is a singer, and as a singer she is confronted by a musical score to which she, naturally, responds by attempting to 'sing' it. The sonic and video material is presented as either captured during the performance, or as being in some sense a part of the memory of the original patient that has been captured by the reprographic machine (so that, for instance, the sounds of a piano may be thought to be derived from her confused memory of a song by Schumann).

Narrative of the finished performance

The performance presents a singer who enters the performance space and is confronted, as are the audience before the performance begins, by the image of the score on the screen. She tries to make sense of this fragment of text, singing it in an exploratory fashion into a microphone on a stand. In doing so she uploads her interrogations and interpretations into the modern machine of reproduction, in the same way that the schizophrenic patient of 1899 was required to record his/her speech into a phonograph. As the performer uploads her voice into the machine, the machine itself responds. It seems to have its own life, processing and regurgitating the visual and sonic material she presents, also offering animated versions of Kraepelin's graphs and bar charts. And the machine also contains fragments and memories of the original patient: ghostly digital emanations; a short 'primitive' film sequence of a woman speaking the text whilst strapped into a device designed to record muscular tensions (based on illustrations taken from the Kraepelin); another such sequence of the same woman standing in front of a phonograph to have her speech recorded. As the piece progresses the live performer develops a relationship with her double on screen, ventriloquizing, and in one instance apparently animating, the screen image. The physical being of the performer seems to be increasingly absorbed into the screen-machine, until her voice is completely synthesised; eventually she appears to change places with the woman on the screen, and finally disappears into the depths of the screen space, from where the screen woman had initially emerged.

Conclusion

This project was an example of practice as research (sometimes called practice-led research). Practice as research involves the formulation of a clear set of research issues – conceptual, aesthetic, technical – that are to be addressed through the process of development of a creative project. It is the nature of all creative projects that they evolve in the process of development, and in the case of practice as research it is important that the initial parameters are kept in mind when artistic decisions are being made, so that the expedient of effectiveness is not the sole criterion for making choices. Nonetheless, as I admit above, there may be instances where one has to abandon avenues of enquiry because they simply don't work – in particular those dependent on technological applications that may be insufficiently advanced to achieve one's aims. A second danger of practice as research is that the outcomes may have the nature of practical demonstration rather than fully achieved artistic creation. This was certainly the case with the work-in-progress showing of the piece in London, when it became evident that the material needed to be developed aesthetically and dramatically as well as technically and conceptually. In relation to the research aspect of such a project the responsibility here involves a constant process of critical reflection on such decisions to ensure that new understanding is gained of why certain dramaturgical or aesthetic decisions seem to work better than others, always understanding that aesthetic and dramaturgical issues cannot be separated from broader conceptual and, indeed, ideological questions.

References

Abbate, Carolyn (1991) *Unsung Voices: Opera and Musical Narrative in the Nineteenth Century*, Princeton, NJ: Princeton University Press.

Abrams, M. H. (1953) *The Mirror and the Lamp: Romantic Theory and the Critical Tradition*, New York: Oxford University Press.

Adorno, Theodor (1999) *Sound Figures*, Stanford, CA: Stanford University Press.

Bioy Casares, Adolfo (2003) *The Invention of Morel*, New York: New York Review of Books.

Cone, Edward T. (1974) *The Composer's Voice*, Berkeley, Los Angeles, London: University of California Press.

Didi-Huberman, Georges (2004) *Invention of Hysteria: Charcot and the Photographic Iconography of the Salpêtrière* (trans. Alisa Hartz), Cambridge MA: MIT Press.

Greenberg, Clement (1965) "Modernist Painting", *Art & Literature*, 4, Spring, pp. 193–201.

Heumann, Michael (1998) *Ghost in the Machine: Sound and Technology in Twentieth Century Literature*, unpublished PhD Dissertation, University of California, Riverside, 1998. Available at http://www.hauntedink.com/ghost/index.html. Accessed on 12 March 2006.

Kemp, Martin and Wallace, Marina (2000) *Spectacular Bodies: The Art and Science of the Human Body from Leonardo to Now*, Berkeley, Los Angeles, London: University of California Press.

Kittler, Friedrich A. (1999) *Gramophone, Film, Typewriter* (trans. Geoffrey Winthrop-Young and Michael Wutz), Stanford, CA: Stanford University Press.

Kraepelin, Emil (1896–1914) *Psychologische Arbeiten*, Leipzig: Verlag von Wilhelm Engelmann, 6 Vols.

—— (1919) *Dementia Praecox and Paraphrenia* (trans. R. Mary Barclay), Edinburgh: E. & S. Livingstone.

Miller, Karl (1985) *Doubles: Studies in Literary History*, Oxford: Oxford University Press.

Ronell, Avitall (1988) *The Telephone Book: Technology – Schizophrenia – Electric Speech*, Lincoln, Nebraska: Nebraska University Press.

Royle, Nicholas (2003) *The Uncanny*, New York: Routledge.

Till, Nicholas (2004) "'I don't mind if something's operatic, just as long as it's not opera': A Critical Practice for New Opera and Music Theatre", *Contemporary Theatre Review*, Vol. 14 (1), pp. 15–24.

Wingfield, Paul (1992) "Janáček's Speech-Melody Theory in Concept and Practice", *Cambridge Opera Journal*, 4 (3), November, pp. 281–301.

Chapter 10

Composing Theatre on a Diagonal: *Metaxi ALogon*, a Music-centric
Performance

Demetris Zavros

Prologue

Composing a music-centric theatre

The 'musicalisation' of theatre or 'theatre as music' is a term that has been recently discussed in contemporary theatre *praxis* – especially since the publication of Hans-Thies Lehmann's book *Postdramatic Theatre* (2006) in English – and involves approaching the theatrical staging from a musical standpoint. The musical composition of the theatrical spectacle is offered as an alternative to the more usual forms of dramaturgy that prioritise the text, characterisation and narrative structures to create "the representation of a closed-off fictional cosmos, the mimetic staging of a fable" as Karen Jurs-Munby explains in her 'Introduction' to Lehmann's book (Lehmann 2006: 3).

Lehmann discusses the idea of "musicalisation" (Lehmann 2006: 91) as one trait among others in "the palette of stylistic traits of postdramatic theatre" (Lehmann 2006: 86). Eleni Varopoulou, whom Lehmann quotes almost exclusively in his section on 'Musicalisation', discusses the term based on the practice of several contemporary theatre directors[1] and notices a shift in the directorial approach, which pertains to a musical organisation of all theatrical means. Theatre becomes "'a theatre of musical structures' where musical phrases, sounds, tones and noises constitute acoustic facts, which, instead of converging, act as autonomous elements". Rhythm comes to the foreground with the use of "impressive changes; long pauses; repetitions and motifs; and the alteration between very fast or slow tempi". The language is musicalised through a "denaturalisation of the usual utterance" of the text and through *polyglossia* (the use of several different languages). The intercultural and musical aspects of language emerge through foreign accents and special characteristics that surface through the identities of actors with multicultural backgrounds. Directors make use of the chorus and the chora-tic dimension of the composition on stage, as well as multiple castings to divide the dramatic personae. Props gain a musical life creating an "'acoustic stage' that runs in parallel to, and achieves, the same degree of importance to the visual stage" (Varopoulou 2002: 141–65, my translation).

---

1. Marthaler, Wilson, Vasiliev, Schleef, Brochen, Brook, Mnouchkine, Vitez, Serban, Nekrošius, Societas Rafaello Sanzio etc.

The process of musical composition undoubtedly relates to the creation of 'musical structures' and this is certainly a very important issue that we must take into account when approaching the process of devising a performance of 'theatre as music'. But, I believe that 'theatre as music', is not only a theatre that uses music and utilises musical strategies of organisation, but equally as importantly, it is one that establishes itself as a non-logocentric medium of communication. Within the field of experimental music-theatre, my understanding of the term 'composed theatre' is a 'music-centric theatre': theatre that uses *all the means in its disposal* to create an audio-visual equivalent to the experience of music devoid of *logos*.

Accordingly, the two driving questions of my practice-based research into music theatre, thus far, are formed as follows:

1. How can we use musical models (which are based on a conceptualisation of music as an 'other' to *logos*) in order to create a music-theatre performance?
2. How can we use music as an organising principle (musical structures, rhythm, dynamics, etc.) in a way that the compositional choices are derived from these specific conceptual/ musical models?

In conjunction with these research questions, my practice also involves the theatrical composition of material derived from myth. Myth is used as a textual source of inspiration based initially on Levi-Strauss' thesis on the similarity between music and myth (on a structural and conceptual level). My focus on myth is based on the hypothesis that if the two domains share an affinity (structurally and conceptually) then myth could provide a very important source of material for the composition of a performance as music.

The processes I have employed are quite unique in each performance. However, since I have been investigating different yet related issues in each one, these processes could be enumerated in the following way:

1. Deriving inspiration from mythical texts (accepting initially the assertion that music as a conceptual and structural domain is closer to mythical than to other types of texts).
2. Questioning and re-evaluating the proposition of the relationship between myth and music being based on the creation or existence of categories of binary oppositions.
3. Re-conceptualising mythical texts based on non-logocentric approaches to music.
4. Utilising musical types of composition that are akin to the conceptual model of the relationships between the motifs supported by the research into the mythical context.
5. Transposing these compositional types into the visual domain (placement into the frame of space/stage, movement (direction, rhythm, texture etc.) both with regards to structuring the performance (in the creation of a performance score) and to approaching the process of reception and 'meaning-making' or the general conceptual driving force).

My research, then, elucidates the process of using one or more dramatic mythical texts in a way that in their music-centric treatment and composition, they produce a non-logocentric

– or, in fact, a music-centric – theatrical performance. In *Clastoclysm* (2007), I took Lévi-Strauss' structural analysis as a point of departure. Yet, I built the performance on an alternative structural/conceptual model ('the continuum') based on musical discrepancies that exist in Lévi-Strauss' analysis.[2]

In my analysis of *Clastoclysm* I spoke of the 'continuum' (as a model derived from a particular musical type) that reveals the sign as 'a process of becoming'; I argued that the 'continuum' is one conceptual and structural strategy in the creation of a theatrical performance that exposes the sense data (auditory and visual) as referring to "answers that are not (yet) graspable" (Lehmann 2006: 99). Here I would like to extend this idea in discussing some of the issues involved in the creation of a rhizomatic performance through approaching music as a "becoming" (as this notion appears, in Gilles Deleuze and Felix Guattari's *Mille Plateaux/A Thousand Plateaus* and primarily, in Plateaus 10 and 11: "1730: Becoming-Intense, Becoming-Animal, Becoming-Imperceptible..." and "1837: Of the Refrain").

Metaxi ALogon and the process of 'composing' a rhizomatic performance

Metaxi ALogon was performed at *stage@leeds* (School of Performance and Cultural Industries, University of Leeds, United Kingdom, 11 June 2008). The title could be interpreted in a variety of ways as it includes words that have been appropriated in English, but still retain alternative meanings in Greek and could additionally infer multiple interpretations in their conjunction. 'Metaxi' could mean both 'in-between' and 'silk'; A-logon is that which lies outside *logos*, but also means 'horse' or 'horses' in Modern Greek. The performance was divided in four sections: Introduction, Plateau I, Plateau II, and Plateau III.

> Let us summarize the principal characteristics of a rhizome: unlike trees or their roots, the rhizome connects any point to any other point, and its traits are not necessarily linked to traits of the same nature; it brings into play very different regimes of signs and even nonsign states. [...] It is composed not of units but of directions, or rather directions in motion. It has neither beginning nor end, but always a middle (*milieu*) from which it grows and which it overspills [...] The rhizome operates by variation, expansion, conquest, capture, offshoots.
>
> (Deleuze and Guattari 2007: 23)

---

2. Lévi-Strauss creates binary categories that expose myth as a system structurally comparable to music since both of them are structured simultaneously on vertical (harmonic, synchronic) and horizontal (melodic, diachronic) axes. Based on the notion of the 'continuum', I have offered an alternative conceptual model upon which I structured the performance, problematising, thus, some of Lévi-Strauss' musical presuppositions. For a more detailed analysis of this performance look at Zavros, D. (2008), "Flooding the *concrète*: *Clastoclysm* and the notion of the 'continuum' as a conceptual and musical basis for a postdramatic music-theatre performance", *Studies in Musical Theatre*, 2:1, pp. 83–100.

The creation of a rhizomatic performance (based on the myth of Oedipus) was the principal objective of *Metaxi ALogon* (2008). In the following sections I will try to briefly explain mainly three of the processes that were utilised in the creation of this music-centric performance. These adhere to the general processes as they appear at the beginning of this article but they are more specific in their focus and to the particular project.

Process I: Re-conceptualising the myths

A 'becoming-molecular' of mythical texts based on Deleuzian notions of music

In "Of The Refrain" (Plateau 11 of *A Thousand Plateaus*), Deleuze and Guattari reject the idea of music as a self-contained structure, by using birdsong as a point of departure in a discussion of how music is used to delineate territories in nature. Based on this discussion, they formulate the notion of 'the refrain' as the content proper of music. At the same time they stress that "whereas the refrain is essentially territorial, territorialising or reterritorialising, music makes of the refrain a deterritorialised form of expression" (Deleuze and Guattari 2007: 331). They argue that the territorialisation of the refrain happens due to the fact that its musical qualities have become expressive, but at the same time

> expressive qualities entertain variable or constant relations with one another …; they no longer constitute placards that mark a territory, but motifs and counterpoints that express the relation of the territory to interior impulses or exterior circumstances, whether or not they are given.
>
> (Deleuze and Guattari 2007: 351).

This 'deterritorialisation' of the 'refrain' is a process which Deleuze and Guattari call 'a becoming'. While the content of music is the refrain, Deleuze and Guattari claim that the preoccupation of so many musical works with subjects that relate to children, women and animals is not an accidental coincidence. "Music is pervaded by every minority" and this is how it produces its "immense power" (Deleuze and Guattari 2007: 330). In using 'a child, a woman, a bird' musical expression does not restrict itself to an imitative exercise. The deterritorialisation of the refrain is real because of a becoming-child, becoming-woman, becoming-animal that is inseparable (according to Deleuze and Guattari) from the content proper of music. The identity of these becomings as Bogue explains "is molecular rather than molar, that of a multiplicity of elements that somehow cohere without entering into a regular, fixed pattern of organization" (Bogue 2003: 34).

In my process of using a musical model as a methodological/conceptual tool in creating music-theatre, a question arises in the treatment of the mythical text: how can a 'becoming-molecular' be effectuated in a music-theatre performance which begins from a mythical text? This question formed the basis of the creative process and was applied on several levels of this procedure. In the following analysis I will concentrate on some of the processes utilised and the way that Deleuze and Guattari's understanding of 'music as a becoming' is embedded in those processes.

It is quite important to state from the beginning that Deleuze and Guattari are not proponents of the use of mythical narratives. After all, in *Anti-Oedipus* they attack the use of the myth of Oedipus as that which gave rise to the comprehensive model of the Oedipus complex in Freudian psychoanalysis. With regard to myth, and especially in its connection to the idea of the becoming, their stand becomes apparent in the following passage:

> In his study of myths, Lévi-Strauss is always encountering these rapid acts by which a human becomes animal at the same time as the animal becomes … (Becomes what? Human or something else?). It is always possible to try to explain these *blocks of becoming* by a correspondence between two relations, but to do so most certainly impoverishes the phenomenon under study. Must it not be admitted that myth as a frame of classification is quite incapable of registering these becomings, which are more like fragments of tales? Must we not lend credence to Jean Duvignaud's hypothesis that there are 'anomic' phenomena pervading societies that are not degradations of the mythic order but irreducible dynamisms drawing lines of flight and implying other forms of expression than those of myth, even if myth recapitulates them in its own terms in order to curb them?
>
> (Deleuze and Guattari 2007: 262, emphasis in the original text)

While they urge for other forms of expression, they also admit that myth recapitulates the 'anomic' phenomena, which effectuate becomings even if in the myth's terms these phenomena are 'curbed'. Even when curbed, must they not, necessarily (according to their general theory) exist, at least, as innate 'lines of flight'? Based on this idea, the approach to myth became one of extracting those 'anomic' phenomena from it. Through this objective, I am essentially offering a re-conceptualisation of the myths under investigation, according to a concept that is essentially musical: the 'becoming'.

Creating at n-1 dimensions: Oedipus re-imagined as three instances of the same 'refrain'

Deleuze's most extensive treatise on theatre appears in his essay "Un manifeste de moins" on the theatre of Carmelo Bene in which he explains how in confronting a classical text (*Richard III*), the director creates through subtraction: in writing 'at n-1 dimensions'. He suggests that in subtracting with 'chirurgical precision', a director can question and problematise those logocentric systems of power that pervade the 'theatre of representation'.

The popularisation of the Oedipus myth seems to have happened greatly due to its connection with psychoanalysis, which universalises (based on the story of the myth) an urge that emits from the unconscious of a male child to consummate a sexual relationship with his mother, in an effort to substitute the father. By subtracting the idea of incest from the mythical text, other ideas were allowed to come to the forefront, as if the myth was approached through a different 'prism'. The focus shifted to three instances of 'deterritorialisation' in the myth. All three are Oedipus's meetings with the 'Other': Laios as 'Other', The Sphinx as 'Other', and Teiresias as 'Other'. In this way, Oedipus's journey was discharged from its fatalistic teleology and the myth was re-imagined musically: the 'meeting with the Other' was treated as a 'refrain'.

Overlaying extremities by rendering them mutually implicit through the idea of 'transcoding'

> Jakob von Uexkull has elaborated an admirable theory of transcodings. He sees the components as melodies in counterpoint, each of which serves as a motif for another: Nature as music. Whenever there is transcoding, we can be sure that there is not a simple addition, but the constitution of a new plane, as of a surplus value. A melodic or rhythmic plane, surplus value of passage or bridging.
>
> (Deleuze and Guattari 2007: 346)

An example of 'transcoding' that Deleuze and Guattari offer in their discussion is that of the fly and the spider. The spider, they suggest, builds its web (in its very precise specifications) before it has encountered a fly. Consequently they state that "the spider web implies that there are sequences of the fly's own code in the spider's code; it is as though the spider had a fly in its head, a fly 'motif', or a fly 'refrain'" (Deleuze and Guattari 2007: 346). This idea of the transcoding is one that we utilised in re-imagining the myth in a way alternative to the use of binaries.

In his book *Lévi-Strauss*, Edmund Leach looks at several myths, exemplifying Lévi-Strauss' structural analysis. In his brief discussion of the myth he entitles 'Theseus, Phaidra and Hippolytos' he remarks that

> [T]his is very close to being the inverse of the Oedipus story [...]. Here the father kills the son instead of the son killing the father. The son does not sleep with the mother, though he is accused of doing so. The mother (Phaidra-Jokaste) commits suicide in both cases.
>
> (Leach 1973: 78)

There are two points here worth mentioning: the first is related to the process of subtraction that gave rise to our initial re-conceptualisation of the Oedipus myth; the other is related to a process associated with the problematisation of binaries. Leach notices a coincidence in the two myths, which proved quite important in the creative process: both of the mothers commit suicide. In using this point of coincidence (the mother) as the point of subtraction (one that has already been subtracted from the myth of Oedipus), the Hippolytos myth could also be re-imagined through an idea that Deleuze connects to music (the becoming-animal) and could be seen as being curbed in the myth itself.

Hippolytos's name means 'loose horse' and this pointed to his fate, which pre-inscribed that he would be dragged to death by his loose horses. In the becoming-animal I found an alternative understanding of his name that escapes the teleology of fate. In the tragedy by Euripides, Hippolytos is shown to be the tamer, the man who is in control of the animal (in a manifestation of a hierarchy that supports the dualisms man/animal). In effect, my reading of the relationship with his horses questioned the logocentrism that is inherent in such dualisms by introducing a re-imagination of such a relationship in *a becoming-horse*. I treated this becoming-animal as a phenomenon/process that is curbed in the myth of Hippolytos (if we were to follow Deleuze and Duvignaud's hypothesis) and I extrapolated it to re-invigorate the myth through a concept that is, according to Deleuze and Guattari, indisputably musical. Furthermore, through implanting the idea of a becoming-horse (or the horse 'motif' or 'refrain') in the presentation of the Oedipus myth, I didn't treat the myth of Hippolytos as its inverse. The performance was envisioned as the creation of a multiplicity that is produced in their simultaneity: It is not a representation of the Oedipus myth or the Sophoclean tragedy; nor is it a staging of the Hippolytos myth or the Euripidean tragedy. And their simultaneity was conceived (because of the becoming-horse module that appears in both) not as "a simple addition, but the constitution of a new plane, as of a surplus value. A melodic or rhythmic plane, surplus value of passage or bridging" (Deleuze and Guattari 2007: 346). It was imagined as a simultaneity that produces an 'in-between' which is already always *a-logon*.

Process II: Musical composition and de-composition as a driving force in the process of creating the theatrical event

My quest to compose musically a theatrical performance based on myth pre-supposed the treatment of a necessarily pre-existing mythical text. Thus, I saw fit to use a pre-existing musical text in parallel, which I treated through a methodology similar to the one applied on the mythical text. The piece of music that was chosen was Vivaldi's *The Four Seasons* (1723).[3]

Deleuze and Guattari differentiate between three periods of music: the Classical (a classification that also subsumes the Baroque), the Romantic and the Modernist. They base this classification on their three permutations of 'the refrain' (as point of order, territorial circle and cosmic line of flight). Nevertheless, these three aspects of the refrain, they insist, do not follow a hierarchised evolutionary sequence; instead they function as "three aspects of a single thing" (Deleuze and Guattari 2007: 344). As a consequence, they adopt a

---

3. In the process of de-composing the musical work I chose to focus on one of the movements of the concerto ('Summer') and more particularly the 'Presto' section.

modernist orientation with regard to musical creation (one which emphasises innovation), but they find this element of innovation in the work of great artists of all periods. In effect, they regard the great composers as innovators of the musical medium of their day and true musical creation as a process of introducing innovation through 'lines of flight' that always already exist within the territories of the medium with which they work; or by inventing "a kind of a diagonal running between the harmonic vertical and the melodic horizon" (Deleuze and Guattari 2007: 327).

The question, then, with regard to the music, took a similar line to the one I used for the treatment of the mythical text: based on this piece of music, how could I use those elements that exist already in it as 'lines of flight' even if they are plugged into the pre-existing forms of Western tonal music (i.e. Baroque) to which the piece adheres? The de-composition process of the music did not happen irrelevantly to the process of composing the performance. Through the de-composition of both the myth and the music, I hoped to produce a sort of a 'becoming' as an event; a performance which starts from a found text (both mythical and musical), but which spreads out as a kind of a rhizome with different nodes and stems sprouting out to create affects and intensities; as a multiplicity that grows out and affects all of the sources out of which it comes. Through the de-compositional process, then, I was trying to allow to surface through the myth and the musical text creative forces, which would make the performance an 'event' in the Deleuzian sense.

Representing the 'refrain' through the becoming-animal module and the 'dividual'

In a practical manifestation of the idea of a 'transcoding' between Oedipus and Hippolytos, all of the moments in the performance were presented in conjunction with the rhythms and intensities of a becoming-horse. In the process of rehearsal, the performers and I began thinking of the concept of 'becoming-animal' and, more specifically, 'becoming-horse' from the very beginning. Even if the process began with an imitation of horses, we tried to move from that to a process wherein we extracted from that mimetic practice a sense of being alongside this new notion of the horse or a 'this-ness' that was embodied in the rhythms, intensities and gestures that we tried out.

> Do not imitate a dog, but make your organism enter into composition with *something else* in such a way that the particles emitted from the aggregate thus composed will be canine as a function of the relation of movement and rest […] into which they enter.
> (Deleuze and Guattari 2007: 302, emphasis in the original text)

In '1730: Becoming-Intense, Becoming-Animal, Becoming-Imperceptible…' Deleuze and Guattari insist that "the word 'like' is one of those words that change drastically in meaning and function when they are used in connection with haecceities, when they are made into expressions of becomings instead of signified states or signifying relations" (Deleuze and

Guattari 2007:302).[4] In our imitating the horses in rehearsal we tried to find those rhythms and intensities that belong to a horse, extract them and use them in our final presentation. One of the processes for example included using a harnessing apparatus and considering the physical qualities of a creature that is harnessed, yet has the natural strength to revolt and liberate itself at any time. In the horse's physicality we found a slow and delicate round movement which was always impregnated with the potentiality of a more violent outburst; a potentiality that occasionally found expression in faster, more abrupt and angular movements; ones that reminded us of the threat that always lies underneath its serene exterior.

This 'becoming-horse' module was implanted in the process of the presentation of the three Plateaus in all aspects of the performance: the visuals, the sound (text and music) and the movement. Plateau I, for example, begins with the meeting of Oedipus and his father Laios (who is on his chariot). Looking at this meeting through the prism that allows a becoming to arise through the co-existence of the two myths (Oedipus and Hippolytos as re-imagined), I re-visualised Laios as a multiplicity, as 'a pack of horses' that is trying to deter Oedipus from returning to the cage (the striated/state space, from which Laios displaced him when he was an infant). Out of this multiplicity – the 'pack' that appears in front of the cages – emerge individual performers each taking up the character of Oedipus in turns. No performer is representing Oedipus or Laios more than any of the others. It is a multiplicity that changes with every movement and gives rise to stem-like points of individuation through the movements and rests that are implicit in it.

The way in which we presented the first meeting suspended the dualism chorus/ protagonist that exists in Greek tragedies. The question effectively is one of treating a group of performers as the *Dividual*. Bogue notices that what Deleuze and Guattari call the 'Dividual' is a collectivity that is described by Debussy as a goal in his choral writing:

> What I would like to make is something more sparse, more divided, more relaxed, more impalpable, something inorganic in appearance and yet fundamentally ordered; a true human crowd in which each voice is free, and yet in which all the united voices together produce one impression and one movement.
>
> (Debussy cited from Barraque in Bogue 2003: 42)

My effort, then, was a struggle to erase the line between chorus and protagonist. To create protagonists that sprung through a *chora*-tic multiplicity and fell back upon it. The goal was that in every instance of individuality the performers always still carried within them a sense of this multiplicity that s/he temporarily came out of; and every time the group represented an individual as a 'multiplicity', they were acting as a 'pack', a 'choral crowd'.

---

4. When Robert De Niro, they argue, "walks 'like' a crab in a film sequence, it is not a question of his imitating the crab; it is a question of making something that has to do with the crab enter into composition with the image, with the speed of the image" (Deleuze and Guattari 2007: 303).

The de-composition of the music and the generation of theatrical material in the presentation of the 'refrain'

There is a further connection between Laios as 'Other' and the chariot (or the horses), which is not referred to in Sophocles' tragedy, but became important when we re-imagined Laios and Oedipus' meeting under the 'becoming-horse' molecule. Laios abducted and raped Chysippos ('golden horse'), the son of Pelop, alluring him with the excuse of helping him with chariot practice. It is as 'Other' but also King that Laios falls in a crime of his own entrapping and entrapment. Consequently, in the resulting simultaneity he is presented as a 'pack of horses' but also as an authoritative figure. In this latter part of the simultaneity, it is the reverbaration of the myth with the de-compositon of the music that creates the rhizomatic growth. If we were to look at the score of Vivaldi's 'Presto' closely, one thing that springs out is the continuous use of scalar patterns for the different parts of the score. In thinking about the use of scales in musical education and performance training we sought to re-imagine theatrically this latter part of the presentation of Laios. A bass-clarinettist is called on stage by an authoritative figure to 'come and practise, boy' (see figure 1). As he moves from the scalar patterns and the proper quality of sound to improvised sections

Figure 1: The simultaneous presentation of Laios as a 'pack of horses' and an authoritative figure who pulls the bass-clarinettist into his cage. Photograph by Georges Bacoust.

Figure 2: The performer's continuous unsuccessful struggle to stand on his two feet. Photograph by Georges Bacoust.

(which include unconventional timbres), the authoritative figure pulls the chords of control to put him back in order and every time pulls him closer to his 'cage'. When he is finally in it, she feeds/rewards him. Taking the scales out of context, then, this section theatricalises the process of musical training as a harnessing/limitation of the creativity of the individual performer in the name of an all encompassing law of 'proper' technique and 'proper' sound quality, and points to the practice of improvisation and the play with unconventional timbres that became central in the de-composition of the music in the performance.[5]

---

5. The decomposition of the music in the performance did not only consist of such an abstraction of the scalar pattern, of course. This is only an example of how the music assisted with the generation of material in the presentation of this first plateau. In other sections, the decomposition took several other forms such as extracting pitch-sets, over-imposing them, using them in correlation with specific syllables from Euripides' *Hippolytus*, playing with different tempi and rhythms and experimenting with improvisation and the creation of different timbres.

Figure 3: A female performer is weaving the thread coming out of another's mouth while uttering definitions of the word 'norm' in the style of telling a fairytale. Photograph by Georges Bacoust.

Process III: Approaching the notion of form as process

As Bogue notices, Deleuze and Guattari borrow from Maldiney their conception of form not as "a static shape or a set of fixed relations", but "understood dynamically as a process of spontaneous emergence and self-shaping" (Bogue 2003: 118). The form is, in fact, more a process than a product. It is a process of folding, unfolding and refolding between all different components that may belong to entirely different milieus, of different natures. As such, a rhizomatic performance can only be created, perceived and analysed in relation to the process that gave rise to it.

Going back to the 'Introduction' section of the performance, we established the two initial extremities (Oedipus and Hippolytus) through presenting the respective extremities of the body (feet and head). The visual establishment of the 'feet' is comprised by a performer's continuous unsuccessful struggle to stand on his two feet (see figure 2). The extremity of the 'head' is shown simultaneously through the process of creating a harnessing structure to be put on another performer's head. We used these visual motifs later as elements in order to facilitate the creation of most of the movement material that appears in all three Plateaus. These motifs also gave rise to entire sections themselves that are irrelevant to the stories of the myths but rhizomatically connected to the construct of the performance.

However, in the presentation of these motifs an accidental coincidence emerged; an accident that we used to approach the notion of the form of the performance "dynamically as a process of spontaneous emergence and self-shaping" (Bogue 2003: 118). In the establishment of the 'head' motif a performer weaves together a thread that is coming out of another's mouth and at the end of this section forms a construct that is put on the performer's head (see figure 3). This is followed by a linguistic 'game', which is interrupted by one of the performers asking the question: 'But, what if I want to be a butterfly?' The 'Introduction' finishes with this question, which seems almost irrelevant to the context of this scene. The particular choice of animal (butterfly) was not accidental. Yet, it was the product of a 'diagram' that came out of an accident.

In his essay on Francis Bacon, Deleuze talks about a 'diagram', which is formed out of accidents in the process of painting and which allows the image (in deformation) to evade the naturalism of representation. The idea of creating through a 'diagram' that is produced out of the process of creation itself is akin to the concept of form that I mentioned above. In this particular case, the accident was a realisation that came about through the working title *ALogon Metaxis* and the process of representation of the 'head' motif.

Using the accident as the impulse for a 'diagram'

'Metaxis' is a term used in performance studies to mean: "The state of belonging completely and simultaneously to two different autonomous worlds" (Boal 1995: 43), or, as William Echard explains, "to denote the state of mind in which performers and/or audiences are simultaneously inhabiting two different worlds: in [the case of a musical performance], being aware of both the virtual and actual sides of a musical event" (Echard 2006: 12). It is derived from Greek where the word 'μεταξύ' means 'in-between'. Interestingly, in its appropriation into English, and the replacement of the 'υ'[6] with an 'i', the word in its new spelling resembles another Greek word 'μετάξι', which means 'silk'. This created an accidental coincidence between the word 'silk' and the representation of the vocal thread coming out of the performer's mouth and woven into the linguistic construct. While no text on silkworms was used in the 'Introduction', the question at the end of this section, points towards the idea of the becoming-animal as well as the process through which the silkworm becomes a butterfly. Having posed the question in the 'Introduction', the rest of the performance is comprised out of three plateaus that essentially offer an answer. Interestingly, while we can

---

6. The 'υ' sounds like an 'i' in 'milk'.

Figure 4: The group of performers representing Teiresias; All the performers have earphones on their eyes and they offer a pair to the female performer representing Oedipus. After she places them on her eyes a blinding light will flood the stage. Photograph by Georges Bacoust.

easily observe with a naked eye all other stages of the life of a silk worm, the 'metamorphosis' process is hidden in the cocoon. And it is that which we cannot see with naked eyes that the performance is attempting to present as a process. This way of seeing was re-invented (as it is presented, for example, in Plateau III – the meeting with Teiresias) through a different way of experiencing what lies hidden inside: one that obliterates the dualism in/out and transcends our usual ways of experiencing through seeing and hearing.

In Plateau III, Teiresias is presented as a 'choral crowd'. The piece of music that accompanies this scene was built on a line from Sophocles' *Oedipus Rex*, in which Oedipus (ironically) tells Teiresias: 'τυφλός τα τ'ωτα τον τε νουν τα τ'όμματ'ει' ('You are blind in the ears, in the mind and in the eyes'). The phrase is most well known because of the strong degree of tragic irony it encapsulates, but also because of the very strong assonance of the 'τ'.[7] In

---

7. The letter 'τ' translates to a 't' in English, but the actual corresponding sound is something between a 't' and a 'd'.

fact, in this line, the consonant 'τ' is paired with almost all the vowel sounds of the Greek language. The accompanying piece of music resulted from improvisation sessions in which the performers were asked to begin with producing vocal sounds based on the consonant 'τ' (with its different pairings with vowels) and gradually to move to a section where the vowels were used alone. The vowels in this new section corresponded to the notes of the first two introductory chords of the 'Presto' section. However, this time all of the notes were presented together. In the resulting composition of the improvisations, the goal was that there was neither a protruding melodic line nor a sense of a harmonic movement. While there was a definite sense of movement, it happened through the change in intensities and timbres along with the change in vowels: the notes feel like they are suspended in an ocean of sound. This piece accompanies the entrance of the multiplicity 'Teiresias' (represented by a group of performers – again based on the notion of the 'dividual') and 'its' meeting with Oedipus (who is now represented by a female performer). The blinding of the natural eyes happens through a way that points to an alternative way of seeing: she 'blinds' herself by placing earphones on her eyes (see figure 4). Teiresias 'sees' what others cannot see, because s/he can hear through the eyes. It is this alternative way of seeing that Deleuze's theory, and by extension the performance, is asking the audience to embrace.

> Paul Klee says that the object of painting is not to render the visible – to reproduce visual entities – but to *render visible*, to make visible that which is not visible, the forces that play through the visible.
>
> (Bogue 2003: 44)

This appears as a doctrine of modernism according to Deleuze and Guattari and it can be said to hold true in any field of the post-romantic era: poetry, music, theatre etc. If the goal of art were to render visible the invisible, then the goal of 'music-theatre as music' would be to render audible the invisible (as well as visible the inaudible). This is the importance of this meeting with 'Teiresias': his mind (νους) is not blind (τυφλός) because (unlike Oedipus, at this stage) he is not trying to see things with his eyes. He knows how to hear things with his eyes and see things with his ears. In effect, this section represents the overall aim: the composition of a performance where sound (music) is used to present the audience with a form of 'deterritorialised' seeing and the visual is used to allow a 'deterritorialised' form of hearing.

Final thoughts

In the Prologue of this article I stated that my research centres around two principle questions: How can we use non-logocentric musical models in order to create a music-theatre performance? How can we use music as an organising principle so that all compositional choices are derived from these specific conceptual/musical models? Deleuze and Guattari certainly offer a non-logocentric conceptualisation of music which provided the theoretical basis upon which the performance was formed. While this article is by no means an exhaustive account of all the processes that took place, I tried to exemplify some of the most important ones derived from Deleuze and Guattari's notion of music as a 'becoming' and the wider philosophical implications suggested by their notion of the rhizome.

To recapitulate, then, the three main processes that I have described are:

- Reconceptualising the myths under investigation based on ideas that Deleuze and Guattari provide in their discussion of music (the 'becoming-molecular' of the mythical texts; the 'subtraction' process, in order to re-imagine the myths musically through the creation of a 'refrain'; the 'transcoding', in order to obliterate the notion of binaries in the conceptualisation of the myths).
- Composing and De-composing Music as a driving force in the creation of the theatrical event (the use of the 'refrain' and the generation of material for presentation; the use of the 'Dividual', in order to utilise the 'refrain' in a way that we surpass the issue of binaries not only in the re-conceptualisation of the myths but also in the presentation).
- Practically approaching the notion of form as process ('the diagram' as a creative tool that is formed through the use of an 'accident').

The embedding of the theoretical background in my practical exploration allows one thing to surface: the use of musical strategies *alone* in the organisation of a music-theatre performance is not enough to achieve a 'theatre as music'. To achieve this goal we need to go a step further: we need to extrapolate those musical strategies of organising theatrical material from specific *music-centric conceptual models*. This is something that I proposed at the beginning of this article not only as an outcome of this particular performance project but as a more general outcome of my practice-based research into what I thus-far called 'music-centric' music theatre. This belief led me to turn to Deleuze and Guattari and use their notion of music as a 'becoming', which is part of their more general conceptual model. This was done in such a way that the utilisation of musical strategies of organisation adheres to (or is, in fact, extracted from) the theoretical backbone and uses it as a driving force in the creation of the performance. Through Deleuze and Guattari's notion of music as a 'becoming' and the different ways it was used to compose the performance (visually and aurally), I have reached the conclusion that the creation of a theatre performance 'as music' is attainable in the sense of music-theatre as 'a becoming-music'. In other words, even if music-theatre can never in actuality *be* music, it can be perceived as such in its 'becoming-music'; a 'becoming' that (like every 'becoming') may not be actual, but is real. It is through the Deleuzian concept of the 'becoming', then, that I can approach this understanding of the term 'music-theatre as music' and suggest the alternative term 'music-theatre as a 'becoming-music'.

Acknowledgements

I would like to thank my Ph.D. supervisors Dr George Rodosthenous and Prof Jonathan Pitches for their ongoing support and help with the preparation of my thesis, which served as the starting point for this article.

References

Boal, A. (1995) *Theatre of the Oppressed* (trans. Charles, A. and McBride, M. L.), London: Pluto Press.

Bogue, R. (2003) *Deleuze on Music, Painting, and the* Arts, London: Routledge.

Buchanan, I. and Swiboda M. (2006) *Deleuze and Music*, Edinburgh: Edinburgh University Press Ltd.

Deleuze G. and Guattari, F. (2007) *A Thousand Plateaus (Capitalism and Schizophrenia)* (trans. Massumi, B.), London: Continuum.

Deleuze, G. (2005) *Francis Bacon: The Logic of Sensation* (trans. Smith, D. W.), University of Minnesota Press.

Echard, W. (2006) "Sensible Virtual Selves: Bodies, Instruments and the Becoming-concrete of Music", *Contemporary Music Review*, 25: 1/2, pp. 7–16.

Kowsar, M. (1986) "Deleuze on Theatre: A Case Study of Carmelo Bene's 'Richard III'", *Theatre Journal*, 38: 1, pp. 19–33.

Leach, E. (1982) *Lévi-Strauss*, Glasgow: William Collins Sons & Co. Ltd.

Lehmann, H. (2006) *Postdramatic Theatre*, Wiltshire: The Cromwell Press.

Lévi-Strauss, C. (1970) *The Raw and the Cooked* (trans. Weightman, J. and Weightman, D.), London: Cape.

Varopoulou, E. (2002) *Το Ζωντανό Θέατρο: Δοκίμιο για τη σύγχρονη σκηνή*, Athens: Εκδόσεις Άγρα.

Zavros, D. (2008) "Flooding the *concrète: Clastoclysm* and the notion of the 'continuum' as a conceptual and musical basis for a postdramatic music-theatre performance", *Studies in Musical Theatre*, 2:1, pp. 83–100.

Part III

Processes and Practices: Portraits and Analyses

Chapter 11

'Ça devient du théâtre, mais ça vient de la musique': The Music Theatre of Georges Aperghis

Matthias Rebstock

G eorges Aperghis is certainly one of the most prominent, influential and active figures in the field of Composed Theatre. Especially in the late seventies and the eighties he determined the genre of the *théâtre musical* in France in a way that today this term seems to be directly linked with the name of Aperghis.[1] And even though today Aperghis has reduced his work within the *théâtre musical* to give more space to concert music it still can be seen as anchor of his whole Œuvre and a lot of the features of his working process spread from his experiences in music theatre to his concert pieces – and back again.

To grasp the aesthetics of the music theatre of Aperghis is a difficult task as the only constant element in his work is the constant search for new ways, new possibilities, new adventures, is a great dynamics with which he explores and combines what even might at first look like antipodes. There is – different from Heiner Goebbels, for example – nothing like a certain working method Aperghis would try to follow, no wish to work under the same preconditions or circumstances twice. But there are some basic assumptions and convictions that shine through the different pieces and often enough there is a certain tension between these "regles du jeu" (see Durney 1990), so there is always a rest that doesn't seem to fit, that you cannot explain or grasp, just as in his pieces.

Early experiences with music and theatre

Aperghis' way to his personal style of music theatre is as interesting as it is revealing for his further career. Born in Athens he grew up in an artistic ambiance. Both his parents were fine artists and for a long time Aperghis was uncertain whether to follow his artistic or his musical talents. In 1963 the 18-year-old Aperghis went to Paris where he has lived and worked since. Actually, coming to continue his studies in music, right from the beginning he got in touch with the theatre scene of Paris. Among others he met the actress Edith Scob, whom he later married, and became close friends with the theatre writer Arthur Adamov and the director Antoine Vitez. On the other hand he devoted himself to composition but never enrolled at Conservatory. He followed the concert series of Pierre Boulez, the

---

1. See Gammel 2002: 7. And different from the English 'music theatre' and the German 'Musiktheater', which are both rather wide and unspecific. The French 'théâtre musical' is interwoven with the concept of contemporary music. See Hahn 2008: 9.

Domaine Musical, and was deeply impressed by a performance of *Sur Scène* in 1964, one of the first pieces of the Instrumental Theatre by Mauricio Kagel. In 1971 he presented his first music theatre piece, *La Tragique histoire du nécromancien Hieronimo et de son miroir* at the Festival in Avignon. 1973, also at the Festival of Avignon that had become a kind of artistic home for Aperghis in those early years, he premiered his first opera *Pandaemonium* and in 1976 a second: *Histoire de loups*.

But not enough writing for both the théâtre musical and the opera Aperghis also wrote music for theatre plays working regularly and very closely with Antoine Vitez and the set designer Yannis Kokkos. So Aperghis is one of the very few composers of his generation who have worked in all three fields of music theatre (excluding the musical) and who got to know the different working methods, the different ways of producing, the different institutional contexts and, last but not least, the different compositional possibilities, challenges and demands the different genres offer.

Moving in these different fields between music and theatre Aperghis started to develop his own visions for the kind of music theatre he wanted to explore: "I have always dreamed of creating a working space where actors, musicians and painters can work together on projects and explore the relationships between music, theatre, painting and film" (Aperghis 2001: 156, translation M. R.) In 1976 Aperghis got the chance to realise this vision. With subsidies of the *Ministry of Culture* and the *Festival d'automne* he and his wife Edith Scob founded *l'Atelier Théâtre et Musique (ATEM)*, first in the suburbs of Paris, later hosted at the *Théatre des Amandiers* in Nanterre. And it was only after 20 years of directing *ATEM* that he left in 1997.[2]

With the work at *ATEM* Aperghis' approach to music theatre changed radically. Looking back from today Aperghis describes two topics he wanted to explore in his work with *ATEM*, topics that determine his aesthetics up till now:

> Le travail était comment trouver un autre genre de personnage qui ne sont pas des personnages de Tchekhov, mais qui sont des personnages musicaux. Donc il y a un accent rythmique, une intensité de couleur particulière. Voilà des personnages qui existent comme ça, par une intensité différente. Et ça devient du théâtre, mais ça vient de la musique. Et l'autre problème était – venant alors de l'opéra – comment est-ce qu'on peux mettre sur le même plan la voix, les éclairages, l'installation, le son et le texte – ou pas texte –, musique – ou pas musique –, musique visuelle et tout ça. Il y a donc une hiérarchie à l'opéra. C'est une pyramide en fait, avec un texte qui est mis en scène par la musique, qui est ensuite mis en scène par un metteur en scène, et tout ça converge pour faire un objet unique autour d'un seul texte et avec des situations théâtrales comme dans le théâtre classique en fait. Donc, comment libérer tous les éléments et essayer de

---

2. Since then it was run by his companion Antoine Gindt.

faire une autre syntaxe qui n'a rien à voir avec une histoire unique mais qui a plusieurs histoires, qui est polyphonique.[3]

And in addition to these Aesthetic concerns, the searching for musical characters and for a non-hierarchical way of organisation of the theatrical elements, there was also a strong social or even political aspect to his work at *ATEM*:

C'était quelques années après 1968 donc c'était une utopie. Mais il n'y avait pas un intermédiaire entre l'artiste et le public. Là, il y avait un public qui ne connaissait pas du tout le théâtre, qui connaissait la télévision, et c'est tout. Alors, qu'est-ce qui se passe s'il y a des gens qui travaillent sur le théâtre et la musique, comment ça se passe? C'était la question. Et c'était très intéressant parce qu'il y avait des ateliers d'amateurs, des vieux, des petits, et ça a créé un public en fait.[4]

The social aspect of his work in that explicit way has certainly become less important since Aperghis has stopped his work at l'ATEM. But it gave rise to two more threads that have kept to characterise his whole work: on the one hand his interest to work together with other people and his curiosity to get to know them, to discover their abilities and to challenge them; and on the other the experience with what one could call *oral composition*:

C'était pour moi très important que c'était des acteurs parce que je ne voulais pas me cacher derrière une facilité musicale où je pourrais écrire des choses musicales. Mais je voulais simplifier pour faire un travail oral comme au théâtre, et dicter la musique juste

---

3. "The task was how to find a different kind of character who would not be like Chekhov's characters but rather more like musical characters. That means there is a rhythmical accent, an intensity of particular colours – so there are characters that exist of nothing but a special intensity. And that becomes theatre, but it comes from music. And the other problem was – coming from writing for the opera – how is it possible to put the different elements on the same level, the voice, the lights, the stage, the sound and the text – or even no text, music – or even no music, visual music and all that. In opera there is a certain hierarchy. It is basically like a pyramid, with a text that gets presented by the music in a certain way that is scenically presented by a stage director, and all this comes together to create a single object, around a single text and with theatrical situations as in classical theatre. So the question was how to free all these elements and try to build a different kind of syntax that has nothing to do with a single story, but one that produces different stories, that is polyphonic" (Aperghis 2010).
4. "That was a few years after 1968, so that was an utopia. But in those days there was no intermediary between artists and the public. There was a public that did not know the theatre at all, that only knew the TV and that was it. So what would happen if there were people who were working on theatre, on music with them, how could that happen. That was the question. And that was very interesting because there were workshops with amateurs, with elderly people, with children and that actually built a new audience" (Aperghis 2010).

par cœur parce que les acteurs ne lisaient pas la musique. Pour moi ça a été un travail très, très difficile. Un acteur n'est pas un musicien mais un acteur. Il faut arriver à lui faire sortir la musique ou le théâtre par lui-même, avec lui, qu'il fasse tout un travail intérieur. Le musicien lit la partition et ca va.[5]

These topics form the core of Aperghis' aesthetics and in the following I will explore them in further detail. At the same time they seem to be essential for the whole field of Composed Theatre, even though each composer will find different answers to the same questions.

'C'est la musique qui amènet le theatre'

One prerequisite for the kind of theatre that Aperghis strives for, one that retains its musical nature, is that characters and narratives should not be classifiable within existing schemata. Characters should not be psychologically legible, and narratives should not be contiguous in a conventional logical way.

Je ne parle pas des situation théâtrales. Ca ne m'intéresse pas. Mais il faut faire une sorte de personnage, de musique que quelqu'un joue ou chante – qu'est-ce que j'écris pour lui amener l'idée d'un personnage vague, abstrait ou parfois pas précis – qui se contredit et change. Mais je n'ai pas envie que les gens jouent du théâtre. Je suis content si la musique et le travail qu'on fait ensemble les amènent à exister de manière très forte. Et on est touché par l'énergie ou la qualité de ce qu'ils font. Mais mon effort, c'est qu'on ne sait jamais ce qu'ils font vraiment. On peut approcher un peu mais quand on sait, on n'écoute plus la musique. Si on dit: 'Ah bien ! C'est ça !', c'est fini. Les gens rentrent les antennes et c'est fini.[6]

---

5. "For me it was very important that they were actors because I did not want to hide behind a musical ability, where I could write musical things. I wanted to simplify in order to make an oral work, like in theatre, and dictate the music only by heart because the actors could not read music. For me that was a very, very difficult task. An actor is not a musician but an actor. You have to come to the point where the music or the theatre originates from him, with him doing enormous inner work on his own. The musician reads the score and that's it" (Aperghis 2010).
6. "I don't mean theatrical situations. That doesn't interest me. But you have to do it in a way that the music, that some one plays or sings – that what I write for him – that that carries the vague idea of a character, abstract and often imprecise, that is contradictory, that changes. But I don't want them to play theatre. I am happy if the music and the work we do together makes them exist in a very strong manner and if one is touched by this energy or quality of what they do. But my aim is that one never really knows what it is that they are doing. You can come a bit closer but if you knew, you would stop listening to the music. If you say: 'Ok, this is that', it's all over. People pull in their antennae and that's it" (Aperghis 2010).

Aperghis' rejection of theatre and theatrical situations is shaped by a more classical idea of the theatre. Nevertheless, this passage is of particular interest because it suggests how Aperghis' approach may be differentiated from forms of Postdramatic Theatre (Lehmann 1999) as well as the anti-psychological approaches of the twentieth-century avant-garde, for example, Edward Gordon Craig or Oskar Schlemmer's Bauhaus stage studio or other forms of abstract or mechanical theatre. These theatrical forms also push back the basic theatrical principles of psychological characters and logically sequential narration, focussing instead on the performativity of actions. And in this context, it is revealing that Lehmann repeatedly highlights the trend towards the musicalisation of contemporary theatre. Yet Aperghis is not concerned with the renewal of theatrical language – thinking it from the problems of classical theatre – but rather with enabling listening in the theatre, that is to transport the audience into a musical perception mode. And this musical perception mode is disturbed by characters and actions that are immediately comprehensible and classifiable because one involuntarily switches to a perception mode that tries to *understand* what is perceived, that looks for psychological coherence, reasons and causes and brings it under concepts instead of focussing on what is perceived as such, on its phenomenological qualities. For Aperghis, making the theatre musical is not a means to an end, but rather an end in itself; it is about making the musical organisation of elements – and that is what music comes down to – truly available to apperception. Musical structures need not compensate for the possible lack of coherence that results from dispensing with the context previously supplied by narration. Instead, the dissolution of narrative allows the basic musical character and musical syntax of Aperghis' theatre to unfold and reach the surface of the audience's perception. Meaning as the goal of the theatre experience is not simply suspended; it is splintered into a kaleidoscope and placed as an assignment, a challenge, to each individual audience member.

> We cannot do anything other than impart meaning to things, and that's what I find interesting: how the audience can understand something even before it reaches their consciousness. What has it understood? The whole thing works as long as the viewer's mind is telling itself stories. You have to hold their attention for one and a half hours; they have to tell themselves stories constantly without me telling one.
>
> (Aperghis in Singer 2001, translation MR)

In order to achieve this openness and plurality of possible horizons of meaning, and not a theatre of 'histoire unique', it is not only necessary to avoid clear contexts of meaning; one must also load the different elements with proposals of meaning. And that is precisely how Aperghis views his work as a composer.

> If the interpretive possibilities are so multifaceted that I can no longer control them, then I stop writing because I have managed to understand something different each time I read the score. In the final analysis, one has to build something that is very abstract.
>
> (Aperghis in Singer 2001, translation MR)

Another motif appears to surface here that is typical of Apherghis' working process: he constantly seeks a position from which he can encounter his compositions from the outside, as a reader or performer, in order to find something that he has not yet seen: something that is hiding in the music, in the score, without him being aware of it during the writing process.

> On entend des choses, on se dit, mais c'est pas possible que ces choses étaient dans cette musique-là. On la croyait gaie, par exemple, et voilà une musique terrible. Ou l'inverse. [...] Ça m'excite beaucoup de voir une musique qui change d'aspect, et du coup, ça me donne des idées de *mise en scène*, de mouvement ou de jeu. Et donc ça fait une espèce de boule de neige en fait, par-ce qu' un élément amène un autre. Et il y a tout ça qui joue ensemble.[7]

For Aperghis, psychology is circumvented in three ways: the figures of his musical theatre do not comply with psychologically motivated patterns of signification; Aperghis attempts to touch upon an understanding that precedes the conscious act of comprehension; and he himself tries to locate in his compositions that which has made it past his conscious control and been inscribed into the music.

Independence of elements

Aperghis has developed a fundamental conviction from his experiences with *ATEM*, among others, that remains unassailable to the present day:

> The visual elements should not be allowed to reinforce or emphasise the music, and the music should not be allowed to underline the narrative. Things must complement themselves; they must have different natures. This is an important rule for me: never say the same thing twice. [...] Another thing has to emerge that is neither one nor the other; it is something new.
>
> (Aperghis in Singer 2001, translation MR)

The individual elements should remain independent of one another and self-sufficient – meaning not in the service of illustrating another element – as well as related to one another. This approach has nothing to do with the unrelated juxtaposition of various events that we know

---

7. "You hear something and you say to yourself: that's impossible that this acually is in that music. You thought it was, let's say, happy and the music turns out to be furious. Or the other way round. I find that very exciting to see a music changing its aspects, and all of a sudden, that gives me ideas for the scenic part, for movements or playing. And that's like throwing a snowball as one thing is coming to another. And all that plays together." Interview with Georges Aperghis by Marcus Gammel, Strasbourg, 10 February 2002 (in Gammel 2002).

from the works of Cage. The musical model here is polyphony. When we speak of polyphony and counterpoint, we are not speaking in a purely metaphorical manner; rather, we are describing precisely the point at which the organisation of heterogeneity according to musical principles comes into play: tempo, rhythm, colour, density, direction, variation, morphogenesis of motifs, repetition, movement types, etc. are categories according to which different materials can be structured and set in relation to one another. Aperghis structures his musical theatre at a level that has nothing to do with the content or the dimension of meaning. It does not revolve around the question – a typical one for (traditional) theatre – of 'what should be narrated', a question that provides orientation for material and structure, but rather the reverse: to build up a complex structure that is so loaded with potential meanings that the viewer can – and must – distil his own stories from it. This is also what the phrase 'la musique amène le theatre' means.[8]

This aesthetic programme is inherent within Aperghis' individual pieces. But there is no piece in which it was actually so schematically and completely realised as I have just described it. Music (understood as the organisation of sounds and noises) stands fundamentally in the foreground for Aperghis. Unlike in Goebbels' or Tsangaris' works, there are relatively few moments that are completely determined by visual or scenic action in which the musical dimension is fully absent. The beginning of the piece *Zeugen* (*Witnesses*, Witten 2007), with hand puppets by Paul Klee and texts by Robert Walser, is all the more striking for this. The piece begins in absolute silence, and the audience sees nothing other than the slow, macroscopic movement of a video camera over the planks of the puppet stage, relayed to a projection screen above as a strange, inhospitable landscape. The music abruptly begins after over two minutes. More often, there are passages in his pieces in which text is simply spoken, as semantic islands in a polyphonic flow of signs, so to speak.

The working process begins most often with musical compositions that – in contrast to the early years at *ATEM* – are written down as scores. Aperghis frequently makes use of the fragment form. For his children's musical theatre *Le Petit Chaperon Rouge* (Cologne 2001), for example, he initially composed 23 'extraits': individual short pieces that, although they had some relationship to one another, did not have a set sequential arrangement and did not correspond to the final version of the piece. It is typical for Aperghis that these fragments are not composed for the subject of the related piece and have neither a clear beginning nor end:[9]

---

8. What is striking here is the way in which a certain tension is articulated: on one hand, the elements should remain self-sufficient. And that would also mean that they must be constructed according to their own logic and rules. On the other hand, the overall structure of all of the elements follows an *organisation musicale*, meaning that they are subjugated to musical principles. Marcus Gammel has found an appropriate way to describe this tension: "The structure of [Aperghis'] pieces is determined by musical principles, without the music dominating the other elements" (Gammel 2002: 9).

9. However, even in this first phase of composition, Aperghis is always clear about the people for whom he is writing. I will return later to the significance of the performers in the compositional process of Aperghis.

Le but est que la musique soit indépendante, qu'elle n'ait pas à raconter quelque chose de la pièce, qu'elle existe pour elle-même. Et si après il y a le choc avec le texte, c'est là où elle devient le théâtre. Mais si la musique change le texte, ça fait un autre théâtre. La musique n'est pas colorée au début pour jouer tel ou tel rôle. C'est du matériel sonore.[10]

This 'shock', in which the variously prepared materials collide, occurs at the rehearsals. Aperghis then works together with the musicians and/or performers to develop the piece out of what emerges from this collision – some 'third entity' – so that the musical 'extraits' also find their place and their final form within the overall musical structure. Accordingly, Aperghis considers it his task during rehearsals to discover what the fragments 'want':

La difficulté, c'est d'identifier l'interet de chaque fragment. Sachant qu'un fragment tout seul n'existe pas, qu'il n'existe que dans une syntax. Ensuite il faut déterminer à partir de quel moment un fragment se met à vivre. À respirer. À quel moment il peut se confronter à une autre. Un fragment est faible et tout de suite avalé par ceux qui sont autour.[11]

On one hand, the form of the fragment has a technical compositional rationale. Long, self-contained musical compositions cannot be integrated in an open and equal conflict with other materials at rehearsal, leading to the imposition of hierarchy from the beginning. The fragment as a form however has an ideological aspect that only finds its equivalent at the level of procedure:

I don't believe – how should I say this – in a world where harmony and coherence of thought rule the day. I don't see any connections between things. That doesn't interest me. I believe more in small fragments, pieces of life, that randomly come into contact.

(Aperghis in Maximoff 2006)

Unlike, for example, Heiner Goebbels, who after a phase of intensive rehearsal and improvisation backs out and composes the piece alone, this phase of Aperghis' composition, in which different materials are brought into relationships with each other and create a compositional form, can only be done in rehearsal with the collaboration of participating musicians and performers. Sometimes, this last stage of composition is not even written into a score; instead, it is based

---

10. "The goal is that the music is independent. That it does not need to tell something of the piece. That it exists just for itself. And when later it comes to the shock with the text, then it becomes theatre. But if one changes the text it becomes a different theatre. The music is not made from the beginning to play such and such a role. It is just sound material" (Aperghis 2010).

11. "The challenge is to find out what's the interest of each fragment. Knowing that a fragment never exists alone, that it only exists within a syntax. Then, you have to find the point when it starts to be alive. To breath. At which moment can it be confronted with another fragment. A fragment is weak and easily swallowed by the others around it" (Aperghis in Houdart 2007: 60).

on agreements and intensive rehearsal work, similar to a theatrical working process.[12] This phase recalls the techniques of oral composition and can be traced directly to the experiences at *ATEM*. In the context of the composition of the various extraits in *Le Petit Chaperon Rouge*, this process is particularly evident in the sextet, which is performed as concluding music in accordance with the moral of the fairy tale, before the piece starts from the beginning again with the repetition of the beginning text.[13] Yet there is no sextet in the musical fragments that Aperghis brought with him to the rehearsals. The sextet arose from two other overlapping fragments that are both played in their original form in the final score, namely as the duet for two pianos that stands in the first place in the fragments and is played in the score at the letter *F*, and the quartet for two clarinets, saxophone and violin, which is on page 26 in the 'extraits' and is located in the score beginning at the letter *I*.

This compositional process can also be observed in *Machinations* (2000) for four women,[14] electronics and video. The piece is distinguished by a powerfully stage setting: the four performers sit in a row at small tables. They produce a music that is comprised solely of phonemes. At the same time, they are working with small objects on the tables, and these are being filmed by a mini-camera and projected onto a projection screen above each performer. The objects are simple and primarily organic things: leaves, bark, hair, seeds, the performers' own hands, etc. Across from them, Olivier Pasquet – no accident that he is a man – stands behind his computers and operates the live electronics, which work exclusively with material from the female vocalists, collecting, alienating and thereby manipulating the voices (and perhaps the women). A text by François Regnault is woven throughout the piece, "a kind of time travel that begins with the game of dice and, through various stages, leads to the programs of our contemporary computers" (Aperghis in Polzer and Schäfer 2001). The first step in the composition of *Machinations* was the composition of individual phonetic texts for the four women. These texts were also composed without regard to staging or subject. The second step consisted of rehearsals with the four women in which the texts were read and assigned to the performers. Only after this did Aperghis ask François Regnault for a text that could provide a brief history of devices up to the computer. This means that the semantic context in which the music of language and phonemes would surface in the performance was determined in retrospect, independent of the musical material. Aperghis pursued the same process for the electronic music, first making recordings with the performers and then using these recordings as the basis for electronic processing. He then returned to the rehearsals with these electronic recordings and worked on the overall structure together with the performers. The stage arrangement first developed in this final rehearsal phase.

---

12. For example, the majority of the score of *Le Petit Chaperon Rouge*, currently in print with *Durand* publishers, was prepared by Marcus Gammel, not by Aperghis himself.
13. Letter 'W' in the score. I am grateful to Marcus Gammel for granting me permission to view the original fragments.
14. Sylvie Levesque, Donatienne Michel-Dansac, Sylvie Sacoun and Geneviève Strosser.

These two examples allow us to discern another important feature of Aperghis' aesthetics that seems symptomatic for Composed Theatre in general: there is no separation between composition and staging. Or, to put it differently, the creation of relationships between the various elements of the theatre, such as music, text, action, crafting audiovisual connections and the development of the overall structure, does not fall under staging as it would in classical opera; instead, the creation of correlations between these elements is an important part of composition itself. Aperghis extends the compositional process into the rehearsal process, including the entire path to performance.[15] The entire score of the piece is not the point of departure, as it is in classical productions, it is the end point. Only after going through the entire process does the score arrive at its fixed result. Up to that point, notation serves to fuse together the musical material, meaning the individual 'extraits'.

In this way, composition touches to an important extent on what the performers bring to the piece. In *Machinations*, for example, Aperghis largely left the selection of visual objects to the performers: "Ils ont aussi beaucoup amené sur le plan visuel, parce que tous les accessoires, tous les objets – je leur ai demandé d'amener ce qu'ils veulent. Ces sont que des choses d'eux. Ces sont des choses que j'ai jamais imaginé."[16] This also shows on one hand how Aperghis takes seriously the people with whom he works, and on the other hand how he allows himself to be surprised by material that emerges in this way and to a certain degree how he deals with his own conscious control of the material.

If composition is related to the (musical) organisation of all elements of the theatre, in which composition includes working with the staging material, it would be obvious that this would also be reflected in the scores. One would expect that – as for example with Mauricio Kagel – stage actions, passages, spatial dispositions etc. would be notated in the score. But Aperghis only does this in rare exceptional cases.[17] For the most part, the scores contain only the music and the text. In *Le Petit Chaperon Rouge*, for example, alongside the music and the text, there is no information what so ever that points to the visual dimension of the piece. Even the tuba and the tap shoes, which play a major role in Aperghis' production of the premiere, are not in the score. In *Machinations*, the score only contains the texts and the cue points for the electronic music; everything else remains open. Aperghis, who is a great admirer of Kagel, clearly draws from his experiences with Kagel's works: "C'est dommage

---

15. For example, Manos Tsangaris would have pursued the opposite strategy: the staging would have already been predetermined to a certain degree in the act of composition. The score would allow scarcely more latitude for the scenic than for the musical elements, meaning that the interpretative scope of the scenic part would be reduced to the interpretive scope that scores always permit for musical interpretation.
16. "They are also very much involved in the visual aspect of the piece, because all these accessories and all these objects – I asked them to bring with them what they liked. These are their things, things I never would have imagined on my own" (Aperghis 2010).
17. For example in *Sept crimes de l'amour*. Here, odd basic physical positions are written for the three performers. For each of the seven pieces one position is to be maintained throughout.

qu'il n'y ait pas la possibilité pour chaque interprète d'un peu tout respirer. Ca m'a donc beaucoup conforté avec l'idée de ne pas écrire dans ce sens là. Moi, je suis aussi maniaque que Kagel mais je laisse des paramètres ouverts."[18]

This desire to avoid specifying stage components in the score is associated once again with the special relationship to the performers:

> Le corps d'un acteur ou d'un musicien et sa façon de se tenir, ses intérêts, sa vie, son passé et tout ca, c'est très important pour moi. L'action n'est donc pas la même si c'est Jean Paul Drouet ou Françoise Rivalland qui joue par exemple. C'est complètement différent pour moi. Pour moi, c'est toujours très important de partir des gens qui sont là. En fait, je n'aime pas écrire en général. Alors une fois, c'est écrit, et après je fais confiance aux gens qui suivent.[19]

Viewed analytically, Aperghis' approach holds a certain contradiction: what does a certain composition consist of? What are its conditions of identity? If the scenic part were an essential component of a composition, then, strictly speaking, it would be impossible to choose a completely different stage production for a new performance of the piece in which the relationship between music, text and action could be completely different. The scenic part necessarily becomes just as much a component of the piece as the music itself.[20] If the staging or the scenic part, however, is not essential for the composition, then the argument for balance between the theatrical elements and their interplay within a musical structure cannot be maintained in a strict sense. And the example of Kagel actually demonstrates that – at least in some of the early works of his Instrumental Theatre – he used a similar rehearsal process as Aperghis. The scenic part of *Sur Scène*, for example, was done initially in collaboration and testing with the performers. The difference is that afterwards Kagel wrote down the found version exactly, thereby making it binding. Kagel does this not only to determine the character of future performances, but also to secure the status of an artwork of his scenic compositions. Only stable conditions of identity that are fixed in the score

---

18. "It is a pity that none of the players has the chance to breathe a little bit. So this confirmed my idea not to write in this sense. I am just as manic as Kagel, but I leave some parameters open" (Aperghis 2010).
19. "The body of an actor or a musician and the way he behaves, his interests, his life, his past and all that, this is all very important to me. So a certain action is not the same when Jean Paul Drouet or Françoise Rivalland performs it, for example. That's completely different for me. For me it is always very important to start with the people that are there. Actually I don't like to write in an impersonal way. But once it is written, I have confidence to other people that will follow" (Aperghis 2010).
20. The line of demarcation in question here does not run simply between the music described in the score and the staging (as in opera). Instead, the music owes its structure – as described above – to the process of developing the musical *and* the scenic part. The music therefore bears the traces of the scenic work, although this is not represented in the score itself.

guarantee the work's individual character (see Rebstock 2006: 310). Aperghis, in contrast, does not assign much value to such theoretical or even ontological considerations. He views his compositions as a processes; for him, his pieces are not closed or finished objects. They are written for the moment of performance. And new performances, new performers, new spaces etc. may necessitate changes for new performances.[21] "It's free: you can make a new version, another stage, etc. I like that. The first time I am happy to make that because it is part of my work of the composition. But after it's ok" (Aperghis 2010).

Immanent and imaginary theatre

In addition to the polyphony of elements, there is another form of theatricality in Aperghis' works that arises directly from the musical gesture of composition and is therefore immanent in the music itself. This form is found not only in the explicitly musical-theatrical works, but also in his instrumental music and especially in his vocal music. Of central concern here is the virtuosity of Aperghis' music. The vocal works in particular require a special physicality, a physical energy, to master their enormous difficulty, an act that inherently ventures into the territory of the theatrical. Accordingly, the *Quatorze Jactations* (2001), a collection of 14 solo works for baritone that Aperghis wrote for Lionel Peintre, are described in the program notes as 'théâtre vocal', although explicitly there is no theatrical layer composed:

> I am attempting to collect a number of phonemes or sounds until I get a texture that, when they are spoken or played, are no longer just music after a certain point; I hope that they lead to a comportment (*comportement*). It only works with a certain kind of energy, in a certain situation, a physical condition.
>
> (Aperghis in Maximoff 2006)

This type of theatricality is based on the performativity of vocal and instrumental actions. It is composed in the sense that it is evoked by the musical text. It is not composed in the aforementioned sense of a polyphony of elements, because it cannot be understood as self-sufficient material and accordingly cannot be expressly arranged but has to stay immanent: "Si tu as besoin de bouger pour respirer et chanter, tu le fait. Mais il ne faut pas le faire consciemment. Si c'est conscient où tu commences à jouer un truc, là, c'est fini."[22]

The immanent theatricality of the *Jactations* is not based solely on these 'comportements', but rather on the type of composed texts, namely a special form of composition with

---

21. In his work, Marcus Gammel shows how *Le Petit Chaperon Rouge* has changed from performance to performance, at both the scenic and musical levels. See Gammel 2002: 15.
22. "If you need to move in order to breathe and sing, then do it. But you should not do it consciously. If it is conscious, or if you start to play something, it's finished" (Aperghis 2010).

phonemes, that has become a red thread in Aperghis' entire oeuvre since 1976. This unique kind of music of language appears for the first time in his opera *Histoire de Loups*, which deals with Freud's *Wolf Man*:

> [L]'homme était russe. Freud était Viennois. […] Et donc, c'était là que j'ai commencé à fabriquer des syllabes qui ne voulaient rien dire mais qui me donnaient la couleur russe et la couleur allemande. Et c'est ça qui m'a donné après l'idée que ces syllabes pourraient fabriquer des mélodies. Pas des mélodies de sons, […] mais des mélodies de syllabes, des couleurs de syllabes. Et donc j'ai commencé comme ça.[23]

The first work to be based entirely on this new compositional form were the *Quatorze Récitations pour voix seul* (1978) for female voices, which were the prototype, so to speak, for the *Quatorze Jactations* for male voices. These compositions are among the most popular pieces of New Music in France. In these works, phonemes that resemble French, German and English sounds are invented and combined, yet without making any sense; and, unlike the *Histoire de Loups*, without any thematic context. Existing words and syllables are mixed in among the imaginary images. The listener always believes that they have extracted a certain amount of meaning that does not actually exist. The audience member attempts, with this hermeneutic attitude towards listening, to *understand* the music like a language, but collides again and again with the syllables' pure tonality and colourfulness. This desire to understand, to comprehend, coupled with the inability to do so, ensures the 'open ears' with which the listener inevitably must follow the *Récitations*. At the same time, the listener begins to associate meanings through the Fata Morgana of semantics. And together with the rhythmic gestural character that Aperghis imparts to this music of language, the great physicality that the work's virtuosity demands of the (female) vocalist, small scenes appear before the mind's eyes or ears of the audience. A kind of imaginary theatre is created. The audience begins to narrate stories, each to their own, even though a story is not being performed. The clue is that the singer must remain completely immersed in the music for this imaginary theatre:

> The problem is that it can become too precise. That people think, 'oh yes, they're shouting at each other…' When you come to such a conclusion, then you aren't listening anymore. Then you aren't listening to every individual sound. As long as you are constantly scrutinising the whole event, the ears are unlocked and listening.
>
> (Aperghis in Maximoff 2006).

---

23. "This man was Russian. Freud was from Vienna […] So it was then, that I began to build syllables that didn't want to mean anything anymore but that gave me the colour of Russian and the colour of German. And this later gave me the idea that these syllables could form melodies. Not melodies built with notes, […] but melodies made of syllables, of the colours of syllables. That's is how I started" (Aperghis in Gammel 2002: 98. Translation by Lee Holt).

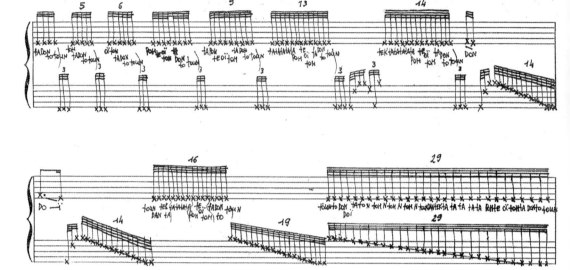

Figure 1: Georges Aperghis: *Le corps à corps* (1978). In the first line the vocal actions are notated, in the second the percussion actions on the *tombak*. Copyright by Edition Salabert, Paris.

This textual form and writing for voices define Aperghis' oeuvre. The vocal works, with the operas, the *théâtre musical*, the solo vocal works and oratorios comprise the majority of his complete works. But in a number of instrumental pieces, performers also have to speak or perform vocal actions. André Gindt has gone so far as to say that the instrumental voices in Aperghis are treated basically as vocal parts. But the opposite is the case, too: the vocal parts are dealt with like instrumental parts. This is expressed most clearly in passages in which text and music are closely associated in a special way. The best example of this is *Le corps à corps* (1978) for the tombak, a hand-held Persian drum.

This piece focusses on the unity of syllable and rhythm as is typical of playing the Indian tabla: "Back then, I was much more excited by Indian music. The Indian tabla players are known to begin by speaking the beat."[24] Whether language is turned into music or music into language is a question of perspective. This kind of association between music and language is also found today in Aperghis' works, in which he often divides the unity of rhythm, spoken melody and syllables among several performers:

The forms of the immanent and imaginary theatre therefore are not in opposition to the polyphony of elements; instead, they surface during moments and passages within the

---

24. Interview with Georges Aperghis by Patrick Hahn, Bern 17 April 2007 (Hahn 2008: 15). Patrick Hahn goes on to suggest that Aperghis' textual composition has more to do with this line of thought than with Dada, Futurism or Lettrism. Aperghis tends to view Joyce or Beckett as his literary influences. See Gindt 1990: 90.

polyphonic structure of the *théâtre musical*. In *Avis de tempête* (2007), for example, there is a passage in which Johanne Saunier speaks a highly rhythmitised text at extreme speed. The physical effort this text requires is clearly experienced as its own performative dimension. The syllables develop that haze of signification that the audience attempts to follow by making associations and imagining. At the same time, Johanne Saunier turns around herself constantly in a rapid yet flowing movement that contrasts with the staccato rhythms of the text. In her outstretched hand, she holds a small video camera that she looks into constantly. The image is projected live onto a screen. What we see there reverses the live action yet again: the singer rotates about her own axis while seeming to stand still in the projection, with the world revolving around her. In the projection the moment of physical action is extinguished by the relative stillness of the camera in relation to the moving body.

Process and motivation

We can examine the artistic process from an aesthetic perspective. Approaches and methods then appear to be intentional and functional, oriented towards a certain planned aesthetic experience. Yet we can also observe the artistic process through the lens of motivation: it is not just a certain result that drives forward (artistic) processes; the process itself must have some motivating character. In the final analysis, the driving forces for the work – at least for Aperghis – are not simply the results; it is primarily the artistic question that wants to be solved. It is also for this reason that Aperghis refuses to work according to a specific method: "Les expériences les plus anciennes ne te servent pas. [...] Je veux me lancer dans des aventures nouvelles, plus difficiles parce qu'il n'y a pas une expérience."[25]

For Aperghis, working with and for other people is a crucial motivating factor. During the *ATEM* period, this was expressed in the social and political utopia associated with *ATEM's* founding, and was demonstrated concretely in workshops with laypersons from the suburbs of Paris. Today, this impulse towards collaborative motivation can be seen in two ways: first, the collective processes involved in the development of the pieces, and second, the idea, characteristic of Aperghis, that his compositions are not only dedicated to specific performers, but are also to a certain degree portraits of these performers.

To write for someone you know is something different, because from the beginning you are taking possession of this person – at least that's how it is for me – and observing him. [...] Whenever I observe a performer in his daily life, during rehearsals, while drinking coffee, their everyday gestures, then I discover him as a person and from that point I am convinced that, while I am writing for him, he is much stronger than in reality, from a musical perspective. Often, when they receive the score, they are excited yet afraid at the

---

25. "Your prior experiences don't help you. [...] I want to dive into new adventures, more difficult as there is no experience" (Aperghis 2010).

Figure 2: Letter 'S' of Georges Aperghis: *Little Red Riding Hood* (2001). Copyright by Edition Durant, Paris.

same time of its difficulty. Because I am convinced – and this comes from love – that they can do everything, and this is true because they do it, but at what a price! (laughs) It is a way of sublimating the performer. [...] Whenever I decide to write something for them, I give them an enigmatic puzzle. They open the score, and I'm interested in seeing their reaction, what they will do with it.

(Aperghis in Maximoff 2006)

This motivation also releases a special motivation among the musicians and performers. Lionel Peintre, for whom Aperghis wrote the *Quatorze Jactations*, describes very clearly how the score for *Jactations* – which initially seemed completely impossible – soon took over his life: "That wasn't a composition, it was a monster that had it in for me. Really! (laughs) This thing was very aggressive towards me. As soon as I began working on it, it came out of me like a wild animal" (Aperghis in Maximoff 2006). The way in which Aperghis develops his *théâtre musical* together with the musicians and performers is not based solely on aesthetic considerations and intentions. One cannot simply decide to work together in such collaborative way; it must correspond to one's very being, and this just is the case for Aperghis. Marcus Gammel, who was assistant director in the production of *Le Petit Chaperon Rouge*, and a participating observer at the same time, provides this valuable insight into this aspect of the working process:

The most striking feature of his leadership of the group is his extreme reserve about making direct statements. [...] If he begins to give directions, Aperghis often keeps his formulations in the subjunctive: "Ce qui serait bien, c'est que tu..." is one of his most frequently used turns of phrase – sometimes also expressed as a question: "Et si tu allais là-bas...?" [...] At the same time, the composer is extremely open to ideas and input from his colleagues. He demonstrates a high degree of sensibility for their needs ("C'est faisable ou pas?") and he is concerned constantly about their safety during rehearsals or on the stage. [...] After work is over, the entire group often ends up in a restaurant, where Aperghis displays his brilliant talent for conversation. [...] At the personal level, he also shows great interest for the needs of his colleagues.

(Gammel 2002: 56)

Gammel emphasises that this form of gentleness in no way means that Aperghis is not always in control, "effectively steering rehearsal out of the arcane" (Gammel 2002: 56). Conversely, this familiar atmosphere, similar to the aforementioned composed portraits, generates a special motivation among his performers:

> With his understated authority, those who work with Aperghis become even more attentive to his wishes and goals – they read it straight from his eyes. [...] Just as he is constantly and palpably considering the needs of the musicians, the musicians are trying to make his work easier. [...] This is how Georges Aperghis manages to collapse diametrical oppositions, even in group leadership; he only resorts to his authority in the rarest of cases, yet the performers recognise his absolute authority. He doesn't make any direct demands and receives extraordinary effort from everyone working with him, and he is very talented at channelling this energy. This is how Aperghis creates a working atmosphere that guarantees him maximal creative latitude.
>
> (Gammel 2002: 56)

Looking back to his work with the musicians of *Le Petit Chaperon Rouge* Aperghis himself describes the challenge and the benefits – both personal and artistic – of this kind of collaboration in the following way:

> [M]oi, pour faire ce que je fais avec eux, j'ai besoin de les aimer beaucoup. Donc d'avoir vraiment envie de travailler avec eux. La moindre chose qui va pas, un retard le matin, quelqu'un qui rigole au mauvais moment [...] tout de suite, je me rétracte, et je peux plus travailler en fait, parce que il y a quelque chose qui me refroidit. Donc c'est assez fragile tout ça, comment ça se fait. Mais ici je suis bien. Avec eux par exemple je me sens très en confiance, donc ça se passe bien, quoi. Et ça se passe souvent bien d'ailleurs. Et c'est une drôle de chose, parce que c'est aussi une façon de dévoiler beaucoup de ses faiblesses devant tout le monde, de dire: "Voilà, j'ai pas d'idée. Je sais plus, je suis fatigué." Donc c'est une façon de demander beaucoup mais de donner aussi beaucoup. Comme ça, on est tous dans une espèce d'exigence et je trouve ça bien.[26]
>
> (*Translation: Lee Holt*)

---

26. "In order to do what I do with them I have to really like them. That means that I really want to work with them. The smallest thing that doesn't work, some one being late in the morning or laughing at the wrong moment [...] I am immediately discouraged and I cannot go on working because there is something that cools me down. So, it's all rather fragile how it is done. But for me it is fine. With them, for example, I feel mutual trust so it is going well. And by the way, it's often going fine. And that's kind of a funny thing because that's also a way to show one's own weaknesses to everybody if you say: 'Ok, I have no idea. I don't know, I am tired.' So it is a way of asking for a lot but also of giving a lot. And like that you are involved in a kind of pretension and I like that" (Aperghis in Gammel 2002: 63).

References

Aperghis, Georges (2010) Interview by Matthias Rebstock, Paris, 01/05/2010.

—— (2001) "Werkstattgespräch *Machinations.* Nathalie Singer im Gespräch mit Georges Aperghis", in Odo Berno Polzerand and Thomas Schäfer (eds.) (2001), *Katalog Wien Modern 2001*, Saarbrücken.

Durney, Daniel (1990) "La règle du jeu", in Antoine Gindt: *Georges Aperghis: Le corps musical*, Arles.

Gammel, Marcus (2002) "Rotkäppchen ist der Wolf. Kreativität im Musiktheater von Georges Aperghis", MA thesis, Berlin: Humbold Universität.

Hahn, Patrick (2008) "Stoff-Rest-Stoff. Zum künstlerischen Umgang mit Resten in einem spectacle musical von Georges Aperghis", MA thesis, Köln: Köln University.

Houdart, Célia (2007) *Avis de tempete*, Paris: Intervalles.

Lehmann, Hans-Thies (1999) *Postdramatisches Theater*, Frankfurt: Verlag der Autoren.

Maximoff, Catherine (2006) *Georges Aperghis: Storm Beneath a Skull*, DVD documentary, Juxta Productions.

Rebstock, Matthias (2006) *Zwischen Musik und Theater: Das instrumentalen Theater von Mauricio Kagel*, Hofheim: Wolke Verlag.

Chapter 12

Musical Conquest and Settlement: On Ruedi Häusermann's Theatre Work(s)

Judith Gerstenberg

At first, a heap of randomly dumped objects. In the dim light one recognises the odd instrument within the pile. Four figures fawn over a white surface, leaving strange forward-pointing tracks. They plan and calculate, we know not what. They issue brief commands, something seems to motivate them to put helmet-like constructions with sound pickups onto their heads, long strings are being put up across the room, forming bottlenecks. A knot is disentangled, two new ones develop, recordings are made, a thunder sheet painted, slippers prepared for optimal suction. Amid all that, there are sections in which the characters retire to their original places, bury themselves in their instruments; sections of abstract sound worlds, of improvised music (for the four performers, including Ruedi Häusermann himself, are exceptionally gifted multi-instrumentalists). At the end of the evening, but really only at the very end, one realises that one has witnessed a musical exploration and sounding: the four men of the type: 'elderly Swiss' – in love with their home country, a song on their lips, with a dash of awe and a lot of seriousness, hard-working and well aware of their important task and hard working – take a break, sitting within the result of their day's work, namely the painfully erected parlour, puff a pipe and listen to the self-produced sounds of a village idyll. They are very pleased with themselves – until they begin to hammer and saw again. This production at the theatre at the Schauspielhaus Zurich was called – not without affectionate irony – *Väter unser [Our fathers]* and was created in 2000, the first year of artistic director Christoph Marthaler's tenure there. It was a theatrical event of a then-elusive category.

For when *Väter unser* was invited to be the Swiss entry to the Bonn Biennale, a festival of contemporary European theatre, there was bewilderment – at least for those audience members and critics not yet persuaded by recent changes in the notion of authorship: after all, the dramatic text of the performers was limited to a repeated 'good' and 'continue' with an occasional 'Achtung für…' [look out for…[1]]. 'Look out for big birds', for example, or 'Look out for: Catholic Church'. The four performers spent the rest of the evening enacting the above-mentioned meticulous surveys of the stage space for which they used very strange implements and devices. The sounds, which were apparently created unintentionally, joined together – on reflection over time – to become a sophisticated composition. And in the end we had heard a concert, a whole world had been created, a life depicted and a mentality and attitude portrayed.

---

1. The German/Swiss 'Achtung' has a double meaning: it can signify both a call for attention as well as respect (note from the translator).

As early as 1998, when Ruedi Häusermann received the most distinguished German theatre award, the Bavarian Theatre Prize, for one of his earlier works, *Das Beste aus: Meschliches Versagen (Folge I)* [*The Best of: Human error (Episode I)*], a certain helplessness prevailed, since this production would simply not fit any category or genre: it was neither a play, nor an opera, nor dance. The prize was finally awarded under the newly established rubric 'other theatre events'. In fact, there still is uncertainty among newspaper editors about whether to send a theatre critic or a music critic to a Häusermann production. While the theatre critic often lacks the vocabulary to describe the abstract music, the colleague responsible for opera or concerts is confused by the theatrical playfulness of the work.

Its own category

Quite obviously, the theatre work of Swiss Ruedi Häusermann constitutes its own category or genre. He is a musician – by training; a musician, however, who since childhood has developed an eye for the stagings and the *mise en scène* of everyday life, using his sensitivity to joyfully set the occasional trap for others with the help of subtle manipulations. Both, the music and this attention to the theatrical potential of his environment determine his world view; a view that one cannot put on and take off like a pair of glasses but which instead constitutes an understanding. Both have been formative for Häusermann as a person, which is why he has continued exploring how musical and theatrical awareness can open spaces for each other since those first performances. His interest is always in the process as well, which remains visible in the result, negotiating the manufacturing of the theatre event in performance. Häusermann is driven by the question: what ingredients transform a casual, unassuming moment into a poetic one? It is a question about perception and revaluation, about what we see and hear. In an existential sense, for Häusermann – both as an artist and

Figure 1: Ruedi Häusermann. Photograph by Sebastian Hoppe.

as a human being – all his productions are stations of a music-theatrical exploration of the world.

Resisting categorisation, Häusermann's works are labeled 'projects', a term he avoids. Ultimately, all artistic work is a 'project'. Each is an enterprise, a design, a plan, or – as business jargon would have it – a time-limited development project. This includes those of his works which feel their way into an already established literary or musical world and appropriate it or – on the contrary – make their difference from this world apparent. One distinction, however, that the term 'project' marks in theatre is that at the end of such a period of work nothing remains which has any continuance outside the actual performance, nothing that could be handed down. Therefore, projects are particularly indebted to the mediality of the live performance, its unique features emphasising that theatre is only at one's disposal in the instance of experiencing it. Häusermann stagings are marked by this awareness. They confront the task of shaping this very melancholic and ecstatic privilege, this ephemerality, this non-consolidating volatile nature. It is this space of uncertainties and transitions that Häusermann continues to explore.

Music-theatrical self-assurance

Ruedi Häusermann's motor is a fascination with the spiritual, not the material world. This fascination has biographical origins. He comes from a family of artisans. His father was a stove-fitter, whom Häusermann accompanied to construction sites. There, 'Kunst' ('art') was the term for the stove bench through which the firing chamber was laid. The kind of thinking Häusermann learnt there was guided by objective criteria: was something bent or straight, will it fulfil its function or does it need correction? If the firing chamber ended up short, the Kunst (art) had to be torn down. There was no room for other concepts of quality, and certainly none that related to a mere idea. This other, artistic, non purpose-oriented world had yet to be conquered by Häusermann as a part of his life. This is what makes it so precious to him. He knows its fragility and also that it comes apart when its legitimacy is denied.

Initially he had to push aside all standards known to him. The resulting relief, which he continues looking for today time and time again, is the prerequisite of creativity. Exploring this creative impulse (with all its recurring doubts, but understood as possibilities and potential) was and is a key interest. Häusermann does not model himself on other artists, but tries to maintain a productive naivety as a kind of shelter. The danger of inventing something and claiming it as one's own just to be different, rather than searching for it in oneself, the danger in other words of a quest for mere novelty that overshadows true originality would then be too great. For each sequence of notes has been played before, every thought has been thought before. Häusermann tills only those fields that he can later plant himself. He would not skip any step. Thus each production is to be read as a further step in a large-scale project of life. The individual productions refer to each other, continue their narrative and remain solely committed to the subjective interests of their author. Consequently, it isn't possible to suggest new *sujets* or ideas for productions to Häusermann. He remains searching his own identity, which still wants to be defended against the very concrete and solid world from which he originates.

He started late. Only after finishing his economics degree did he decide to study classical flute. As a clarinettist and saxophonist, he had already played in the compulsory Swiss cadet corps and worked his way through the entire history of jazz. During his music degree he turned to free improvisation, liberating himself from harmony structures, fixed-time structures and predetermined forms. He had to eradicate the boundaries for himself in order to be able to draw new ones, or perhaps to rediscover old boundaries as non-binding. During the concerts in which he plays today – most often with cellist Martin Schütz, percussionist Martin Hägler and sound specialist Philippe Läng – they bounce ideas off each other without any specific expectations. Being able to understand these ideas as such, to accept them from each other or – what is sometimes most difficult – to let them go by, is the art of this concerted playing. These four very unique musician-personalities thus roam musical worlds together, places whose existence they didn't even know before. It is always this kind of music, constantly and inherently renewing itself, that Häusermann places within theatrical contexts.

Drawing from complexity

The original cell of Häusermann's theatre work can be found in his solo programme *Der Schritt ins Jenseits [The step into the next world]* (Tuchlaube Aarau, 1992, see Figure 2). He himself was on stage in two roles; he was both sound manager (director) and employed artist (actor) in a small recording studio. The artist produces sounds on cue and records music tracks on various instruments, while the voice of the sound manager keeps interrupting him, humiliating him, demanding new takes, until finally commissioned artist Häusermann, who is doing his best, hisses under his breath: 'S schiist mi aa' [Swiss dialect for: 'It pisses me off', note from the translator]. We can just hear the voice of the director/sound manager – a God that overhears everything: 'Du muesch ned säge, s schiist mi aa, Ruedi' ['Don't say, it pisses you off, Ruedi', note from the translator] – when the frustrated musician sinks the loudspeaker from which this warning emanates in a bucket of water. Finally freed of the admonitions and instruction on how to do things, a miracle happens. All the interrupted trials and truncated noises (including deliberately provoked audience reactions) that were entirely devoid of any aura suddenly produce a great concert. The live recorded takes from the first part are now intertwined into a surprising story, to which Häusermann improvises brilliantly on his instruments. Out of the previous chaos a biography grows, a whole world. In fact, as a listening audience we have witnessed an act of creation. To confirm this experience and, above all, to capture it and counteract any pathos, Häusermann has a Punch doll (Kasperlipuppe) give an encore as God, who releases the audience with a rendition of the song 'Oh, wie wohl ist mir am Abend ...' [German traditional canon, 'Oh, how content I am in the evening ...', note from the translator].

Figure 2: Ruedi Häusermann in *Schritt ins Jenseits*. Photograph by Judith Schlosser.

The charm of Häusermann's productions is in their humour and their refusal to take themselves too seriously. He avoids the crowing gesture. That's why he often interrupts his music with naive scenes, with what could also be understood in the oldest theatre in the world, the kind of theatre where people began to tell stories, as children with few resources, a theatre in the attic or in the barn.

In fact, a principle is established in *Schritt ins Jenseits* that can be re-encountered in many of Häusermann's later works: something suddenly emerges as if from nowhere, out of a random complexity, from seemingly insignificant aspects, and we later discover and realise that every detail was premeditated and according to a mysterious plan.

Figures 3 and 4: Scenes from *Trübe Quellenlage*. Photographs by Sebastian Hoppe.

'Blue-skies' compositions / Sound research

Since his first solo programme, Häusermann's name can be found more often in a theatre context than on the concert stage. Nevertheless, he thinks of himself first and foremost as a composer. To justify this understanding, he takes time off before each new theatre work; time to retire in order to develop new music. 'Blue-skies' compositions are the result. The only criterion guiding Häusermann in this is a quest for personal new territories. He sits down and starts at random – he may for example improvise with different instruments on several recording tracks[2] (he only fixes a certain time signature and tempo and later assembles and composes the tracks into a 'piece' in retrospect in order to avoid a surreptitious flirting with certain reactions), or he may make some notations. He simply begins, unencumbered by an idea, a concrete project. Once something has gained some form, it can be considered described, can be discarded or further developed. The familiar, which initially occurs in this process, shows Häusermann at least where its boundaries lie, towards which he wants to advance. When he arrives at these margins, the yet unbroken ground becomes gradually visible, which he then can start to till. Over time, an inner necessity evolves for the composition. Once this is recognised as such, it turns out to become an incorruptible measure.

The music precedes the beginning of any theatrical work. When a composition is sufficiently developed for a start, it relieves Häusermann of a lot, as he can then develop a unique non-musical narrative from it (or from one of its musical side-lines or marginal notes), a narrative that grows out of the music. This often only becomes recognisable during the creative process of the theatre rehearsals.

For *Randolphs Erben [Randolph's heirs]* (Staatsoper Stuttgart 2009), for example, in which the stage is transformed into a music shop, including an instrument workshop, he had written compositions for a brass and a string quartet that weren't aimed for any specific theatrical use. He brings this finished piece of work into the rehearsal process the way that others might bring a text. It is an open question, what images it may create, or vice versa:

---

2. In the case of *Trübe Quellenlage. Opera Conserva [Murky Sources. Opera Conserva* (Theater Basel, 2002)] this created a particular challenge for the staging process, as the composition couldn't be reproduced live. In the centre of this production there was then necessarily a multi-track recorder. The performer literally acted as 'Tonträger' [the German word for sound storage medium means 'sound carrier' in literal translation; note from the translator] and realized a live 'hearing' in which they visualised multiple layers of the recorded tracks, without simply illustrating them. With their live interferences, the performers subverted and transgressed the score of the recorded music. Solo performances alternated with choral arrangements. At times the performers resembled devotedly grazing farm animals when crossing the stage with their gigantic speakers on their heads (see Figures 3 and 4). One performer opened his coat like an exhibitionist and bared his sound device; long-time collaborator Annalisa Derossi created cable spaghetti when swinging her hips and hip- and wire-leads as she entered as a lascivious lasso cowgirl with her loudspeaker tucked away in her behind.

how images – still to be found – may interlink with the musical events in order allow this composition to unfold in sound.

Now, while on the lower part of the stage, there is hammering, beating out, lacquering, constructing and repairing of instruments, a customer enters the shop; a customer who wants to buy a trumpet. The shop has few visitors these days and so the staff gets into a frenzy: it brings one trumpet after the other (each running up and down stairs sounds, as we realise, like an introduction to a piece of music and provides a rhythm). Even every closet door that is opened makes a sound – in the right pitch of course – which the violin mimics, continues and transforms shortly after. The customer tries out the various instruments, plays something barely recognisable as a melody, which nonetheless later proves to be a central motif of one of the previously composed string quartets. The tones that sound like arbitrary try-outs of the instruments are being picked up more and more by the string quartet – at first the violin shadows the sounds, while the other instruments gradually tune in and the sound is condensed, almost incidentally into that earlier composition. All of a sudden the customer drops a mouthpiece. This is the sign for the drill, which with its shrill noise blocks out and destroys the sounds that had just emancipated into music. This difference in the materiality of tones and sounds is something that Häusermann continues to investigate, since it is through their difference that these sounds unearth each other's value. The compositions which he develops before the theatre rehearsals give him an indication of the direction in

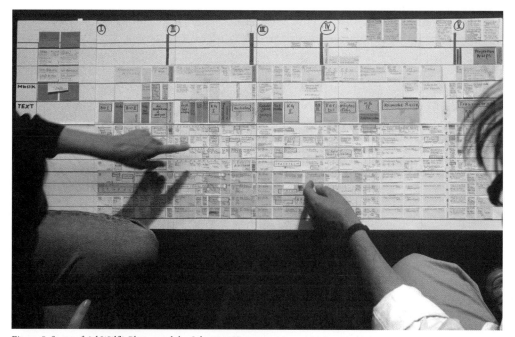

Figure 5: Score of *Ad Wölfli*. Photograph by Sebastian Hoppe.

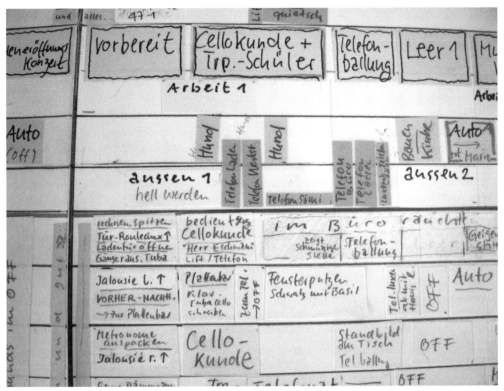

Figure 6: Detail of the score of *Randolphs Erben*. Photograph by Ruedi Häusermann.

which he then proceeds, force him to inventions that in retrospect expose how they came about. Since the musicians are present throughout the rehearsal process, Häusermann is free to continue composing pieces such as the previously mentioned introduction on the stairs, in which the theatre gives something back to the music.

At the beginning of such theatre work, we literally have the proverbial blank page. Three sheets of A2 paper, taped together. They match exactly the dimensions of the table that is available in Häusermann's studio on the Goffersberg, that place near the railway line between Basel and Zurich where all his works originate. The sheet of paper is prepared to collect all the ideas (or better: finds) which accumulate in the course of weeks, months, sometimes years, and which are put on small post-it notes of different colours that are constantly being resorted and repositioned (see Figures 5 and 6). Finding things is more important to Häusermann than searching, since searching is generally already guided by an expectation, tempting one to judge and dismiss what is encountered too early. Häusermann takes his time. Necessarily. There is no other way of arriving at his aim. His dream always remains the same: to create onstage a world that becomes a home. But this world is not generated by a collection of beautiful ideas. The biggest and most time-consuming task is to find out what questions to ask, how to develop criteria so that decisions can be made. Before rehearsals start, Häusermann merely determines an approximate sense of direction, rather than settling for a fixed definition of an idea.

Developing this sense of direction, he invites guests from the mostly familiar and long established pool of people of the production team to the Goffersberg. These are not ordinary work meetings to which one is summoned, but small productions, presented as gifts, small scenic arrangements with puns, which are personal and recognisable only to their addressee, heartfelt presents that create the right temperature, prerequisite for a possible free flow of ideas. Even the scores he has written, he wants to be read merely as a rough map. Together with the musicians involved in the project he will investigate which of the branching paths are actually accessible by exploring the possible worlds of sound with them over a long period of time during monthly rehearsal weekends. Together with the string quartet assembled for his production of *Gewähltes Profil: Lautlos* [*Silent mode: on*[3]] (Staatstheater Hannover / Staatsoper Stuttgart / Munich Opera Festival 2006), for example, Häusermann was searching for sounds that he described by an image of a slightly waving curtain at an open window, which reveals that the wind carries barely audible music into the room. The very fine stroking of the strings, the extreme *flautando*, produces sounds that disappear almost immediately after ringing out. There is not the familiar string sound; the music opens up to a theatrical process that is enhanced by sound worlds, which sometimes drowned it out before it then re-emerges.

Another search word for this sound laboratory was 'beetle music'. This refers to the creaking and rasping of beetle shells, which become audible when listening to beetles up close. These are sounds one has to listen to intently in order to distinguish their diversity.

Häusermann regards this joint research activity as a vital second step in his composition. It is also within this collaboration that the set of rules is found, which determines the theatrical process. Incidentally, Häusermann considers his task to be creating a kind of territory in which certain natural laws apply. The longer one looks at the initially unfamiliar, the more clearly one begins to see, hear, and recognise, slowly becoming acquainted and at home with something that eventually can be called a world. In the end, it is up to viewers and listeners to realise how each detail joins and becomes an overall composition.

Enduring uncertainty

Ultimately, Häusermann asks of his collaborators (and later the audience) to endure a sustained period of uncertainty, during which it is permissible to think and try out without strain or the need to focus on a result. Enduring this uncertainty is a real challenge. Häusermann knows how hard it is, because it prohibits the individual (whether musician, actor, set designers,

---

3. The title refers to the silent mode option in mobile phone settings (note from the translator).

etc.) from sorting out his or her own area too early. Only after the language and the sound for the project are found – and that is always a delicate process – can the individual fine-tune his or her own personal profile. This point in time sometimes occurs only just before the premiere. It is possible then to look back and realise what has already been created. As a result, Häusermann is especially indebted to and dependent on his performers – professional musicians who become actors, actors who support the music and also people of essential warmth and cordiality, in whose world Häusermann is more interested theatrically than in their education or training. Their manner and attitude is part of what he finds in them. And just in what he finds, in what is already there, he discovers his stories, the theatrical material.

Häusermann devotes his whole attention to the details of his environment and thus gives them an earnestness that often unearths their philosophical dimension. Sometimes one has to wait long until the various ideas, the exploratory processes, develop a necessity that only then needs pursuit. At all levels – music, design, text – certain moments emerge from the rehearsal process with which one falls in love. However, to shape and organise these moments into a form that unites all these individual movements proves to be the real and always new challenge. A single element that remains with no context interferes with this coherence and has to dropped. Recognising this necessitates the perspective of all parties off stage. Describing to each other what we see on stage gradually creates the narrative context and makes decisions possible. It is not uncommon for Häusermann to see himself confronted with a situation where the original idea of the project has taken itself offstage in the end. It remains of crucial importance nevertheless because it is essential as a starting point where one can begin to unload one's thoughts.

Composed coincidences

And so Häusermann collects all chances and coincidences in order to ultimately leave nothing to chance. Every detail has been arrived at conceptually; each moment corresponds with all others in the production. Häusermann has a central dramaturgic device in his pre-composed music. The music is not just an ingredient or mere addition to the theatrical work, but determines its design. It is the music which enables him to meticulously arrange the seemingly random, to zoom in and out of events, to overlap, fade and cut, and thus to steer the viewer's perception.

This virtuoso play with the perceptual mechanisms of the audience marks the particular quality of Häusermann. It facilitates the experience of the immediate presence of a performance, since hearing and seeing is subjected to continuous fluctuation. This presents a challenge to continually reorient oneself, not least because Häusermann juxtaposes very different worlds in almost all his works. Their essence and characteristics are particularly evident at their edges and boundaries, where one merges into the other, overlaps the other and takes its place. It is Häusermann's desire that the impressions, the colour and shape of his productions remain in constant flux, just like the weather or the sea.

In reality, his works remain fragile. In the end, as a spectator one leaves the theatre with an idea, a hunch; one supposes oneself to have seen something, remembers having heard something. The author Peter Bichsel once likened Häusermann's pieces to landscapes seen only from afar, yet heard.

There is, however, one thing remaining at the end of a Häusermann production: the blank page has been transformed into a score (see Figure 5) on which many small coloured pieces of paper have found their places in an evidently strict order. These are notes with peculiar abbreviations and references such as 'image pushing', 'chair music', 'text vehicle', notes on which the complex texture of music, scene, foreground and background events was mapped during rehearsals. It can only be deciphered by those who were part of its emergence.

(Translation: David Roesner)

Chapter 13

Composing with Raw Materials: Daniel Ott's Music-theatre Portraits and Landscapes

Christa Brüstle

Composition is generally understood as doing something constructive, a creative activity. Composition or *compositio* is the "science of producing harmony by assembling and joining consonant and dissonant notes" (Walther 1732: 178)[1] as Johann Gottfried Walther defined it in 1732. Composition was then seen as a science; it later became the creative act of a genius and, in the twentieth century, a method, process and construction – whereby the activity and creativity (of a composer) has always remained in the foreground. As Arnold Schönberg wrote:

> After many unsuccessful attempts during a period of approximately twelve years, I laid the foundation for a new procedure in musical construction which seemed fitted to replace those structural differences provided formerly by tonal harmonies. I called this procedure *Method of Composing with Twelve Tones Which are Related Only with One Another.*
>
> (Schoenberg 1941: 218)

Taking pleasure in the creative act, even physical pleasure, was stressed by Stravinsky:

> All creation presupposes at its origin a sort of appetite that is brought on by the foretaste of discovery. This foretaste of the creative act accompanies the intuitive grasp of an unknown entity already possessed but not yet intelligible, an entity that will not take definite shape except by the action of a constantly vigilant technique. [...] The very act of putting my work on paper, of, as we say, kneading the dough, is for me inseparable from the pleasure of creation. So far as I am concerned, I cannot separate the spiritual effort from the psychological and physical effort; they confront me on the same level and do not present a hierarchy.
>
> (Stravinsky 1970: 65–67)[2]

One can imagine the craftsman right in front of us, piecing things together bit by bit and in so doing creating a complete whole. The archaic English term for this activity is 'to perform',

---

1. If not stated otherwise all translations of quotations originally in German are by Nick Woods.
2. For the questionable authorship of Stravinsky's writing and the context of the quoted statement, see Rust 2009.

which has in common with the modern word *performance* only that something is being constructed and completed.[3]

As far as the pianist and composer Daniel Ott is concerned, composition does not start with one's own constructive activity; when composing his musical pieces and music theatre projects, what is there is much more the starting point and field of work at one and the same time. Natural surroundings and landscapes, for example, are resources the Swiss artist, who grew up in picturesque Grub in Appenzell canton, repeatedly uses as venues. Urban and industrial areas are composite locations that are rich in history and have many starting points for audible and visible events. Even transit routes or (forgotten about) non-places create their own atmospheres that one only comes across when used, for example, in the music theatre journey *Südliche Autobahn* (Berlin 2007) or in the music theatre piece *Paulinenbrücke* (Stuttgart 2009).[4] But what is already there relates not only to exterior spaces, as one also finds room for manoeuvre and social relations, personal experiences and memories, an education, a job, a working environment, in short, personal circumstances of the past and present – everything is present, everything is 'there'. The basic condition for creating art with it and from it is a mix of sensitivity, attentiveness, observing, leaving and finding.[5] The first thing to ask is not 'What can I do with the material?' but 'What does the material and/or the material found do with me?' This approach reveals Ott's link to John Cage, whose vision of music theatre he shares: "There is no such thing as an empty space or an empty time. There is always something to see, something to hear" (Cage 1958: 8).

Daniel Ott's music theatre projects are *Gesamtkunstwerke* in a very practical sense, as they emerge from teamwork. The composer sees the performers as co-authors whose experiences, memories and personal circumstances, whose reactions to particular places, and whose relationships to the work flow into the development of a music theatre project. Different artistic fields should also communicate 'without any hierarchy'.

> At the composer/author level, this means that *ideas* are not pre-sorted into categories as soon as they appear. I consider it important to be open to *stimuli/ideas/research*, to accept ideas "as ideas" – to investigate where they might lead is then the second or third step … only later does the question arise: "What can I implement with my skills and possibilities? Where must I depend on experts (co-authors/performers) from other areas?"
>
> (Ott 2001: 51)

Ott attributes this working method partly to his active interest in Pina Bausch. He got to know her dance theatre projects more closely in the late 1980s while studying composition in Essen. He also quotes Hans Wüthrich, referring to the Swiss composer's psycho-acoustic portraits, "that is, composition with another ego".[6]

---

3. Cf. Simpson and Weiner 1989: 543.
4. For further information about Daniel Ott's works and current projects, see www.danielott.com.
5. Cf. Seel 2002.
6. Cf. Ott 2000: 95.

From her piece *Kontakthof* (1978) onwards, Pina Bausch's working method explicitly involved asking questions of her ensemble in order to develop her works, questions intended to "gather material on particular themes; [...] from the personal answers, which depend on the mood and cultural origin of each dancer's personality, and which probably have different forces of expression, emerge words, sentences, gestures, poses, movements – small scenes are created" (Schulze-Reuber 2005: 73).[7] In Ott's work, too, an experimental working process gives rise to performable concepts and stages, or versions of a performance, based on the found (present) material, its context and whatever triggered the material. In other words, syntheses, montages, combinations and compressions of music, images, actions, figures now begin to develop that may, for example, be integrated into an existing landscape or staged independently. In this sense, Daniel Ott's work is also related to Dieter Schnebel's experimental methods, for example, Schnebel's works *Maulwerke* (1968–74) or *Körper-Sprache* (1979–80). The core principle of both these well-known pieces is not based on prescribing a set order of action or a narrative structure; instead they begin with 'drills' or 'exercises' in which the basic elements of speech articulation or individual body movements are isolated to be tried out in sound studies or rhythmic studies. Schnebel intends that 'complete processes' should develop from these exercises, that is, performance versions for a particular group of performers and for a particular place. Daniel Ott also considers the openness arising from this principle to be very significant.

> After all, the '*open form*' – a rather dated concern of the Avant-garde movement – is still an important *precondition* of my work: the *unfinished, fragmentary, temporary, incomplete* as an opportunity to *take ideas further* – the gap that enables me to interrupt a process (my own or from elsewhere) with new ideas. *Working with the open form* also means to me 'work in progress': engaging with themes/materials without having any idea of the form which may later emerge.[8]
>
> (Ott 2001: 54)

This process does not create music theatre, however; music and theatre are 'there' from the beginning. A musician does not need to become an actor; he is one already, although most musicians who have gone through the traditional western musical education would not emphasise this. But in the context of music, the roles are particularly clear: conductor, orchestra musician, soloist, popular musician, bass, organist – a whole range of social frameworks and contexts, which could be extended, demand not only the appropriate music but also the 'embodiment' of particular roles to satisfy the audience's expectations. In everyday life, we encounter the unity of music, sound and action directly, when walking or running, in traffic, when cooking and eating (the list could be extended at will). Ott presupposes the

---

7. Cf. also Schmidt 2002: 87–98.
8. The stages of work which go into a journalistic portrait, starting with reflection on themes and research, are also comparable; cf. also von Matt 2008.

'permeability' of the artistic and everyday dimensions in his music theatre projects. "The effort necessary to maintain 'open boundaries' within artistic fields and the exchange between them, resulting in a *complete work of art*, also applies beyond these fields; that music theatre 'relates to' – *stands in a relationship* to – its social and political environment – directly or indirectly" (Ott 2000: 54). Daniel Ott's music theatre is always socially reflective art. This process includes making music together, for example with improvisation. It also implies letting the individual music of the musicians themselves – such as dance music, folk music, favourite pieces – become part of the composition of what already exists and what is being created.

skizze – 7½ bruchstücke (1992)

Five musicians with five instruments are present: bass clarinet (Uwe Moeckel), percussion (Christian Dierstein), violin (Melise Mellinger), viola (Barbara Maurer) and cello (Lucas Fels). The percussion comprises two saw blades, eleven glass bottles (to be broken), a bottle piano, a caña rociera (an instrument made from a split bamboo cane and used as a rattle), a pair of cymbals (lined with felt, completely damped), a metal rod, a felt and a wooden drumstick, a double bass bow, a metal sheet on which sand is rubbed by the feet, branches, two wooden boxes, a large glass bell jar, three 'tuned' wine glasses, a water container, gravel, sand and a small drum on which sand trickles. As an initial orientation, the question mentioned above is posed: What does the material and/or discovered material do with me? In addition, one might ask: What elements, aspects, questions, effects do the musicians and their instruments produce? The composer is confronted with this question and later the audience considers it in a different way. First, the musicians are virtuosi on their instruments. How did that come about? Which instruments do they play, and why? Has Barbara Maurer always played the viola? What made Christian Dierstein choose percussion? Did Melise Mellinger learn to play the violin as a child? Did Uwe Moeckel always want to play the clarinet? It is easy to imagine these questions arising during private conversation, just by the way. The answers are to be found in the piece, whereby it becomes clear that the musicians are reflecting on what has made them and is still making them what they are. Musical autobiographies or portraits? Does this mean that the piece is directly linked to the people who developed it or who contributed to its development? Would it be different with different musicians? "The musicians' *answers* to my questions influence the composition process in various ways. Either through quotations or the direct inclusion of found material – or through structural ideas – an *idea* from outside often arouses the necessary *resistance* to my intentions, thereby teasing out new ideas. How directly this joint formation process leaves *traces* on the performance depends particularly on the willingness and possibilities of the musicians. The aspect of *reproduction* of a composition by other performers fades into the background: sometimes it is possible to make an *adaptation* for new performers. Some of my works remain *unique*; they can only be staged by the performers with whom they were created" (Ott 2000: 53).[9]

---

9. Cf. Rebstock 2005.

The piece *skizze – 7½ bruchstücke* was first performed in Witten in 1992. It comprises 7½ images in which the musicians alter their basic actions and positions on the stage. A score documents precisely what structures and topics were discussed and decided on during the formation process. So the score is documentation that also gives instructions for the performance. It contains the sounds to be played, note by note; the rhythm of actions, words and sentences to be spoken are set down precisely. The musicians are also actors; they act themselves and about themselves; their roles emerge from their profession. For example, take Christian Dierstein, a percussion specialist for new music, a perfectionist with an extraordinary sensitivity to sound. His range of instruments, described above, is not unusual in new, experimental music: it is the norm. Breaking branches rhythmically, which he does at the opening of the piece over a quiet background of music from the other players, or throwing glass bottles violently into a wooden box, are quite familiar sound events in this context. They recall pieces by Nicolaus A. Huber, for example, where similar events occur (Daniel Ott studied composition under Huber from 1985 to 1990). So the percussionist is very active; in the second image, he takes seven precisely measured steps from left to right at the back of the stage, turning on his heels each time; in addition to the aggressive bottle breaking, he throws gravel at the saws, stirs in the broken glass, and throws sand at the drum. And what does he say while doing this? "It's simply – you get it – simply unbelievable – get it – simply not – never get rid – unbelievable – you get – it's un- – it's simply un- – you simply never – get rid of it".

An echo of the softer, more reflective sound events in the following third image provides a quiet moment before all the performers start speaking again. The percussionist starts pacing feverishly again and now more details are revealed: "It's unbelievable – you can hardly get rid of it – such a – such violence, that comes from marching – such militarism is almost always there with percussion."[10] What actually is percussion? The monologue and the reflections continue. "The way of using exotic instruments is somehow colonial – even the expression – 'beating a drum' – as if it's all about beating – the rociera or caña rociera – an instrument made of bamboo – used like castanets – at the fiesta del rocio – 'beating a drum' – beating is the least of it – 'drum' – the words themselves are violent – beating a drum also means: plucking, pulling, shaking and." As if to show possible continuations, in the next image, the fourth, the musicians are all standing in a row, looking towards the back of the stage and working with their feet. The fourth image develops into a joint step-dance with accompaniment.

The example of the percussionist shows that Ott does not simply provoke answers to his questions, but also initiates monologues. Chains of linked thoughts are expressed, associations woven in, related topics mentioned. This may recall Robert Ashley's 'involuntary speech' in his *Automatic Writing* (1979) or the musicians murmuring as if in their sleep in Michael Hirsch's *Hirngespinste* (1996). Speaking while music-making, speaking about music-making while music-making, reflecting on speaking about music-making while

---

10. All quotations from Daniel Ott, *skizze – 7½ bruchstücke*, score, dated 8 March 1992.

music-making; this also links with Mauricio Kagel's 'instrumental theatre', for example *Sur Scène* (1959/60) or *Sonant* (1960/…).[11]

In Daniel Ott's piece, speaking is also story-telling, recounting one's own experiences, and not suppressing the related emotions but giving them space. The speaking and actions are not simply carried out, do not simply happen, but transport anger, grief, regret, contentment and calm. The string players also take their experiences with their instruments, their relationships to their instruments, as their starting point. Barbara Maurer first played the violin, then the viola: "well yes, it was nothing special – just an average instrument, and when it's a gift you don't look so closely – end of last century". Melise Mellinger, who starts speaking with Barbara Maurer in the second image, was forced to; in the penultimate image she is finally able to articulate more clearly: "I would – I was forced to practice the violin – I got postcards showing landscapes or beautiful actors as a reward." Lucas Fels, cellist in the Arditti Quartet since late 2005, is less personal in his report, talking (probably) about his instrument. He also first presents speech fragments, hints, in the second image ("was a bit too big – a bit sawn off – was too big") that later come together to form a coherent statement, especially in the fifth image – after the step-dance – when all three strings players come forward and describe and praise their instruments. Now the cellist chants:

> seventeen-twenty bologna, it's the only cello made by the violin-maker florinus guidantos of bologna, made in 1720, a bit was sawn off here because the instrument was too big – a very special instrument, fantastic sound – there was woodworm in the f-holes.

Mixed with his resentment and pride in his instrument's history is his anger at having to suppress his south Baden dialect, and the cellist lapses into his dialect now more than ever. Again a chain of associations is triggered, which leaves open the question of its origins and continuation in the piece.

A film version of *skizze – 7½ bruchstücke* was produced in 1993 in collaboration with Reinhard Manz, entitled *7½*, and its first public viewing took place in Witten the same year. In the announcement of a television broadcast of the film in August 1993, the author gave this interpretation: "Scenes of pristine natural beauty for the opening – followed by the musicians' world, full of neuroses, compulsive repetition and legitimation crises, each musician trapped in an imaginary cage and each sound the product of alienated work."[12] But is the ensemble really in crisis, are the musicians autistic and is the music they play really the product of alienation? This interpretation hardly seems appropriate to the highly professional formation of the *ensemble recherche* from Freiburg, which is playing here. But how can one interpret the players' interactions that occur quite naturally, that in fact hold the piece together?

---

11. Cf. also Rebstock 2007.
12. "Zwischen Cage und Fellini: Daniel Otts *7½*", in Basler Zeitung, 11 August 1993. Cf. also www.danielott.com/presse/ (06 June 2010). The film was broadcast on the Swiss TV channel DRS.

The percussionists' actions dominate the beginning of the piece; the other instruments 'accompany' them. Sustained notes from the strings (violin and viola *flageolet*) and clarinet and brief rhythmic accents are the quiet background or sound shadow for the breaking of the branches. In the second image, the dynamics change; impulsive sound-gestures by the ensemble seem to heighten the breaking bottles in the box. This is followed by all the performers speaking, showing isolation but also a group dynamic – everyone has something to say. The word 'chaos' is mentioned – and not by chance. In the third image, a thoughtful pause takes place, which may succeed in reorganising the articulation emerging out of the silence. Yet the complex overlap of the sentences recurs, more intense in its dynamic withdrawal. Image four provides perhaps the greatest contrast: all performers standing in a row, all looking in the same direction, all performing to the same rhythm. Image five synchronises the string players' speaking; a further rhythmic link is attempted in the sixth image, but now there is a protest. "No, that's not quite true!" Melise Mellinger interrupts the procession of her male colleagues, who are moving in an orderly line from right to left on stage. The move away from this is gradually linked to a return to individualisation.

"The 7½ images must be staged during rehearsals", writes Daniel Ott in his score for the piece. He requires neutral stage lighting, a "well lit stage during the whole piece". The performers should have individual dark clothing and shoes with hard soles. He also specifies the initial positions of the chairs on stage and the precise position of the percussion. The staging is accordingly less a performance strategy than a creation strategy; the latter "creates the actuality of what it shows" (Fischer-Lichte 2004: 324).

ojota (1997 onwards)

The different versions of the *ojota* cycle are examples of Daniel Ott's 'work in progress'. *Ojota* uses shoes, steps, paths and traces. "I looked into different languages and cultures for synonyms for shoes or steps when searching for an overall title for the cycle. I finally discovered the word '*ojota*' in Quechua, a pre-Columbian indigenous language still spoken in the Andean Highlands of Peru and Bolivia. There is no word in Quechua for shoe – as the word 'shoe' appears to be of European origin – but there is a word for (wood) sandals, namely *ojota*" (Ott 2001: 55).[13] The starting point for the shoe pieces are elementary and personal experiences of walking. Mixing sound and movement into walking in different shoes and on different paths recreates a new basis that needs no seeking out, rather, and at most, emphasised or stage managed in the sense of "letting something current emerge" (Fischer-Lichte 2007: 22). There is also a broad cultural historical and artistic perspective in which walking has a role to play.[14] We may think of Thomas Bernhard's story *Gehen* from

---

13. See also Ott 2000: 94–8.
14. Cf. for example de Certeau 1988.

1971, another key text for Daniel Ott. Extracts from texts become material for him, such as five pairs of shoes made of leather, wood and iron that were used in the first version of *ojota* in 1997, in which a drummer goes on his way. In this contribution to the collective composition *Zwielicht – Hornberg. Sonnenuntergang/Sonnenaufgang* (Rümlingen), the drummer Christian Dierstein walks a stretch "almost one kilometre in length with changing surfaces underfoot: forest floor, gravel, meadow, wooden boards, grit and a tarred road". He moves "wearing different shoes (made of different material) on his feet and hands – and the mobile sounds produced this way could interact with the sound events and images that crossed the drummer's path" (Ott 2001: 56). Structuring and shaping walking, above all giving it rhythm, belong to the essential, compositional aspect of the piece. One cannot see the drummer in this piece as a musician merely performing one of Ott's scores, however, as Dierstein's own additions are integrated into the piece.

> The composition consisted ultimately of *sound events* while walking, of *pauses* and *changes of shoes* as well as of *virtuoso sections* 'trodden' into acoustically appropriate points in the piece. As he changed his shoes, Dierstein gave accounts of experiences with *shoes* and *stretches of path* that he had remembered during rehearsals, as well as recalling associations with the process of *walking* from various cultural journeys.
>
> (Ott 2001: 56)

One can call Daniel Ott's approach to his work as encyclopaedic in the widest sense. This touches very closely on the working methods of Mauricio Kagel. However, Ott's use of material is less about pre-structuring and preparing it (with Kagel, as well as with Schnebel, a consequence of parametric thinking) and much more about linking it. The heterogeneous material is not pre-arranged, but rather composed on the basis of aspects of its effect – not only in the sense of symbioses or synergies, but also in the sense of contrasts and contradictions. Composition becomes staging, staging composition. Matthias Rebstock asked an important question in this respect when he asked the composer how he went from the "improvised building blocks, that have a lot to do with the musicians, to a finalised composition" (Ott 2000: 97). It is worth studying the answer, but only the first paragraph can be given here for reasons of space. Ott replied:

> You can basically say that yes there are pieces in which everything develops from a point, and those that are based on a find to which the composer responds. You can see such finds, which were not my invention, in *ojota III*, and there isn't just one such point, but different ones. I currently find it exciting to link both together. I did not invent the shoe, nor samba. They are like pins on the map – and it is the path between them I compose.
>
> (Ott 2000: 97)

After the sound events of walking on a small stage were conveyed in *ojota II* (1998), and the shoe sounds combined with a mobile instrumental ensemble (*musica temporale*, Dresden), new personal and musical arrangements were presented in *ojota III*. For the premiere of *ojota III* at the Donaueschinger Musiktage in 1999, Ott worked with Anna Clementi (vocals), Françoise Rivalland (santur and cymbal), Chico Mello (guitar, clarinette), Simone Candotto (trombone) and Christian Dierstein (drums).[15]

> The starting point for the composition was improvisation and the performers' memories of *shoes/steps/paths/traces* from the five cultural journeys and in their five mother tongues: Italian, French, Portuguese, Friulan and German. I linked these finds with my own associations and refined them, created compositional sequences from them, and discussed them with the stage designer Sabine Hilscher and the dramaturge Matthias Rebstock. The performers became co-authors, their mother tongues music.
>
> (Ott 2001: 57)

Even the structure of this version of *ojota* is based on three 'sound finds' that emerged during rehearsals: fandango, serenade and waltz.[16] These also structure the dramaturgy, the density and the tempo of the sequences. There are two 'shoe changes' that end parts one and three and which initiate a 'cloakroom situation' – personal accounts from the performers that are simultaneously interpreted in the languages 'present'. However, this rough arrangement provides no information about the wealth of aspects that are implicitly and explicitly interwoven and made into a theme in this piece about shoes. The pairs of shoes that come onto the stage one after the other at the start, from high-heeled shoes and clogs to worn-out brogues, pumps and sandals, is possibly an allegory of this arrangement. Each pair of shoes could tell a story. The stage designer Sabine Hilscher specialises in such items and naturally selected the shoes on the basis of their sound. This selection criterion was surely important in part three when some of the pairs of shoes perform solo.

You can not only tread paths in shoes, as the shoes themselves become trails on the stage, the rows of shoes giving the space a clear shape at the start. The drummer positions them in rhythmic sequences and Anna Clementi uses them as pathways, as if they were rocks in a stream, the water flowing between them.

In the south Brazilian fandango, musicians play complex rhythms using their wooden shoes and the musicians in *ojota III* hark back to this tradition. Continuing this tradition freely is also intended. While the first part presents group work that ends with 'frozen' scenes and a silent fandango, the middle section of the piece focusses on the 'lonely balladeer' Chico Mello with his guitar. His performance is contrasted by the musician Anna Clementi, loud and hysterically invective in a dressing gown ('Aunt Rosina') in the 'long corridor of a house in Catania', as well as by Françoise Rivalland stomping around clumsily on stilts. The trombonist later enters and exits the stage in the role of a character from a small Italian

---

15. Cf. the DVD documentary of the premiere in Donaueschingen by Reinhard Manz, point de vue DOC, Basel 1999/2008.
16. Cf. Ott 2001: 57.

Figure 1: Scene from Daniel Ott: *ojota III* (1999).
Copyright Sabine Hilscher.

town. His small, exhilarating gestures are enough to identify him as an actor. The panorama of the shoes and their contexts thus overlap with the functions of the characters on the stage: private individuals, folk musicians, and the performers of a piece, actors, stage workers, narrators, translators and living sculptures.

This spectrum is extended in the next project – *ojota IV* (2000, Theater Bielefeld) – and is directed towards the audience's situation as well as the duration of the performance and the number of performers (seven singers, two actors and six musicians).

> Together with the dramaturges Matthias Rebstock and Roland Quitt, a version emerged in which location changes by the performers and audience divided up the evening into smaller sections. This meant that spectators could experience aspects of the *pathways/ steps/walking* theme.

> (Ott 2001: 60)

The arrangement of the piece is close to open-air theatre, but it is more akin to music theatre projects of the 1960s and 70s, for example Meredith Monk's *Juice: A Theatre Cantata in*

3 Installments (1969) and *Vessel: An Opera Epic* (1971). Both of these projects by Monk are performed in three different stages. The locations in *Juice* become smaller and more private, while those in *Vessel* become larger and more public.[17] The fourth *ojota* project by Ott "kidnaps" the listeners and spectators in a hall on the outskirts of Bielefeld before the audience is then brought (in part two) into the "bitter February cold" where, "from behind a massive *gravel/sand/waste* landscape", a "self-luminous *procession*" emerges, "which is chased off by the actors (with Bernhard texts)" (Ott 2001: 60). The performance of *ojota III* follows in part three ('inside') after an acoustic transition in full darkness. *Ojota IV* "is a workshop and journey of self-discovery, a trip to the frontiers of art and an allegory for vagrancy" (Loskill 2000: 64). For the middle section outdoors, Ott interweaves sentences from Thomas Bernhard's *Gehen* into the panorama of the 'shoe work'.

Bernhard's story must have been more than a mere source of text for *ojota*, however. The complexity of its descriptions of events, the overlay of quotations, the merging of voices as well as the presentation of people and objects in this text, and the similar expressions relating to speaking, walking and thinking that are frequently repeated though in a different way, were certainly formal reference points during the creation of *ojota*. This refers not only to the increase in the number of associations with shoes in the individual pieces, but also to the working process divided into several parts. The cycle in *Ojota V* was further developed for three performers with shoes, tables, stools and an accordion (Drochtersen-Hüll, 2002).

Hafenbecken I & II. umschlagplatz klang (2005/2006) and other compositions for public spaces including landscapes

Alongside pieces that use the concert hall as a stage, or pieces for extended theatre spaces, Daniel Ott regularly develops projects for public venues such as city spaces, industrial areas or natural landscapes. Even ski-lifts have been used, for example in *skilift / klang*, "open air music for trumpet, brass band, ski-lift masts and ringing bells" (Heiligkreuz/Entlebuech 2003). He has even created his own experimental field in this area with the *Festival Rümlingen* in Switzerland, in which many international artists now take part.[18] The starting points for these projects are again the characteristics of the existing environment, particularly buildings, functional industrial facilities, scenic water structures, hills, woods, meadows, railway lines or roads running through. (*Hafenbecken I & II. umschlagplatz klang* for 68 instruments was conceived for a performance at the Rhine Harbour in Basel and received its premiere in 2006 with the Basel Sinfonietta). It was created together with the director Enrico Stolzenburg, the costume designer Angela Zimmermann and the lighting designer Michael Gööck.[19]

---

17. Cf. Jowitt 1997.
18. Cf. Ott 2005.
19. Cf. Manz 2007.

Behind the sound event 'Hafenbecken I & II. umschlagplatz klang' were the musicians Guido Stier and Numa Bischof from the Basel Sinfonietta (of which Bischof is the former managing director), who were looking for music for a 'moving orchestra' in a particular location in Basel – i.e. they were explicitly looking for music to be played outside of a concert hall. After considering various locations (Lange Erlen, Kasernenareal, etc.), we opted for Rhine Harbour in Basel. The first sound experiment took place in November 2002 with ten musicians from the Basel Sinfonietta in the large hall of the transhipment yard. There were further experiments over the next three years to continue to investigate the acoustic and 'theatrical' possibilities of the entire location more precisely.

(Ott and Stolzenburg 2006)

As with the music theatre projects mentioned above, a performance plan used at the end was developed gradually during the rehearsal phase. "The first question we asked ourselves was 'How does the location "itself" sound without using any additional sounds?' On first inspection, we noted the strong smells at the harbour and we heard the sound of water, seagulls squawking, ship horns, metal welding, sounds from the railways, cranes, ships and the unloading of goods from containers – a different acoustic environment with sounds from all four directions and which fluctuated heavily depending on the time of day and light. How could additional sounds from musical instruments be linked with the harbour sounds without disturbing the existing sound characteristics of the location? We adopted an improvisational approach to the music in the different sound experiments that began three-and-a-half years before the first performance. Many ideas came about jointly with the orchestra musicians involved in the project" (Ott 2008: 37).

A 'constructed' level of sound was added to the improvised harbour music and this emerged from the number 17. A 17-tone series was derived (with quarter tones) from the 17 stations in the first part of the project. "Each of the 17 stations in the first part of the performance has its own 'main music' and its own interval; the 17-note chord emerges at the beginning, and the first tone is naturally the 'Rhine sound' E flat major" (Ott and Stolzenburg 2006). One can see here how Ott finds the tones for his music. Even rhythmic structures stem in part from data he has 'found', for example in *ojota I* they emerged from the proportions of changes in light (sunrise, sunset, civil twilight, nautical twilight, darkness).

Hafenbecken I & II. umschlagplatz klang was performed in three stages. In the first section, with 17 stations, live sounds were 'installed' or sound sources were set in motion in particular locations of the harbour. The audience wandered between the different locations or with the 'moving orchestra'. There were drums on a filling system, electric guitars on a travelling railway carriage or double bass players on a boat and trombonists on construction cranes. The second stage, after sunset, saw "common sound signals and 68 very quiet chords, harmonies with minimal differences that the harbour 'coloured' in the advancing twilight" (Ott 2008: 39). The third section was room music for the harbour's large freight hall.

The musicians streamed into the hall at the beginning of part three, distributed themselves in the playing positions on the various floors around the spectators and then left the hall at the end in the opposite direction. In doing so, they continued the movement they had started, the stream of sound disappeared in the distance and they traced an arc to the open start of the evening.

(Ott 2008: 39)

Daniel Ott's place-related projects and landscape compositions provide particular evidence of his impulse to create musical and theatrical perceptual offers, but which can barely be perceived as stagings. One has to see them as artistic settlements and remove them from the given setting in order to make the 'natural' surroundings apparent. Ott thereby brings the audience into 'experimental' situations in different ways. If the public loses its orientation in *ojota IV*, as the path and goal were not revealed when the spectators were kidnapped and taken from the theatre, then everything in the landscape composition remains open: so where do the listeners and spectators go in order not to miss the 'artwork'? Ott's 'communication' with the public is explained more clearly using two concluding examples.

Ott was in charge of the musical arrangement of Peter Zumthor's Swiss Pavilion for the Expo 2000 in Hanover. Zumthor had built a wooden house – called Swiss Sound Body – that was an open structure whose inner space was organised like a labyrinth with many corridors and open spaces that opened up like yards. Ott's musical furnishing and 'performance' in the building was part of a complete staging concept: alongside Ott, Plinio Bachmann was responsible for writing/words, Max Rigendinger for gastronomy, Karoline Gruber for staging and Ida Gut for clothing.[20]

The music formed one element in the house: "There was *music* for 12 hours on each of the 153 days the Swiss Pavilion was open. Each of the fifteen musicians played for five to six hours each day between 9.30am and 9.30pm in shifts of roughly three hours and in accordance with a changing plan in the *sound rooms* and *corridors* of the *sound body*: six accordionists, six hammered dulcimer players and three musicians who improvised with changing instruments (trombone, tuba, trumpet, alphorn, saxophone, voice, etc.)" (Ott 2001: 64). It was envisaged from the outset that there would be 'acoustic rooms' in Zumthor's building, for example, certain open spaces or places where people could communicate. They encouraged people to linger and listen. The music thus grabbed the visitors' attention for a certain period of time and at the same time created an individual atmosphere. In this way, the building was a 'tuned space' from which individual voices stood out.

The basic sounds provide sound material above which the musicians improvise; accordionists and hammered dulcimer players investigate the possibilities offered by the basic sounds during the rehearsal phase. Improvisation rules and variation possibilities

---

20. Cf. Ott 2001: 63 et seq.

Figure 2: Sketch by Daniel Ott, programme book *Wittener Tage für neue Kammermusik* 2009, p. 15.

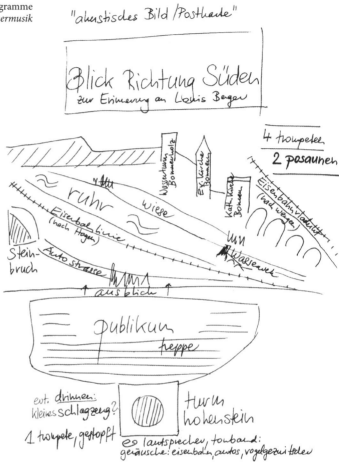

are tested/discarded/developed further; in the sound body, the freely improvising musicians respond to the basic sound and provide additional stimuli: the basic sound is different every day, is always changing.

(Ott 2001: 65)[21]

---

21. The basic sound "is made up of 153 sounds and 23 eruptions [...] The sounds are rather flat, wide – sound colours making their way through the space. The eruptions are loud, flamboyant, rhythmic, imprecise, intermittent – i.e. they surprise. The basic sound and eruptions always alternate differently. The basic sound is a new plan each day. The existing or pre-composed sounds were adjusted to the *sound body* during sound tests early in 2000 in which almost all the musicians took part. During the tests, the musicians responded to the basic sound with their own scenic ideas and sound improvisations. To a certain extent, the musicians are therefore co-composers" (Hönig 2000: 88).

Visitors were also surprised by particular sound events (e.g. *eruptions* or *breaks*). By turning a corner in the labyrinth, one could suddenly find oneself in an opening that was immersed in a particular atmosphere. The wood acted as a sound absorber, so although one suspected that something was happening, one was not prepared for what exactly would happen. An acoustic homogenisation of the building was linked with numerous local events.[22] It was not intended for the focus to be on the allusions to Switzerland, but it seems obvious that the country is being symbolically transported into an architectural body that is open on all sides and a home and resting place for ramblers. This also relates to sound ecology, the presence of natural or social 'soundscapes' that were captured in Ott's project for the pavilion and installed there.

> The interpreters play their own music in the *windows*: folk music from their native countries, their own style of music. For me, this is an opportunity to make the diversity of the 350 participating musicians and their music audible throughout the exhibition.
>
> (Ott 2001: 66)

In contrast to many music projects where sounds from landscapes or urban spaces are 'captured' in electro-acoustic compositions and displaced in other spaces, musicians performed the soundscape of the Swiss Pavilion fresh each day. The focus of the work was not on a constant, identical musical arrangement of the space, but on its 'living' metamorphosis.

Daniel Ott's landscape composition *Blick Richtung Süden* was conceived for the Witten New Chamber Music Days 2009. The composer and the director Enrico Stolzenburg commented on the project as follows:

> The public stands on the platform at the foot of the tower at Hohenstein that was built in memory of the industrialist and parliamentarian Louis Berger in 1902. There is a breathtaking view south of the floodplains of the Ruhr, a panorama of nature and civilisation: road traffic and trains pass through the idyllic riverscape with small islands, meadows and hill ranges, the Ruhr swells up at the water works, and the quarry, the Witten-Bommern Bridge and the neighbouring industrial site show the area was shaped by man. One can hear traffic and industrial sounds alternating with rather chance sounds produced by nature and animals. For beholders of the scene, a sound postcard opens up that captures the contradictions of the southern Ruhr region in a unique and concentrated way. The acoustics of the area are largely dependent on the season – e.g. the water levels of the Ruhr determine the intensity of the noise at the power plant – we form the final dramaturgy of our sound image during the rehearsals before the performances in which both amateur musicians and clubs from Witten and the surrounding area also took part.[23]

---

22. On the sound homogenisation of the space, cf. Straus 1930. On the creation of atmospheres, cf. Schouten 2007.
23. *Wittener Tage für neue Kammermusik 2009*, programme book, Saarbrücken: Pfau-Verlag 2009, p. 14. Cf. Rohde: 2009.

Figure 3: Daniel Ott: *Blick Richtung Süden* (2009). Copyright Enrico Stolzenburg.

In the landscape composition for five trumpets, two trombones, one clarinet, percussion, live electronics, homing pigeons, canoeists and brass band (in Witten), the brass instruments are predominant and enter into a dialogue with far off places.

> Sounds are captured and blasted out; from a far-off meadow, even from the platform of a sluice, four trumpeters and two trombonists send out [...] their sound signals in the direction of the Berger Tower from where a fifth trumpeter replies. Tape recordings boost the landscape's sounds. The sound image is enhanced by lively gestures from sport and play activities far off and close by, among the latter a squadron of canoes approaching the sluice from a distance.
>
> (Rohde: 2009)

The scenery is described differently in another report: "A 'concert installation' made up of sounds from nature, civilisation [...] and echo-like brass calls between valley and tower, and in which art and reality, chance and purpose mix together until they can no longer be recognised. Whoever had the opportunity to attend this 'sound postcard', which exaggerates the aesthetic contradictions of the southern Ruhr region [...] on several occasions was able to experience how the visual and acoustic colours of the staging were subject to change on a daily basis" (Wieschollek 2009: 80).

Working with existing natural, architectural and industrial elements, and those developed by society, a staged, perceptual offer was created. The recipients, those present, on the one hand absorb a *Gesamtkunstwerk*, listen to a staged overall situation and observe an artistically arranged big picture, at least in some sections, but on the other hand they understand the performance of the artwork's various components in individual and selective reception stages, that is, they follow the artistic linking of the individual elements.

Conclusion

Music and theatre are inseparable in a very specific way in Daniel Ott's works. It is not just that a musician, a visible artist on the stage, becomes a stage character at the same time, or is one already; biographical, professional and social influences, individual characteristics, inclinations and aversions, short-term and long-term goals, interests, associations and special skills – all of a person's characteristics and contexts imaginable play a role in or feed into Ott's works of music theatre. Everyday life becomes *music* theatre. This not only concerns the people involved in the works; even harbour basins, ski-lifts or railway viaducts and sections of landscape are themselves natural or constructed theatre locations that become *music* theatre. Music is attached to existing sounds, embedded in a soundscape and used as a staging tool, the latter noticeable at varying degrees of intensity. One may ask why the composer has dedicated himself more intently to public spaces and large scenic dimensions in recent years and what development possibilities they offer him. Firstly, the research work to be carried out ahead of a project is changing considerably: more time for the development of the landscape, historical factors or land-use plans and the social as well as acoustic structure of an occupied landscape need to be considered, for example. The information collected at this stage is probably more substantial and comprehensive than that acquired in the work with musicians from a small ensemble, but it is probably less personal and acquired from a greater distance. In any case, the composer is still always the one that registers, that is, takes in, what 'is there' in the first instance and the impressions of his work colleagues are added to this. In this way, Ott is a filter and a coupling that respectively sorts and connects the existing elements, associated thoughts, new material, far-off geographical areas as well as aspects that are immediately to hand. Communicativeness, openness and loose ends are all part of this working process. The performers involved do not merely execute Ott's instructions but are co-creators of the pieces and projects. There is no question about the authorship of the works, however, as the artistic direction and organisation of processes is in the hands of just one person's (or a management team). That said, Ott is not a supervisor who gives orders during these work processes; he is more a contact man and an instigator, a catalyst and an achiever.

(Translation: Nick Woods)

References

Cage, John (1958) "Experimental Music", in Cage, John (1961), *Silence*, Hanover: Wesleyan University Press.

De Certeau, Michel (1988) "Praktiken im Raum", in Michel de Certeau, *Kunst des Handelns*, translated by Ronald Voullié, Berlin, pp. 179–238.

Fischer-Lichte, Erika (2007) "Theatralität und Inszenierung", in Fischer-Lichte, Erika, Horn, Christian, Pflug, Isabel, and Warstat, Matthias (2007) *Inszenierung von Authentizität*, Tübingen and Basel: A. Francke, pp. 9–28.

—— (2004) *Ästhetik des Performativen*, Frankfurt am Main: Suhrkamp Verlag.

Hönig, Roderick (ed.) (2000) *Klangkörperbuch, Lexikon zum Pavillon der Schweizerischen Eidgenossenschaft an der Expo 2000 in Hannover*, Basel, Boston and Berlin: Birkhäuser Verlag

Jowitt, Deborah (1997) *Meredith Monk*, Baltimore and London: The John Hopkins University Press.

Loskill, Jörg (2000) "Reise in das Schuh-Land. Daniel Otts *Ojota IV* in Bielefeld", in Opernwelt 41, vol. 4.

Manz, Reinhard (2007) *Hafenbecken I & II*, DVD, point de vue DOC, Basel.

Von Matt, Sylvia Egli et al. (2008) *Das Porträt*, Konstanz: UVK Verlagsgesellschaft.

Ott, Daniel (2008) "Am Umschlagplatz Klang: Anmerkungen zum Experimentellen in der Musik", in Neue Zeitschrift für Musik 169.

—— and Enrico Stolzenburg, *Musik für ein "bewegtes Orchester" an einem besonderen Ort*, www.sinfonietta-archiv.ch/PPL/Saison06/Text_S1_2006.htm (accessed on 18 June 2010).

—— (2001) "Voraussetzungen für ein Neues Musiktheater – Gesamtkunstwerk", in Kolleritsch, Otto (2001) *Das Musiktheater – Exempel der Kunst* (= Studien zur Wertungsforschung, vol. 38), Vienna and Graz: Universal-Edition, pp. 50–81.

—— (2000) "ojota – Schuhe, Schritte, Wege. Gespräch zwischen Daniel Ott und Matthias Rebstock", in Sanio, Sabine, Wackernagel, Bettina and Ravenna, Jutta (2000), *Klangkunst – Musiktheater. Musik im Dialog III* (= Jahrbuch der Berliner Gesellschaft für Neue Musik 1999), Saarbrücken: Pfau-Verlag.

Rebstock, Matthias (2007) *Komposition zwischen Musik und Theater. Das instrumentale Theater von Mauricio Kagel zwischen 1959 und 1965* (= sinefonia 6), Hofheim: wolke Verlag.

—— (2005) "'Just do your Job': Rollenkonzepte im neuen Musiktheater", in Ott, Daniel, Ott, Lukas and Jeschke, Lydia (2005) *Geballte Gegenwart. Experiment Neue Musik Rümlingen*, Basel: Christoph Merian Verlag, pp. 44–7.

Rohde, Gerhard (2009) "Klingende Landschaften: Wittens Tage für neue Kammermusik drängen ins Freie", Neue Musikzeitung 58, vol. 6, www.nmz.de/artikel/klingende-landschaften (27 March 2010).

Rust, Sarah (2009) "Igor Strawinskys Poétique musicale – Ein musikästhetisches Credo", MA thesis, Freie Universität Berlin 2009.

Schoenberg, Arnold (1941) "Composition with Twelve Tones (1)", in Schoenberg, Arnold (1975), *Style and Idea*, edited by Leonard Stein, London: Faber &Faber.

Schmidt, Jochen (2002) *Pina Bausch 'Tanzen gegen die Angst'*, Munich: Econ & List Taschenbuch-Verlag, pp. 87–98.

Schouten, Sabine (2007) *Sinnliches Spüren: Wahrnehmung und Erzeugung von Atmosphären im Theater* (= Recherchen, vol. 46), Berlin: Theater der Zeit.

Schulze-Reuber, Rika (2005) *Das Tanztheater Pina Bausch: Spiegel der Gesellschaft*, Frankfurt am Main: R. G. Fischer.

Martin Seel (2002) *Sich bestimmen lassen. Studien zur theoretischen und praktischen Philosophie*, Frankfurt am Main: Suhrkamp

Simpson, J. A. and Weiner, E. S. C. (ed.) (1989) *The Oxford English Dictionary*, vol. 11, Oxford.

Straus, Erwin (1930) *Die Formen des Räumlichen. Ihre Bedeutung für die Motorik und die Wahrnehmung*, in Straus, Erwin (1960), *Psychologie der menschlichen Welt. Gesammelte Schriften*, Berlin, Göttingen, Heidelberg: Springer, pp. 141–78.

Stravinsky, Igor (1970) *Poetics of Music in the Form of Six Lessons*, Cambridge: Harvard University Press [1947].

Johann Gottfried Walther (1732) *Musikalisches Lexikon oder musikalische Bibliothek*, Leipzig, reprint: Richard Schaal (ed.) (1953), Kassel and Basel: Bärenreiter.

Wieschollek, Dirk (2009) "Landschaft mit Klangwolke. Die Wittener Tage für neue Kammermusik gehen hinaus ins Freie", Neue Zeitschrift für Musik 170, vol. 3.

Chapter 14

Permanent Quest: The Processional Theatre of Manos Tsangaris

Jörn Peter Hiekel

The music theatre œuvre of Manos Tsangaris is characterised both by continuously changing choices with regard to formats, arrangements and instrumentations, and by the fact that these changes also occur within individual works of separate groups of works. All his works seem to wrestle free from the customary frontality of presentation, as we have known it from the history of opera and classical concerts, in order to explore new solutions. This also usually means that traditional roles and responsibilities of vocal and instrumental performers are eliminated or at least extended. It is characteristic of Tsangaris' approach that his works consist of individual stations in different rooms through which one migrates – an approach that has for some time been called 'Processional Theatre'.[1] Due to the different formats and changing strategies, the question of the perception of music becomes the centre of attention, independently at first of the semantic constellations evoked by certain texts, which change in every project and provide different levels of concentration and intensification.

Spaces of/for awareness

Such delimitations and transgressions in the works of Manos Tsangaris can be characterised without exaggeration as an act of resistance against the conventions and norms of the music industry. In this respect, Tsangaris follows the tradition of his former teacher, Mauricio Kagel. But even more determinedly than Kagel he has coined and variegated this creative form of transgression time and again, often in conscious deviation from familiar locations of music(-theatre)-performance. This approach, based not on a radical break but on the idea of a permeability of different strategies of presenting music, benefits from what the age-old, tried and tested performance situation shares with the existing strong dramatic imprint on musical or theatrical works or with its inherent teleological aspects: all these factors are rooted in our consciousness so strongly, and the dominance of the marks they have left over a long time period is so unchallenged, that a composer can continuously rebel against them in a number of ways.

---

1. The German term 'Stationentheater' refers to a similar aesthetic principle as its counterpart 'processional theatre'; it is, however, more neutral with regard to its political implications (often described as an empowering form of street theatre) (note from the translator).

This rebellion by means of strategies of using different spatial arrangements provides a perspective that for Tsangaris is not an end in itself but a basic requirement of most of his projects. Again and again these unlock unusual spaces or approach familiar spaces in new unusual ways, invoking innovative and unique theatrical situations in the often minaturesque music-theatre pieces. These can be characterised – following Hans-Thies Lehmann's descriptions of a postdramatic theatre – by their renunciation of a given artistic macro-structure providing coherence, such as the dramatic text (cf. Lehmann 1999, here and for the following). Here, the dissemination of text and meaning are not ostentatious factors. Instead, there is a multitude of prismatic refractions. As a recipient, one is drawn into situations that manage to sustain one's aesthetic curiosity by means of many surprises. It becomes apparent that what is being (re)presented might be an excerpt of a larger context. Instead of a solid, stabilising synthesis of the different levels, there are always open fragmented moments as well as 'figurations of self-eradications of meanings' (Lehmann 1999: 140). But in addition to moments of contingency, there are repeatedly condensations of clusters of meaning. These can be characterised as flashes of insight, which sometimes reveal their orientation to real daily life experiences and emphasise the fleeting, casual and ephemeral, but are sometimes far removed from everyday life and seem almost surreal. In all this the essential experience is that of an oscillation between understanding and not understanding – which constitutes a fundamental experience in contemporary music theatre.

When Manos Tsangaris' theatre operates with texts, it succeeds in creating event-like situations, which may distance themselves from logical sequentiality in many ways. Examples include the Dresden production *Lot's Weib [Lot's wife]* (2006) and the Donaueschingen *Batsheba*-project (2009) – both oscillate in remarkably diverse ways between the representation of stories and a variety of elements which lead away from these stories. Central to Tsangaris' Composed Theatre are perceptual constellations, which are characterised by permanent transitions between representation, association and seemingly unrelated playful performance. This transitionality draws our attention to the common difficulty in interpreting something seemingly unrelated as a consistent string of signs.

Tsangaris' preferred mode of text presentation ironically suspends the conventional dissemination of text – particularly in the media – without exaggerating it in a pointedly grotesque way. Reflections on the plethora of sensory stimuli in our reality are also central. The composer's miniaturesque compositions (which consist of small, mostly two- to eight-minute scenes) are attempts to condense this abundance into concentrates, which in their unique mixture are often terse and enchanting, and sometimes poetic.

Interrogation of sites

Visitors in the processional theatre of Manos Tsangaris are *flâneurs*, who, in the sense of Walter Benjamin's emphatic descriptions of ideas of passages, end up in unusual constellations of experience and thus begin to marvel. This can be read as a critical comment on those public passages called 'shopping malls', which may be seen as a signature of our present time. Their abundant (over-)staged event-worlds rely on the suggestion of individuality while tending towards a collective, ecstatic experience. Suggestively, Tsangaris reflects on the persuasive nature of the commercial strategies of *mise en scène* without adopting them. His theatrical works discover distinctive, delicate possibilities for passages and unexpected links.

The composed passages in works by Tsangaris are in some respects the exact opposite of all those light-flooded commercial arcades. In work as early as his *Studie [Study]* for performer and lighting (1978), labelled 'Opus 1', one can clearly see how important it is for him to operate with darkness. A completely dark room is transformed into a partially perceptible space through the use of a single spotlight. The result is a dull brightness, which clearly reflects the difficulty with which it was wrested from the darkness. A crescendo of the main spotlight from 0 to 100 per cent and other finesses of lighting follow. It is precisely the lighting design and timing which is minutely determined in the scores of Tsangaris. This highlights the artificiality of what is depicted. Brief moments of turning on lights full beam in otherwise dark spaces are characteristic of many of his projects. This often happens by means of torches, which either eliminate the usual ritual of seeing-and-being-seen in the concert or opera situations, or reduce it to a brief moment of wonder due to a sudden encounter. Ushers are thus an indispensable part of some of his works.

Time and time again the key issue is the interrogation and interpretation of very specific places. The venue as a community space, which offers the possibility of a collective experience, is contrasted with small-scale situations, in which the usual rituals – such as applauding or taking a bow as well as similarly clearly recognisable finale effects – are suspended. The works of Tsangaris are thus often situated on the border between a 'situational'[2] and a progressively structured design. They are not unfamiliar with traditional forms and sequences, but continue to disrupt the conventional continuum of the temporal art of music with regard to their actions, gestures and sounds.

Overall, the deviation from traditional theatre performance settings is more obvious in Tsangaris' work than for example in the instrumental theatre of his former teacher, Mauricio Kagel – a concept which certainly influenced his understanding of theatre. Today, as Kagel's music has already found its place in municipal symphonic concerts or in conservative–representative festivals and is being presented as a genre-typical music with a conventional dramaturgical format (one may welcome or regret this), it appears that his former student has in many respects taken Kagel's place. By now Tsangaris' projects can also no longer – as used to be the case at festivals such as Donaueschingen – be pigeonholed as a mere addition to the 'actual' concert activities. The boundaries of what is supposed to be at the centre and on the fringe have been largely blurred, particularly evident in the strong presence of the performance of *Batsheba: Eat the history!* at the Donaueschingen Music Festival in 2009.

---

2. With regard to this notion see Tsangaris 2006.

Even though Manos Tsangaris responds to specific sites with his works, almost all of them can still be transferred to other places without a loss of substance. This is particularly true for the project *Winzig [Tiny]*, first realised in Cologne in 1993, a variably fanned out 'music for a house'[3] consisting of highly unusual situations. One walked through surprising, sometimes disturbing spatial arrangements. These resemble the sensation-promising show booths at a fun fair, which can indeed be regarded as the epitome of developing and staging a world of its own and its poetic possibilities. Rooms, which are not usually accessible, are being filled with musical and theatrical activities and are (re)activated, as if it was the most natural thing in the world.

Tsangaris' projects occur preferably in historic buildings. Ideally, these historical spaces come with a unique aura to which he can respond. The project *Drei Räume [Three Spaces]*, seen and heard at the Donaueschinger Music Festival in 2004, may serve as an example. The object of reflection was the Fürstliche Hofbibliothek [Donaueschingen Court Library], which had been emptied out (due to the sale of manuscripts) and was now presented and made resonant in all its charm and its dignity by Tsangaris. Amongst other things this was achieved through the exquisite sounds of a harpsichord, which was embedded in a candlelight setting with Dirndl dresses from the Mozart era. A setting like this cannot easily be transferred. Some things in this project were even specifically related to Donaueschingen and the festival which sprawls over the whole city, such as scenes in the upper floor of the library or the cellar, where the 'prince' and the 'artistic director' were brought into view in addition to showing video recordings of festival visitors. The aim was to playfully exemplify and model the essence of the festival structure in Donaueschingen. Tsangaris even suggested that these sorts of concretisation could be compared with reality television.[4] It is precisely in *Drei Räume* that the question about what reality could ever be arises. And from the eponymous spaces of the title the most significant one proves to be the inner space of the spectator.

Winzig, with which Tsangaris first gained international attention, is already one of those projects that explore a house, make it sound in different places and bring its hidden charms and possibilities into view (beyond the accepted performance spaces even all the way to the boiler room), as well as its limitations. In this, Tsangaris' concept may not be unique, but it has a special suggestiveness. The places where one has intensively experienced one of his projects (and which obviously revert to serving other purposes afterwards), can hardly be re-entered later without the memory of this project. It is all the more attractive, then, when some projects – especially his *Diskrete Stücke [Discrete Pieces]* – are realised in public places that are not otherwise used for music-theatre. At its world premiere, this was the main building of the WDR in Cologne;[5] a place whose rich history is also to some extent reflected in this composition.

---

3. This refers to the subtitle of the composition: *Winzig: Musik für ein Haus* (note from the translator).
4. Cf. the conversation between Armin Köhler and Tsangaris documented in the programme notes of the Donaueschingen music festival 2004, p. 108.
5. The main building of the federal broadcasting company for the West of Germany (note from the translator).

Changes of perspective

It is important for Tsangaris' processional theatre to keep perspectives flexible. At each performance, visitors can give up their chosen direction of movement in favour of another. This includes at least three aspects: first, the succession of the stations that the spectator traverses is deliberately not determined. The *parcours* through these staged imaginary worlds is consequently individual and – according to the notion of passages by Walter Benjamin – characterised by a non-directional movement which suspends a clear succession. Also, in some theatre situations one is invited to linger as briefly or long as one wishes, or to revisit parts of the performance, which have a fixed duration and are repeated, and see them several times. Second, the question of one's own position is interrogated each time: there are various concepts that either allow strolling during the performance or facilitate different viewpoints of the same event from different perspectives. And third, the spatial arrangement alternates between moments of close proximity and distance, not unlike a camera moving from a close-up to a long shot.

The latter, rendering perspectives flexible, is particularly significant: the close-up culminates in installations which guide the viewer's eye into a keyhole situation. With the help of small invisible magnets or similar techniques, movements are evoked in small showcases which can only be seen by one or two spectators simultaneously. Here a kind of proximity is achieved, which we are otherwise at best familiar with in the visual arts.

Closeness can be encountered in a very specific way in a miniature, which Tsangaris presented at various performances of *Winzig* under the title *Sessellift [chair lift]* – and which used a particularly small room performatively (see Figures IV.4.1 and IV.4.2). The piece consists of a lift moving up and down crowded by two spectators and one performing musician. Not only is this space mobile; it also creates a kind of proximity between performer and audience that is highly unusual in traditional concert life. We are familiar with it in contemporary theatre, particularly during its 'activist' phase in the 1960s and 70s, if we think about the many productions in which actors performed in the middle of the auditorium between the rows of seats (see Lehmann 1999: 291). The proximity of this 'elevator music' by Tsangaris, however, is linked in a quite different way to spatial intimacy and security. The aesthetic experience intertwines extremely different qualities such as luxury and distress by means of this unusual closeness: the exclusivity of a private performance with an almost claustrophobic narrowness as an indicator of being at someone's mercy.[6]

In *Sessellift* one can identify the specific way in which Manos Tsangaris composes different media. In this section of *Winzig* the following instruments are used: a large galvanised aluminium pot, the bottom of which is played on, a mouth-pipe, a light pendulum made from a blinking flashlight, which hangs by a thread from the ceiling, and another blinking

---

6. Other music-theatre works have meanwhile taken up this aesthetical strategy, for example in the piece *Avenir! Avenir!* by Hamed Taheri and Dror Feiler, 2006 in Stuttgart.

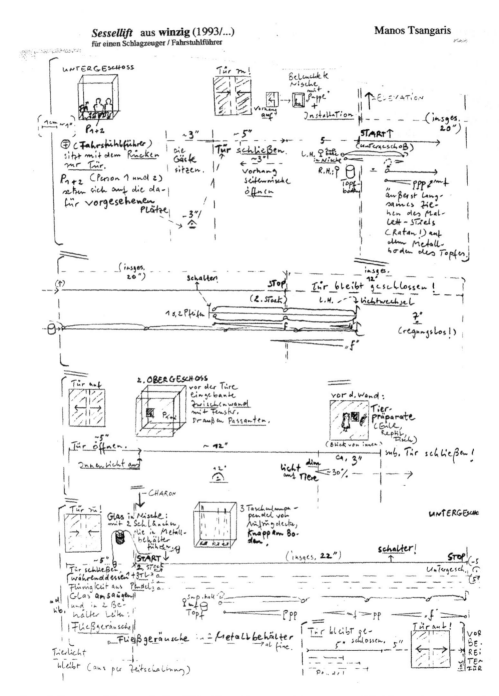

Figure 1: First page of the score for *Sessellift* by Manos Tsangaris. With permission of the Thuermchen Verlag, Cologne.

Figure 2: Scene from *Sessellift*.
Private Photograph.

flashlight. In this orchestra of simple everyday objects, the visual level is quite naturally intertwined with the acoustic level. A look at the score of this piece reveals that the use of all elements is coordinated quite accurately by Tsangaris (by providing timings by the second). The same applies to the closing of the lift door as well as its journey to other floors. In this arrangement of sounds and visuals there are both continuously flowing and deliberately surprising elements. The latter consists, for example, in suddenly exposing two prepared (stuffed) animals – a flying bird and a fish – which have been kept hidden until that point. Playing with surprise and mysteriousness turns out to be the central dimension of the *Sessellift* section. Playing the mouth pipe and the aluminium pot also contributes to this significantly through its alternation between loud and quiet moments. Just when the lift doors first close according to the score, a threatening atmosphere is created. The narrowness of the space is first experienced; gloomy expectations are evoked. Shortly thereafter, the departure of the lift leads to the first climax of the whole piece, before opening the view on the stuffed animals. In a peculiar way, they signal something of a departure from the vitality of life, associating a rather negative feeling. The two stuffed animals appear in a black box, which has been set up in front of the lift door on the targeted floor. Thus instead of leaving the lift, as one would expect after its arrival, the audience is confronted with these mysterious animals. The door closes again and the lift returns to its original floor. What follows then is certainly a kind of *lieto fine*, namely the reopening the door – and the spectators realise on exiting the lift that they have witnessed a small and ominous musical theatre scene. The ironic undercurrent of the scene – due to its setting and its aura and the simple materials – forms a vital part of the experience of this scene.

Tsangaris has often been drawn to this aspect of a strict limitation of the audience and the essential play with different perspectives it includes. It represents a deliberate inversion of the relationship between performer and spectator and he tested this in a particularly radical way some decades ago: in the composition *o.T.* (i.e. *Untitled*) from 1980, a seven-piece ensemble plays for a single listener. At its first performance, this listener was Mauricio Kagel.[7]

Characteristic of many projects of Tsangaris are also moments of distance, indebted to the Brechtian theatre. This distance juxtaposes at times the effects of immediacy (such as those in the lift), which result from the limited space. Similar to the frames of paintings, Tsangaris' theatrical situations are also often framed.[8] These frames are related to the repetitive structure of what is being shown. Each visitor is led by an usher into a small room, feels the concentrated characteristic of a miniature piece, but is aware that others have preceded and will follow his/her brief presence in this room. The aura of uniqueness, which even in the age of mechanical reproduction is still an essential element of our culture, is thus suspended or at least put into perspective.

Tsangaris' projects are often framed in original or consciously defamiliarising ways, for example by creating a cage or aquarium situation in the *Vegetarische Lounge [Vegetarian Lounge]* within *Nacht-Labor [Nocturnal Laboratory]* – which forms part of another cycle of music-theatre-miniatures called *Die Döner Schaltung [The Kebab Circuit]* (2004): an artificial laboratory-like world outside of the continuous flow of time. The same applies to the constellations which revolve within themselves in which objects – in *Riesig aus Winzig [Gigantic from Tiny]* these are small metal beads – are led by an invisible hand.

Some works of Tsangaris develop a dialectic between the setting of a framework and a continuous flow. In the ensemble piece *An die Vorwelt [To the Ancestoral World]* (1996) this means that the composition "sneaks unnoticed from the everyday world into the art world" (Mörchen 2001: 49). The large room to which this piece responds is Cologne Philharmonic Hall. On its podium scenes are being performed, that reduce all the familiar activities of this place to absurdity. The artistic director for example is called away in the middle of

---

7. See also David Roesner's comments on *o.T.* in the context of his discourse analysis in chapter 16.
8. Tsangaris has reflected on the importance of framings himself, see Tsangaris 1998: 59.

his announcements to give way to a free anarchical proliferation of activities, such as the warm-up of an ensemble of musicians. A space is thus being relieved of its rituals, its usual hierarchical formations are rendered obsolete and everyday activities take their place. This, too, is a typical example of postdramatic theatre in Lehmann's terms. And the transitionality that unfolds could be read as a transgression between fiction and factuality along the lines of Gérard Genette's concept of metalepsis (2004).

Surprising experiences

This breakdown of the theatre of Manos Tsangaris into its different stations corresponds clearly with the widely discussed abandonment of the metanarrative and the end of the grand unified theories with a claim to truth. This reflects the salient modesty that this processional theatre radiates, no different by the way than most of the lyrical texts of the author, which are often laconically short. This modesty may be the opposing force to the tendency towards the *Gesamtkunstwerk* [total work of art], which is undoubtedly inherent in this approach to theatre. It corresponds with the linking of different formats, which are crucial for much of Tsangaris' work. Titles such as *Winzig [Tiny]* and *groß und klein [large and small]* point to this already. For this, the composer's experience with radio plays and incidental music is likely to have been formative.

The small format – having become a defining feature of the art of Tsangaris – raises a variety of associations. It brings to mind little toy worlds, or model-scale (re)constructions to help to understand the world. And it also raises the question of the division of the seemingly important and the supposedly unimportant, as the radio play from 1988 *Grundfleisch [Groundflesh]* did with its enjoyable parody of Herbert von Karajan's self-importance. This problematic has since become a recurrent basic tendency of Tsangaris' works. His concepts know about complex connections and technical sophistication, but they also contain distinctively simple moments, which in the tradition of the *arte povera* undermine the widespread digitisation and rendering technical in all fields of art.

The liminality between observation of events and contribution to them marks a further aspect of Tsangaris' aesthetics. An example from the core of the project *Winzig*, bearing the terse title *winzig aus winzig [tiny from tiny]* attests to this. This piece places three spectators on an audience platform, just where a 'pretend audience' has already taken its place, which begins to become theatrically active after the show has started. The spaces between performers and audience overlap so much that the spectators soon expect – shockingly or exhilaratingly – that they ought to participate in the events themselves.[9] At same time, the

---

9. This is also paralleled by other contemporary theatre *auteurs*. The performance-installation *Human Writes* by William Forsythe and Kendall Thomas from 2006 is an example in which the question whether the spectators become actors themselves becomes a central aspect during in the course of the performance.

small format leads back to the aspect of the fragmentary nature of the (re)presented. Is what we see and hear – one wonders as a visitor of the processional theatre – part of a greater whole or rather its blueprint? At any rate, the inside and the outside engage in complex relationships.

In *Nachtlabor* the relativity of our perception is brought to our attention. In this case, that includes exposing the audience. Thus a general tendency of Tsangaris' work can be pinpointed here: to bring to the forefront the disappearance of the individual spectator in the crowd. The audience is first outside, positioned between an old brick wall and a modern glass wall, initially even blinded by the light, in a limbo between narrowing restriction and an opening.[10] The eyes rush ahead and take part in a theatre event, while the ears are committed to strikingly different impressions. The inner stage of the recipient – an essential space in Tsangaris' Composed Theatre – thus becomes surprisingly lopsided. This situation resolves itself when the same event is perceived from a different perspective in the adjacent room and one becomes aware of the next cohort of spectators in their helplessness, their exposure.

This precisely composed imbalance points to a characteristic of unlocking, which is typical for Manos Tsangaris' composing. His concepts lead to an experience of self that is diametrically opposed to the dissipating, desensitising tendency of public passages. This aspect is reminiscent of Leonardo's cave wanderer who can be incited to pursuit of knowledge and understanding by a plethora of the unfamiliar, but sometimes also of Plato's cave dweller, who must be dragged into the light by force. Certainly, the experience of Manos Tsangaris' projects in their surprising and awe-inspiring moments is an exciting and pleasurable affair. But with their moments of mystification or even obfuscation, with the flexibility of perspective, with the constant play of closeness and distance, with the different proportions and the reflection of the specific aura of a place there is also a consciously disorienting and question-raising impulse. And in experiencing some of his projects one nurtures the faint hope that the music industry as a whole, in so far as it is determined by the fixation on certain performance modes and forms of reception, gets some injection of life through the artistic laboratory nature of Tsangaris' work – a stimulus which is neither meant to eliminate concerts not to lead to trivial decoration, but to a creative reflection and revitalisation of their rituals.

Manos Tsangaris takes musicians and listeners on an exploratory journey with his works. His music embodies a permanent quest, precisely because of the non-obviousness of the formats; a kind of basic research into what the interaction of music with other elements such as texts and spaces can achieve. The oscillation between closeness and distance – between the discrete proximity of sounds very close to the ear of the perceiver on the one hand and the normal hearing distance on the other – illustrates this particularly well. It is naturally

---

10. This at least was the arrangement in the performance in Witten. Other staging solutions would also be possible.

important to the overall development of the composer that he does not want to be locked into certain formats. And thus specifically the large-sized *Batsheba* project aims not to simply eliminate the bearing of great classical opera: this presentation of the Biblical story is familiar with both its close-up perspective with discrete, almost imperceptible movements and its grand operatic gestures. These elements of traditional opera have taken aback many viewers at the premiere in Donaueschingen. But the tendency to change formats, if brought into play consistently, can hardly be thought of without creating some unexpected twists. And that is precisely what constitutes a crucial aspect of the work of Manos Tsangaris and its invigorating effect within contemporary music theatre.

(Translation: David Roesner)

References

Genette, Gérard (2004) *Métalepse: De la figure à la fiction*, Paris: Seuil.

Lehmann, Hans-Thies (1999) *Postdramatisches Theater*, Frankfurt am Main: Verlag der Autoren.

Mörchen, Raoul (2001) "'Und wenn es gelingt, verschmilzt auch alles': Das mediale Theater von Manos Tsangaris", in: *MusikTexte*, 91 (2001), pp. 45–50.

Tsangaris, Manos (1998) "Wahrnehmungsphänomene als Auslöser des kompositorischen Prozesses", in: *Musik im Dialog. Jahrbuch der Berliner Gesellschaft für Neue Musik*, ed. by S. Sanio and Chr. Metzger, Saarbrücken: Pfau-Verlag, pp. 55–66.

—— (2006) "Was heißt situatives Komponieren?", in: *KunstMusik*, 6 (2006), pp. 30–5.

Further information on Tsangaris works can be found on his website at www.tsangaris.de.

Part IV

Discussion and Debate

Chapter 15

Composed Theatre - Discussion and Debate: On Terminology, Planning and Intuition, Concepts and Processes, Self-reflexivity and Communication

Edited by Matthias Rebstock and David Roesner

Excerpts from two round-table discussions on Composed Theatre conducted at the Drama Department, University of Exeter (UK) 19 April 2009 and the Music Department, Universität Hildesheim (GER), 17 May 2009

Introduction

The following text contains excerpts of two long discussions each of which concluded a three-day workshop meeting at Exeter and Hildesheim respectively, to which we had invited practitioners and scholars in the field of Composed Theatre to introduce us and each other to their work and their working processes.[1] Several of the participants were able to attend both meetings, which created and intensive and ongoing discussion and debate about key aspect and questions in relation to Composed Theatre. In particular the debate centred around five topics: Terminology, Planning vs. Intuition, Concepts and processes, Self-reflexivity, and Communication. The discussions were open to the public and attracted a small specialist audience, some of whom participated in the discussion as well.

The text contains contributions by Cathie Boyd, Director, Artistic Director *Cryptic*, Glasgow; Paul Edmondson, Performer and Martial Artist, Exeter; Michael Hirsch, Composer/Director, Berlin; Jörg Laue, Composer/Director, Artistic Director *LOSE COMBO*, Berlin; Jörg Lensing, Artistic Director Theater der Klänge, Düsseldorf; Roland Quitt, Freelance Dramaturg for Music Theatre, Mannheim; Matthias Rebstock, Professor for Scenic Music (Hildesheim) and artistic director of *leitundlause*, Berlin; George Rodosthenous, Composer/Director, Artistic Director *Altitude North*; David Roesner, Senior Lecturer, University of Exeter; Hannah Silva, Poet and Performer, Plymouth; Nick Till, Professor for Music Theatre at University of Sussex and Artistic Director *Post-Operative Productions*; Demetris Zavros, Composer/Director, Associate Director *Altitude North*, Leeds.

On terminology

David Roesner

While being well aware that a single definition of Composed Theatre may neither be possible nor desirable, can we perhaps still talk about your various understandings of this as a process and practice and try to map some areas which the term seems to cover?

---

1. More information on the workshop series can be found at http://humanities.exeter.ac.uk/drama/research/projects/composedtheatre/.

George Rodosthenous

It's obvious that we've become comfortable with the term 'Composed Theatre'. The only clarification I would like to make at least for myself is that, what I understand by Composed Theatre can also be a piece of theatre which is not music theatre, but a piece that is being created with musical structures in mind.

Jörg Laue

I don't want to criticise that title at all, but I was wondering: when Michael [Hirsch] showed us some compositions everybody tried to find out what composition is in theatre, what theatre is in composition, but I wonder why we can't just call it a concert? There are all those different aspects but to me it is not important to connect those with terms and to define whether it is theatre in composition, Composed Theatre, theatrical composition or whatever – it's just not my main concern.

Michael Hirsch

Yes, for me terms are also not important. But of course it's another point of view for you as scholars – you have to write about it and think about it. I have to make it and for me it is of no importance what my work is going to be called.

Cathie Boyd

That's fine from an artistic point of view, but what about the people producing you and what about the people presenting you? There's a huge responsibility for them to describe the work and to think about how to sell that. It's a massive problem because in music theatre, if that's what we're talking about, there is always the question: do you send in theatre critics or do you send in music critics? And there's a terrible generation in Britain of music critics, who only want to see traditional opera and if you try and do anything contemporary they'll slander it. But if you bring in a theatre critic, they have no idea of the technical skills of that musician, and I go ballistic. Sorry, but I do think it's slightly irresponsible of us to say I don't care what you call my work, because if someone misrepresents you, you would be annoyed artistically.

Michael Hirsch

Well, I agree that I am responsible for it, but when my work is produced somewhere I always describe my work to the people who present me and they can then decide what it is I'm writing. In all the festivals I have to write comments about my work and I am happy to do that, but I'm not interested in having a headline or label for all my works – 'Hirsch makes Composed Theatre'. That's not my problem, I think.

Matthias Rebstock

Maybe it is misleading to understand this as question about labelling work. It is not about labelling, it's about understanding what we do. So if we talk about Composed Theatre I'm much more interested in what we actually mean by that, and whether it is the right term.

If we take 'theatre' as a field and then we make the field smaller and say, well, we're talking about devised theatre, so Shakespeare is out (laughs), it's already smaller. And then we say, well, we're not just talking about devised theatre, we're talking about devising Composed Theatre, presumably that this again would make the field you're talking about smaller. Now the question is: is this a good way to make the field smaller, does it really have to get more precise, or would it be an alternative to say that we are talking about devising music theatre? Could be. But, as you immediately sense, it would be something very different, because as George has rightly said: Composed Theatre is not necessarily music theatre, you can apply musical thinking on all sorts of theatre, you can apply it to films, you can apply it to going shopping – I don't know.

So if we stick to the term, we're not talking about music theatre – it is part of it, but not all music theatre is Composed Theatre – and not all Composed Theatre is music theatre. A straightforward opera performance for me is not necessarily a Composed Theatre piece.

Jörg Lensing

I think Demetris [Zavros] said it very well when he said: It is theatre with musical structures in mind. It's exactly that. And I agree with this very much, especially with the term 'Composed Theatre', because I find it important to make the point that it is something else than, for example, intermedia theatre. Intermedia theatre is one *form* of Composed Theatre but it's not the only one.

What also became clear to me in these three days is that there are different notions about Composed Theatre between the British and the Germans. I think we [Germans] are quite clear about what Composed Theatre is, because we have all these references to Kagel and Schnebel.

I think the criterion is, whether the subject of the performance is 'Gegenstand der Komposition' – the topic of the composition. If I write music, it is not important for me what the string quartet will look like; they have to perform my music well, but the visual aspect is not the topic of the composition. But the minute I care about the visual aspect and the performance then it becomes the topic of the composition and in that moment the same string quartet becomes Composed Theatre.

David Roesner

But what happens when the Kronos Quartet commissions a piece and then dress in designer clothes and have a bit of a lighting design?

Jörg Lensing

I think that is the *mise en scène* of music, that's something else. So if a director is coming who says I take some music and now I stage this music, then he makes something in addition, but it's not topic of the composition.

David Roesner

And what happens if you look at Heiner Goebbels' *Eraritjaritjaka*?[2] This piece is based entirely on pre-existing string quartets of the twentieth century, with one exception of a Contrapunctus by Bach. None of them were written with a theatrical performance in mind, but Goebbels takes those existing structures, inserts voices, inserts lighting, inserts film, and the result is something I would definitely call Composed Theatre.

Jörg Lensing

Yes, but that is what we call a meta-composition. So he is a composer and he takes the string quartets as a material for a bigger composition, a meta-composition.

---

2. Premiered in Lausanne, at the Theatre Vidy (2004).

David Roesner

I would like to come back to another term, that of integration or integrated theatre, because one of the recurring criteria of Composed Theatre seems to be that it's not a phenomenon of addition where two or more elements are added together in one way or another, but that there is an integration forming a much more inseparable connection and synthesis. Cathie: your direction for example emerges so much from the individual score you work with that if you changed the music it would make no sense whatsoever. Or in Heiner Goebbels' *Eraritjaritjaka* I mentioned earlier, there is a video sequence in which every movement of the actor and every movement of the camera is composed bar by bar to Ravel's string quartet. Yes, the music was there before, composed with no theatre piece in mind, but it's now closely integrated in that sense. It is like the difference between sewing two bits of cloth together – you can still take them apart again, relatively unchanged, or knitting or weaving to threads together, which form a blanket or jumper or something, and if you take them apart they are no longer that, they are in some sense destroyed.

Cathie Boyd

Isn't that ultimately what we're talking about: it is about a performance which is layered, but ultimately it's the musicality which is predominant within it.

Matthias Rebstock

I still think there are two ways that we need to distinguish when trying to define what Composed Theatre could be. One way is to try to look at a performance and decide whether it is Composed Theatre or not. That is a kind of an ontological approach. But what Jörg and George have emphasised strongly is not an ontological approach but a focus on method, on 'Verfahren', procedure, and a way of thinking.

Hannah Silva

I just wanted to say something in relation to the notion that composing is a way of thinking about how to organise material. Musical composition provides the clearest code or language for talking about theatre; academically and in rehearsal, the structures, principles, notation systems, modes of thinking compositionally are so well established that they provide the possibility to work compositionally within and outside of those parameters. They allow the composer to compose for the piano, also to compose for prepared piano, a wine glass, light and bodies in time and space.

It's inherently interdisciplinary but this doesn't necessarily mean that it involves collaboration with practitioners from other disciplines during the compositional process, but it could also involve collaboration across disciplines within the one composer, also providing room for collaboration within the scores. And when composing music you might work with rhythm over melody, when composing theatre you might emphasise light over dance, but that doesn't mean that the dance is impeded. When no element of performance is restricted by any other element the composer has a choice, and where that choice exists a field of compositional process exists, otherwise it would be coping rather than composing.

Jörg Lensing

Following this logic you can, of course, compose on paper and never work together. Someone has thought about everything and constructed everything and has the lighting and the dance in his mind when he creates the structure. But the other process is to try it, to find the possibilities how to play this instrument. But that is what I mean with 'integrated'; it really means to have both together in order to arrive at a result which depends on both. And then you could not take away the lighting and only look at the dance because it is not the whole. The lighting is not illustrating the dance, which is normally the case in conventional theatre. You can rehearse for weeks with the dancers with neon light and then at the last technical rehearsal the lighting designer comes in and adds light for making it emotionally or aesthetically fitting. But in an integrated process or in a composed process you cannot add on or take off the lighting – they are depending on each other.

Paul Edmondson

It seems to me as though the notion of Composed Theatre operates on a continuum as opposed to being in a definite, established position, and that that continuum operates either on a continuum between freedom and restraint – but I don't know, that may be too restrictive – or between integration and differentiation. Then the question of whether something like Stockhausen's *Trans*, which was mentioned earlier, can be considered Composed Theatre may mean placing it at one end of the continuum and the kind of work Jörg does, where everybody's co-collaborating and involved in the performance space as an instrument, may find itself on a different side of the continuum.

Cathie Boyd

But isn't the difference that Jörg devises; you work, if I understand it correctly, as a collective, and you try lots of ideas, whereas in the other extreme you go in with a fixed existing score and then look at how you break that down.

Jörg Lensing

But the finalising of the work, even if you work collectively, consists in arriving at a structure, how the piece is finally performed. And this structure, of course, is composed. We may call this structure, Air and Sonata and Rondo and all these things – I really take old forms to organise the improvised material. So for example there is the introduction of the sonata and you determine which material it contains and how long it can be, before you want to move on to the development [Durchführung], which may consist of three dances together with a particular video and a particular music and there are fixed connections and meeting points for the performers in order to use the music in a certain way – that's composition for me. It's not that I write down every single moment for every fraction of a second; I give the dancers a certain freedom within the performance to handle the material as they have done it before in the creation process.

What I have learned as a composer is that in the beginning, if I write for violin, I meet a violin player and really talk with him and ask him to show me what he's able to do. And as a composer you ask: could you do this? Could you also do that? And he may say, yes, normally we don't do it that way, but I'll try it, and it sounds nice. Then we discuss how to fix this in notation, so that it would sound again like that later on, or if played by someone else. So whenever I make a solo composition for violin the process would be exactly that. I know the possibilities of the instrument and I know a little bit more about the possibilities that are not conventional, and I have been told how to write it down. And if I take the means of the theatre it's exactly the same. I am fascinated by what MAX/MSP jitter offers as a tool; for me it's an instrument full of possibilities. So if I have a good programmer there I would ask him to show me this and that, all that's possible, and how to fix it. I don't notate it any more, but I would want him to come up with a patch, which works exactly in a certain way in a certain moment. That is playing this instrument: I am not the player, it is the one who's programming it, operating it – we call it operator, but in fact he's an instrumentalist for me, he's playing Jitter.

It is something that I learnt from Kagel: when I first met him, he said, we have a piece of lighting equipment in the basement, so why don't you compose something for the lighting equipment – we have eighteen channels. The lighting board was programmable so we could make programmed compositions only for changing lights, for composed light. And Kagel understood it as an instrument: take it, try it and make a composition for light.

And importantly, this is not depending on a process of dramatic narration, it's more a structure, an abstract structure; composing structural processes in time. It could be dramatic, it could be narrative – but it doesn't have to be. And I think that is a different approach to what directors and choreographers are taught.

On Planning vs. Intuition

David Roesner

The notion of 'composing theatre' may suggest a high level of planning, premeditation and conceptualisation in advance of an actual rehearsal process – does Composed Theatre adhere to this traditional sense of classical musical composition?

Cathie Boyd

I don't go in fully planned on what I'm doing. I have a sort of idea, but I really work off what I've been given, so I'm responding instinctively all the time. It's constantly what you're getting. You have to see what performers give you, otherwise you treat them as puppets.

Michael Hirsch

I think it's both: in the artistic process you are jumping between clear structural ideas and then suddenly you have very irrational feelings about how it could be. The first moment before I start a composition may launch from a very unclear and irrational idea – I don't know exactly what I want. And then I use the structure to find the way to it. The structure is the means of coming to what is in the first instance a very irrational, very vague imagination, even less than an imagination, only a kind of atmosphere you have in mind. But then you have got the structure as the means to capture it.

Matthias Rebstock

I really think there's a third thing that comes in when you work with other people. It is not just about you being sometimes structural and logical and sometimes irrational, but if you work with people and you don't know what's going to happen with them, what they will bring, what do they think, it is neither irrational nor logical, but a third thing.

Jörg Lensing

For me it is the selection of material that is entirely instinctive: whether you are being inspired by something or deny it, whether I say yes or no, that is a totally instinctive process. But of course I consciously propose something or ask for something and then I get certain responses. For example with musicians: if your musician comes and plays a score he is not offering very much, but if you meet him and you ask him to show you the possibilities he has, what and how he can play, then he is offering something. And then I can instinctively react to that.

Demetris Zavros

I think it's very different to work and develop with other people rather than composing music for instruments, where you can think about a lot of different things in advance. I tend to overthink before I go into the studio to try things out, especially compositions. And when I get to the point where I actually start writing music, I write specific music because I have a specific action in mind that I want to go with it, and at some points in the music I want to allow some space for what's going to happen visually, to avoid that the same thing is happening visually and aurally. A lot of times when I go in the studio to work with the actors, dancers or performers who are going to move in the space visually, I find out that there are a lot of things that they cannot do as I first imagined them, and I have to find compromises. And in that compromise and in that difficulty you have to become creative to find other solutions, and then maybe I will go back and change things in the music because I want a certain relationship to continue to exist.

So with regard to the idea of a polyphony of theatrical means, I think for me as a director/composer it means that I always go back and change the music if something is not working visually. There is a relationship between the different lines in that polyphony. I mean, they are all important in themselves, but somehow they have to come together as they would in any polyphonic piece of music at the end of the day. I think the difficulty is how do you compose visually and aurally at the same time so that these levels complement each other.

Matthias Rebstock

It is interesting that you say you have to make compromises and that that forces you into creativity, because for me it is completely different. I go into rehearsals and I'm really curious what the performers are going to do today. I have no idea at the beginning. There are certain limitations within the rehearsal process, of course, but I would never say it is a compromise; I just get creative with the performers if they can't do something that I wanted them to do.

I rather probably just have questions or exercises I want to do with them in order to see what's coming. So the main reason I work with people is really to get ideas I wouldn't have on my own and to create something none of us could have thought of individually.

Michael Hirsch

Even for me as the 'old-fashioned composer' at this table, it is also important for whom I write a piece. I write totally different pieces whether I write for the *Stuttgarter Vokalsolisten* or for the *Maulwerker*. And I'm inspired if I know who will play it.

Demetris Zavros

I'm not saying that what I have described is the only way things happen in my process. I do of course allow my performers to create material and I get inspired by what they are doing – I'm not thinking about everything in advance. But the things that I *am* thinking about in advance don't always work in the studio and it is a great part of the creative process to find solutions to things that do not necessarily work exactly in the way that we have visualised them initially.

Hannah Silva

I think the idea of compromise is actually quite important when you're working with several disciplines. I think there are always compromises. That is not to say that the director's vision is necessarily compromised, but within those different layers there is always compromise and it is through those compromises that a new form emerges. So it's perhaps through the compromises within different disciplines that you arrive at Composed Theatre, which is something new.

On concepts and processes

Matthias Rebstock

I was wondering if we could take up this point about the concepts of these pieces, because I found it quite interesting that almost all of you have very strong concepts in your work and everybody knows exactly why they are doing what but, as Jörg said very clearly, it's not important whether the audience understands these concepts in the end. So I would like to talk about the function of these concepts and how important it is for you that parts of the concepts can be understood, can be conceived, can be picked up, or not. I also wonder if working conceptually in this way is actually one of the characteristics of Composed Theatre, maybe because we don't have the narrative, because there's something missing which we normally have in theatre, and it might be something to give you a purpose for the working process, a sense that you're not lost. So it's important for you in order to work, but perhaps not important for the audience to grasp? On the other hand, I do sometimes have the feeling, that had I known about a concept I might have appreciated the work more.

David Roesner

Can I add that I wonder whether there's a similarity to 'actual' music in the sense that anyone can sit down and listen to a piece of music and appreciate it for what it is without necessarily understanding how it was made, what the conceptual ideas were, how the composer worked, what orchestration is, what counterpoint is, etc. So it works on that sort of surface level and people appreciate it for what it is – they don't leave concerts necessarily saying "I didn't understand this piece of music" unless perhaps when it is New Music. But at the same time, of course, musicologists and other people invest a lot of time in doing the analysis of the music, and they look at relations of motifs and themes etc. And sometimes musicologists are very concerned about the process and look into how the third draft of that particular passage that Beethoven did and why he crossed out the first two notes, and so on. But you don't hear that in the result. So, I wonder whether there is something about music that 'works' despite being ignorant about its concept or conception and whether Composed Theatre makes use of that by using musically inspired or derived concepts, or whether there is broader characteristic of the post-modern at play, which is very strong on being conceptual, without necessarily needing to be musical.

Demetris Zavros

Well, I think that a lot of people who have seen my work think that I don't think about the audience (laughter), whereas I think that I do think about the audience quite a lot (laughter). That leads back to what I was saying earlier: I don't think of the audience worrying that I'm not giving them enough information about what I mean by this work, but because I *don't* want to explain it, because that would limit its meaning to one thing, where I want them to take several meanings out of it, to construct it in their own minds however they want to. I don't want this to be a cop-out either: I don't mean to say that I do whatever I want and you get whatever you want out of it. So when it's not something that relates to one meaning, how do we organise something to open up these pages of meanings so that we can make sure that there are a lot of things that the audience can take out for them. …

Jörg Laue

… maybe by not thinking about the audience?

Demetris Zavros

Well, I think that would be a cop-out, really, simply not thinking about the audience.

David Roesner

Perhaps a notion of 'coherence' is useful instead of meaning? Composed Theatre shifts towards different guarantors of coherence I think. And that's where the strong concepts come into play: you don't abandon coherence, you don't abandon the fact that you need to organise relationships and also discriminate and say why something is in the piece and why something is not, or why you like this, but not that? But the sense of coherence comes from a different origin or is argued for from a different position and that's a musical position. And I think for the audience it's a similar process, where if I find it coherent at some point in Jörg's piece to reflect about me spending time in a particular place, about how time passes, about how I react to an environment that invites me to a particular mode of spending time, then I've brought in a different kind of coherence than spending three hours trying to find out what is he trying to tell me, what does it all *mean*?

Jörg Laue

It is for that reason that I said I did not want to tell you about that concept and the way I presented it.

Matthias Rebstock

But the interesting thing is, I mean you spend hours and hours to do these transformations[3] ...

Jörg Laue

Yes, of course.

---

3. See Jörg Laue's chapter (6) in this book about his process or adaptation and transformation of materials.

Matthias Rebstock

And you say there's no point for the audience, they don't need to know, they don't need to perceive …

Jörg Laue

Why should they be interested in how many hours I spend …?

Matthias Rebstock

No, what interests me is not the audience, but you: why do you do it? Does it help to feel that you know what you're doing, or why do you spend so much effort on it? I think I do understand why you do it, but I think it might be a characteristic point for this conceptually based theatre. So, why is it so important for you to be so precise in your work?

Jörg Laue

Maybe it's just me (laughter). No, but …

Roland Quitt

Is it part of the structure that is important for the audience, or could it have been made up in a much simpler way? Would it have changed the experience of the audience if you just had taken much less time in doing this and if you had made it up according to much simpler principles?

Jörg Laue

Could be. But for me to work out such a piece has got to do with those processes and a way of thinking about – about media and technical aspects in the work. And so it's just my way of doing things.

Matthias Rebstock

So it is not like the idea in homeopathy that even if you take out all of the material, all of the atoms, there is something left; you can't see it, you can't prove it, but it helps? In other words, is it not this idea that something of this process, of this precision of all the work you did, will somehow remain in the piece?

Jörg Laue

Yeah, hopefully it does.

Nick Till

I'm trying to think what we mean by saying that it is conceptual, because I mean that's quite an abstract conceptual process that you put in place, and in which actually, as you say, it is not even revealed. I don't know whether anything I do is conceptual in that sense of giving myself some kind of conceptual process to work with. I think it may be conceptual, but it's more specifically engaged with certain problematics. I'm interested in setting myself problem-solving kinds of exercises. Well, yours is a problem-solving thing, too, but mine aren't so abstract, I suppose, (laughs). I'm just questioning assumptions about certain kinds of relationships or certain understandings of how meaning is constructed, or whatever. So I mean I'm probably always more dealing at a semantic level than a purely conceptual…

David Roesner

… but with your Stuttgart piece[4] there's a clear indication that you were given a setting which was not conceptual but pragmatic, which meant there were certain rules of the game and you did follow them – and this is what the experiment is about: I have two projectors and two microphones, what can I do with that?

Nick Till

Well, you see, I would say we didn't. I mean, I would make a distinction there, because certainly 'experimental' in the Cagean sense means you engage in a very important way

---

4. See Nick Till's chapter (9) in this book.

of thinking: what if I put that together with that and that together with that and see what happens? That's an experimental process, you don't know the outcome and you have no intention to control the outcome, you want to see what will happen if … Whereas in our case, I didn't say 'let's see what happens if?', or at least we did a little bit of 'let's see what happens if?' but at a certain point we started to decide actually there are other ways we needed to construct the piece. But I suppose there was a conceptual process in terms of here are the givens, and rather than saying 'let's see what happens', saying, okay, what do I find interesting or problematic about this as a set of givens that I can start to question and unpack and so on? So I suppose the conceptual step is the one that says, okay, why am I dissatisfied with the way in which most people use the relationship between the live performer and the screen image without questioning what those relationships are and how can I do something that starts to ask questions about that.

Matthias Rebstock

But I think with Nick's work it's important for the piece that you get some idea of the process.

Roland Quitt

I don't *see* the process of your work. I mean, I would know that you didn't work that way, I might think that you could have thought this up on paper, too.

Nick Till

I think that's true, but I mean the way the piece worked was that to some extent it replicated parts of the process we went through, like when you're presented with an object which is a sheet of music and someone tries to make sense of it and in that process embarks on a journey. That in effect is what we did, we gave ourselves an object and we tried to make some sense of it in different ways, and that included doing research into what its significance might be, it included starting to think about the relationship of that piece of music to technology and the fact that we were using contemporary technologies. And all of that gets, as it were, thematised in the piece. So to that extent I think although aspects of the process are not in there, in another sense I guess the piece does really quite explicitly thematise its own process of investigation.

David Roesner

It may be helpful with regard to Composed Theatre perhaps not to talk about 'criteria' but about 'tendencies', for example by saying that the kind of work we are talking about has a tendency to be self-reflexive, without suggesting that is always the case. For example including the discussion about the piece in itself, or Jörg's performance lecture[5] which talks about his work while also exemplifying it: that's highly self-reflexive, asking: what am I talking about? Why did I start here? Why didn't I start there? So tendencies is one word that might be useful. The other word I'd like to throw in is renegotiation. I think one common thread through all the pieces is that they, again, in one way or another, renegotiate the relationship between the elements and particularly the musical elements – whatever they are, sounds and structures and actual music etc. – with the other theatrical means of expression. And they engange in certain relationships – whether they're hierarchical or whether they're about how music and stage action make meaning together – and they don't take that for granted, they renegotiate it. So in the process you all think about how you work: "why don't we start with the music here, why don't we start with the music and then build the film on that, that would be new, wouldn't it etc.". And then your process either carries that thinking through to the performance, where you can see it and where you as an audience become part of that renegotiation and can acknowledge that these are new terms, now conditions. So the performance then carries the terms of those renegotiations to various degrees – some spell it out and sometimes the terms of those renegotiations are more implicit.

Roland Quitt

It came to my mind that the first situation in the arts where process was really put into the foreground was probably Pollock's action paintings. And when Pollock did his pictures there was this misunderstanding because someone made a film which showed how Pollock was painting whereas Pollock insisted that the pictures are the piece of art and not the performative situation of him dancing on the pictures and going around with all this colour. But, from this, performance art developed. While Jackson Pollock himself said that is is all about the pictures and even if we show the process it is the picture which is the art work, is was still a very, very big influence and somehow created performance art or was part of the creation of performance art. Performance art has become very important within today's theatre. I mean, to me it seems it has almost overtaken theatre, traditional theatre, in some way. And performance is always process itself.

---

5. See Jörg Laue's chapter (6) in this book.

Nick Till

I mean, there may have been a hidden complex conceptual process in Jörg's piece – well, there was – but the end result quite clearly didn't, as it were, give us certain kinds of indications that we needed to understand that to understand the piece, whereas other pieces may be giving you indications that there's something that you're not understanding, and that's when it can be frustrating because you're aware there is a set of intentions here of understanding something, but you can't quite piece them together.

On self-reflexivity

David Roesner

Do you feel that Composed Theatre often comes with a sense of self-reflexivity and a kind of meta-discourse, that is, is it particularly frequently about the relationship of music and theatre? To elaborate on this question briefly: Opera, for example, is often about human relationships and emotions, love stories, tragedies etc. whereas in Composed Theatre, it seems to me, the topic often is the relationship between the two media itself, or the act of composing, or the question about what constitutes music, composition, or performance.

Jörg Lensing

I think it's not necessarily a question about a meta-discourse in the theatre performance itself. I really think it's more a reflection on questioning the traditional workflow. I find that very important, because the traditional workflow results in certain aesthetics, and if you don't like these aesthetics you have to question the traditional way of working itself. I think a lot of work, not only Composed Theatre, but also advanced theatre and intermedia theatre, find other models for the workflow, and the result is totally different from what you see in the traditional theatre. In Germany it's interesting to see, for example, that the *Schauspielhäuser* (municipal theatres), now begin to import the kinds of workflows for example from the French theatre companies, in order to find something alternative languages to those they have established for a lot of years now since the Second World War. That's a very interesting process.

On communication

David Roesner

I had one last complex in mind which is about communication. We talked a lot about concepts and we talked a lot about how you conceive your work. What I was wondering is, if you could comment on the communication process in the work. I mean, obviously in very few examples it's all about one person and there's kind of an internal communication, but actually all of your performances and projects include other human beings in whatever function – as co-designers, as performers, as co-composers and so on, and I was wondering whether you felt that in this area of Composed Theatre the collaboration and the communication were in any way different. Do they require different languages?

George Rodosthenous

I remember what Heiner Goebbels said two days ago[6] about his experiences working with people he knows well: "I don't have to talk" – I think that is really wonderful if you work with people you don't need to explain your whole ethos, your whole principles, your whole aesthetics. Instead he can say: we don't talk.

Matthias Rebstock

I think Nick said something very interesting on this in his lecture[7], that because you had all these different people to deal with, you had to write scenarios, and because you had to write these scenarios the whole piece changed, because you had to fix them in a way, which you usually don't.

Nick Till

To some extent, yes.

---

6. See Heiner Goebbels' chapter (4) in this book.
7. See Nick Till's chapter (9) in this book.

Matthias Rebstock

And do you mean writing scenarios in the classical way as instructions, someone coming on stage doing this or that, or what's the scenario in your case?

Nick Till

Well, the scenario was two things: there was a sort of technical scenario and then there were lengthy verbal descriptions – such as "I want a noise like a train hitting a piano …".

David Roesner

I think that's really interesting, because we've talked about ways of structuring all the time, many of which were quite abstract, and now you're saying that the descriptions of the sounds, the abstract objects, are in fact very much a narrative, quite metaphorical, full of images …

Nick Till

Yes, because that was the only way I could communicate to the guy who was doing the sound what sort of things I was wanting.

Roland Quitt

I have just a couple of things that came to my mind out of my work, which is not about working in theatre and that maybe not even have much to do with Composed Theatre. If you want to work together with people you have to find people who you don't have to explain the basics to any more. I have often experienced this: the more successful people get in theatre the more they tend to surround themselves with a fixed team of people to work with. And if you are Joachim Schlömer and you are invited to come to Mannheim, then Mannheim will have to pay for all these people because otherwise he won't come. He brings his own lighting designer and all these people with him. And you can experience that when you work with him that there's some mutual understanding within this group of people and the way that they work with him. It's just exactly what Heiner Goebbels described.

David Roesner

Thank you. I'm wondering, looking at the time, whether we should come to a close.

Roland Quitt

So, have we changed the world? (laughter).

Matthias Rebstock

The world has changed while we were talking here, we just didn't notice (laughter).

(Transcription: Susan Lumb)

Part V

Discourse and Analysis

Chapter 16

'It is not about labelling, it's about understanding what we do':[1] Composed Theatre as Discourse

David Roesner

---

1. Matthias Rebstock in one of the round-table discussions, see chapter 15.

Introduction[2]

This chapter attempts to collocate, compare, explore and interrogate some of the key themes and questions that the different preceding chapters (and the related research activities) have offered.[3] At the same time it is consciously avoiding the title

2. I would like to express my gratitude to Nita Schechet for her meticulous proofing and stylistic improvements on this text. Any remaining flaws or errors, however, are mine. I also thank all those mentioned in the text for providing me with feedback, clarifications and encouragement.
3. The key material for this analysis was generated predominantly in the course of the AHRC funded workshop series 'Process of Devising Composed Theatre' (April/May 2009), the proceedings of which have been audio-visually documented and can be accessed through the Digital Archives of both University of Exeter's Drama Department as well as the Institut für Musik und Musikwissenschaft at the University of Hildesheim. The full details of my primary sources for this chapter are:

   Workshop Series *Processes of Devising Composed Theatre*, University of Exeter, Department of Drama, 16–19 April 2009, University of Hildesheim (GER), Institut für Musik und Musikwissenschaft, 14–17 May 2009. With Cathie Boyd, Director, Artistic Director Theatre Cryptic, Glasgow; Freda Chapple, Voice and Performance Consultant (Sheffield), Johanna Dombois, Director/Author (Cologne); Heiner Goebbels Composer/Director (Frankfurt/ University of Giessen); Michael Hirsch, Composer/Director (Berlin); Jörg Laue, Composer/ Director, Artistic Director LOSE COMBO, (Berlin); Jörg Lensing, Artistic Director Theater der Klänge (Düsseldorf); Roland Quitt, Dramaturg, free-lance dramaturg, (Mannheim); Matthias Rebstock, Professor for 'Szenische Musik' (Hildesheim) and artistic director of leitundlause (Berlin); George Rodosthenous, Composer/Director, Artistic Director Altitude North (Leeds); David Roesner, Senior Lecturer, University of Exeter; Nicholas Till, Post-Operative Productions, Professor of Music, University of Sussex; Manos Tsangaris, Composer, Director, Author (Cologne); Demetris Zavros, Composer/Director (Leeds).

   Symposium *Zusammenarbeit und Autorschaft im Neuen Musiktheater* [Collaboration and Authorship in New Music Theatre], 7 October 2007 at the Haus der Berliner Festspiele. Concept and organisation: Irene Kletschke (KlangKunstBühne, UdK Berlin, HFM Hanns Eisler Berlin). Podium: Heiner Goebbels, Ruedi Häusermann, Julian Klein and Manos Tsangaris. Chair: David Roesner.

   My interview with Leo Dick, composer and director, on 8 May 2008 in Bielefeld, about the world première of his production *Kann Heidi brauchen, was es gelernt hat? – Szenisches Musikpanorama für 12 MusikerdarstellerInnen* (composer and director: Leo Dick, libretto and dramaturg: Felizitas Ammann, stage and costume design: Tassilo Tesche) on 6 June 2008.

'conclusion': as mentioned in the introduction, we offer *Composed Theatre* as a starting point rather than a closing statement. The practices and processes we seek to analyse within this framework are continuously being developed and proliferated and we hope the academic discourse will remain in dialogue with the emerging arts practices.

There are two key premises to the following attempt at a discourse analysis of conversations and discussions Matthias Rebstock and I initiated and have pursued since 2007: what we had – tentatively at first – called Composed Theatre referred to a music-theatrical practice that appeared relatively clearly defined and coherent from a distance, but on closer examination became more and more multifaceted, even contradictory and certainly difficult to define. It is a genre that undermines the idea of genre. It is a form of music-theatre that sometimes contains no music. It is an interdisciplinary practice that questions the nature and materiality of its disciplines.

What emerges, then, is the notion of a field: seen from above, it looks distinct, its outline clearly defined. Seen from within, boundaries blur and the question of whether this or that landmark is still definitely part of the field becomes equivocal. We realised that Composed Theatre could not sensibly be defined ontologically (exclusively) by its phenomena: the works and performances that we felt were somehow situated in the field. Composed Theatre, we argued, requires a close look at the practices and processes of its creation in order to understand it and to identify – if not a clear-cut definition with necessary and sufficient criteria – at least a set of tendencies, gravitational centres around which key aspects tend to orbit. Thus the first aim of this chapter is to achieve a surveying of this field.

The second aim (and premise) of this text is to access practice and process discursively: When talking about some of the key tendencies of process in Composed Theatre, I will not present an essentialist view of 'what it is' but an analysis of how practitioners themselves have described and characterised their processes, concepts and understandings. In this specialist discourse about the aesthetics and ethics of making Composed Theatre, I will seek to tease out the key topics, themes and discursive formations.

Phillips and Jørgensen's 'preliminary definition of a discourse' describes "*a particular way of talking about and understanding the world (or an aspect of the world)*" (2002: 3, original emphasis). Discourses are, they say, historically and culturally specific. They link knowledge and social processes, but Phillips and Jørgensen stress an anti-essentialist notion of knowledge: it is "contingent and thus anti-foundationalist" (2002: 5). It is with this clearly in mind that I have approached the material discussed in this chapter. In addition, Roger Fowler has pointed out that discourse not only represents a way of "talking about and understanding the world" (2002: 3) as it is, but also expresses how the world should be.

> 'Discourse' is speech or writing seen from the point of view of the beliefs, values and categories which it embodies; these beliefs etc. constitute a way of looking at the world, an organization or representation of experience – 'ideology' in the neutral non-pejorative sense. Different modes of discourse encode different representations of experience;

and the source of these representations is the communicative context within which the discourse is embedded.

(Fowler cit. in Mills 1997: 6)

Discourse can thus be generated at the interface between observations and utopian ideas and encompass both reflective and imaginative, visionary aspects; both are present in the exchanges on Composed Theatre.

One of the tendencies of the discursive fragments[4] is to attempt to define Composed Theatre by means of exclusion or *ex negativo*. Consequently, a question often paired with how the practitioners characterise the nature of their work(ing) is concerned with what they distinguish it from. In a field that sits between and/or straddles established notions of performative formats such as straight theatre, opera, music theatre,[5] dance theatre or concert, the question of how its process of creation differs became a running theme of the conversations, inevitably incorporating generalising ideas of what those processes 'typically' and 'traditionally' are in those neighbouring formats.

Within Michel Foucault's distinction of three different levels on which he uses the notion of discourse, the second one is most apt for the kind of exploration this chapter undertakes. He writes:

Instead of gradually reducing the rather fluctuating meaning of the word 'discourse', I believe I have in fact added to its meanings: treating it sometimes as the general domain of all statements, sometimes as an individual group of statements, and sometimes as a regulated practice that accounts for a number of statements.

(Foucault cit. in Mills 1997: 6)

---

4. I am following the terminology and systematic of Siegfried Jäger (1999) who distinguishes discourse threads (Diskursstränge): overarching, thematically connected discursive processes; discourse fragments (Diskursfragmente): individual contributions, texts, or parts of texts; discourse events and contexts (Diskursive Ereignisse und Kontexte): form the relationship between an event and its treatment in the discourse based on and influenced by the political and social dominances; discourse levels (Diskursebenen): levels such as science, politics, education, on which the discursive threads operate; discourse positions (Diskurspositionen), the individual ideological position of the speaker or medium.

5. I am using music theatre here not as an umbrella term, but in its more defined historical, aesthetic and ideological sense that emerged from a variety of attempts at reform and reinvention of the operatic genres in the 1960s and 1970s by composers such as Luigi Nono, Luciano Berio, Gvörgy Ligeti or Karl-Heinz Stockhausen (see Andrew Clements article on music theatre in *The New Grove Dictionary of Music and Musicians* for a clear outline of this notion of the term [Clements 2001: 534–5]).

While one could argue that *any* practice of statements will be regulated in one way or another, I do not think that in the case of our 'individual group of statements' the aspects of regulation, power relation and hegemony[6] are at the forefront of the discussion. Nonetheless it is worth mentioning the context of the statements and thus the status of the material on which I am basing the following observations.

The discursive threads all unfolded in an academic context and within a research incentive. The discourse positions of all contributors are similar in that all have a direct, often artistically practical involvement in what we have coined Composed Theatre. There are, of course, also significant differences in discursive positions with regard to artistic standing, international acclaim, national background, institutional support, artistic identity etc., whose significance will emerge when relevant in the following analysis.

I have organised the analysis of discourse fragments and threads around four key questions: What do we mean when we talk about Composed Theatre? Who do we work with and how? How is the working process different from other forms of theatre and music practice? What are the consequences of the above?

What do we mean when we talk about Composed Theatre?

There is an extensive discursive thread concerned with questions of terminology.[7] The aim is to capture the diverse practices embraced by a shared concept.[8] While working through the proposed term 'Composed Theatre', the discourse seeks to identify the common ground, the through-lines and shared aspects that make grouping the range of practices sensible and productive. This is done in two ways: by means of suggesting alternative terms that highlight different aspects of the field and by aiming to find strong points of contact (with less interest in what these should be called or labelled).

I will first discuss some of the alternative or supplementary terms with regard to how they may help to map and shape the field. I will then explore two notions that have become dominant in our attempts to describe common features of the different processes of Composed Theatre: the application of compositional thinking, and the way in which material is connected and layered, often in relation to scores and musical notation.

---

6. Discourse analysis has, particularly in Michel Foucault's work, also been a method to discuss questions of power and hegemony, which are both established, represented and maintained in discourse. In a discourse with by and large like-minded artists and scholars, analysis of what themes or groupings our discourse suppressed or marginalised, was not, I feel, of great enough significance to be a prominent focus of this chapter.
7. See for example the discussion in chapter 15.
8. See also Jörg Laue's reflection and problematisation on the act of defining in his chapter (6) in this book.

Terminology

Some of the terms that have been suggested highlight the question whether and how Composed Theatre renegotiates the relationship between the 'acoustic and the visual stage'[9] (Goebbels). Roland Quitt, for example, suggests that "a post-Wagnerian theatre of composers has come into being, which is concerned not only with organising parameters of the acoustic but also of the optical field".[10] Michael Hirsch, when speaking about his combinations of *musique concrète* with theatrical elements, refers to it as 'audible theatre', suggestion thus a complementary term to Dieter Schnebel's idea of 'visible music'.[11] Jörg Lensing introduces the notion of an 'integrated theatre', stressing the close-knit, mutually dependent relationship of elements like sound, movement, video and lighting in some of his company Theater der Klänge's work.[12]

These terms focus, it would seem, more on the phenomenological side of Composed Theatre: what feels, looks, sounds different about it? How is its intermodality[13] different to that of other genres of performance art? It is a form that changes some of the perceptive expectancies and dominances traditionally established by other genres.[14] They are all useful in describing specific groups of practices, particularly with regard to their reception, but do not encompass the amount of aesthetic variety we encountered when introduced to the range of Composed Theatres. There are, for example, specimens of Composed Theatre such as Heiner Goebbels' works, which defy the notion of 'integrated' and instead insist on the compositional *separation* of elements (see e.g., Goebbels 2002). At the same time, the dual thinking of acoustic and visual elements or aural and optical stages, which Quitt's and Hirsch's terms seek to modify, is in itself problematic: Composed Theatre often actively seeks to render this distinction obsolete, to 'ravish the senses' (Cryptic[15]) into synaesthetic receptivity, hearing with the eyes and seeing with the ears.

A second group of statements reflects on how the process differs from other practices. In his presentation, Quitt suggests both the terms 'project theatre' and 'advanced theatre', which

---

9. All quotations from discourse participants are taken from the sources outlined in footnote 3.
10. In this chapter I mainly refer to Roland Quitt's keynote contribution to the symposia that formed part of the basis for this book (see Exeter Digital Archive). This is largely distinct from the additional argument he provides in his chapter (2) in this book.
11. For example, his piece from 1962 *nostalgie [or: visible music II]* for solo conductor. Publisher: Schott Music.
12. Hans-Joachim Hespos, a very prolific composer in this field, who was not part of the discourse itself, similarly calls his work 'integrales Theater' (integral theatre). See Steiert 1988 for a detailed discussion of the term and Hespos' work, as well as Brüstle 2007.
13. See for example Schouten 2007 for a discussion of intermodality in performance.
14. In a theatre production, for example, audiences expect to understand the text and would be reluctant to see a play in a language they do not speak; while in opera a lack of enunciation or a foreign language are rarely seen as a major deterrent.
15. See http://www.cryptic.org.uk/cryptic-projects/cryptic-and-technology/ [20 May 2010].

emphasise its experimental nature, increased collaborativity and a sense of progression from more engrained modes of working and creation.

In a different way this is also reflected in Hirsch's notion of the 'Konvolut'[16] or Manos Tsangaris' metaphor of music-theatrical 'molecules': both are conceptual and notational premises which fragment the work into smaller, more independent units, which refrain from suggesting a single linear order and thus change the nature of composing, notating, rehearsing and staging the works. Hirsch's term also encompasses the inclination to consciously play with and cite different genres within units of his 'Konvolut', even arranging elements in such a way that audiences will experience a piece as a different genre depending on where they are situated in relation to the music-theatrical event.

By referring to some of his work as 'music for actors', Hirsch also introduces the notion that Composed Theatre could be defined not only by specific (intermodal) modes of perception or specific (experimental/advanced) working processes but also by performer. Composed Theatre often addresses and exploits the specific musical and theatrical frictions that occur when a certain training background and a certain creative and/or performative task do not quite match. Heiner Goebbels' decision to let the highly trained musicians of the Ensemble Modern recite texts or play instruments foreign them (e.g. in *Black on White*, 1996[17]), and to ask his actor André Wilms to cook an omelette and recite Canetti strictly adhering to the bars of Ravel's *String Quartet in F* (in *Eraritjaritjaka*, 2004) are examples of this.

Compositional thinking

Despite defying a clear common genre, style, aesthetic surface or topic (a generally agreed-upon feature of Composed Theatre), its definition or characterisation reflects a shift in the dramaturgical approach towards creating coherence: Composed Theatre, we argued and agreed, is the implementation of (musical) compositional thinking to all or most aspects of the process of creating a music-theatrical performance.[18] Demetris Zavros calls this the

---

16. See Hirsch's chapter (5) in this book for a more detailed account of this format.
17. Details of the productions I refer to in this chapter are listed as part of the bibliography.
18. The exploration of aspects of 'composing' and 'compositional thinking' in Composed Theatre should be prefaced by explaining how the word 'composition' was commonly understood in our discursive thread. In its most general sense, composition denotes 'the activity or process of creating music, and the product of such activity' (Blum 2010). Blum further explores the rich varieties with regard to the sense of fixity, authorship and level of originality required in different times and cultures to justify the term 'composition'. In the present discourse, however, composition was referred to based on its development in Europe from the thirteenth century and the development of counterpoint in the Ars Nova period and onwards with a clear emphasis on the 'high art' practices of canonical composers and their notated works.

application of "musical strategies of organization in the composition of 'all theatrical means' (Hans-Thies Lehmann) from music-centric conceptual models".[19]

This idea of 'compositional thinking' became a throughline of the discussion: it provides common ground while remaining sufficiently flexible to embrace different *kinds* of compositional thinking. For example, part of the discourse is concerned with musical form, structures and models. Thinking in abstract relationships of form (Roland Quitt and Nicholas Till talk about this) becomes a key stimulus and challenge; sometimes this even means applying or superimposing historical forms (Lensing mentioned Sonata, Suite and others for their work) and de-constructing them with new technologies and theatrical means of expression.

Closely related to thinking in musical microstructures is an interest in musical microstructures and musical rhetoric, and consequent explorations of structural relations like repetition and variation, establishing and working with what amounts to motifs, making musical forms of permutation more generally applicable not only to the acoustic material but to theatrical action as a whole. All these are explicitly compositional ways of approaching speech, gesture, light, scenography and other elements.

Thinking thus within and working on musical parameters (pitch, volume, duration, timbre) is discussed as another way of 'directing as a composer' (Goebbels): Goebbels 'confessed' that although he had overheard a visiting director at the theatre department in Giessen warn his students never to give actors instructions like 'faster/slower or louder/softer', this was something he, Goebbels, precisely practiced, not least because he trusted his actors to translate these musical instructions into their respective languages effectively and relate them to whatever level of interior imagery, subtext, energy direction etc. they might need. Similarly, George Rodosthenous reports his techniques of 'conducting' his theatre rehearsals and improvisations by establishing with the actors and dancers which gestures mean *crescendo*, *decrescendo*, *accelerando* or *rallantando*, which enables him to steer compositional aspects of an ongoing improvisation without having to interrupt or give verbal instructions.

Generally the discourse frequently touches upon how all creation of music and theatre is centrally concerned with questions of rhythm and timing. Applying parametrical thinking in Composed Theatre, I would suggest, is demarcated from the rhythmical considerations in a straight play in that rhythm no longer serves primarily as a psychological and narrative device. It is also different from purely musical composition in that it extends beyond the acoustic realm to kinetic rhythms, visual rhythms, rhythms of spoken language, rhythms even of inanimate materials.[20]

---

19. For this reason Zavros also suggested the alternative term 'music-centric music theatre' in this context, which – like Composed Theatre – places the focus on the conceptual and processual aspects, but is, as a term, perhaps less user-friendly. There was also some discussion on whether Composed Theatre was inevitably 'music-theatre' and quite a few discourse positions disagreed. See below for more detail on this aspect.

20. In Heiner Goebbels' *Stifters Dinge* (2007), for example, the real time rhythms of water flowing into basins, its undulations reflecting light onto moving gauze curtains and finally its chemical

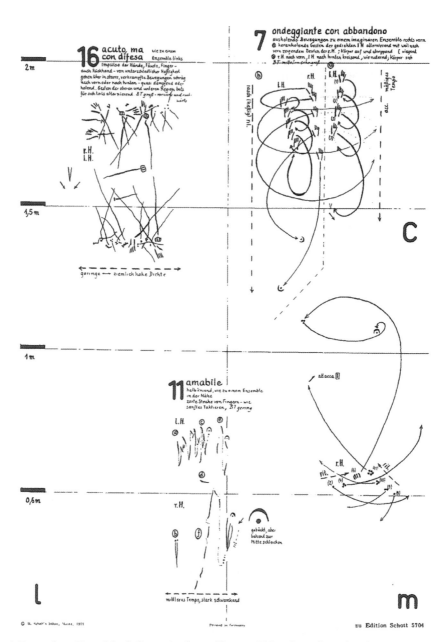

Figure 1: Excerpt from Dieter Schnebel's *nostalgie [or: visible music II] for solo conductor* (1962).

A few additional pinpointed remarks help to clarify and sharpen the notion of Composed Theatre. In relation to the composite term music theatre, Rebstock feels that there are certainly examples of music theatre that are not Composed Theatre (where the compositional thinking only applies to its music, not to the somehow separate aspects of staging, which may even amount to a practice of 'Bebilderung' 21 of the score). Quitt adds the reverse perspective, that Composed Theatre is not necessarily music theatre. A piece like Dieter Schnebel's *nostalgie [or: visible music II] for solo conductor* (1962) for example does not, in a stricter sense, contain any music, but evokes imaginary music through the precise composition of a conductor's gestures (see figure 1[22]) and instructions to an imaginary ensemble.[23]

Consequently, as Jörg Laue elaborates, Composed Theatre calls into question its materiality: it is not, he says, about specific starting points or kinds of material, but about processes of musically organising, transforming and shaping material in space and time.

This question is also pertinent when the act of composing theatre is based on or incorporates an existing musical composition. Laue and the LOSE COMBO, for example, structured an entire performance (still (*LAST/Trilogie 2*, 2000), note by note, using a complex process of conversion, on a composition by Bach (Contrapunctus III from *Die Kunst der Fuge*, BWV 1080); Heiner Goebbels an his team composed an entire live film, bar by bar, to Ravel's *String Quartet in F* (in *Eraritjaritjaka*, 2004) and Johanna Dombois uses specific recordings of, for

---

reaction with a powder, which results in beautifully slow eruptions of puffs of steam, foreground the rhythmical qualities of a natural element in a highly technological stage environment and invite a contemplative way of watching and listening not unlike the nature descriptions in Adalbert Stifter's writing, on which the production is based, but also not unlike, of course, absorbing music.

21. 'Bebilderung' or the mere addition of images/illustrations to the music has become a pejorative topos of music theatre criticism in German-speaking theatre practice in the past few decades. For the purpose of this investigation it may suffice to note that the act of composition is different in Composed Theatre from (other forms of) music theatre: in Composed Theatre it extends to and is fully aware of the ensuing theatrical presentation.

22. The verbal instructions translate, for example, as: "16: high tone, but defensive. As if towards an ensemble to the left. Impulses of the hands, fists, fingers – also backhand – of different intensities proceed into stiff, rigid movements, diagonally to the front or downwards, quasi muting or fetching . Gestures of the upper and lower region alternating individually" or "7. Undulating with abandoment. Wide-ranging motions to an imaginary ensemble to the front right. Gathering gestures of a turned left Hand alternating with forward pointing of the right hand, bouncing movements of the body [...]" and "11. Amabile (dulcet), half-kneeling as if to an ensemble close by, delicate strokes with the fingers – like subtly beating the time". Copyright by Schott Music, 1971, Mainz – Germany. Reproduced by permission. All rights reserved.

23. See for example Salzmann/Desi 2009, p. 149ff. and Jarzina 2005 for a fuller discussion of this piece. Also see http://dsounds.netzwerkneuemusik.de/ausgabe-1/dieter-schnebel-visible-music-ii.html [07 July 2010] for a description and video recording of the piece.

Figure 2: Johanna Dombois' *Ring-Studie 01 Richard Wagners »Rheingold«-Vorspiel in Second Life'* (2009) – from the composed animation of the Zurich Operhouse, composed exactly to a recording of the Prelude from Wagner's *Ring*.

example, Beethoven's *Fidelio* or Wagner's *Ring der Nibelungen*, when directing multimedial and/or virtual stagings, not only paying extremely detailed attention to each bar of the score, but even using the various acoustic and expressive parameters of the individual recording as stage directions or virtual camera instructions on a micro-second level. In each case there is an act of transformation and translation of someone else's compositional thinking onto the real, filmed or virtual stages of the individual theatre production, their design, lighting and performances by the actors, avatars or figurative design elements (see figures 2 and 7).

In this context, however, Quitt raises the question about whether the term 'Composed' is actually metaphorical. Can we really say that we are composing theatre as music or is it still composing theatre *as if* it were music? A literal meaning, Zavros agrees, would ignore the "Eigengesetzlichkeit des Materials" (Adorno 1991: 158), that is, the unique (and differing) material qualities of theatre and music, as well as the unique (and differing) modes of reception of acoustically (music) and visually (theatre) dominant stimuli. Again, I suggest that the problem with this – otherwise perfectly valid – question lies in the assumption of a clear binary between the aural and visual, between music and theatre. Both are and always have been composite media and many of their contributing aspects, such as language or sound, contain both acoustic and optical elements and appeal to both the listener and the viewer inseparably. I would argue that on a continuum of materiality stretching from musicality to theatricality, the notion of composition gradually shifts from its literal sense (composing theatre as music), via presence as simile (composing theatre like music), to metaphor (composing theatre musically).

The freedom and complexity of 'compositional thinking' as understood by different discourse positions, according to different notions and emphases of what they understand to be 'composition', is paralleled by the level of variety in the processes in which this compositional thinking is applied.

According to the varying reports and descriptions of working processes, compositional thinking is applied by some in a comparatively 'traditional' individual process of composing, in which theatre elements keep 'sneaking in' (Hirsch), or in which there is an element of theatrical action involved in creating and recording sounds for tape music and *musique concrète* (see Hirch's chapter (5) in this book). Other practices are ascribed to 'creation' (Cathie Boyd). While Boyd describes a clear division of labour between the (often commissioned) composers and herself as director, there is a significant amount of communication, exchange of ideas and concepts, collaborative editing and shaping that takes place in the process, with impact on the score and the staging concept. Other processes place great emphasis on different forms of improvisation from the beginning, including composer(s), director(s) and performer(s) – in some cases (Goebbels) even staging, costume, light and sound design.

Some processes, then, are more collaborative than others, some more devised than others.[24] It is the desire to extend musical models and principles across the expressive and structural spectrum of the theatrical event as a whole that unites these different practices and makes it worthwhile to look at them as a grouping despite their heterogeneity.

One of the most recurrent features of the discourse on what compositional thinking means in the context of Composed Theatre is the exploration of horizontal and vertical connections and relations influenced and inspired by the predominant symbolic notational language of music: the score. For many practitioners, Composed Theatre means thinking of theatre as a score and exploring the connections, the 'joints' (Tsangaris), the 'polyphony' (Goebbels), the 'track-work' (Wilson[25]) and the 'layers' (Zavros).

Making connections: Thinking in and working with scores

Scores, or at least precursors of scores, which I will call proto-scores, are described and reflected upon in many of the discursive fragments on Composed Theatre. They both reflect and guide practitioners' compelling interest in creating and shaping events in relation to a

---

24. See the more detailed comparison of processes and working methods in part 4 of this chapter.
25. While Robert Wilson did not actively contribute to the discourse on Composed Theatre here, Heiner Goebbels refers to him and his practice, which has a great significance for Composed Theatre, in his chapter (4). For a fuller discussion of the notion of track-work in Wilson's theatre also see Roesner 2003: 234–38.

rhythmic unfolding of time and in specific functional abstract relation to each other. They described scores and proto-scores as a strategic planning and communication device, an 'Aufschreibesystem' 'notation system', (Kittler 1985) to record and remember, an organising principle and overarching metaphor.

Where in traditional drama the guiding organising principles are led by the character relations and motivations which drive (or are driven by) unfolding events with a cause-effect relationship as well as the dialogic principle of dramatic narration, Composed Theatre is guided by the structural and semantic relations of a complex array of intermedial 'voices'. Again, the discourse on the score as device, practice, principle and metaphor identifies a number of positions on a continuum; a continuum that ranges from pragmatic ways of organising heterogeneous events across media to politically motivated uses of certain notational systems; from strategies of abstraction associated with musical notation to strategies of narrativisation; from the desire to separate the 'ingredients' of Composed Theatre to the facilitation of synthesis and cohesion. There is a shared concept, however, which forms a steady *basso continuo* of the discourse: the notion of polyphony.[26] Polyphony in Composed Theatre is the transference of a compositional principle: a simultaneity of voices that allows an independence of its parts while providing structural linkage. For Composed Theatre, Jörg Laue suggests calling it 'performative polyphony', and with reference to Freda Chapple's thoughts on intermediality,[27] I suggest one could also speak of an 'intermedial polyphony'. Either way, the notion of polyphony carries a sense of an autonomy of individual voices, layers, and media within a greater whole in which the structural and semantic relations can be renegotiated and form new and previously uncommon connections, hierarchies and patterns of mutual impact.[28]

The discourse then diversifies three different polyphonic tendencies in organising the material. The first replaces other forms of organisational connections (such as semantic or even narrative links) of distinct events or 'voices' with *structural* relations from the repertoire of the musical polyphonic 'grammar': counterpoint, imitation, complementary rhythms, echoes, inversion, retrograde, retrograde inversion, etc. The second embraces techniques that avoid meaningful juxtaposition in favour of mere simultaneity – putting things side by side, without indicating how they might be connected. Jörg Laue's reference to John Cage ("to gather together what exists in a dispersed state"[29]) and his work with time brackets, purely formal units in which seemingly unrelated events occur at the same time, attest to this. Also

---

26. See also Roesner 2008 on this topic.
27. These are documented both on the DVD of her presentation which is part of the Exeter Digital Archive as well her co-edited publication (Chapple/Kattenbelt 2006).
28. This is where Chapple's concept of intermediality as "an approach to look at assessing impact of one medium upon the other" and not a proliferation of lots of screens on a stage is very helpful (see also Chapple and Kattenbelt 2006).
29. See Laue's chapter (6) in this book.

Heiner Goebbels' aesthetic recommendation: "Explain nothing. Put it there. Say it. Leave."[30] allows things to remain separate and encourages a kind of polyphony that does not aim to provide the 'semantic glue' holding things together and fixing their relationship and mutual interference in one particular way. This resonates with Baudrillard's notion of the 'radiation of the signified': "[…] ambiguity, polysemia, polyvalence, polyphony of meaning: it is always a matter of the *radiation of the signified*, of a simultaneity of significations" (Baudrillard 1993: 217, original emphasis).

And thirdly, in a meta-structural way, both Hirsch's notational strategy of the 'Konvolut' (see above) and Manos Tsangaris' thinking in performative 'molecules' (as well as the historical examples of Kagel's *Staatstheater* [1967–70] and John Cage's *Songbooks* [1970], to name but two) are also extensions of this thinking: they are attempts to find a balance, as Hirsch puts it, between independence and organisation. Where the latter still focusses on the joints, links and connections of voices, even if the connections are forged musically and not semantically as one might expect on a theatre stage, the former seeks to emphasise the "cracks, the spaces in between", as Chapple puts it.

Rebstock provides an important distinction with regard to polyphony: while the performative or intermedial polyphony[31] is a strong working principle in the process of *creating* Composed Theatre, there is still an undeniable tendency of the receiver as a 'mono medium' (Tsangaris) to synthesise the diversity into a meaningful, cohesive whole regardless of the strategies of separation and simultaneity. However, I would argue, polyphony – in music – is precisely the technique that strives to afford the listener the choice between concentrating on the connections of voices, their harmony and joint coherence, or focussing on one voice at a time. Due to each voice's relative autonomy, it makes sense for the listener to follow it individually while only occasionally eavesdropping sideways to hear what the other voices are doing. Similarly, the performative or intermedial polyphony affords the viewer/ listener a continuum of levels of 'zooming' in and out of the web of 'voices' and a continuum of knitting and disentangling relations between them. While no audience member as a mono medium can ever truly perceive a multiplicity of voice simultaneously with equal attention, the polyphony in Composed Theatre, which itself operates on a fluctuation of hierarchies and dependencies, allows for perceptual and experiential choices to be made by the audience.[32]

In order to demonstrate the varied nature of the engagement with questions of notation and scoring in Composed Theatre, three further individual cases are interesting to consider.

---

30. Title for a lecture Goebbels gave 2009 in Stockholm – see http://www.egs.edu/faculty/heiner-goebbels/videos/heiner-goebbels/ [19 May 2010].
31. I actually suggest using either term, depending on the tendencies of the individual performance, that is, whether it foregrounds polyphonic relationships between different (technological) media, such as Theater der Klänge's *Suite intermediale* (2008) or between different kinds of physical, vocal and instrumental performance, such as Heiner Goebbels' *Black on White* (1996).

Nick Till talks about his project *Hearing Voices* (Stuttgart 2006) and the attempt to make use of the transcript (into musical notation) of a phonogram recording of a schizophrenic patient as starting point and material for the production. Rather than starting with a notation as a piece of art, as most music-theatre would, here a document intended for a medical diagnosis becomes the key material for a music-theatrical diagnosis of the uncanny effects of mediated bodies and voices in a contemporary music-theatrical attempt to look at 'essential conditions of narrative forms in musical theatre' (Till). At the same time, almost ironically, this document of a highly individual mental disorder aids Till's attempts to 'get away from certain notions of subjectivity and expression and interiority that go with conventional notions of operatic singing' (Till) as it question the conventional and habitual use of notations and scores in music theatre and requires new, experimental approaches.

While there was a general sense in the discourse that the notion of musical scores for the theatre provided a means towards more abstraction, form and structure, there were interesting exceptions. Cathie Boyd's work with *Cryptic* almost inverts this process. Boyd starts with what is often a commissioned piece of music: for the most part this is highly abstract instrumental and/or electronic music and sometimes vocal music. She then translates or enriches the musical score into a graph or proto-score which overlays the structure of the music with both visual, performative and technical aspects of the performance, but first of all consists of a kind of visual representation of the 'emotional journey' (Boyd) she and her musicians associate with the music – not necessarily the composer's emotional journey, she says. This then becomes the (hidden) narrative trajectory and subtext of the piece. Theatrically/visually presenting music then is not just aligning theatrical elements compositionally to an existing or emerging piece of music, but also an attempt to 'pad' music with some of the narrative and dramaturgical thinking of theatre. On a practical level, the proto-score (see Figure 3) is a planning tool and *aide memoire*, not intended for documenting or handing down, but for maintaining an overview and helping the communication of all those creatively involved in the production.[33]

George Rodosthenous also uses a graph as a notational device and reference point for himself and the performers and collaborators on a project. Its function, however, is slightly different. Envisioning the performance as a segmented event in time and making decision towards a clearly structured and balanced overall rhythm of the piece early in the process allow Rodosthenous a great deal of improvisational freedom *within* that structure. The graph, which outlines the sequence, duration and formal and narrative relation of its parts, also provides orientation for the often non-chronological work on the scenes themselves.

---

32. See also Heiner Goebbels' (2007) chapter in Lechtermann/Wagner/Wenzel (Eds.) *Möglichkeitsräume – Zur Performativität von sensorischer Wahrnehmung* for a further exploration of this question of the 'performativity of sensory perception' (my translation of the book's subtitle).
33. See also the passage below on establishing a common language.

OPTICAL IDENTITY BREAKDOWN

TIME LAPSE	INDIV TIME	MUSIC	PLAYERS	JOURNEY & COLOURS	VISUALS	DESIGN	LIGHTING	NOTES
30.43								
Part 8	23.40	FRANGHIZ ALI ZADEH Mugam Sayagi Time TQ in March.	Cello only on stage Players join later with percussion instrument, played from memory	Prayer time turns to rage The cello calls the players back to the stage Tough, beautiful, angry, hopeful *Black and white*	Edited B&W video which is being mixed live by Jasch - 12 short videos to be mixed Video to end on still image.	Yu-Ying brings on Gong for Leslie.	Stage to be very dark, cello solo only with shadows of TQ players against cyc? The climatic section towards the end punctuated by LX.	Other players start off stage, viola joins, then VI I. Viola later play tam tam, VI II plays triangle and tamburo. Ends with cello solo.
54.23								
Part 9	5.03	ROLF WALLIN Phonotope 1 Part 4 Metal – FIRE – earth	.	Confusion - Is this place right for us, Destruction - lets leave our mark. Regret at what has been damaged *Reds and yellows*	Jasch to leave table area with glove –2D to 3D For first 80 seconds then Live camera switching - Use tang in pairs, Vn1/va – Vc/Vn2.		(no scores used by quartet)	Metal =1.18, FIRE =2.45, Water –1.00 FIRE LX focus Leslie to leave cello DS at end Spy cameras being used which are preset down stage.
59.26								
Part 10	8.32	JOBY TALBOT	TQ DS v close to audience closest moment in the piece	Masculine adrenalin Saturated colours and light *Rich blues*	Projections using all surfaces All visuals grow at this point in scale	sci fi over saturation	(no scores used by quartet) harsh beams across the stage	Octet – TQ playing with manual override soundtrack. Starts standing DS.

Figure 3: Excerpt from a graph/notation of Boyd for *Optical Identity*.

Within this macrostructure, Rodosthenous then actually works like a theatre director on motivation, narrative, character etc., but often uses pieces of music in the process to emotionally map a scene. Music acts as an emotional pacemaker or prompter in developing a quite naturalistic scene, like a rhythmically fixed subtext, or rather: subscore. Other than working with subtext, the subscore provides atmospheric and emotional cues in real time rather than discursive instructions the actor needs to give him/herself. This frees the actor's imagination to improvise alongside the 'railing' provided by the music and also acts as a shared rather than individual and internal set of instructions for a whole group of performers.

Finally, political implications of the notion of the score and the practices of notation are discussed. Manos Tsangaris reflects on his inner resistance to writing scores in the sense of an authoritative text by a hierarchically superior composer to be executed by voiceless musicians, who do as they are told. Jörg Lensing expresses similar dissatisfactions with common, traditional classical music practice. Tsangaris refers to John Cage when suggesting that we should be using the written space to invent new social models rather than reiterating established power structures. Many of the scoring and notation techniques described in the context of Composed Theatre display an active and critical engagement with the implicit politics of the score. Notation is used to facilitate a more transparent exchange with the whole creative team (Boyd, Rodothenous), scoring is used to actively strive for a balance between the artistic means of the theatre (Tsangaris, Goebbels), new, non-linear forms of scores are invented or explored in order to enhance the importance and uniqueness of the performance itself as one possible reading of the put-together[34] material and strengthen the artistic influence of the creative production team (Tsangaris, Hirsch, and of course, historically, Cage and Kagel).

This aspect of the discourse on Composed Theatre, then, would imply that it is characterised not only by an employment and application of compositional thinking in a theatrical environment, but also by an invitation to critically reflect on the practice of musical composition itself. It is perhaps no coincidence then that two people independently use the term de-composition (Tsangaris, Zavros) to describe certain aspects of Composed Theatre processes. If one were to follow the double meaning (to decompose = to musically deconstruct, but also: to rot, to decay), there is a suggestion that Composed Theatre is an act of musical and theatrical construction based on and fertilised by acts of disintegrating previous materials and practices. If a moment of poetic exuberance can be forgiven, one might say that Composed Theatre is the worm feasting on the corpse of Opera, the flower growing out of Theatre's compost, the Phoenix rising out of Concert's ashes.

Who do we work with and how?

Discussing Composed Theatre inevitably involves talking about the individuals whose work we feel constitutes features and landmarks in the field we are trying to map. One premise was that if our notion of Composed Theatre challenged certain engrained characteristics and expectations about process, aesthetics and perception(s) in the more established varieties of performing music and theatre, then role definitions and kinds of collaborations, perhaps even the creative communication would also demonstrate significant changes. In this part I will look at discursive threads reflecting the key differences and challenges that Composed Theatre poses to the composer, director, performer, designer and technician who work in this field.

The composer

The role of the composer is described as undergoing both limitations and extensions with the context of Composed Theatre. Lensing and Boyd stress the importance of the composer's openness to the opportunities and necessities of the performative dimensions interwoven with the organisation of sound, whether s/he is immediately involved in the project or

---

34. Hirsch reminded us that composition derives from the Latin 'componere', which means putting together, assembling. Blum offers the same etymology in his *New Grove* entry: "The term belongs to a large class of English nouns derived from the participial stems of Latin verbs (here *composit-*, from *componere*: 'put together') followed by the suffix *-io/-ionem*. Etymologically, the primary senses of 'composition' are 'the condition of being composed' and 'the action of composing'" (Blum 2010).

just a commissioned partner. For Boyd in particular there are at times negotiations about the different dramaturgical requirements for the material: while a newly composed piece of music might work in a pure concert setting, it can prove too long, too complicated or dramaturgically ineffective when scrutinised for theatrical effectiveness. Both director and composer have to negotiate and agree that the amalgamation of the acoustic and the visual layers is more than their sum and therefore compromise on the perceived 'purity' of each.

Lensing outlines that several of the composers who have collaborated on various projects (Hanno Spelsberg, Tobias Schlierf, Michael Sapp) often compose and improvise during rehearsal on their instruments or – in the case of founding member and composer Thomas Neuhaus – improvise digitally with laptop and Max/MSP/Jitter in the context of the sensor-equipped stage. Processes of composing, directing, and textual or movement improvisations thus often happen simultaneously and affect and pervade each other. Other composers, such as Wolfgang Heiniger, draw our attention to the fact that extending the materiality of what is 'composable' also has a strong effect on a composer's identity: in his own practice, which he describes as dealing with 'meta-instruments' or 'transmedial instruments', compositional activity may for example no longer involve a keyboard and pen and paper, but a programmable lighting desk, or, again, a computer operating Max/MSP/Jitter.

Heiner Goebbels' production *Stifters Dinge/Stifter's Things* (Lausanne 2007) went full circle in this respect, when his technical team (particularly Hubert Machnik) programmed a keyboard for him in such a way that it controlled all the elements of stage action at its disposal of this performance without performers. The electronically controlled pianos, the gauze curtains, the lights, the remote controlled dragging of stones, slapping of long tubes, hisses of dry ice – all this had become programmable through Max/MSP/Jitter and intuitively playable through a musical instrument, which facilitated a much more intuitively musical control for Heiner Goebbels as a composer and musician and allowed him to 'think' as such not only cognitively but also physically by using his own pianist-body knowledge.[35]

Theater der Klänge go yet one step further and dissolve, one could say, the role of the composer, by means of fully sensor equipped and mediatised stages, which by means of Max/MSP/Jitter become the instrument on which no longer one person plays, but which integrates all performers into the *in situ* composition process.[36]

While in *Cryptic*, Boyd's process of composing may still be predominantly the individual creative pursuit in shaping time and sound, opened towards and extended by visual and/or theatrical considerations for presentation, the latter examples (Lensing, Heiniger, Goebbels) mark a more profound change in the role of the composer. They embed the act of composing more strongly within the act of rehearsing and shaping performance itself, and turn

---

35. See Labouvie 2006 for a discussion of the notion of body knowledge.
36. See also Lensing's chapter (7) in this book and in particular the technical setup documents for different productions (figures 2, 5 and 6 in Lensing's chapter) as well as the section 'Technology' in this chapter.

composers into directors to a stronger degree, sometimes transforming sound technicians/ programmers into co-composers. This means that some of the often substantial ego of the composer – created and enforced by romantic notions of the genius in the nineteenth century and a corresponding celebrity cult of the twentieth century – has to be sacrificed or at least qualified in this transition.

Consequently, Lensing poses the question whether the pursuit and the training of a 'serious' composer is somewhat threatened or diminished by the amalgamation of composition and performance, for example when exploring the comic potential of a new compositional interface between movement and live sound electronics (*Figur und Klang im Raum,* 1993).[37] Composed Theatre is not, as the discourse suggests, about taking oneself or artistic tasks less seriously, but it relies less on certain formulaic strategies and poses which ordinarily seek to 'guarantee' the nimbus of a serious composer and his/her work. Instead they quite often actively engage in playful acts of questioning or undermining that very notion.

Introducing the theatrical as a frame of creation and perception[38] re-introduces the human body to the process and performance of composition. We have been trained and accustomed to ignore the physicality, the flesh and blood, of making music in those dominant developments of (classical) music that privilege music as an immaterial idea and form over the visceral, multisensory experience it affords the player and listener.[39] Composed Theatre forces the composer to engage the performer as a physical, performative entity and presence and bid farewell to the ideal of the barely noticeable, "as transparent as possible" (Small 1998: 154) intermediary. Obviously, this 'ideal' has not only been upheld by composers, but also by performers themselves, who also have to confront the changes and challenges of Composed Theatre.

The performer

While the composer needs to stretch his/her 'Instrumentarium'[40] and open up his 'attic' for new kinds of processes and collaborations in Composed Theatre, the performer likewise needs to widen and bridge his/her professional training and abilities towards other disciplines and often engage more actively and creatively with the process of creating the work itself.

This creates certain friction with some of the professional habits of artists. For example, the discourse describes the difficulty in getting musicians to give a project the necessary

---

37. See for example: http://www.theater-der-klaenge.de/produktionen/figur/zentrum.php?pa=3& lang=1 [06 July 2010].
38. See also Roesner 2010b.
39. See Cesare 2006 for a further discussion of the changing relationship of music, performance and the body.
40. 'Instrumentarium' is a German term, for which the dictionary suggest 'orchestra', but it also includes the notion of 'set of tools/instruments', which could also be for examples a surgeon's instruments, and even more widely the range of methods/approaches available that could prove 'instrumental' for a certain task.

Figures 4 and 5: Mark O'Keeffe in Cathie Body/Cryptic's *Apocalypse... The Seven Angels* (Glasgow 2006) and Members of the T'ang Quartet in Cathie Boyd/Cryptic's *Optical Identity* (Singapore 2007).

Figure 6: A musician in Heiner Goebbels' *Black on White*, reading Edgar Allen Poe through his trumpet microphone. Photograph by Priska Ketterer.

time commitment to go beyond a well-crafted execution of a finished score. The economic constraints of a freelance musician generally permit only a few days of rehearsal before the actual performance. That does not accommodate the altered demands of Composed Theatre. Lensing, for example, wants the performers to be an integral part of developing the piece; Boyd needs them to memorise complex pieces of music and embrace their physicality on stage by playing during difficult movements and positions, in costume or even naked (see figures 4 and 5); Goebbels asks them to be part of the musical and theatrical process of arranging, and Tsangaris, Zavros and Rebstock encourage them to engage with the theatrical aspects, the *mise en scène* of their performance.[41] Generally speaking, all performers in Composed Theatre need to stretch their abilities and their understanding of their professional selves beyond that to which they are habituated by their training, their career experience, and sometimes their contracts. Musicians need to embrace their physicality and their theatricality; they are asked to speak text, dance, operate theatre machinery, dress-up and wear theatre make-up. Actors or dancers are required to sharpen their musical skills:

41. Most of these aspects apply across the board and are not limited to those artists I associate with certain characteristic here – they are merely examples.

act precisely to a musical score, sing or play instruments, pay increased attention to the rhythmic and sonic qualities of what is happening on stage.

The strategies of finding and developing these hybrid performers are manifold: many composers/directors of Composed Theatre provide some of the training needed: Boyd did theatre workshops with the Latvian Radio Choir or the T'ang Quartett, Leo Dick or Matthias Rebstock make room in the rehearsal schedule to train with their actors musically, and Ruedi Häusermann spends time with all performers together singing and thus creating a culture of mutual attention and musical sensitivity through the study of traditional vocal scores. Others, like Heiner Goebbels, are sometimes deliberately interested in the *lack* of professional training in certain areas: he likes, for example, the way a non-actor reads a text or the natural voice of untrained singers (see figure 6).

Very often the necessary mutual trust and understanding, the common language of composer/director and performers, has been built over considerable time and is the result of many individual collaborations. While there is a danger, as Goebbels puts it, in becoming too comfortable, too familiar with each other, there is – in this work where one cannot fall back on certain disciplinary standards and basics – an increased need for a continuity in the collaboration in order to afford the performer the courage to embrace new kinds of tasks and challenges and for the composer/director to know and 'collect' (Goebbels) the individual and unique qualities of the performers.[42]

The director

Three topics emerge from the discourse on directors and directing in Composed Theatre: a difference in trust, directorial style and self-description.

The first discursive thread can be summarised in Cathie Boyd's statement of one of her maxims: "Let the experts do their job."[43] This is seconded by Heiner Goebbels' recommendation to 'trust in the competence of the other'. He thus suggests a counterconcept to the dictatorial style of some representatives of the so-called Regietheater, theatre that amplifies and makes absolute the solitary vision of one director, subordinating all other

---

42. On the whole there is a stronger sense within the discourse that Composed Theatre is often more closely tailored to and emerging from quite specific skill sets and personal qualities of individual performers. Where a theatre form questions given standards of performance, both musically and theatrically, artistic individualities and idiolects have a stronger impact on process and product. Several discourse contributors described how their projects became specific to and un-interchangeable to individual performers, such as, for example, the yodelling actress and singer Barbara Berger for Leo Dick's *Heidi* (see Roesner 2010b) or the extended voice artist and drummer David Moss for Heiner Goebbels' *Surrogate Cities* (1994).

43. Boyd's statement refers to singers and musicians ('let singers sing and musicians play'), but can be extended to other areas of expertise in Composed Theatre, as I maintain in this chapter.

creative input to that director's 'trademark'. In Composed Theatre we encounter many strategies of arriving at a shared vision, a multiplicity of creative inputs. Practitioners may go into rehearsal with an open question, a piece of material, and leave it to the actor, designer, instrumentalist, sound programmer, etc., to respond to that question or material on the basis of their area of expertise. While there still is often a central figure responsible for final decisions, there is a heightend level of artistic autonomy and mutual respect. The polyphony of theatrical voices described above is not surprisingly the result of a sense of polyphony also at the level of personnel. Or, employing another musical metaphor, one could say: many theatre and music-theatre productions operate like an orchestra with a conductor; Composed Theatre production processes rather resemble a chamber ensemble.

This model extends, I maintain, even to the kind of collaborations where Boyd's notion of the expert is rendered problematic. Jörg Lensing describes how in the work of Theater der Klänge often no one yet knows 'how to do it', which opens new possibilities and opportunities since there are fewer preconceptions. This results in a different approach, based predominantly on improvisations and a kind of trial-and-error process of selection, but again places responsibility and ownership in the hands of all involved, not just a sole directorial figure.

As a consequence, the directorial style tends to differ from that of traditional theatre or opera. There, a director interprets a given material (text/score) with and for the actor/singer and creates a dense web of instructions (gestural, vocal, psychological). In the discourse on Composed Theatre the word 'instructions' rarely came up, replaced by the notion of 'setting challenges'.

These were often described as exterior challenges; formal, spatial or physical settings that acted in opposition to being too comfortable on stage. According to Heiner Goebbels, "performers feeling at home on stage are not interesting for the audience". So Boyd putting an actress on her back, not allowing her to move and asking her to find her own cues for the text in the music, or Goebbels scattering musicians from the same instrumental families (strings, woodwinds, brass) across a large stage, making their musical coordination quite difficult, are conscious performative challenges that help the performers maintain an acute awareness of the overall interplay of all theatrical and musical elements. In other words, the performers are challenged to think of the overall composition, not just their own individual parts.

Equally, the composers and directors say that challenging themselves is one of the key instigators of this kind of work. Goebbels, for example (and this resonates with others), explicitly states that he never stages a piece if he already knows how it will work: "I need to be surprised by it as well."

This also means that there is a questioning of the role of the director. With few exceptions none of the discourse contributors was 'only' a director, but often held and shared other roles as well: composer, producer, dramaturg, video or lighting designer, text author, etc. This represents an interesting twist of the earlier point on expertise, since 'letting the experts do their job' can also extend to the range of multiple artistic personalities *within* one person.

Creating an 'I as other', stepping in and out of adopted and trained roles, was described frequently as a strategy to balance the diverse and multiple tasks.

Manos Tsangaris, for example, describes how he composes a piece with certain liberties for the performer. When it comes to rehearsals, he then 'as a director' encourages the performer to take certain decisions over others and tells the performer not to obsess about the written music at that point. "The composer then becomes my natural enemy" he says with a sense of humour, referring to himself in the third person.

Johanna Dombois, when talking about her intermedial opera projects, which amount to digitised virtual stagings of operatic scores in multimedia environments and/or in *Second Life*,[44] talks about the necessary

> willingness to change the profession you are trained to do, to change into something else. Our conductor, for example, is in fact the choreographer of the images, our dramaturg is the conductor, our system designer is the cameraman, the assistant to the director is the score manager. So everyone does something they are not trained to do, but has to do it on a professional basis.

This then extends the idea of the work as challenge beyond the group of performers and includes the whole creative team, who have to think and act 'as other' and balance the risk of looking amateurish with the benefits of a fresh, original take on processes and materials and on the very idea of professionalism.

Goebbels goes one step further when he says: "I make an advantage of both professions in order to get a distance: when I compose I compose as director. [...] and when I direct I work as a composer."[45] So not only does he act in different capacities in the process, he also relates them crosswise in order to provide different viewpoints and step out of disciplinary professional habits.

On the whole, there was a clear sense that Composed Theatre requires a redefinition of the professional identities of those involved; or rather a move towards fluid definitions of their roles and tasks, since Composed Theatre does not merely replace one concept of a composer, performer, director with another, but questions the idea and value of a stable artistic profile. Nonetheless, the discourse also frequently returned to questions of skill, expertise, even virtuosity, and there seemed a shared understanding that, as Julian Klein from the collective *a rose is* put it, "good interdisciplinarity can unfold where everyone is also firmly at home in one discipline". Ruedi Häusermann supported this view by adding: "It is difficult to work with people who only know about 'mixing' things."

---

44. See in particular Dombois' latest production *Ring-Studie 01 | Rheingold-Vorspiel (Richard Wagner)* (Berlin/Zurich 2009). A detailed description can be found at http://www.jhnndmbs.net/ de/projekte/ 2009/ring/projektbeschreibung.php [12 August 2010].
45. See also Heiner Goebbels' chapter (4) in this book.

It appears that the question of artistic identity has no single answer in Composed Theatre, but finds itself on another continuum from a team of experts to a multi-role individual, from undermining performative standards to their virtuoso extension. The continuum is held together, however, by the shared conviction that the relatively clear and fixed assumptions about the roles of composers, directors, musicians, actors, dancers, technicians, designers, etc., which are expressed in the curricula of the relevant training institutions, have to be interrogated in the process of making and performing Composed Theatre.

I will now look more closely at descriptions of these processes and how they are said to differ from conventional and established practices.

How is the working process different from other forms of theatre and music practice?

In this part I will reflect on some of the major discursive threads about the nature of the processes of creating, devising and rehearsing Composed Theatre, with a particular view to what distinguishes them – again, not by way of a strict demarcation but through tracing a significant tendency – from processes in theatre, music theatre or concert practices. I will look at timescales, the nature of the collaboration, working conditions, communication and the role of technology.

Timescales

There are certain assumptions and expectations created by the large-scale opera and theatre houses in Western Europe about the timescale for a new opera or theatre production and about who gets involved at what point.[46] If it is a new piece of work, there is a writing period by the author or the librettist and composer, often already on commission from a particular venue, which begins about two to three years before the premiere. Next is casting the actors and singers and contracting the artistic team (director, musical director, stage designer, etc.); the latter will start working on the concept and design about six to nine months ahead of the premiere, and finished plans for the set will go into the different workshops before the first day of rehearsal. Rehearsal time varies from about four to twelve weeks for the actors and singers and significantly less for the musicians.

The first key difference in Composed Theatre, as the discourse revealed, is that the process is less linear; there is, for example, a much less rigid division between planning (composing, conceptualising) and verifying/developing (rehearsal, workshop, try-out) processes. These elements and aspects form a more dialectic and circular relationship, compared to the teleological nature of standard production methods.[47] Secondly, the process allows and asks for a much earlier contribution and involvement of what the industry treats as the

---

46. See Conte/Langley (2007) and Röper (2001) for an introduction on standard procedures.

'secondary' or merely 'executing' group of artists: the actors, performers, musicians, and also the technical team. And thirdly, the process of Composed Theatre eradicates or at least problematises the distinction between creation and rehearsal.[48]

Most practitioners describe circular forms of working processes. After an initial period in which a group or individual develops a sense of a topic, question or starting point for a project – be it through travelling (Boyd), extensive reading (Goebbels) or other stimuli – there is often an early exploratory phase of work with others, including prospective performers.[49] It is called 'workshop' (Goebbels), 'sponge stage' (Boyd) or 'playground' ('Spielwiese', Häusermann) and is characterised by openness, playfulness, the fact that 'anything is possible' (Goebbels). Often this is not a highly conceptual phase, sometimes even a 'pre-lingual' sharing of ideas, sounds, images. For Goebbels, this period lasts only a few days, but most of the material, which can later be seen in his production, is already developed at this early stage and then, in a process of sedimentation, selection and arrangement, formed and shaped by Goebbels. This is almost the inverse of standard practice, where an individual small group develops material, which then takes shape in the collective rehearsal process. In Goebbels' process, however, the collective process in the rehearsal room becomes a key generator of material subsequently shaped by an individual.[50]

Rodosthenous' model of rehearsal emphasises the iterative process on a smaller timescale: he often schedules rehearsals only every other day, so that there is a constant alternation

---

47. Boyd, Lensing, Rebstock and Zavros, for example, reflect on the relationship between planning (as a conscious process) and emergence (as an unconscious, intuitive process) and how they individually seek to strike a balance between the two. They all describe an iterative process, not a linear development (be it from intuition to planning or vice versa). The key difference to comparable processes in large-scale opera or theatre productions is that the emergent aspects of rehearsal, the unexpected collaborative outcomes and ideas can have an immediate effect on the 'text' of the performance itself. In Composed Theatre, text and music are often rewritten, changed and adapted due to developments in the rehearsal process. The linear process 'from page to stage' becomes a circular one: 'from page to stage to page to stage etc.'.

48. Cathie Boyd for example states: "Theatre Cryptic refers to the word creation for rehearsals and the creative process – a term we learnt through our collaborations with Montreal based artists. The word rehearsal is derived from the French word repetition (to repeat), which is too narrow for the creative process. We believe that creation allows for a more open mind. We only enter a rehearsal period once the work has been established, usually after its Premiere and before we go on an international tour" (Boyd n.d.).

49. Tsangaris, Hirsch and Häusermann, who still compose in a more traditional sense alone at their desks, still engage in these kinds of processes in that they tend to be involved in the actual production of their work as directors and or performers. Tsangaris revises his scores in the work with the performers and in between different productions and adaptations of his scores for different occasions and Häusermann works closely with the musicians at an early stage of drafting his compositions.

50. Lensing describes a similar process of collective creation (through improvisation) and subsequent more individual selection and arrangement (see his chapter in this book).

between rehearsing (which includes a great deal of improvisation and generation of material) and evaluation/planning.

This shifted emphasis and character of the planning, creating, evaluating, and fine-tuning stages of production has a particular effect on the normally clearly separate groups of people involved in (music) theatre production: those on and those off stage. By involving as many of the performers and 'executors' at the stage of creating material, Composed Theatre not only creates a different sense of involvement, responsibility and authorship of the performers who become co-creators (thereby making the production more reflective of their abilities, biographies, artistic convictions), but it also renegotiates the power relations between the aesthetic elements. Heiner Goebbels rightly says that any element that is added at a late stage of the process will only ever be illustrative of the others. This is why he and others insist that 'secondary' elements, such as sound amplification, lighting, costume and the respective designers and technicians in charge participate from the start. This is clearly not only a chronological decision, but also a statement about the nature of the collaboration.

Nature of collaboration

In theatres and opera houses, collaboration is quite heavily regulated with a view to avoid ambiguities of power and responsibility as well as to promote transparency and efficiency of the working process. Composed Theatre has, as the discourse suggests, developed a two-pronged approach to sidestep some of these regulations in order to avoid the inevitable aesthetic consequences:[51] on the one hand, it questions and shakes up the notion of responsibility and clear divisions of tasks by conflating and amalgamating roles, sharing tasks and rethinking chronologies and causalities of different steps in the process, as discussed above.[52] On the other hand, it often tends towards long-standing collaborations between certain individuals (LOSE COMBO since 1994, Theater der Klänge since 1987, Heiner Goebbels e.g. with André Wilms since 1993, with Klaus Grünberg since 1997) to balance the consciously 'destabilizing' effects of abandoning certain 'industry standards' through a sense of stability and continuity on the level of the individuals involved.

This balance needs perpetual maintenance, since continuity can erode into a fixed system with predictable aesthetic outcomes. Heiner Goebbels thus stresses the importance of sustaining and nurturing *differences* between collaborators. He is wary of the notion of the 'collective' since it suggests a unity he tries to avoid. He is much more interested

---

51. Heiner Goebbels even claimed that the German subsidised repertory system was "uniquely apt for artistic reproduction, but completely unsuited for the inventive processes of the entirely new".
52. In Leo Dick's *Heidi* (2008), for example, Dick was composer, director and at times répétiteur, his performers took part in the editing process of the score, stage design and assembly of props was as much a musical task as a visual task, the musical director was also a theatrical performer, parts of the score were (re-)written during rehearsal, etc.

in identifying the divergences in opinion than the convergences and refers to his notion of polyphony as a metaphor for the kind of his collaboration with others: polyphony as a musical/social technique that privileges the dialogic working through and embracing of friction over harmonisation and unity.[53]

Working conditions

The challenges that this kind of collaboration poses are not only tangible at the level of personnel: as described above, it asks all those involved to step out of their professional comfort zone, which they may at first guard and defend. But the feasibility and success of Composed Theatre also depends on institutional working conditions. Heiner Goebbels has been particularly outspoken about the fact that the current 'Stadttheater-System', the institutionalised working conditions at Germany's leading subsidised repertory theatres, is incompatible with his creative methods. A technical team, for example, working in shifts and rarely the same for two rehearsals, can not develop any creative input and the sense of ownership that Goebbels' productions require.

Working conditions and funding mechanism are a very prominent trope of the discussions and a useful reminder for me as a scholar, who has approached the phenomenon of Composed Theatre with a predominant interest in the creative processes, the aesthetic collaboration and decision-making and the performative results, ignoring at times the significance and immediate influence of seemingly 'external' factors of production, commission, venue, funding, marketing, etc. Here are a few examples: Cathie Boyd talks about the double-pressure of being a producer and director and George Rodosthenous highlights the potential legal complications with collaborative and devised work: who owns this work, what are the ethical and copyright implications if, for example, a member of the original cast leaves and Nick Till outlines how a very strict brief from a commissioner of work, the *Forum Neues Musiktheater* in Stuttgart, regarding technical limitations determined the working process and even the content of their piece to quite a significant extent. The *Fonds Experimentelles Musiktheater NRW*,[54] a key facilitator of experimental music theatre in Germany, works with the continuing paradox of funding experimental work meant to "question and experimentally explore the interplay of language, music and theatre space"[55] while making

---

53. Manos Tsangaris also taps into this notion with his view that working as a group should be a 'parable for processes in society', while also acknowledging the need to keep eyes trained on the result in artistic processes.

54. Experimental Music-Theatre is, of course, not necessarily Composed Theatre, but there are significant overlaps. For information on the funding body see: http://www.kunststiftungnrw.de/inhalt. php?id=15&lang=de [1 July 2010].

it a condition that the work is then produced by one of the established municipal theatres, which are not designed for experimental work.

None of this is unknown or exclusive to Composed Theatre, but since this is a form that constantly negotiates and queries the relations of its contributing artforms and individuals, working conditions become a more pertinent and intrinsically aesthetic problem, which I will come back to briefly in the final section of this chapter.

Communication: Finding a language

One of the aspects of the institutional question is the necessity to re-invent and establish modes of communication, when the clear sense of professional belonging and responsibility becomes blurred. While in established opera and theatre working processes specialists speak to specialists (the musical director to the orchestra, the choreograph to the dancers, the lighting designer to the technical crew, the director to the actors or singers), in Composed Theatre there is a greater need to cross certain given work allocations and their respective languages or jargons. Many of the discourse contributors describe the necessity, and sometimes the difficulty, of developing and negotiating a common language of different specialists.

This has a variety of consequences. According to Goebbels, he and his team often seem to avoid too much verbal communication in the early exploratory workshops and focus on doing – suggesting a costume idea, a lighting idea, a musical idea by actually preparing the material and allowing everyone to move around the stage in order to show rather than tell. George Rodosthenous reports how he would spend time establishing a certain level of music-technical language with his actors and/or dancers, to get them used to 'translating' instructions like 'make that more staccato' into their respective expressive repertoire. Similarly, Johanna Dombois talks about learning the language of the computer programmers in her virtual projects to the extent she needs in order to effectively communicate her directorial ideas to them.

More than is customary in (music) theatre, which over centuries has created its own jargon as shorthand for the most common instructions in staging, practitioners in Composed Theatre are acutely aware of the linguistic gaps they need to close – or celebrate the misunderstandings between the disciplines as a creative potential. Ruedi Häusermann, for example, talks about the 'secret languages' of the different departments and groupings in a theatre and how he feels that the lack of insider knowledge, the inability to describe or name something 'correctly', offers an element of relief, for example, for the actors and musicians, who feel that their 'secrets' remained intact and allow themselves to open up.

The experimental and interdisciplinary nature of process in Composed Theatre has prompted several practitioners to embrace failure beyond the mere linguistic

---

55. See www.theaterkanal.de/news/fonds-experimentelles-musiktheater-sucht-projektideen-fuer-2009 [14 May 2008], my translation.

misunderstanding. Both Laue and Zavros emphasise the importance of what Laue calls 'efficient failure' in their work. There is, he claims, a precision in the random and the unforeseeable, a potential in incidents and accidents, which despite all the stringency of his concepts and compositional planning is allowed to have impact on his work. Hirsch displays a similar interest in the imperfect, the mistakes and linguistic oddities he encountered in his use of televised interviews of actual people in his transcriptions and compositional transformations of the spoken word.[56]

Both in process and performance then, Composed Theatre – despite its frequent anti-logocentric tendencies – contains in-depth problematisations of language.[57] Manos Tsangaris even goes so far as to suggest that Composed Theatre itself is a linguistic phenomenon in the sense that it can be defined by how it applies a different kind of 'grammar' to the 'vocabulary' of the stage.

Before I aim to draw conclusions from the different fragments, threads and positions that emerged as central to the discourse around Composed Theatre, there is a final element that requires exploration: the role of technology in Composed Theatre.

Technology

While none of the contributors claim that Composed Theatre is necessarily linked to a proliferation of technology/-ies of any kind, the level of discussion of technological aspects in the process of making Composed Theatre is considerable. My impression is that the experimental nature of this theatre form, the desire for the "unseen image, the unheard sound" (Goebbels) creates an affinity of its makers for experimentation and venturing into new territories in areas of science and technology.

The ongoing development of software that allows for live manipulation of sound, light and stagecraft, and the integration of diverse technical elements into one musically programmable and playable system, is one of the areas embraced by several practitioners. For her production of *Orlando* (Glasgow 2010), Cathie Boyd worked directly with software designers of the Digital Design Studio, Glasgow School of Art (DDS) to advance the visual possibilities of body projection. The resulting new software, *Living Canvas*, is an interactive tracking technology that facilitates projecting images precisely onto moving human bodies. For her production of *The Paper Nautilus* (2006) with composer Gavin Bryars, Boyd worked with bioluminescence scientists from LUX Biotechnology, Edinburgh. Julian Klein and *a rose is* created a performance *Brain Study* (2004) in which brain waves of the performers

---

56. See also the respective chapters in this book.
57. See also Petra Maria Meyer's insightful analysis of Valère Novarina's *Le théâtre des paroles* in her chapter (3) in this book.

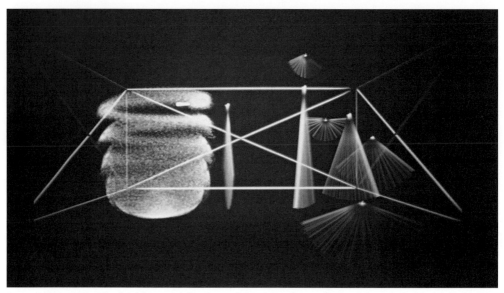

Figure 7: Johanna Dombois' *Fidelio, 21. Jahrhundert* – a 'virtual opera' as an abstract interactive live visualisation of the music, Beethoven-Haus Bonn (2004).

were measured by EEG, analysed and transformed into sounds in a technological setup that resembled a (simple) brain itself.[58]

Nick Till, Jörg Laue and Heiner Goebbels have in different ways thematised historical developments of technology. Till interrogated early film in his use of a silent film version of Carmen (*Silent Movie Opera*, 1999) and used early diagnostic sound recordings and transcriptions of a schizophrenic patient as a starting point of his project *Hearing Voices* (2006). Laue's production *BRAUN Light* (2008) explored the first printed image of a cathode-ray tube as a visual score for a Cageian music in his performative installation, and Heiner Goebbels featured the earliest ethnographic recordings by the Austrian ethnographer Rudolf Pöch of the aboriginal people of Papua New Guinea in his production *Stifter's Things*.

Johanna Dombois' *Fidelio, 21st Century* (Bonn 2004, see figure 7) transcribed Beethoven's score parameter by parameter into programme code for a 3D virtual reality technology, so that the music itself, combined with interactive aspects for the audience, animated the *mise en scène*, thus creating a new "equitable unity of sound and image".[59]

---

58. For more information see www.aroseis.de/eabout.htm, under "Projects", "Brain study" [16 June 2010] and aroseis 2004 in the bibliography.
59. The quotation is taken from a detailed online documentation of the project. See: http://www.beethoven-haus-bonn.de/sixcms/detail.php?id=39119&template=&_mid=39119 [07 July 2010].

In order to avoid reflecting on the role of technology in performance in general, which would go significantly beyond the scope of this chapter, I would like to focus on a few discursive fragments which unpacked the specific challenges and opportunities of technology in Composed Theater in particular.

One recurrent topic was the relationship between the compositional/technological concept and the audience's experience. At the Theater der Klänge, for example, the technological set-up is not a mere vehicle for a performative composition – it actually transforms the stage into an instrument and becomes a determining part of the compositional process itself, which is collaborative and, to a degree, contingent. One might call Theater der Klänge's setup for *Suite intermediale* (2008) or *Figur und Klang im Raum* (1993) the specific 'actor-network'[60] of the respective production. The use of technology functions here as a specific way to disperse authorship and control in the act of composing theatre: the use of trigger microphones, light sensors and motion detection, connected with sound and image editing/producing software, divide the responsibility for the music multimedia outcome between the composer/programmer, sound and image designers, the performers – who evoke specific sounds and images with their movements – and the director, who sees the results and feeds back to the above. There is also contingency because the movements are derived from improvisation and never completely fixed, hence the ways in which the triggers and software respond are never identical.

The question is, however, to what degree the audience needs to be able to fathom the process in order to appreciate and enjoy the result. We encountered different strategies and reactions here. Theater der Klänge sometimes decide to introduce a 'pedagogical' (Lensing) element into the performance, where the technological setup is playfully made transparent; at other times the specific relationship between movement, sounds and projected image remains hidden and could, from the audience's perspective, have been devised separately in more independent processes. Reactions within the discourse range from those who feel it indispensible to understand the techno-compositional interrelations in order to fully appreciate the result, while others are happy to abandon the attempt to re-enact the process and relate purely to the aesthetic outcome.

As mentioned above, Heiner Goebbels' *Stifter's Dinge* is an example of an interesting variation on this. Again, the technological control gained over all or most aspects of the theatrical performance by means of robotics, remote control, MIDI and related software that controls and visualises these aspects and their parameter in a form that is similar to music recording and production software (such as *Logic, Cubase* or *ProTools*) makes the theatre 'composable'

For a fuller discussion of the project see Dombois 2007, 2009, Walz 2008 and the project description at http://www.jhnndmbs.net/de/projekte/2004/01/projektbeschreibung.php [11 August 2010].

60. According to sociologist Bruno Latour (and others) an 'actor network' consist in the totality of interactions of individuals, but also technologies. It maps both the material and semiotic relations between 'actants' and investigates how they form and constitute a whole (see Latour 2005). "ANT is a conceptual frame for exploring collective *sociotechnical* processes" (Ritzer 2004: 1).

in a particular way. The connection of this setup to a piano keyboard reintroduces elements of intuition and a musician's body memory, where computer screens and mouse control may otherwise form a barrier or at least an element of alienation. Composed Theatre, then, becomes a process of composing at the keyboard as it was and still is for many composers, with two significant differences: the material of the composition is the theatrical stage and the recording media are not pencil and staved paper, but software and hard drive.

Nick Till describes how, in his project *Hearing Voices*, the engagement and interaction with technology in music theatre becomes not only a vehicle for questioning some of the assumptions about music theatre, about its "formal structures and modes of representation",[61] but also the topic of the piece itself: an exploration of the "ghost in the machine" and the "uncanny" (Till) effects of technology. Technology here is not only a facilitator or interface of a compositional approach to the theatrical stage, as we have seen in Goebbels' or Lensing's reflections, but also, in its problematisation, a key compositional strategy: the central criterion of difference. In light of this, it is only logical that in Till's production, as he describes it, the technological effect was sometimes more important than the actual technical "integrity" of its execution, so that he was happy to "cheat" (Till) certain technical effects performatively.[62]

I have looked at how processes have been described and characterised and have attempted to tease out some key differences to other forms of theatre. In the final section I reflect on the consequences of the above, specifically on the particular relationship and interplay of music (as idea and practice) and theatre (as form and material) in what we call Composed Theatre.

What are the consequences of the above? A conclusion in form of four theses

Just as this book is intended to *begin* what we hope will become a vibrant discourse and exchange about Composed Theatre rather than its summation, this analysis and attempt to outline consequences of the discourse described above is also intended as a point of departure, a signpost towards a number of directions rather than the definitive end of a journey. With that in mind, I propose four theses about Composed Theatre as they arise from the 'close-up' view of the self-reflexive discourse we have followed and in part initiated. These should be read in dialogue with the 'wide-angled' historical contextualisation by Matthias Rebstock in chapter 1 as well as the entire range of contributions assembled in this book.

---

61. See Till's chapter (9) in this book.
62. Lensing describes a similar problem: the audience often does not 'believe' the nature of the relation of dance and sound in their productions and thinks the performers simply dance to a pre-recorded tape. They solve this by including elements of a 'pedagogical' introduction to how the system works, which can be quite performative and even comical, but is sometimes frowned upon by composers who feel it undermines the seriousness of their work.

Thesis 1: Composed Theatre becomes a field, when looking at process behind process

The investigation of Composed Theatre started with the premise that the criteria for assembling phenomena under this heading would not easily be found at the level of aesthetic surfaces of the performative results themselves. A first look at the material evidence suggested that these outcomes were vastly different and that there were no universally valid criteria to be found: some performances are abstract, others are not; some are 'audibly' musical, others are not; some use texts, instruments, advanced technology, or musical speech – others do not. The results are multi-faceted, aesthetically diverse and show at least as many differences as similarities. Our focus thus shifted from product to practice and process.

The assumption was that similarities of practices and a sense of 'group identity' would be found at the level of the creation process, and part of the aim of this chapter has certainly been to extrapolate similarities and convergences in how practitioners describe their working methods, artistic motifs and identities, and the environments they create for themselves. But again, despite significant links, the processes still betray an equally significant amount of difference. Some are more collective, others more individual. Some rely more on concepts, others on improvisation. Some are characterised by technology, others much less. Some are very generously resourced, others are not.

What seems to be the central uniting factor in grouping these diverse practices and analysing them comparatively is the process behind the process: all the diverse practices and working methods are founded on and inspired by compositional thinking applied to creating live theatrical performance. It is compositional thinking derived from music as idea and practice in a wide range of ways: sometimes more ontological (reverting to certain parameters as the fundamental defining aspects of a musical tone), sometimes more historical (using and applying specific forms, techniques and approaches from musical styles and genres from polyphonic singing via instrumental counterpoint to jazz and rock). But in all cases there is a conscious engagement with a particular kind of transference: from music to theatrical performance. This transference prompts Thesis 2.

Thesis 2: Composed Theatre requires a continuous reflection and working through the ontological conditions of music and theatre, often including a profound questioning of these ontologies and their usefulness or validity

Because there is the intermedial and/or interartial[63] transference at the heart of Composed Theatre which I have described above, I would argue that the practitioners continuously need to establish how they understand both music and theatre as art forms, strategies of communication, and ways of shaping time and space. Composed Theatre is always a

---

63. For a detailed discussion of both intermediality and interartiality see Müller 1998.

conscious work not only on a piece or production but on the notions of 'Composing' and 'Theatre' themselves, which interrogate each other in their interplay.

This may take form in the acknowledgement of differences in materiality. Manos Tsangaris, for example, talks about the impossibility of simply 'transposing' across different media – an increase in light was not simply a 'crescendo' of light. The challenge is nonetheless to try to compose a piece for conductor and light (*Molto Molto*, 1980), which deals with these differences in materiality. More generally, Tsangaris describes his pieces as 'phenomenological experiments': for him they are research into modes of artistic perception, but also sociological research, since they are an 'examination of the conditions of aesthetics' (Tsangaris). For his first piece for his teacher Mauricio Kagel, *o.T.* (1980), he centred all musicians around one person's (Kagel's) head: the main topic of the composition, says Tsangaris, was the question of how to stage music, of the significance of physical proxemics, of the impact of placement of sound within a theatrical setting. It is Composed Theatre about Composed Theatre. It also is, consciously, a piece that could never become a repertoire piece given how uneconomical it is.

Other practices are concerned with the necessity to reflect the relationship of notation in performance, where this relationship is not (yet) as established and universally accepted as standard musical notation. There are transferences of linear structural relationships or vertical relationships of voices in the musical setting into the extended 'Instrumentarium' of Composed Theatre, even though again there are no simple analogies to the descriptive and normative rules of composition and arrangement. In the multimedial setting of the theatre, there are no hidden parallel fifths one ought to avoid, no deceptive cadences, no close harmony or bi-tonality – nonetheless, Composed Theatre employs a kind of thinking that seeks to create structure, meaning and effect in ways similar to music, and thus continuously dealing with analogies and subtle medial differences and becoming highly aware of itself and its related disciplines and genres.

Nick Till, for example, describes his and Kandis Cook's practice (coined as 'post-operative productions'[64]) deliberately as a critical practice which seeks to investigate the use and function of media in opera and operatic forms, to thematise the very problems and conditions of making music theatre, and to "develop non-score based devising and improvisatory processes for music theatre challenging the hierarchical meta-physics of most music-theatre production" (Till).

I would argue that Composed Theatre thus differs from a wider field of contemporary or 'new' music theatre[65] in the nature and scope of its experimental nature. Contemporary Music Theatre can be innovative *within* a given institutional, hierarchical and aesthetic framework that it may 'bend' at times. Composed Theatre, however, often explicitly or implicitly abandons this framework and its assumptions and premises. Its experiments

---

64. See http://www.post-operative.org/ [07 July 2010].
65. See Salzmann/Desi (2008).

operate on more levels than on the aesthetic surface of the work: it tries new forms of authorship, of production methods, of understandings of 'skill' or professional identities. It also seeks to re-negotiate relations of spatial, sonic, performative, visual, atmospheric, notational and conceptual aspects of music theatre and experiments with new causalities, simultaneities and interferences.

Thesis 3: Composed Theatre stems from incentives of distancing, from a notion of différance

Composed Theatre, in both artistic incentives and in its outcomes, is marked by *différance* in the Derridean sense of being defined by how it differs from other, similar or related things. Most practitioners reported a dissatisfaction with the artistic processes and aesthetics they observed during their early professional years and actively sought to negate and abandon certain preconceived artistic identities, entrenched processes, established aesthetics and dramaturgies in order to create new work.

Similarly, our attempts to describe and define key characteristics of Composed Theatre frequently employed techniques demarcating borders to related forms of performance, while fully aware of the problematic of those boundaries. The key point is perhaps the concern of practitioners and scholars with aspects of *différance* when it comes to Composed Theatre. Because it negotiates such a small and volatile area between opera, music theatre, theatre, concert, installation, dance and performance, Composed Theatre is acutely self-aware and almost inevitably strongly self-reflexive. As it continuously defines and redefines what it is and how it is different, it mostly takes shape as an inherently experimental and innovative practice.

Quite a few practitioners describe, for example, meta-theatrical/meta-musical motivations and incentives for their work. Cathie Boyd talks about 'pushing the performers', in this instance the T'ang Quartet, as a key drive to make *Optical Identity* – this desire to explore new expressive qualities in accomplished, but also very specialised performers is something she shares with Heiner Goebbels and Ruedi Häusermann.

As such, Composed Theatre is in the tradition of other avant-garde theatre and music: it is less concerned with new topics, new audiences or new levels of sophistication within an established frame. It seeks to reflect and experiment with the tools, the conditions, the mindsets and ideologies of music and theatre themselves in an active and critical engagement with the dominant artistic culture.

Another aspect of this engagement relates to the question of meaning-making and conventions of *signifiance*. I shall explore this in my final thesis.

Thesis 4: Composed Theatre engages in a complex process of meaning-making, social interaction and political significance by employing the 'detour' of musical thinking as a means of abstraction

The activity of transference mentioned above has implications for the creative process and for the affinity of Composed Theatre to *mise en abyme*. One the one hand, due to its expanded material and to being 'tainted' by the meaning-laden spatial, temporal and physical conditions of theatre as a semiotic process, Composed Theatre cannot, I believe, ever be 'absolute' in analogy to absolute music (a problematic concept itself).

On the other hand, by engaging with and drawing on the more formal 'grammar' of music and musical composition, Composed Theatre inevitably both complicates and sidesteps the more immediate semiotic strategies of *mimesis* of human action, psychological plausibility of dialogue or overall dramatic narrativity.

Manos Tsangaris employed a metaphor which I find very useful and would like to extend here. Asked about the meaning of his pieces, he called his compositions abstract constructions, which however had a semantic cave behind them. This brings to the forefront the particular relationship of abstraction and meaning, of signification and association, thematised as a unique relationship in Composed Theatre. It is, I would argue, a variation of the Platonic allegory of the cave. Plato famously likens our capacity to perceive reality to that of people in a cave, forced to see only shadows on a wall cast by things passing in front of a fire behind their backs. People ascribe form and meaning to the shadows and perceive them as reality.

In Tsangaris' metaphor, which I believe to apply to more examples of Composed Theatre than just his own work, the relationship is somewhat different: it is about the relationship of (abstract) form (of sound and vision) and semantic meaning. In theatrical forms dominated by narration ('straight' theatre, opera, narrative ballet), the physical entities on stage (the bodies, sounds, lights, props, etc.) usually have relatively unequivocal semiotic meaning and narrative function. They are not limited to this function, but it is closely 'attached' to them. In Composed Theatre, this connection is often much looser and more ambiguous. Since in most cases the physical entities have been introduced and placed for *compositional* reasons, their meaning is not predominantly semantic or even narrative. However, within a performance space that can be understood as 'theatre', they find themselves in a semantically charged cave. Their abstract form is reflected and echoed from 'den Brettern, die die Welt bedeuten'[66] [the boards that mean the world] and are thus charged with and tainted by associations and echoes of meaning that we cannot directly attribute to the entities themselves. One might liken this to the way that wine or whiskey take on some of the aromas of the casks in which they are kept, allowing us to detect flavours in the finished drink that do not have their origin in the grape or grain they are distilled from.

---

66. This phrase, coined by Friedrich Schiller in his poem "An die Freunde" (1803), has become a stock phrase in German metonymically referring to the stage or the theatre in general.

In contrast to Plato's prisoners, in Composed Theatre we see and hear both the thing itself and its shadows or echoes, but, one might say, the position of the fire is unknown and changing, so that the act of attribution of meaning to a source or signifier is "unfinalizable", as Mikhail Bakhtin would call it.[67]

An interesting example of this is the introduction of (a) 'listener(s)' by both Hirsch and Till in two unrelated pieces.[68] Hirsch described his decision to introduce this/these theatrical figure(s) into an otherwise largely abstract piece of 'tape music' as an element of irritation to a concert piece. The added layer, the fact that we are not merely listening to a piece of music but also watching and listening to someone on stage who is also listening to the music, makes us aware of the 'boards that mean the world' and creates those semantic reflections and reverberations noted above.

There is, as I have mentioned earlier, also an animated discussion of whether the audience needs to understand or grasp the conceptual setup, the compositional and structural coherence of a piece. Does Composed Theatre need to 'reveal' or even explain its processes, concepts and strategies in order to be understood? In theatre, audiences react to aesthetic surfaces ('I liked the costumes'), to meaning ('I understood what it was about') and to emotion derived from narrative ('I empathised with the character'). With music, there tends to be a slightly different tri-fold attraction: the pleasure of music is derived again from its aesthetic surface ('I liked the singer's voice'), from analytical insight ('I understood how it was done') and from emotional responses to the sounding phenomena and their capacity to create or evoke emotional memories ('It was beautifully sad'). Audiences can freely switch between these different aspects, but the point is that Composed Theatre takes on some of the qualities of music in that it caters to a perception that is allowed to be less concerned with 'what it means' and more with 'how it is done', together with aesthetic and emotional appreciation.

As I have discussed elsewhere (Roesner 2008 and 2010b), there is also a political aspect to this shift in perception. It is the emancipation of the aesthetic form from its immediate semantic functionality. In a world where any sound, light, button, image or gesture has a clear, often economically driven, function and serves as a coded message ('press me', 'buy me', 'watch out', 'come here', 'go away', 'trust me' etc.), the problematisation of the interplay of aesthetic and function and of form and meaning, experimented with and provided by Composed Theatre, is a political statement and a political act.

---

67. See Morson/Emerson (1990), pp. 32ff.
68. Michael Hirsch's *1. Studie* [*1. Study*] from *Das Konvolut, Vol. 2* and Nick Till/Kandis Cook's *At Home with Art* (2001/03).

References

Cited works

Adorno, Theodor W. (1991 [7th edition]) *Dissonanzen: Musik in der verwalteten Welt*, Göttingen, Vandenhoeck and Ruprecht.

Baudrillard, Jean (1993) *Symbolic Exchange and Death*, Translated by Iain Hamilton Grant, Thousand Oaks, CA: Sage Publications.

Blum, Stephen (2010) "Composition", *Grove Music Online: Oxford Music Online* at http://www.oxfordmusiconline.com/subscriber/article/grove/music/06216 [19 May 2010].

Boyd, Cathie (n.d.) "Creation Process – An interview with Cathie Boyd", at http://www.cryptic.org.uk/PageAccess.aspx?PageId=10 [09 October 2008].

Brüstle, Christa (2007) "Zeitbilder. Inszenierung von Klang und Aktion bei Lachenmann und Hespos", in D. Altenburg et. al. (eds.) *Kongressbericht Weimar 2004: Musik und kulturelle Identität*, Kassel: Bärenreiter.

Cesare, T. Nikki (2006) "'Like a chained man's bruise': The Mediated Body in Eight Songs for a Mad King and Anatomy Theater", *Theatre Journal*, 58, 2006, pp. 437–57.

Chapple, Freda/Kattenbelt, Chiel (eds.) (2006) *Intermediality in Theatre and Performance*, Amsterdam/New York: Rodopi.

Clements, Andrew (2001) "Music theatre", In S. Sadie (ed.) *New Grove Dictionary of Music and Musicians, 2nd edition, Vol. 17*. London: Macmillan, pp. 534–35.

Conte, David M. and Langley, Stephen (2007) *Theatre Management: Producing and Managing the Performing Arts*, Hollywood (CA): Quite Specific Media.

Dombois, Johanna (2007) "Musikstrom: Inszenieren mit Neuen Medien am Beispiel 'Fidelio'", *Musik & Ästhetik*, 11/41, January 2007, pp. 91–107. Also at: http://www.jhnndmbs.net/de/projekte/2007/01/pdf.php.

—— (2009) "Master Voices: Opernstimmen im Virtuellen Raum. 'Fidelio, 21. Jahrhundert'", in D. Kolesch, V. Pinto, J. Schrödl (eds.), *Stimm-Welten. Philosophische, medientheoretische und Ästhetische Perspektiven*, Bielefeld: transcript, pp. 127–42.

Goebbels, Heiner (2002) "Gegen das Gesamtkunstwerk: Zur Differenz der Künste", in W. Sandner (Ed.) *Heiner Goebbels. Komposition als Inszenierung*. Berlin: Henschel, pp. 135–41.

—— (2007) "'Manches merkt man sich bloß, weil es mit nichts zusammenhängt': Fragen beim Bau von Eraritjaritjaka", in Chr. Lechtermann, K.Wagner, H. Wenzel (eds.) *Möglichkeitsräume – Zur Performativität von sensorischer Wahrnehmung*, Berlin: Erich Schmidt Verlag, pp. 141–52.

Hiß, Guido (2005) *Synthetische Visionen: Theater als Gesamtkunstwerk von 1800 bis 2000*, München: Epodium.

Jarzina, Asja (2005) *Gestische Musik und musikalische Gesten: Dieter Schnebels 'visible music': Analyse musikalischer Ausdrucksformen am Beispiel von Abfälle 1,2. Für ... und Nostalgie. Solo für einen Dirigenten*, Berlin: Weidler.

Jäger, Siegfried (1999) "Diskurs als 'Fluß von Wissen durch die Zeit'. Ein Strukturierungsversuch", at http://www.philso.uni-augsburg.de/soziologie/sozkunde/diskurs/content/s_jaeger.html [29 June 2010].

Jäger, Margarete/Jäger, Siegfried (2007) *Deutungskämpfe: Theorie und Praxis kritischer Diskursanalyse*, Wiesbaden: Vs Verlag.

Kittler, Friedrich (1985) *Aufschreibesysteme 1800/1900*, München: Fink.

Labouvie, Eva (2006) "Alltagswissen – Körperwissen – Praxiswissen – Fachwissen: Zur Aneignung, Bewertungs- und Orientierungslogik von Wissenskulturen", *Berichte zur Wissenschaftsgeschichte*, 30/2, pp. 119–34.

Latour, Bruno (2005) *Reassembling the Social: An Introduction to Actor-Network-Theory*, Oxford: Oxford University Press.

Mills, Sara (1997) *Discourse*, London: Routledge.

Morson, Gary Saul and Emerson, Caryl S. (1990) *Mikhail Bakhtin: Creation of a Prosaics*, Stanford (CA): Stanford University Press.

Müller, Jürgen E. (1998) "Intermedialität als poetologisches und medientheoretisches Konzept: Einige Reflexionen zu dessen Geschichte", in J. Helbig (Ed.), *Intermedialität: Theorie und Praxis eines interdisziplinären Forschungsgebiets*, Berlin: Erich Schmidt Verlag, pp. 31–40.

Phillips, Louise and Jørgensen, Marianne W. (2002) *Discourse Analysis as Theory and Method*, London: Sage Publications.

Ritzer, George (2004) "Actor Network Theory", In G Ritzer (ed), *Encyclopedia of Social Theory*, Maryland: SAGE Publications, http://www.sagepub.com/ upm-data/5222_Ritzer__Entries_ beginning_with_A__%5B1%5D.pdf [16 June 2010].

Röper, Henning (2001) *Handbuch Theatermanagement*, Wien: Böhlau.

Roesner, David (2003) *Theater als Musik. Verfahren der Musikalisierung in chorischen Theaterformen bei Christoph Marthaler, Einar Schleef und Robert Wilson*, Tübingen, Gunter Narr.

—— (2008) 'The Politics of the Polyphony of Performance: Musicalization in Contemporary German Theatre', *Contemporary Theatre Review*, 18/1, February 2008, pp. 44–55.

—— (2010a) "Musikalisches Theater – Szenische Musik", in A. Mungen (Ed.), *Mitten im Leben: Musiktheater von der Oper bis zur Everyday-Performance mit Musik*, Göttingen: Königshausen and Neumann.

—— (2010b) "Die Utopie 'Heidi'". Arbeitsprozesse im experimentellen Musiktheater am Beispiel von Leo Dicks *Kann Heidi brauchen, was es gelernt hat?*", in K. Röttger (Ed.), *Welt-Bild-Theater. Vol. 1: Politik der Medien und Kulturen des Wissens*. Tübingen: Narr.

Salzman, Eric and Desi, Thomas (2008) *The New Music Theatre*, Oxford, Oxford University Press.

Schouten, Sabine (2007), *Sinnliches Spüren: Wahrnehmung und Erzeugung von Atmosphären im Theater*, Berlin: Theater der Zeit.

Small, Christopher (1998) *Musicking: The Meanings of Performing and Listening*, Hanover: University Press of New England.

Steiert, Thomas (1988) "Die Konzeption des Integralen Theaters in den Musiktheaterwerken von Hans-Joachim Hespos", in *Musiktheater im 20. Jahrhundert, Hamburger Jahrbuch für Musikwissenschaft*, vol. 10, Hamburg: Laaber.

Van Dijk, Teun A. (1985) *Handbook of Discourse Analysis. Vol 1: Disciplines of Discourse*, London: Academic Press.

Walz, Sophie Barbara (2008) *Mediale Analogien von Musik und Bild: Theatrale Abstraktionen in Musikinszenierungen*, MfA Thesis at the Ludwig-Maximilians-Universität München, at: http:// www.jhnndmbs.net/de/projekte/2004/01/ WALZ_Mediale-Analogien_Diplomarbeit_2008.pdf [11 August 2010].

Performances/practitioners

a rose is (Julian Klein) (2004) *Brain Study – Installation für vernetzte Gehirnspieler*, Berliner Festspiele MaerzMusik. With Christian Buck, Sara Hubrich, Jule Kracht, Kristina Lösche-Löwensen, Eva Müllenbach, Ulf Pankoke, Matthias Neukirch, Diederik Peeters; neuro-electronic: Marc Bangert; audio-electronic: Gregor Schwellenbach, Thomas Seelig; space design: Jan Meyer, Natalie Zehnder;

sound: Lothar Solle, Thomas Schneider; dramaturg: Stefanie Wördemann; assistant: Anja Keysselt; concept and director: Julian Klein.

—— See also www.aroseis.de.

Cryptic (Cathie Boyd) (2006) *Paper Nautilus* by Gavin Bryars. Text by Jackie Kay and Etel Adnan. First performed at Tramway, Glasgow, 2 November 2006. Conductor: Garry Walker; soprano: Angela Tunstall; mezzo-soprano: Alexandra Gibson; concept and director: Cathie Boyd; design, costumes and film: Pippa Nissen; choreography: Hiroaki Umeda; lighting design: Nich Smith; bioluminescent consultant: Patrick Hickey; producer: Claire Moran.

—— (2007), *Optical Identity*. Premiered on 31 May 2007 at the Singapore Arts Festival. Music by Kevin Volans, Rolf Wallin, Franghiz Ali-Zadeh and Joby Talbot; performers: T'ang Quartet (first violin: Ng Yu–Ying; second violin: Ang Chek Meng; viola: Lionel Tan; cello: Leslie Tan); digital artist: Jasch; director and concept: Cathie Boyd; set design: Jason Ong; costume design and makers: BAYLENE; lighting design: Nich Smith; production manager: Gemma Swallow; sound engineer: Matthew Padden; stage manager: Kelly Butterfield; producer: Joey Chan.

—— (2010) *Orlando*, by Cryptic. Premiered on 30 September 2010 at Traverse Theatre, Edinburgh. Text by Virginia Woolf using Darryl Pinckney's adaptation; directed by Cathie Boyd; music by Craig Armstrong and AGF (Antye Greie); performed by Madeleine Worrall and AGF; visuals: Angelica Kroeger and James Houston; Living Canvas and Point Cloud Data Imaging: Digital Design Studio, Glasgow School of Art (Dr Paul Chapman); producer: Claire Moran; set designer: James Johnson; lighting designer: Nich Smith; costume designer: Theo Clinkard; production manager: Will Potts; assistant director: Josh Armstrong.

—— See also www.cryptic.org.uk.

Dick, Leo (2008) *Kann Heidi brauchen, was es gelernt hat? – Szenisches Musikpanorama für 12 MusikerdarstellerInnen*. Premiered on 7 June 2008 at the Theater am Neuen Markt, Bielefeld. With Danielle Bonito, Barbara Berger, Annekatrin Klein, Swantje Tessmann, Christin Mollnar, Daniele Pintaudi, Stefan Imholz, Helmuth Westhausser, Martin Klein, Mathias Z. Bühler, Samuel Stoll; composer and director: Leo Dick; libretto and dramaturg: Felizitas Ammann; stage and costume design: Tassilo Tesche; musical direction: Titus Engel.

—— See also: http://www.weitwinkel-web.net/?img=9&pro=6&language=de.

Dombois, Johanna (2004) *Fidelio, 21. Jahrhundert*. Premiered on 2 December 2004, Bühne für Musikvisualisierung, Bonn. Concept, director, dramaturg, artistic direction: Johanna Dombois; director visual effects: Uli Lechner; idea, concept, project leader: Florian Dombois; musicological collaboration: Sebastian Klemm; sound: Joachim Goßmann, Aeldrik Pander, Gerhard Eckel, Falk Grieffenhagen; computer graphics/software: Martin Suttrop, Frank Hasenbrink, Alexander Lechner, Jürgen Wind, Sina Mostafawy, Lialia Nikitina.

—— (2009) *Ring-Studie 01 | Rheingold-Vorspiel* (Richard Wagner). First rendering on 5 May 2009, Berlin, Remise. Concept and director: Johanna Dombois; dramaturg: Richard Klein; Machinima/ Consulting virtual worlds: YOUin3D.com GmbH. A collaboration with YOUin3D.com GmbH, Nathiel Siamendes (Swiss City/Second Life®), Silef Fisseux/Ligeia Westwick (Zurich City Opera House/Second Life®).

—— See also: www.jhnndmbs.net.

Hirsch, Michael (1992–93/1995) *Lieder nach Texten aus dem täglichen Leben* (for 1 speaker). First performance Version 1: 1994, Berlin; Version 2: 1995, Donaueschingen (speaker: Michael Hirsch).

—— (1996) *Hirngespinste. Eine nächtliche Szene für 2 Spieler mit Akkordeon*. First performance in 1996, Munich ("Musica Viva"). Accordion: Teodoro Anzellotti; accordion and speech: Robert Podlesny.

—— (2001) *Das Konvolut, Vol.1* (for female singer, piccolo-flute, clarinet, tuba, string-trio and CD-playback). Commissioned by the Berliner Festspiele for the festival MaerzMusik 2002 in Berlin. First performance on 9 March 2002 (Kammerensemble Neue Musik Berlin and Anna Clementi, vocal).

—— (2002) *Das Konvolut, Vol.2* (for 7 performers/speakers, flute, violin, piano, 2 percussionists and 2 CD-Players). First performances in 2002, Berlin.

—— See also www.hirschmichael.de.

Goebbels, Heiner (1994) *Surrogate Cities – For Big Orchestra, Voice, Mezzosoprano and Sampler.* Premiered in Frankfurt. Performed by Junge Deutsche Philharmonie, with Jocelyn B. Smith and David Moss.

—— (1996) *Schwarz auf Weiss – Black on White.* With the Ensemble Modern; composed and directed by Heiner Goebbels; stage and light: Jean Kalman; costumes: Jasmin Andreae. Frankfurt am Main: Bockenheimer Depot.

—— (2004), *Eraritjaritjaka – museé des phrases.* Words by Elias Canetti; with André Wilms and the Mondriaan Quartett; music by Shostakovitch, Mossolov, Lobanoc, Scelsi, Bryars, Ravel, Crumb, Bach and Goebbels; composed and directed by Heiner Goebbels; stage design and light: Klaus Grünberg; costumes: Florence von Gerkan; live video: Bruno Deville; sound: Willi Bopp. Lausanne: Theatre Vidy.

—— (2007) *Stifters Dinge/Stifter's Things – a Performative Installation/Music Theatre.* Composer and director: Heiner Goebbels; light and stage: Klaus Grünberg; sound: Willi Bopp; programming: Hubert Machnik; co-produced by Theatre Vidy Lausanne with T&M-Nanterre Paris, Schauspielfrankfurt, Berliner Festspiele – Spielzeit Europa, Grand Theatre Luxembourg, Teatro Stabile Turino; co-commissioned by artangel, London.

—— See also www.heinergoebbels.com.

LOSE COMBO (Jörg Laue) *still (LAST/Trilogie 2)* (multimedial musictheatre for two performers, piano trio, audio and videotapes). Premiered on 26 May 2000, Theater am Halleschen Ufer, Berlin. Performance: Sophie Huber, Nicolai Reher; viola: Dorothee Kraus, Eva Oppl; piano: Susanne Huber; sound: Hans-Friedrich Bormann; design, music, text, video: Jörg Laue.

—— (2005), *HERTZ' FREQUENZEN.* First performance on 16 September 2005, tesla in the Podewils'schen Palais, Berlin. Performance: Claudia Splitt, Nicolai Reher; violin: Lisa Lammel; viola: Eva Oppl; clarinet/theremin: Nils Hartwig; concept, design, text, tape: Jörg Laue; video: Jörg Laue, Esther Ernst; sound: Hans-Friedrich Bormann.

—— (2006), *FARADAY'S CAGE.* Performance, concert, installation with the Kammerensemble Neue Musik Berlin. First performance on 1 September 2006, St. Elisabeth-Kirche, Berlin. Performance: Claudia Splitt, Nicolai Reher; Kammerensemble Neue Musik Berlin (flute: Rebecca Lenton; clarinet: Winfried Rager; violin: Ekkehard Windrich; viola: Sophie Bansac; violoncello: Cosima Gerhardt; piano: Heather O'Donnell; percussion: Friedemann Werzlau); concept, lighting, text, video, design, tape: Jörg Laue; visuals, harp: Esther Ernst; sound: Hans-Friedrich Bormann.

—— (2008), *BRAUN light Performance. Konzert. Installation feat. Trio Nexus.* First performance on 15 May 2008, Villa Elisabeth, Berlin (Mitte). Performance: Claudia Splitt, Nicolai Reher, Trio Nexus (piano: Pascale Berthelot; flute: Erik Drescher; percussion: Claudia Sgarbi); concept, design, lighting, video, tape, text: Jörg Laue; video: Esther Ernst; sound: Hans-Friedrich Bormann.

—— See also www.lose-combo.de.

Theater der Klänge (Jörg Lensing) (1993) *Figur und Klang im Raum – eine polyphone szenische Bühnenkomposition von Jörg U. Lensing.* Co-production of the Theater der Klänge with the Bauhaus Dessau. First performance on 25 March 1993 at the Bauhaus Dessau. Performers: Clemente Fernandez, Jacqueline Fischer, Jean-Jacques Haari, Kerstin Hörner, Maria-Jesus Lorrio, Heiko

Seidel, Ismini Sofou; author: Jörg U. Lensing; co-author music: Thomas Neuhaus; co-author light design: Jürgen Steger; dramaturge: Dr. Andreas Bossmann; director: Jörg U. Lensing; music and sound: Thomas Neuhaus.

—— (2005) *HOEReographien*. Artistic director: J. U. Lensing; music/sound: Thomas Neuhaus; video: Thomas Neuhaus, J. U. Lensing, Lucy Lungley; choreography: Jacqueline Fischer; costumes: Caterina Di Fiore; dance: Jenny Ecke, Jelena Ivanovic, Caitlin Smith, Hana Zanin; lighting design: Christian Schroeder; sound and videotechnology: Thomas Neuhaus, J. U. Lensing; costumes: Caterina Di Fiore; stage design: J. U. Lensing, Christian Schroeder.

—— (2008) *Suite intermediale*. Interactive Intermedial Performance. Artistic director: J. U. Lensing; music: Thomas Neuhaus; video: Falk Grieffenhagen; choreography: Jacqueline Fischer; costumes: Caterina Di Fiore; dancers/musicians: Bernardo Fallas, Majorie Delgado, Fatima Gomes, Catalina Gomez, Nina Hänel, Hyun-Jin Kim.

—— See also www.theater-der-klaenge.de.

Till, Nicholas with Kandis Cook (1999) *Silent Movie Opera (Carmen, 1910): Music Theatre for Three Singers, Electronics and Video*. Post-Operative Productions/English National Opera Studio. Battersea Arts Centre, London.

—— (2001/03) *At Home with Art*. Presented in September 2011 at the Battersea Art Centre, London. Revised version shown in April 2003 at "Soundings" Festival, Rose Bruford College. Conceived and devised by Kandis Cook and Nick Till; performed by Laurence Harvey; sound and lighting: Nick Till and Kandis Cook.

—— (2006) *Hearing Voices: Transcriptions of the Phonogram of Schizophrenic, for Female Singer, Laptop and Interactive Audio-Visual Media*. Commissioned by Forum Neues Musiktheater, Stuttgart Opera. ISCM World New Music Days Festival, Stuttgart.

Tsangaris, Manos (1980a) *Molto Molto* (for conductor and light). First performance in 1980, Cologne, with Wolfgang Badun.

—— (1980b) *o.T.* (for bass clarinet, voices, objects, light, with an unprepared person in the audience). Dedicated to Mauricio Kagel. First performance in 1980, Cologne, with Carola Bauckholt, Chris Newman, Michael Riessler and Stephan Seauvageot.

—— (2002), *Orpheus, Zwischenspiele*. Stationentheater für Sopran, Mezzosopran, Altus, kleines Orchester, Buchstabenprojektion, 15 Darsteller, mindestens 50 Statisten, Fadenorgel, Aufzug, drei U-Bahnzüge und Licht. Text by Manos Tsangaris. First performance in 2002, Bielefeld, with Victoria Granlund, Maria Jonas, Charles E. Maxwell, Simon Stockhausen and the Bielefelder Symphonikern; musical director: Carolin Nordmeyer.

—— (2004), *Drei Räume Theater Suite. Musiktheaterminiaturen für Räume mit begrenzter Zuschauerkapazität, Theater für ein Haus für Sprecher, Sänger, Instrumentalisten und Akteure in Ensembles verschiedener Größe oder solistisch*. First performance in 2004, Donaueschingen, with Dorrit Bauerecker, Markus Boysen, Pi-hsien Chen, Katharina Hagopian, Marlies Klumpenaar, Harm Meiners, Thomas Meixner, Dirk Müller, Ingrid Müller-Farny, Dagmar Ondracek, Matthias Rebstock, Chiho Takata, Petra Torky.

—— See also www.tsangaris.de.

Contributors

Christa Brüstle completed her Ph.D. thesis (published in 1998 as *Anton Bruckner und die Nachwelt*) at the Freie Universität Berlin, where in 1999 she became a lecturer and member of the 'Kulturen des Performativen' research group. Her Habilitationsschrift, *Konzert-Szenen: Bewegung – Performance – Medien. Musik zwischen performativer Expansion und medialer Integration 1950–2000*, was completed in 2007, and in 2008 she was appointed professor at the Universität der Künste Berlin. As of October 2011 she is a senior scientist at the Kunstuniversität Graz. She has also taught at the Hochschule für Musik Hanns Eisler, the Technische Universität Berlin, and the Universität Wien. Current research projects concern performance issues in contemporary music, sound and media art, and relationships between music and theatre. She was president of the Berliner Gesellschaft für Neue Musik in 2002–3. She has co-edited the books *Klang and Bewegung* (2004), *Music as a Bridge* (2005) and *Aus dem Takt: Rhythmus in Kunst, Kultur und Natur* (2005).

www.chrbru.de

Judith Gerstenberg, born in Hamburg 1967, is the head dramaturg at the Staatstheater Hannover. She has collaborated continuously with Ruedi Häusermann since 1997, for example at the Neumarkttheater in Zurich, the Schauspielhaus Zurich, the Operafestivals of Zurich and Munich, the Staatstheater Hannover and the Burgtheater in Vienna. She is currently contributing to a monograph on Häusermann, which will be published with the Hier&Jetzt Verlag, Zurich.

www.schauspielhannover.de

Composer and theatre director **Heiner Goebbels**, born in 1952, lives in Frankfurt/ Main (Germany), where he studied sociology and music. His compositions for ensemble and for big orchestras are performed worldwide by many ensembles of contemporary music and orchestras (Berlin Philharmonics, Ensemble Modern, Brooklyn Philharmonic New York, London Sinfonietta etc.). Since the early 1990s he has composed and directed his own 'staged concerts' and music theatre plays, which are presented at most major music and theatre festivals in Europe, USA, Australia a.o.: *Ou bien le débarquement désastreux* (1993), *Black on White* (1996), *Max Black* (1998), *Hashirigaki* (2000), *Landscape with Distant Relatives*

(2002), *Eraritjaritjaka* (2004), *Songs of Wars I Have Seen* (2007) *Stifters Dinge* (2007), *I Went to the House But Did Not Enter* (2008) a.o.

He is also the author of numerous articles, lectures and recordings, released by ECM-records and twice followed by a Grammy nomination.

Heiner Goebbels is professor and managing director at the Institute of Applied Theatre Studies at the Justus Liebig University, Giessen / Germany and since 2006 President of the Theatre Academy of Hesse. From 2012 to 2014 he will be artistic director of the international arts festival 'Ruhrtriennale'.

www.heinergoebbels.com

Jörn Peter Hiekel, born in 1963, is professor for musicology as well as head of department at the Institut für Neue Musik at the Dresdner Hochschule für Musik. He also teaches music history and music aesthetics at the Hochschule der Künste Zürich and is a member of the executive committee of the Institut für Neue Musik und Musikerziehung in Darmstadt. He also leads the project 'KlangNetz Dresden' as well as the music section of the Saxon Academy of the Arts. Hiekel has written and edited a number of books on contemporary music, music of the nineteenth century and on aspects of music aesthetics and interculturalism.

Michael Hirsch, born in Munich in 1958, has lived in Berlin since 1981. He has worked as composer since 1976. He has also worked as actor and stage director.

His work has been performed in several European countries, as well as in USA, South Korea and at important festivals, like the Donaueschingen Festival, Musica Viva (Munich), the Ultraschall-Festival Berlin, Maerz Musik Berlin, Eclat-Festival Stuttgart etc.

His opera *Das stille Zimmer* was performed in 2000 by commission of the Operahouse Bielefeld. He has also written operas for different festivals, for the Hannover State Opera and the Stuttgart State Opera.

His recent compositions include: the vocal symphony *Worte Steine* for solo-bass, choir and grand orchestra (2007–9), the madrigal-opera *Tragicomedia* (2009) and *Rezitativ und Arie* for string orchestra and percussion (2010).

Michal Hirsch received the Elisabeth-Schneider-prize for composition in 2001, and the Busoni-prize for composition in 2005.

http://www.hirschmichael.de
http://www.editionjulianeklein.de

Jörg Laue, born 1964 in Gudensberg (Germany), now lives in Berlin. From 1988–93 he studied Applied Theatre Studies at Universität Giessen; in 1994 he founded LOSE COMBO, through which he has been realizing live-art-projects on the borderlines of stage-performance, visual arts and contemporary music. He has also created sound-, light- and video-installations, writings, and lectures, and been the recipient of several scholarships.

http://www.lose-combo.de/bios/08_laue.htm

Jörg U. Lensing is a composer, sound designer and director. He is also the artistic director of the Theater der Klänge (Theatre of Sounds) in Düsseldorf, which he co-founded in 1987. The Theater der Klänge produces intermedial music theatre and dance productions, with a particular interest in collaborative creation and the integration of sound and video technologies. J. U. Lensing has directed nearly all of its twenty productions since 1987. For several productions he also worked as musical composer and choreographer. Since 2001 the kernel creation team of the Theater der Klänge consists of the director and supervising composer J. U. Lensing, the music-composer and programmer Thomas Neuhaus and the choreographer Jacqueline Fischer. The ensemble itself is a project-ensemble, which let dancers work together with actors and musicians in several constellations.

In 1993 Jörg directed the first 'Bauhaus-Stageclass' in the Bauhaus Dessau. Since 1996 he has taught as professor of sound design at the University of Applied Sciences and Arts at Dortmund, Germany.

Publications include: CD: *Bauhaus Bühnenmusik*, Audio-Books: *Die Neuberin; Megalopolis; teufels kreise* and two books: *Theater der Klänge – 10 Jahre auf dem Weg zu einem eigenen Theater* (1999) and *Sound-Design / Sound-Montage / Soundtrack-Komposition* (2009).

www.theater-der-klaenge.de

Petra Maria Meyer is professor of cultural and media science at the Muthesius University of Art in Kiel. From 2004 to 2008 she was the head of the Center for Interdisciplinary Studies (Forum) of the Muthesius University of Art. For fifteen years she was an author and dramaturg at the Studio for Acoustic Art, WDR, Cologne. Her research and publications span: media-philosophy, -aesthetics and -dramaturgy, phenomenology, intermediality, space-theory, performance-art, theatre, dance, film and acoustic art. They include: *Die Stimme und ihre Schrift* (1993), *Gedächtniskultur des Hörens* (1997), *Intermedialität des Theaters* (2001), *Performance im medialen Wandel* (ed. 2006), *Acoustic turn* (ed. 2008) and most recently *Gegenbilder: Zu abweichenden Strategien der Kriegsdarstellung* (ed. 2009).

www.muthesius-kunsthochschule.de/de/hochschule/personenverzeichnis/meyer_petra_maria/index.php

Roland Quitt works as a freelance dramaturg. He studied musicology, German and philosophy in Berlin and has worked with various theatres as a dramaturg in the fields of music theatre and spoken drama. For many years now his work has mainly been centred around experimental forms of music theatre. At the municipal theatre of Bielefeld (Germany) he developed the format 'visible music' comprising new forms of music theatre outside of opera. Here he was responsible for commissioning and for working conceptually on more than twenty new pieces of music theatre. At the Nationaltheater Mannheim he continued this work. Composers he has worked with include Dieter Schnebel, Vinko Globokar, Manos Tsangaris, Carola Bauckholt, Rolf Riehm, Iris ter Schiphorst, Peter Ablinger, Walter

Zimmermann, Georg Nussbaumer and many others. Within the International Theatre Institute (ITI) he curated 'Music Theatre Now' in 2008 – an international competition for new music theatre (together with Laura Berman).

Matthias Rebstock is professor for scenic music at the University of Hildesheim, Germany. He also works as director in the field of contemporary music theatre. His artistic work has been shown at a great number of internationally renowned festivals such as *Eclat Festival Stuttgart*, *Donaueschinger Musiktage*, *Maerzmusik Berlin*, *musicadhoy Madrid*, *New Music Festival Stockholm*, *Musicia Nova Sao Paulo* and others. The opera *Niebla* that he wrote and staged, together with the composer Elena Mendoza, was selected for the Music Theatre Now prize in 2008 by the International Theatre Institute. He is also author of the book *Komposition zwischen Musik und Theater. Das instrumentale Theater von Mauricio Kagel* (Hofheim 2007) and has edited a book on collective working processes in the arts (*Kollektive in den Künste*, together with Hajo Kurzenberger and Hanns-Josef Ortheil, Hildesheim 2008). His research covers topics in aesthetics, phenomenology and the semiotics of art, contemporary opera, new music theatre, devised theatre, performance and sound art. He is member of the *Herder-Kolleg*, the centre for transdisciplinary cultural studies at the University Hildesheim.

www.matthiasrebstock.de

George Rodosthenous is lecturer in music theatre and the director of enterprise and knowledge transfer at the School of Performance and Cultural Industries of the University of Leeds. He is the artistic director of the theatre company Altitude North and also works as a freelance composer for the theatre. His research interests are 'the body in performance', 'refining improvisational techniques and compositional practices for performance', 'devising pieces with live musical soundscapes as interdisciplinary process', 'updating Greek Tragedy' and 'The British Musical'. He is currently working on the book *Theatre as Voyeurism: The Pleasure(s) of Watching*.

http://www.leeds.ac.uk/pci/staff/staff_grodosthenous.html

David Roesner is senior lecturer in drama at the University of Exeter. In 2002 he finished his Ph.D. at the University of Hildesheim, Germany, on 'Theatre as Music' analysing principles and strategies of musicalisation in productions by Christoph Marthaler, Einar Schleef and Robert Wilson (Tübingen: Narr 2003). He taught at the Universities of Hildesheim, Bern and Mainz. As part of his research he has won the Thurnau Award for Music Theatre Studies, 2007 for his article "The Politics of the Polyphony of Performance", which was later published with CTR (1/2008). In 2009 he conducted an AHRC funded project on "Composed Theatre" together with Matthias Rebstock (Hildesheim). Current publications include the article "Musicality as a paradigm for the theatre – a kind of manifesto" (*Studies in Musical Theatre*, Vol 4/3: 2010) and the co-edited book (with Lynne Kendrick) *Theatre Noise: The Sound of Performance*, Newcastle: Cambridge Scholars Publishing, 2011.

David Roesner also works as a practitioner, most recently as composer and sound designer for Bella Merlin's *Tilly No-Body* (Mondavi Center for the Performing Arts, UC Davis).

http://humanities.exeter.ac.uk/drama/staff/roesner/
http://exeter.academia.edu/Roesner

Nicholas Till is a theatre artist, historian and theorist working in opera and music theatre. He is co-artistic director of the experimental music theatre company Post-Operative Productions, and his works have also been presented by the Royal Opera Garden Venture, English National Opera Studio and the Forum Neues Musiktheater of Stuttgart Opera. He is the author of *Mozart and the Enlightenment* (1992), and is currently editing *The Cambridge Companion to Opera Studies*. He is professor of opera and music theatre at the University of Sussex, where he is director of the Centre for Research in Opera and Music Theatre.

http://www.sussex.ac.uk/profiles/168223

Demetris Zavros has a Ph.D. in Music Theatre from the School of Performance and Cultural Industries (University of Leeds). He is associate director of the theatre company Altitude North and also works as a freelance composer for the theatre. His music-theatre works include: *AiAs Mana, Icarus, Clastoclysm and Metaxi Alogon*. He has composed music for several theatre and dance performances in collaboration with The National Theatre of Cyprus, The National Theatre of Northern Greece, West Yorkshire Playhouse, Festival of Philippoi, International Festival of Ancient Greek Drama (Cyprus) and others.